Other Avon Books by
Samantha James

GABRIEL'S BRIDE
JUST ONE KISS
MY LORD CONQUEROR

SAMANTHA JAMES

EVERY WISH FULFILLED

AVON BOOKS ◆ NEW YORK

EVERY WISH FULFILLED is an original publication of Avon Books. This work has never before appeared in book form. This work is a novel. Any similarity to actual persons or events is purely coincidental.

AVON BOOKS
A division of
The Hearst Corporation
1350 Avenue of the Americas
New York, New York 10019

Copyright © 1997 by Sandra Kleinschmit
Inside cover author photo by Glamour Shots
Published by arrangement with the author
Library of Congress Catalog Card Number: 96-96468
ISBN: 0-380-78607-9

First Avon Books Printing: January 1997

AVON TRADEMARK REG. U.S. PAT. OFF. AND IN OTHER COUNTRIES, MARCA REGISTRADA, HECHO EN U.S.A.

Printed in the U.S.A.

RA   10 9 8 7 6 5 4 3 2 1

Prologue

The Outskirts of London, 1815
Hawksgrove Inn

Little by little the haze of twilight seeped between the shutters. The gloom of darkness floated into the room . . . along with the twisting specter of death.

A man lay feeble and spent within the inn's finest bed—Charles Tremayne, Earl of Deverell—his long, noble fingers curled around the silk counterpane. Once Charles Tremayne had been hearty and robust, the stoutest of men. But infection had ravaged his lungs; his illness had stolen his strength, weakened his muscles to mush, leaving but a remnant of all he'd been before. And now what breath remained in his body rattled like that of a sickly old man.

From the corner, a hovering figure surveyed the Earl of Deverell. James Elliot watched with impassive indifference, his legs stretched out before him, arms across a beefy chest. A restless impatience dwelled deep in his eyes; his mouth thinned. *Die*, he willed venomously of the earl. *Hurry and die, man.* He was sorely tempted to snatch up a pillow, smother the wretch and put him out of his misery, for he was anxious to get home to his supper—not that a surfeit of comfort awaited him in that sliver of a cottage he called home. But at least he was his own man. Master of his house and all he surveyed.

And he gave the orders there.

Across from him, Charles Tremayne raised his head. "James," came his raspy whisper. "You have been good to me, James."

Good to him? James Elliot scoffed. He'd done what he'd been told to do—take care of the man during his illness. He'd dribbled gruel into the earl's mouth and mopped his chin. He'd fetched and emptied smelly chamber pots countless times over the last fortnight. Indeed, James thought blackly, Henry Foster, the innkeeper, would have had his hide—and his job—if he hadn't done what he was told.

For an instant sheer malice flamed in James Elliot's eyes. Lord, but he'd like to kick Foster's fat, waddling arse down the nearest stairway.

But he bore the burden of a wife, and—more's the pity—a daughter.

His daughter. His mouth flattened as he thought of her. Sniveling little nuisance. 'Twas because of her he'd lost his left thumb—and 'twas a moment forever burned into his memory.

He'd been on his knees chopping kindling in the fall of last year; the brat had come up beside him and pushed at his arm. That was all it had taken . . . a howl of rage and pain had erupted from his mouth. He'd seized a stump of wood and whirled on her. The little bitch! She had maimed him. . . .

But now she was maimed, too, he thought with satisfaction.

"James. Come closer, James."

Elliot clamped back a vehement refusal. Instead he arose and did as he was bidden.

"The date, James. What is the date?"

"The eleventh of March, my lord."

Charles Tremayne rolled his head on the pillow. "I've been here nearly a fortnight. I was to have returned home by mid-month." A wispy sigh escaped lips that were dried and cracked. "The physician was right. I should have sent for my wife, my Sylvia. But I thought this stubborn infection would pass, that I would soon be well and on my way home to my family in Yorkshire. Never did I dream it would worsen so quickly . . . I was too stubborn, for never again will I see my boys, Giles and Damien. Never again will I hold my sweet wife in my arms." His eyes filled with tears. "I see it now, now that it is too late. . . ."

James Elliot rolled his eyes and sneered. How long must he be subjected to the prattling of this dratted man?

The earl coughed, a shivering, wracking sound that seemed to encompass his whole body. Long moments passed before he was able to speak again.

"You have taken good care of me, James. My Sylvia will reward you for your efforts, I promise. But now I must ask one more favor of you, for I have no one else to turn to, no one but you." The earl raised a trembling hand toward the bureau. "There alongside the bureau, James. There is a cloth sack. Look inside, and in it you will find a jewel case."

Elliot swiveled his head to his left. With narrowed eyes he peered through the shadows. There was indeed a small cloth sack tipped against the side of the bureau. He did as the earl bade him, withdrawing a long silver case.

"This is it? This is the jewel case?"

"Yes, that's it, James." The earl's voice thinned. "James, I shall never see the dawn of another day. But I must ask you to take the jewel case to my wife, Sylvia, in Yorkshire. The coin within will pay for your journey, though I regret it will take some days. I beg of you, please do this for me, for hidden within the case is my legacy to my wife, a treasure I pray she will find beyond price. . . . She will know how to find it, for she alone knows the secret. . . ."

Those were the Earl of Deverell's last words.

The man in the bed was forgotten. For a never-ending moment James stared at the silver jewel case, his mind buzzing.

With a reverent fingertip he traced the scrolled silver edging upon the lid of the case, yet his expression could only be called greedy. There was a word engraved into a small oval in the center of the lid; since he had never learned to read, it meant little to him.

His cruel lips pulled into a wolfish smile. He erupted into laughter, a cackling sound that—had another been present—might have raised the very hackles of their spine.

"'Tis so easy," he said between bursts of mirth. "So bloody *easy* . . ."

He felt no pity for the man who had just died, nor his widow nor family. No shame for what he was about to do.

For James Elliot was a man without pity. A man without shame.

A man without scruples.

An hour later he burst into a tiny cottage that squatted alongside a rutted, muddy lane. His wife, Justine, glanced up from where she sat before the warmth of a meager fire. She rose, tugging a dirty shawl around her shoulders.

"What kept you?" she snapped. "Your supper is fair burned, and no doubt you'll blame me. Well, 'tis your own fault if you go hungry this night, James Elliot, for I'll be damned if I'll trouble myself further!"

Elliot's feral smile displayed a row of uneven, yellow teeth. "Supper be damned," he said baldly. In his hands he held a cloth sack; now he raised it high. "We'll be feasting by the end of tomorrow, or my name is not James Elliot."

Justine had squared her hands against her hips and braced herself as if for battle, as if she expected such from her husband. At his words, she looked him up and down, as if her ears had deceived her. Her eyes narrowed.

"What is this?" she asked snidely. "Feasting on the pittance you make? Or have you been out hunting instead of working, James Elliot?"

In answer he pulled out the silver jewel case, holding it up triumphantly.

Justine's expression changed abruptly as he sat it upon a crooked-legged table. A small, black-haired child had toddled up as well, next to her father's leg. Curiously she stretched out a tiny finger toward the smooth metal.

Her father whirled on her. "Don't touch that, brat!" he snarled. With the back of his hand, he dealt her a blow across the cheek that sent her tumbling to the floor. Her lips trembled, but she made not a sound.

Elliot glared at his daughter. Loathsome little bitch! he thought furiously. God, but he wished the brat had never been born!

Justine paid little heed. "Find your bed," she ordered brusquely, "and don't come out till morning."

The child crawled to a straw pallet in the corner. Shivering, she curled into a tight little ball.

Both mother and father had forgotten her. Justine nodded at the box. "That's a fine piece, indeed, James. How did you come by it?"

"You know the earl I've been tending? Let us say that I relieved him of his belongings just a little early." Elliot grinned his satisfaction at his cleverness. "'Tis a jewel case."

Justine came alive. "A jewel case!" She scrambled to open it, only to see that the compartments in the top layer were empty, and those beneath as well. She spun around in furious dismay. "Why, you lout, 'tis empty!"

Elliot clamped his jaw together. "Watch your tongue," he warned tightly.

Justine looked as if she longed to argue. She must have decided against it, for she said grudgingly, "Well, no matter. It'll fetch a good price, I suppose."

"Oh, we'll not be selling it." Elliot's tone was smug. "Not just yet anyway."

Justine's sunken eyes blazed. "And why not? 'Tis not terribly fancy—I'd have expected a jewel-encrusted box of an earl—but 'tis no doubt worth half a year's earnings at least!"

Elliot's smile vanished. "If you'd stop your whining, I'd tell you why. Here is what the earl said before he died. 'Hidden within is my legacy,'" he quoted, "'a treasure beyond price.'"

Justine stared first at him, then at the case. "What?" she said blankly. "You mean there is a treasure hidden inside?"

"I mean exactly that!"

"What do you think it is? Gold? Jewels?" She could scarcely contain her excitement.

Elliot's eyes shone. "What does it matter? 'Tis a treasure beyond price! Oh, what plans I have for that treasure!" He gloated. "We'll be rich, Justine. Just think of it. We'll be rich!"

Her eyes flew wide. "Oh," she breathed. "Oh, my."

"Oh, my, indeed." Elliot gave a guttural laugh. When his wife stretched out covetous arms toward the jewel case, her intention obvious, he grabbed her hands. "No. Time enough to find it later," he growled. He yanked her body against his. "For now I've something else in mind."

Justine obliged him, tugging his head down to hers. "Ah," she murmured. "You've not had your supper yet, have you?"

Elliot ground the bulge in his breeches against her hips. "To the devil with supper," he muttered. "I've a hunger of a different sort."

But all at once Justine stepped away. "Wait," she commanded. From a cupboard across the room, she reached far inside and retrieved a dark, dusty bottle. When it was opened, she splashed the ruby liquid into a dingy mug. Smiling, she returned to her husband and held it out.

Elliot curled his fingers around the mug, his left thumb but a stub against the dull metal. His humor was well restored. "So you've been hidin' it from me, eh? A pity, wife, for now I'll have it all for myself." He pressed wet lips against the rim of the mug and drank gustily.

Justine surveyed him lazily as he downed most of the bottle. But just before he would have drained the last dregs from the mug, she reached for it.

Two of her fingers slipped into the mug, dipping into the liquid. Parting the front of her gown, she bared naked, jutting breasts. Her eyes never leaving his burning gaze, she swirled the tips of her fingers around and around huge brown nipples, leaving them dark and wet with wine.

A seductive smile curved her lips. "Your supper, James," she purred.

Elliot bared his teeth. A coarse oath escaped.

His hand fumbled with his breeches. He released his manhood into his hand even as he reached for his wife.

In seconds she lay flattened beneath him on their lumpy mattress. His mouth ravaged hers fiercely. With a grunt he plunged savagely into her body.

The air was filled with noisy snores when Justine eased herself from beneath his weight. Naked, she walked toward the silver jewel case. She spared nary a glance toward her child sleeping in the corner, her thin cheeks streaked with tears.

She rubbed a hand across the smooth metal. So James had plans for his newfound treasure, did he?

A sly smile crept across her lips. Ah, but so did she.

By morning she was gone, the jewel case—and the little girl—along with her.

James Elliot fell into a rage that lasted days. In his cups one night, he destroyed the inside of a tavern and killed two men who tried to stop him.

Little wonder he was sentenced to twenty years in Newgate.

As for Justine, poor soul, she did not live beyond a fortnight. So it was that the poor little mite who was their daughter was left with neither father nor mother.

Many would have said 'twas a blessing indeed.

But alas, in time . . . in time destiny would twine their fates together anew. . . .

Father and daughter had not seen the last of each other.

One

Lancashire
Twenty years later

He wished he could say it was good to be back in England.

Nearly four years had passed since his last visit. Of course he'd expected to return. Indeed, he'd been on his way back. . . .

Never in his life had he expected to find his brother dead.

His wrath rose within him like a cloud of blackest rage. The very curses of hell swirled within him, fighting to be free. No, he thought. Not just dead . . .

Murdered.

High atop a glossy black steed, Damien Lewis Tremayne moved not a muscle. 'Twas as if both man and steed were carved in stone. Yet even as a wracking pain squeezed his heart, he was bled with a weary despair. He stared across the distant valley, but one thought crowding his mind . . . his very being.

He was the last of the Tremaynes.

First his father, he thought bitterly, gone those many years ago. His mother had followed but a few short years thereafter. And now Giles . . .

His heart squeezed. It was a vibrant spring morning—warm for the month of April—rich with the colors of life. The sky was a vivid, endless expanse of blue. Across the meadow, masses of buttercup-yellow daffodils crowned the slope, like a sea of golden sunshine. The air was sweet with the scent of country air and morning dew. . . . But if the cold of winter ran in his veins, the darkest shadows of night dwelled in his expression. And it was the blazing winds of a tempest that fired his soul.

It was to him—to Damien Lewis Tremayne—that the responsibility fell . . . no, not as the new Earl of Deverell—but as the brother of a man who died violently, for no reason, at the hands of another. . . .

He would find his brother's murderer.

And he would see Giles's death avenged, for he must not fail.

He *would* not fail.

It was as that very resolve crossed his mind that at last he turned his mount to ride away. 'Twas then that he saw her—a woman watching him from beneath the shade of a gnarled oak tree. She was seated on a coverlet spread upon the ground, her legs tucked beneath her skirts. In one arm a large sketch pad lay propped; in her hand was a piece of charcoal.

Their eyes caught. As she realized she'd been discovered, her hand stilled. She hugged the pad to her breast, somewhat guiltily, he decided.

Damien approached. He stopped within several paces of her, then dismounted and crossed to her. The woman remained where she was, the slender column of her neck arching as she watched him come to a halt. Her wide, unwavering regard made him feel as if he were the very devil himself come to life. Why he should cause such a reaction, he didn't know. Though he was well aware that he was taller than many a man, he was garbed in a loose, white shirt, dark breeches and boots—surely such a picture as he presented should not frighten the chit.

"Hello," he murmured.

Her lips parted. For an instant he thought she would refuse to speak. But speak she did, in a low, musical voice that made him realize she was not frightened at all, perhaps merely wary.

"Good morning, sir."

One corner of his mouth tipped upward. He sought to further put her at ease. "I couldn't help but notice you watching me. Were you sketching me?"

There was just the slightest hesitation before she replied. "Yes. Yes, I was. I do hope you don't mind."

"Not at all," he returned smoothly. He dropped down to his haunches. "May I see?"

She hesitated, her distress obvious—her reticence even more so—but finally she relinquished the drawing.

Damien studied it. Though it was not yet

finished, with bold, stark lines she had managed to capture every facet of his dark mood—his rage, his utter bleakness.

He disliked it. He disliked it intensely.

Slowly his gaze returned to her. "I should very much like to have it." He wasted no time conveying his wishes.

"Oh, but such a hastily done piece is hardly worth keeping." With a shake of her head, she objected just as staunchly. "I should be embarrassed to part with such a mediocre effort."

He remained pleasant, but adamant. "On the contrary, miss. It's really quite good, and I wish to have it. The price is of no consequence."

"Oh, but it's not money I'm interested in, sir. 'Tis—'tis simply not for sale."

A fleeting solution buzzed through his mind. He considered keeping it, withholding it from her, for he was not a man to display his emotions for all and sundry to see; it was as if this girl had glimpsed a part of him he would far rather keep hidden. He felt—oh, as if he'd been caught in some illicit act.

From the corner of his eye he saw a small cart and pony grazing nearby. It would be simple indeed to whirl and mount his stallion, then ride off; if he were on horseback, she would never catch him.

One dark brow arched. "You're very modest," he observed.

Small, white teeth caught the fullness of her lower lip. "Modest?" she repeated, her tone light. "Nay, sir, simply honest. 'Twould be robbery were you to part with money for this piece—and it not yet finished!"

Damien struggled for patience. Why was she being so stubborn? For the first time then he looked at her . . . really *looked* at her.

Her beauty was like a blow to the belly.

She was exquisite, though in a quite unfashionable way. Her gown was rather faded and old, the laces of the bodice undone against the heat; the rounded neckline revealed smooth, unblemished skin that had acquired a light tan. Clearly she was not a London miss who never faced daylight without bonnet or parasol. Nor was her hair a riot of curls, as was the current vogue. It tumbled down her back, sleek and straight, so dark it was almost black. Her feet were bare, small, pink toes peeping out from the hem of her dress, reminding him of a gypsy.

But it was her eyes that held him spellbound, and his own narrowed in unguarded appreciation. In all his days he'd never seen eyes the color of these. They were extraordinary, their hue deepest violet-blue.

The color of heather in full, vibrant bloom . . .

Who was she? he wondered. A girl from the village? And where had she learned to sketch so well? A natural talent? Surely it was so, he mused. But she was well-spoken. Perhaps she was a maid at Lockhaven Park, whose owner he was to visit that very afternoon. At the thought, something knotted within him. He was not looking forward to his meeting with Miss Heather Duval, mistress of Lockhaven. He had a very good idea what he would encounter—a shrewish, calculating virago whose looks would undoubtedly match her disposition. No wonder the chit had yet to find a husband.

Ruthlessly he pushed the thought aside. He would much rather not think about Heather Duval. Indeed, what he wanted was to take this vision of loveliness back to his room at the inn and make love to her until the very instant he had to leave.

Ah, yes, he thought, feeling desire stir his loins and tighten his middle. If this lass were willing, he would strip away every last stitch of clothing from her, bury his heartache—and his hardness—in the depths of her body. Indeed, he could think of no better way to banish the darkness from his heart.

"Do you have a name, lass?"

Again that hesitation, as she surveyed him from beneath the cast of long, thick lashes. "Alice," she murmured at last.

"Well, Alice, are you certain I cannot convince you to part with it?" In truth, the sketch no longer mattered. Oddly, he found himself reluctant to leave. He even wished she would invite him to stay and sit with her.

A hint of rose had come to her cheeks. "I think not, sir," she said softly.

"Then it seems I have no choice."

He returned it to her, dimly speculating that she would be small in stature, for her shoulders were narrow, her waist slim, her hands scarcely larger than a child's. He wished she would rise, for he had a sudden urge to see her move. She would be all lithe, perfect grace as she walked— and he could almost feel her beneath him in passion's dance, her limbs slim and curved and wildly erotic.

As if to tempt him further, a sudden breeze arose, molding her gown to her body, revealing the thrust of firm, young breasts.

Her color deepened as she discerned his gaze on her bosom. Her free hand fluttered upward as she sought to shield herself from his perusal.

"Come now, Alice. There's no need to hide such loveliness."

She was clearly distressed, though for the life of him, Damien could not imagine why. Surely he was not the first man to pay her such attention. "You, sir," she said breathlessly, "are quite forward."

And alas, he was quite regretful, for he was not a man to shower his attentions where they were not wanted.

He smiled slightly. "Perhaps," he agreed. "But I shall trouble you no further, Alice, and I shall bid you good day. 'Tis my hope we'll meet again, and perhaps you will let me make amends."

He rose and, with a low bow, he left her. It was but a short ride back to the Eppingstone Inn, where he'd taken lodgings. Built of brick and timber and stone a hundred years earlier, the inn was a resting place for travelers, a gathering place for villagers who sought respite from their drudgery in the idle hours of the evening. Wide, rough-hewn planks covered the floors, pitted and

gouged and showing the signs of many a guest
and many a year. The smell of ale lingered in the
air, even in morning's earliest hours, yet it was
not unpleasant, for it mingled with the scent of
meats roasting in the kitchen.

A fire blazed in the huge stone fireplace in the
common room; the trestled tables placed adja-
cent to its warmth were deserted as Damien
strode toward his room on the second floor. He
was glad, for he was suddenly in the mood to talk
to no one. Still, a peculiar restlessness plagued
him throughout the next few hours.

He couldn't put her out of his mind—Alice,
the girl with the violet eyes. She possessed a
sweet, bewitching beauty, a beauty that lured and
enticed him in a way he'd not felt for a long, long
time. He was sorely tempted to leave, to go out
and search until he found her. . . .

"Enough!" Cursing himself roundly, he
vaulted off the bed and snatched up his coat. He
was here for a reason—and it was not to bed a
wench named Alice, comely as she was. It was
time, he reminded himself blackly, to get to the
business at hand.

The business of catching a murderer.

Indeed, it was this very vow that had brought
him to Lancashire . . . that hardened his mouth
and stiffened his shoulders. His feet fell like
blows as he descended the smooth, worn steps of
the narrow staircase.

"Goin' out, Mr. Lewis?"

The voice came from the corner of the common room. Damien glanced up and saw the

innkeeper, Mr. Simpson, polishing silver at one of the tables. He tipped his hat to the portly, bewhiskered gentleman, leashing his impatience.

"Indeed, I am, Mr. Simpson. I am meeting Miss Heather Duval at Lockhaven Park this afternoon to speak with her about filling the position of estate manager."

"Ah, yes. Robin passed on quite suddenly, y'know."

A pity, that—but also a stroke of luck. It was Cameron, the investigator Damien had hired to help him find Giles's murderer, who had learned that the Lockhaven estate manager had passed away, and that Heather Duval was anxious to find a replacement. Damien had seized on the opportunity as heaven-sent and dispatched a note to her immediately. Should he secure the position, he would have the perfect opportunity to quietly observe Miss Heather Duval . . . and thus await his quarry.

He tipped his head slightly. "So I'm told," he murmured. "A pity, his death, but I confess, I'm eager to stay on in Lancashire."

Mr. Simpson's head bobbed up and down. "The Lord's pocket, m'wife calls it." He laid down a serving fork. "You'll find no better woman than Miss Heather. She's fair and always does well by her people. Why, a veritable saint, m'wife calls her. But that's little wonder, considering she was raised by the Earl and Countess of Stonehurst. The earl took her in after the carriage accident that killed her parents, y'know."

Damien nodded. Cameron had told him that

was the story everyone believed—but it was not true. No, the man in the carriage with the woman was not her husband—nor the father of the girl . . .

For the husband still lived, blast his rotten, dirty soul!

A fleeting shadow crossed Mr. Simpson's features. He sighed. " 'Tis really such a shame. . . ." His voice trailed off, and he shook his head.

Everything inside Damien seemed to stand at attention. He waited for Mr. Simpson to say more, but the old man did not. He caught his pocket watch in hand and glanced at it. "Well," he said lightly, "I'd best be off. It wouldn't do to be late."

"Good luck," Mr. Simpson called after him.

Outside, he mounted Zeus, a towering black that had been Giles's favorite mount. . . . There was a faint catch in his heart. God, but he would give anything—*anything*!—for Giles to be alive still. . . .

His mood darkened, like a black cloud across the moon. Faces flashed before him as he guided Zeus down the narrow lane that wound through the village. The glances cast his way were curious, yet not unfriendly. He passed two dark-haired women selling baskets at a market stand; the pair was engaged in vivacious discussion, interspersed with laughter.

He envied them their carefreeness.

Outside the milliner's cottage, two young boys wrestled in the dirt, rolling wildly. Damien couldn't help but remember how he and Giles

had often indulged in such play, rough and
tumbling and reckless. As children, they had
been nearly inseparable, for there was scarcely
more than a year between them in age. They had
shared the same bedchamber. Bedeviled their
tutor and plotted antics far into the night. Whispered of grand plans for the future, when at last
they left their youth behind.

The glimmer of a smile curved Damien's lips,
even as a pang shot through him. Giles had often
boasted that he would someday be the illustrious
captain of a vast seagoing vessel with a crew of a
hundred men, charting his course across the seas
and making a name for himself in the far-flung
ports of the world. As for himself, he had been
no less daring and grandiose. He had dreamed of
acquiring fame and fortune, of building an em-
pire of land and wealth the likes of which no man
had ever seen. . . .

But they were the dreams of children, for
nothing had turned out as planned. . . . Both
father and mother had died, and their care was
given over to their mother's sister Gertrude; it
was under Aunt Gertrude's guidance that he and
Giles had grown to manhood. So it was that with
their father's death, Giles's dreams had ended,
for he was the new Earl of Deverell. Instead he—
Damien—was the one who had sailed the seas
while Giles went off to Cambridge; he had traveled to America and left the business of the
earldom in the hands of his elder brother, Giles.

His mouth a grim, straight line, Damien
spurred his mount onward. He ducked beneath

the low-hanging branch of an oak tree, then veered around the bottom of a grassy knoll. His jaw was clenched tight, as if to do battle. Indeed, he had to remind himself that his battle was not with Miss Heather Duval . . .

She was but the means to her father.

It was then that Lockhaven Park came into view. Without realizing it, Damien reined in his mount and came to a halt. As he'd been when he'd first seen it, he couldn't help but admire such an impressive sight. Towering, stately trees paved the lane that swept in a wide half-circle toward the manor house. Verdant lawn surrounded the house in every direction. With a red brick facade and gleaming white portico, the house itself was simple yet aristocratic. Indeed, he reflected almost reluctantly, Lockhaven reminded him more than a little of Bayberry, his home in Virginia.

With a touch of his heel, once again he urged Zeus forward. Within a few short minutes, he stood before the huge double doors. An ornately carved brass knocker in hand, he rapped sharply on the paneled facade.

The sound of footsteps echoed within. A stoop-shouldered butler opened the door wide; there was an air of shabby capability about him as he fixed inquiring eyes upon the visitor.

"May I help you, sir?"

"You may indeed." Damien's tone was brisk. "I am Damien Lewis. I have an appointment to see Miss Heather Duval."

"Ah, yes, Mr. Lewis." The butler's gaze swept

the length of him as he spoke. He must have passed muster, for the butler's lined face relaxed into a warm smile. "Miss Heather is expecting you. Please, come in."

Damien stepped into the foyer. The butler closed the portal, then gestured down a long corridor. "I am Marcus, by the way. Please, follow me. Miss Heather is in her study."

Damien fell into step beside him, slowing his stride to match that of the elderly man beside him. They passed the drawing room and the music room; he caught a glimpse of glossy floors, tall, paneled walls lined with windows, awash with sunlight and filled with soft, inviting divans and chairs. Some strange emotion seized hold of him, something that bordered on anger, for he was reminded once again of Bayberry—yet he didn't want to like anything whatsoever about Lockhaven Park. Not the grounds. Not the furnishings. Most certainly not its mistress . . .

"Here we are, sir," Marcus said cheerfully. He opened the last door on the right and stood aside so Damien could pass through. "Perhaps we'll be seeing you again soon."

Damien caught his eyes. "One can only hope," he murmured. Smiling slightly, he moved past the old man into the study. Marcus gave him a wink, then withdrew. As the door closed behind him, Damien raised his head. His every nerve coiled tight within him as he prepared to confront Miss Heather Duval, daughter of his brother's murderer . . .

But it was a painting on the wall that captured

his attention. It was dark and ominous—a hunchback stood upon a hilltop. Above his head, across the bleak horizon, he was surrounded by masses of black, seething clouds.

The hunchback had no face.

"Mr. Lewis?"

His gaze veered. His mind registered a massive mahogany desk that dominated the far corner. A diminutive figure was seated behind it, her hands folded just so before her.

He reeled.

It was she. His gypsy from this morning. There could be no mistake. Her worn, faded dress had been exchanged for one of crisp, gray muslin; she'd caught her hair up in a prim little bun atop her crown. Oh, she looked older, to be sure. But those exquisitely sculpted features were the same. And those huge, violet eyes gazed mutely into his.

He allowed the merest trace of a smile to curl his lips, for he must reveal no hint of the turmoil that roiled within him.

"So, Alice," he murmured, "we meet again."

She didn't return his smile. "So we do," she observed, "a meeting I suspect neither of us expected." Her voice was quiet and calm, yet her regard had once again turned wary.

He gave a slight shrug. "You may well be right."

He watched as she gestured across from her. "Please," she said, her tone coolly formal, "sit down."

So. This is how it would be. Damien's manner

grew chill. He battled an acid hatred. She should have been ugly. Grotesque. God, but he wished she were! After all, she carried the same blood as a murderer. *Stop it*, reproved a voice in his head. *You judge too harshly and too soon.*

His stride unfaltering, he crossed the room. "Forgive me," he said. "I am not only rude, I've been remiss." He now stood before her. "I am Damien Lewis."

Boldly he reached for her hand; his own, deeply bronzed and much larger, seemed to swallow hers up. As he released her fingers, he saw her looking down at his hands. He was suddenly very glad that his palm was calloused and rough, for he often worked alongside his own men in the fields. If the lady believed he were a city dandy, the game might well have been lost before it was even begun.

He seated himself in a burgundy leather wing chair directly across from her; there was a wooden cane propped against the side of her desk, with a handle of beaten, engraved silver. In some far distant corner of his mind, he registered the feeling that it seemed a bit out of place. . . .

He crossed his booted feet at the ankles and slanted her an easy smile. "I confess, this is a bit awkward. Will your husband be joining us?"

"I have no husband, sir. You see before you the sole mistress of Lockhaven Park."

If he'd hoped to discomfit her, he failed abominably, for her reply was swift, her manner as unruffled as his own. What devil had seized hold of him, Damien couldn't say, for he already knew what her answer would be even before she spoke. The lady had no husband. Indeed, he knew quite a lot about Miss Heather Duval—that she'd been raised under the wardship of Miles Grayson, Earl of Stonehurst, who lived not five kilometers distant. He didn't know why—perhaps because her father had spent the last twenty years in Newgate.

But now it was she who regarded him with keen aplomb. "I trust this poses no problem for you, Mr. Lewis? I know there are some who might consider it an affront to be in the employ of a woman. So I will understand if you wish to discontinue the interview—"

"On the contrary, Miss Duval. Please, let us proceed." There was a glint in his eye; he had the feeling that was what she wanted.

Slim, supple fingers seemed to tense, then visibly relax. Yet her words were the complete antithesis of what he expected. "Then let us get down to business," she said softly. She reached for a small sheaf of papers on the corner of the desktop. "I must admit, Mr. Lewis, I was quite impressed with the letter you sent. It seems you have a good deal of experience to commend you."

His tobacco holdings in Virginia had prospered greatly over the last ten years; ego notwithstanding, Damien liked to think it was because he involved himself in every aspect of the business. "At the risk of sounding rather arrogant, Miss Duval, I believe I do."

She contemplated him, her head tipped to the side. A faint frown flashed across her features.

"Your accent," she murmured. " 'Tis rather unfamiliar."

He chuckled, striving to be at his most charming. "No doubt it's a bit of a mixture. You see, I was born in Yorkshire and spent most of my youth there." Notably absent was the fact that he'd been born the second son of an earl. He must tread carefully, lest his true identity be revealed. Oh, no, he was not about to disclose who he really was, for he could trust no one . . .

Especially not her.

"When I was sixteen," he went on, "I decided to go in search of fame and fortune, and landed in America."

"Sixteen!" She was clearly aghast. "But that's so young to be on your own! Surely someone traveled with you?"

He shook his head. "No," he said lightly. "But I was big for a lad and pretended to know quite well the ways of the world. I settled in Virginia and went to work for a plantation owner. Eventually I came to be in charge of the daily operations there." A roundabout way of putting it, but true nonetheless.

"I see." Her gaze was fixed on his face. He could almost see her mind working, gauging him, weighing and measuring. "Could you describe your duties in more detail?"

"Certainly, Miss Duval. I was the sole keeper of the books, and I was responsible for supervising the planting and harvest of the plantation's chief crop—tobacco. I bought and ordered supplies, and saw to the housing and welfare of those who worked in the fields."

She nodded. "I'm curious, however, Mr. Lewis. What brought you back to England?"

He gestured vaguely, pretending to ponder. "Despite the years I spent in America, this is home," he said at last. "It doesn't matter whether it's Lancashire or Yorkshire. I returned for a visit and . . . 'twas a precipitous decision, I admit. Thus I fear I carry no letters of recommendation with me." He held his breath and waited.

She nodded, yet he sensed her hesitancy. "I must be honest, Mr. Lewis," she said slowly. "I need a man who is not an ogre, for I will not have an estate manager whom my tenants fear. At the same time, I require someone who is able to perform his duties with a firm, capable hand. Thus far I've had precious little luck finding a suitable replacement for Robin, and time grows short. But we are not growing tobacco here in Lancashire, Mr. Lewis. We raise sheep and cattle, and grow what crops are needed to sustain the estate and its tenants."

"I am hardly ignorant of such matters," he said quickly. "My aunt's farm in Yorkshire is very similar to your estate, and it was there that I spent much of my youth."

She gave a tiny shake of her head. "'Tis not that I doubt your ability—"

"Then I have an offer, Miss Duval. If you will engage me as your estate manager, I shall work without wages for the first month." He was driven by desperate purpose, but he dared not let her know it. "Should you be dissatisfied with me, or should my work prove inadequate in any way, you may dismiss me at the end of that time. With all respect, Miss Duval, it would seem to me that you have nothing to lose."

She was tempted; hope flared within him, yet he didn't dare risk pushing her further. With naught but the hold of his eyes, he sought to convince her. Time stretched out endlessly. But just when he thought his plan futile, she rose to her feet behind the desk. For the first time, that lovely mouth softened in a faint smile.

Damien felt he'd been punched in the belly. He'd thought her lovely before, but God above, now she stole the very breath from his lungs.

"You are a persuasive man, Mr. Lewis. I agree to your proposal—but on one condition. I will not cheat you by withholding wages for services given me. In addition to your salary"—she named a figure that was more than generous—"the estate manager is entitled to the use of the house near the east pasture. 'Tis a modest dwelling, but I hope you'll find it adequate. Is this agreeable to you, sir?"

Damien stood as well. "It is indeed, Miss Duval."

"Good," she pronounced. "When would you like to move your things?"

"Tomorrow would be fine, Miss Duval. I can begin after that."

"Excellent, then. If you'll meet me at the stable at ten o'clock, I should like to show you the estate."

"I shall look forward to it." He reached around to retrieve his hat. When he glanced back, he saw that she was still standing. But he had the sensation there was more she wanted to say.

He arched a brow. "Was there something else, Miss Duval?"

"Yes. Yes, actually there is." For the first time since this morning, she seemed almost flustered. "Mr. Lewis, you're quite certain this is what you want? I ask because . . . well, it occurs to me that you may find Lancashire quite tedious. Our village is small and—"

He cut her off, yet there was no sting in his tone. "If I were in search of city life, Miss Duval, I'd have gone to London."

His gaze was unrelenting, yet those unusual violet eyes never left his. "You take my meaning well, Mr. Lewis."

A single step brought him directly across from her. Reaching out, he took her hand. It was small and dainty and feminine, and all at once he found himself torn by conflicting emotions. He fought the urge to crush her hand in his, the way her father had surely crushed his brother. Yet even as he wanted to conquer and defeat all that she was, he longed to rip the pins from her hair, to feel it tumble over his fingers, all warm, dark silk as he urged her rose-tinted mouth to his. He wanted her to come to him. He wanted to see her walk to him, her form all fluid, perfect and agile gracefulness. . . .

"I wish to make my home in a quiet restful place such as this, Miss Duval, so, please, trouble yourself no further." His tone was soft. He brought her fingers to his lips, a fleeting touch that was over almost as soon as it was begun. "I promise you, I shall be quite satisfied here at Lockhaven, for I am just a common, hard-working man like any other."

With that, he bid her farewell and strode from the study. His plan had been set into motion.

Now all he could do was wait.

Two

He was not a man like any other. Nor was he common.

Heather had never been more certain of anything in her life.

Slowly she lowered herself to her seat once more. Her legs felt peculiarly unsteady. And her heart was knocking wildly, the way it had when he'd come upon her this morning.

She chided herself for her foolishness, yet she could not dismiss it so easily. Indeed, his presence was still a palpable force in the room.

He'd kissed her hand. Why. *Why?*

He'd been treading on dangerous ground, for it was a presumption both bold and blatant. And then there was the way he'd looked at her that morning. His gaze had wandered over her unbound hair, the bareness of her shoulders, lingering on her breasts. An odd feeling tightened her middle. Strange, but she wouldn't have said his attention was brazen or even impudent, so much as it had been just . . . intent.

It was unsettling, that's what it was. *He* was unsettling. Since the moment they'd met, he'd scarcely left her thoughts. It wasn't just his looks, though never had she encountered a man so strikingly pleasing to the eye. No, it wasn't that at all. . . .

There had been something compelling about him—a glimpse of some elusive emotion shuttered deep in his soul, and it was that which had drawn her to him. It was that which she had sought to capture in her sketch.

Heather couldn't help it. Her hand stole to the top drawer of her desk. Paper rustled as she pulled the sketch from its hiding place.

Her teeth dug unconsciously into her lower lip. She stared at her depiction of his profile . . . the firm, square jaw, patrician brow and chiseled lips were almost flawlessly classical.

She'd never dreamed he was Damien Lewis, the man she was to interview that very day.

Slowly she let out her breath, lowering the sketch to the desktop. A frown furrowed the smoothness of her brow. Had she made a mistake in hiring him?

In all honesty, there had been only a handful of applicants for the position. Most men were too proud—too lofty, in her mind—even to consider working for a woman. She'd begun to think she would be forced to place an ad in the London daily in order to find a replacement.

Having just reached the age of five-and-twenty, Heather was well aware that she was considered "on the shelf." In truth, she'd always known she would never marry. No matter how hard she tried—no matter how she used to wish otherwise—she'd resigned herself to spinsterhood when she was still a child. She'd known that her life could never be the same as those of other young women of her age and station. 'Twas a simple fact of life, for she could not change what she was. She would always be . . . different.

But she was lucky. On the occasion of her twenty-first birthday, Mama and Papa had bestowed on her a most unusual gift—Lockhaven Park. It was their way of giving her the means to attain both prosperity and her own self-esteem. From the start, Heather had been determined not to disappoint them. She had promptly discovered that being a landowner was no easy task. Being a woman, especially one such as herself, made it doubly hard.

But Lockhaven had prospered and flourished under her care and toil. She had made it what it was today, and she had done it solely on her own.

That was something that could never be taken from her.

Still, Robin's death had been a blow. He had been an old, trusted friend whom she'd known almost her entire life, and she still missed him dreadfully. But her estate manager was also essential to Lockhaven itself. Robin had been a crucial pair of hands—perhaps, more aptly, a pair of legs—for she simply could not travel about the estate as she might have wished.

Papa had hinted that he would be happy to help her find a new estate manager, but, as always, Heather was determined to manage on her own. Some might have said it was stubborn pride, but Heather didn't think so. True, Papa had offered advice from time to time, but he hadn't interfered, and for that she was grateful.

Small fingers curled around the edge of the sketch. Yes, she told herself firmly. Damien Lewis was the right man. Despite her few misgivings, she could feel it. What did it matter that just looking at him made her feel all strange and fluttery inside? He was confident—oh, he was most certainly that! Arrogant? Perhaps a trifle, but there were times when that was not such a bad thing. But it was neither of those things that inspired her decision.

No, she reasoned slowly. It was more a feeling that he would be forthright and honest no matter the cost, a man she could trust implicitly.

Just then the study door burst open. With a swirl of skirts and a flurry of movement, her sister Beatrice rushed in.

At sixteen, Beatrice was a beauty on the verge of full bloom. Slim and petite, her hair a mass of golden-blond curls, Bea was the image of her mother, Victoria Grayson, Countess of Stonehurst.

In truth, Heather was in no way related to the Graysons. But she had grown up the ward of Miles Grayson, the Earl of Stonehurst, and they were the only family she had ever known, for she remembered neither her mother nor her father.

She'd been very young, scarcely four, when she'd come under the care of the earl. Heather didn't remember the carriage accident that had claimed the lives of her parents; she had been the only survivor. The accident had occurred just outside Stonehurst, and the earl had taken her in while she recovered. Indeed, all she remembered of that time was being held safe and warm in the strong and comforting embrace of the man she'd always known as "Papa."

Miles hadn't been married then. He'd met—and married—his wife, Victoria, several years later in London. Heather would never forget the first time she'd seen Victoria—she'd thought her a fairy princess. But Victoria was warm and loving, and from the start there had been a bond between them that nothing could erase. Victoria had had no qualms about taking in another's child as her own.

Heather hadn't been an only child for long, however. Within a year of their marriage, Miles and Victoria had had another daughter. Heather had been eight when Bea was born. Two other children had followed over the years as well. Christina was twelve, and Arthur, as dark as his sisters were fair, had just celebrated his eighth birthday.

Oh, there had been times when Heather had felt a pang of guilt that she could remember nothing of her parents. But Miles and Victoria, Beatrice, Christina and Arthur were her family now. She loved them as much as they loved her. It was as simple as that.

And as usual, Beatrice was her normal, vibrant self. "Heather! I just passed the most divine-looking gentleman riding down the lane. Never say he came from here!"

Heather had quickly shoved the sketch back into her drawer. Now she leaned back in her chair, her expression indulgent. "As a matter of fact, Bea, he did."

"He did?" Beatrice squealed and dashed across the floor. "Oh, Heather, who is he? And whatever was he doing here?"

"I've just hired him as my new estate manager. His name is Damien Lewis."

"*He* is your new estate manager? Oh, Heather, he tipped his hat to me and wished me good day, and I thought I would swoon!" Beatrice pressed her hand to her forehead and pretended to do exactly that, sinking back onto a small settee.

Heather suppressed a smile. Beatrice was a great reader of novels and full of all things romantic. Little wonder that she was smitten with Damien Lewis.

Beatrice popped up an instant later. "He's smashingly good-looking, don't you think?"

Despite herself, Heather's heart lurched. Yet her tone was aplomb itself. "I really hadn't noticed, Bea."

Beatrice clasped her hands to her breast. "But his eyes were so blue, Heather."

"His eyes were gray, love." Her tone was absent.

Bea slanted her a glance. Wicked amusement sparkled in her eyes. "Ah, so you did notice!"

"Of course I didn't!" Heather objected strenuously.

"Oh, come, Heather. He is surely the handsomest man in all England, and if I were you . . . why, I would hire him, too!"

"Of course he isn't! And I'll have you know, young miss, I hired him for his qualifications—

and because I believe he'll do an excellent job."
Even as she spoke, Damien's visage flashed
through Heather's mind—high cheekbones, a
smooth-shaven jaw, his gray eyes arresting and
keen.

"I suppose you're right. Of course you hired
him for his qualifications—and not his looks."
Bea gave an airy laugh. "Why, the notion that
you, of all people, would do so is really quite
silly, isn't it?"

Heather's mouth opened and closed. She
couldn't stifle the pang that swept through her.
Just because she'd never had a suitor in her life
didn't mean she was completely unmindful of
the male race. Most of the time she didn't mind
that there wasn't a man alive who would spare
her more than a passing glance. But for the blink
of an eye, a faint wistfulness overtook her.

Lord, had she ever been as young as Beatrice?
When Bea came out next Season, she would soon
have the world at her fingertips—clothes, parties, gentlemen who would dote on her every
word and write poetry about her beauty. Bea had
so much before her, so much that she would
never have . . .

Bea leapt up from her chair with a snap of her
fingers. "I have it! I shall talk Mama and Papa
into planning a ball. I've begun dance lessons,
you know." She pulled a face. "We can invite
Mr. Lewis. And of course you shall come, too,
Heather—"

Heather interrupted with gentle firmness.
"Bea, Damien Lewis is surely almost twice your
age."

"A man of experience! I should like that, I think." It was as if Bea heard nary a word she spoke. She spun around the room, one wrist delicately bent as if resting on the shoulder of an imaginary dance partner.

"I think you read far too many novels, Bea." Heather's tone was dry. She rose, grimacing a little. Her knee was rather stiff today. Too much sitting, she decided, reaching for her cane.

Beatrice pouted playfully and made another face. "Mama says 'tis because you were always telling me stories when I was a child."

You are still a child, Heather nearly retorted.

"So if I do," the girl went on loftily, "'tis because of you."

"And if I did," Heather said with a chuckle, "'tis because Mama told *me* so many stories."

Bea swirled to a halt. Darting forward, she seized Heather's hand. "'Tis a glorious day, is it not? And far too warm to stifle here inside. Why don't we go out? Christina and Arthur will soon be along. I'll ask Marcus to bring us tea and cookies out on the terrace."

Heather sighed, but it was a halfhearted sound. "Bea, I have work to do."

Bea dismissed her protest airily. "Oh, pooh. You work too hard, Heather. Even Mama and Papa say so. So you may as well come, for I won't leave until you do."

Heather sought to fix her sister with a sternfully reproaching look. She failed abominably, and they both burst into laughter.

But it seemed that Beatrice would have the last word after all. Bea looped her arm through hers as they passed through the doorway. She cast Heather a sidelong glance through curling blond lashes.

"He is, you know."

Puzzled, Heather tipped her head in silent query.

"Damien Lewis," Bea said demurely. "He *is* the handsomest man in all England."

Damien did not return straightaway to the Eppingstone Inn. Instead he rode south and east, to the town of Willoughby. There was a small tavern near the river. Long tables were lined with men, their boisterous laughter and booming voices bouncing off the low ceiling. Tobacco smoke spiraled lazily upward. But in the corner by the door, a man sat alone, his back resting against the wall as he surveyed the scene before him. He was slender and unassuming, dressed in drab brown wool, not at all the sort of man one was apt to take notice of unless pointed out.

Damien opened the door to a burst of laughter and smoke-filled air. The echo of his boots was lost amidst the din as he strode toward the bar. But before he was even halfway there, his elbow was seized by a buxom wench with curling brown hair and a generous, crooked-toothed smile.

"Looking for a spot o'ale this fine evening, sir?"

Damien inclined his head. "That I am," he replied.

"Then you've come to the right place." She nodded toward the barkeep. "Douglas brews the best ale in Lancashire."

"Then I'm all the more eager to sample it." Judging from the laden smell of her breath, she'd had more than her own share already.

The wench grinned. "Maybe you'd like some company to go along with your ale, eh?" She ran her hand down his forearm and thrust her breast against his side; it was an unmistakable invitation.

Damien's eyes wandered over her upturned face. Her cheeks were ruddy and full, her lips chapped but wearing a ready smile. The wench was eager, her body warm and full and soft. It spun through his mind that this was not what he'd come for, but perhaps later . . . But no, for his own body was patently unresponsive—and despite the fact that it had been weeks since he'd lain with a woman, he suspected it would remain so.

He retrieved a coin from his pocket. Pressing it into her palm, he gave a faint shake of his head. "Another time," he said softly, then proceeded on his way.

The man in the corner watched quietly as the barkeep filled a tankard with ale and handed it to Damien, who turned and retraced his steps to the door. Neither glance nor words passed between the two, but a moment later the man in the corner rose from his chair. His ale in hand, he slipped outside where it was quiet, where they wouldn't be noticed . . . where they could talk.

Damien stood with his back to the tavern, his posture rigidly upright, one booted foot braced against the rough bark of an oak tree. The man from the corner approached, the damp ground muffling the sound of his footsteps. He halted several feet away from Damien but spoke not a word.

It was Damien who broke the silence, his voice terse. "I got the position."

"Good. That will put you close to her. You'll be aware of everything that goes on."

Cameron Lindsey's voice held a note of quiet satisfaction. It was more than just money, though he was being amply paid. In all his years as an investigator, he'd never seen a man more driven than Damien Lewis Tremayne. But what was truly his quest? Vengeance? Justice? Satisfaction? It could have been any of these things . . .

Or perhaps all of them.

"She's not what I expected." Damien stared into the encroaching darkness. "I thought she would be like him. Like her father, a conniving, murdering bastard." His tone was bitter, but then it turned almost accusing. "But she's not. She's intelligent. Beautiful. She has this—this air of sophisticated gentility about her. And damn it all, it—it irritates the hell out of me!"

Cameron studied him. "You must remember, she was probably no more than three or four years of age when she was last with her father. He was sent to Newgate shortly after her mother was killed. She may have been too young to even remember him."

Damien turned to face him. "The story the villagers tell is that both her parents were killed in a carriage accident. You're certain the man accompanying the woman in the carriage was not Heather's father?"

"James Elliot is her father." Cameron spoke with conviction. "I spoke with a woman who knew both her parents, James *and* Justine—and she mentioned they had a little girl."

Damien's jaw clenched. It was Cameron who had learned Justine had been killed in a carriage accident in Lancashire. "And you're absolutely certain this is the same Justine who was married to Elliot?"

Cameron nodded. "There are too many similarities for it *not* to be," he emphasized. "The daughter was the same age. We know Justine departed London at that time. The name listed on the passenger list was Justine Duval—her maiden surname. It *has* to be," he said again.

"So why wasn't she using the surname Elliot?"

Cameron's features were grim. "I don't know," he admitted. "Perhaps she was trying to get away from her husband. Lord knows he was a violent man—after all, he murdered those two poor fellows and ended up in Newgate."

Damien's knuckles shone white. His jaw clenched hard.

He asked the question he'd asked a hundred times before. "But that doesn't explain why he would murder Giles. *Why?* As far as we've been able to discover, Giles had no enemies. And James Elliot was in prison for the last twenty years—Giles was just a boy when Elliot entered Newgate. They couldn't possibly have known each other. It makes no sense!"

Damien fell into a brooding silence. His frustration was keenly apparent.

It wasn't the first time tragedy had touched his

life. But he'd come home to England, only to find Giles barely cold in his grave. . . .

Cameron laid a comforting hand on his shoulder. "I know this has been difficult for you."

Damien blew out a weary sigh. "You must think I'm ungrateful," he said quietly. "On the contrary. Without you I'd not know where to turn next. You've been an immense help, Cameron." For indeed, the magistrate's investigation had turned up nothing. *An unfortunate accident*, he'd called it. Damien might have been convinced he was right. That Giles had caught his perpetrator in the midst of a robbery, and thus been killed for it. . . .

But it appeared that nothing had been taken from either the house or the grounds. And more importantly, there was reason to believe James Elliot had deliberately sought out Giles at Deverell, the family estate in Yorkshire—that he'd been after something.

"But it was you who was able to point me in the right direction," Cameron said. "If you hadn't found the maid Corinne . . ."

Corinne. Damien's mind traveled back. All of the household staff but the maid Corinne had stayed on to await his appearance, for Giles had expected him shortly. Indeed, he'd arrived within several weeks of Giles's death. But Corinne, an upstairs maid, had quit the day after the magistrate had interviewed all the household servants—and disappeared.

The magistrate was unable to locate her, and so Damien decided to carry on his own investigation. Perhaps it was nothing; perhaps there was every reason to be suspicious of the way the maid had fled. Whatever the reason, he'd been determined not to neglect the smallest detail.

In talking with those who knew the girl, he discovered she had a sister in Northumbria—and it was there he'd found her.

But all was not as he'd thought. . . .

At first Corinne had refused to talk to him. But when he confronted her about why she'd left, she'd broken down. "Ye cannot think I did it!" she'd cried.

Damien was determined. "What else am I to think? You fled the day after you spoke to the magistrate. Surely you can see why one might think you the guilty party."

"I left because I was afraid to stay on!"

It was true. Damien could see it in her eyes. But an eerie prickling ran up his spine; every sense within him warned that she was hiding something. "None of the other servants left," he pointed out. "You were the only one."

"It wasn't me. It wasn't! Lord Deverell was good to me! 'Twere someone else killed him, I swear!"

"Who, Corinne? *Who*?"

Her eyes darted to the windows of the tiny cottage. She began to shake as if she'd been submerged in an icy brine. Silent tears ran down her cheeks.

She was terrified . . . for her very life.

"I believe you, Corinne." His tone was quietly

intent. "But my brother was murdered. I want to find his killer. I implore you, if you know anything that will help me, please tell me."

It took several more minutes to coax and calm her, but finally she began to talk.

"I slept in a room off the kitchen," she said. "And it was in the wee hours near morn that I awoke, y'see. I heard a man shouting—aye, and there was a terrible pounding, too!—but the man I heard was not the master, mind ye. I knew it, for the earl was not one to raise his voice in anger—ever. And it wasn't coming from above-stairs."

"Was it a voice you knew?" he asked quickly.

Corinne shook her head. "I'd never heard it afore in my life. I'm certain, m'lord."

"What happened then?"

The girl began wringing her hands. "Oh, but I can't believe how foolish I was! I—I crept into the hallway, for by then I could tell the noise came from the earl's study. 'Twas dark, so I hid near the door, which was slightly ajar."

She clasped her hands in her lap. "The man inside . . . he was throwing things on the floor, against the walls. From what little I could see, the room was a shambles. And he was ranting, m'lord, screamin' at the earl about how he'd spent twenty years in prison waiting for this night and he'd not be cheated. 'Where is it?' he demanded. Over and over and over."

"'It'?" Damien's gaze narrowed. "What was he after, Corinne?"

"I've no idea, m'lord. But the earl . . . oh, I

could hear that he was afraid, too . . . he insisted he didn't know. But that horrible man—he wouldn't listen! He cursed the earl—oh, so foully!—and accused the earl of lying. Of trying to keep it for himself."

Corinne's hands began to tremble anew. "The man whirled around and seized the poker from the fireplace. I couldn't see the master, but I heard him . . . 'Mercy,' he cried. 'Have mercy.' But that horrid man had none. I could see his shadow on the wall. He raised the poker high and swung it down. . . ."

Damien's eyes squeezed shut. His body jerked, for the pain that tore through him was like a blow to the center of his soul.

"And then I didn't hear the master anymore. Oh, it was terrible, my lord. Terrible! He is a madman. There was such rage in him. I could hear it. I—I could feel it!" Corinne was crying softly now. "I—I knew what he'd done and I've never been so frightened in my life. I—I ran back to my bed and hid there till morn!"

Damien swallowed, his throat thick and tight. So this was how Giles had died . . . and for what? *What?* What had that bastard been searching for? The bedchambers had been torn apart as well, according to the magistrate.

He had to force himself to steady his voice. "Was this why you didn't tell the magistrate? Because you were afraid?"

"Yes! I was afraid he'd find out I saw him and come after me! That's why I left as soon as I could!"

He handed her his handkerchief. "Did you see this man, Corinne? Did you see him at any time?"

She dabbed at her eyes, refusing to meet his gaze. "No," she said in a tiny little voice.

She was lying. He sought to curb his frustration and didn't entirely succeed. "You saw him, Corinne. Dammit, I know you did."

She raised her head, only now her eyes were blazing. "And what if I did! All I saw was a glimpse. He was older than the earl, with grimy black hair, but so what? And once—once!—he passed by the door, so close I could see the thumb of his hand was missing, but so what—"

"Which hand? Right or left?"

"I don't remember! Don't you see, it doesn't matter. It won't bring back the earl—"

"No, it won't. But with your help we can find his murderer. Would you recognize this man if you saw him again, Corinne?"

The girl leaped to her feet. "I don't know! Don't ye see, I just don't know! And it won't do no good to bring the magistrate here, because I'll just deny it! If that man ever finds out I saw him, he'll come after me. And then maybe one night I'll end up on the floor as dead as yer brother!"

Damien tried to reason with her. "Corinne, please! I'll send you and your sister away where it's safe—"

"No! Ye can't make me see him again. Do ye hear? Ye can't!" She was adamant, but bleeding through her defiance was a world of genuine terror. "I'll never tell another soul what I've just told you, m'lord, and that's a promise."

He'd thanked her and given her enough money to take her and her sister far, far away, then departed.

He didn't blame her for thinking of her own safety; indeed, he was grateful, for now he had a trail to follow.

The man who had killed Giles had spent twenty years in prison . . . and was recently released. It was then that Damien had hired Cameron Lindsey. It wasn't long before Cameron discovered that James Elliot—missing the thumb of his left hand—had left Newgate only days before Giles's murder.

Slowly he brought his mind back to the present. Pain seared his heart, while the evening breeze cooled the fire of his anger.

So it was that his quest had led him here to Lancashire—and to Heather Duval. So it was that he masqueraded under the name Damien Lewis. So it was that questions circled in his mind like vultures around their prey. Was Heather raised under the Earl of Stonehurst's wardship because her father had been in prison? What did she know? What did she remember? Why didn't she use her rightful surname, Elliot? Why hadn't her mother? Was Cameron right? Had Justine Elliot been trying to escape her husband?

"So." Cameron broke the silence. "Do you want me to keep searching for Elliot?"

Damien nodded. "Meet me here six weeks hence, unless you hear from me. Should you learn anything of importance, send word to me at Lockhaven."

Cameron's expression was guarded. "You

know," he said slowly, "Elliot may have gone into hiding to protect himself. It's possible he may not resurface for months, even years."

Damien's jaw locked. "I'll never stop searching. I'll find my brother's murderer, no matter what it takes."

Cameron gave a wordless salute, then slipped away into the darkness.

Damien remained where he was. No, he reflected harshly. He couldn't believe it would end this way. He *wouldn't*. He had no patience for waiting. In time, he told himself. In time he would find James Elliot.

It was a gamble, but one he must take—and one that was worth the risk. James Elliot had a daughter, a daughter he'd not seen in twenty years. Surely he would return to his daughter. . . .

Perhaps he already had.

Three

It was noon, another glorious day. Sunlight streamed down from the sky in brilliant abandon. Birds trilled their songs from high in the treetops, proclaiming the beauty of the day to all who listened.

Heather slanted a smile of thanks toward the groom who helped her into the curricle. She was no sooner settled in her seat than the drumming of hoofbeats reached her ear.

He was right on time.

She inhaled deeply, curling her fingers into her palms. Her stomach had been twisting and churning all morning, for the thought of encountering her new estate manager again was . . . what? *Almost terrifying.* But that was ridiculous. She was a woman full-grown, and he was but a man like any other. . . .

She maintained that very thought as he trotted his mount near; he rode a huge black stallion with massive flanks.

"Good morning," he called out.

"Good morning, Mr. Lewis."

"It's a fine day, is it not?"

"Exceedingly."

He reined to a halt next to the curricle, resting one strong wrist across his thigh. "Should I ride alongside you?"

"Not at all. Please, join me." She gestured to the empty seat beside her.

He dismounted, handing his reins to the groom with a wink. "His name is Zeus," he told the boy. "But don't let that frighten you. He's a pudding-heart if you scratch his nose and give him a handful of oats."

He turned and, with one fluid move, vaulted onto the seat beside her. Briskly she snapped the reins, and they were off.

It was all she could do not to look over at him. Faith, but he seemed enormous—seated next to him like this, she could feel his size with every sense that she possessed. His legs stretched out far beyond hers, almost impossibly long; his breeches fit him like a second skin, clinging to the breadth of his thigh muscles. Had he raised an arm, her shoulder would have fit neatly into the hollow beneath. His hands rested casually on his knees. An odd feeling knotted in her breast, for, even relaxed, his hands were intensely masculine, the backs sprinkled with fine, dark hairs. His fingers were tanned, long and lean; she remembered well the feel of her own swallowed up within his. His skin had been so warm. . . .

You ninny! Stop this! she chided herself furiously. Why, she was acting every bit as foolishly as Bea had yesterday.

She stole a glance at him. "I thought I'd show you the estate buildings first, then stop in the village. I'd like you to meet the vicar, and I'll introduce you to the shopkeepers with whom we trade. From there we can visit the tenants."

He nodded. "By the way, I'm delighted with the house." There was a small pause. "And it was quite generous of you to have the pantry stocked."

Heather felt a rush of heat in her cheeks. "That's quite all right."

The wheel hit a rut in the road, jostling her shoulder against his side. Heather straightened immediately and held herself stiffly erect. If he noticed her reaction, he gave no sign of it.

They soon approached a cluster of outbuildings. She pointed out the smokehouse, the icehouse, the springhouse, a small blacksmith's shop. The largest, she explained, was the dairy. It was there that she reined the curricle to a halt.

Damien leaped lightly to the ground, then immediately turned. She was barely on her feet when she felt her waist gripped by strong hands. He swung her to the ground; she flinched a little, for she was not used to being touched so by a man. Yet instinctively she caught at the wide span of his shoulders. Her fingertips registered hardness and warmth. The contact was over in a mere instant, for she hurriedly withdrew her hands while fighting an irrational fluttering of her stomach.

"Actually I'm quite proud of the dairy," she said brightly. "I'm told our cheese is the best in the shire, and we transport several carts weekly to Liverpool, since we supply many of the shops there. Last year we had to step up production, for the demand far exceeded what I expected."

She was talking as she began to move forward, unaware that her companion was listening with half an ear. . . .

Damien couldn't help it.

God, but she was even lovelier than he recalled. Her clothing was less formal than it had been at their meeting yesterday. She wore neither gloves nor cap, but a simple gown of pale yellow muslin, embroidered with dainty white flowers on the sleeves and hem. Nor had she pulled her hair up in a severe bun; her long, shining tresses were caught back at the nape in a bright yellow ribbon. The color of a sunrise glowed on her cheeks and skin; the soft purple of summer heather came alive in her eyes. He couldn't help but think she was like the gypsy he'd first seen in the meadow. . . .

She turned and stepped toward the dairy entrance.

He felt as if a fist had plowed straight into his belly. This was the first time he'd seen her on her feet, he realized. But her movements were not smooth and flowing, as he'd envisioned. And in that mind-splitting moment, all he could think was that his perfect little gypsy was not so perfect after all. . . .

He couldn't help it. Stunned, he couldn't tear his eyes from her. Her gait was slow and hitched; her right leg lagged slightly behind.

His mind balked. A part of him was appalled. Dear God. It seemed almost obscene that such blemish should mar this beautiful young woman. . . .

Some unknown sense must have warned her of his shock. She turned.

But perhaps she was hurt. . . . "Forgive me, Miss Duval. We could have delayed this if I'd known you were injured—"

Something flickered in her eyes. "I'm not hurt, Mr. Lewis."

Damien was at a rare loss for words. The awkward silence dragged on, for this was surely the longest moment in his life. Shame twisted his vitals. "I'm sorry," he heard himself say. "I didn't mean to stare."

It was a moment before she spoke. "I'm sure you didn't," she replied quite pleasantly. "But no matter, I'm quite accustomed to it."

Perhaps she was. But she hated it. He'd known it the instant their eyes collided—the very instant her gaze became shuttered and cool. He longed to ask what had happened—had she suffered some injury as a child, perhaps? Yet something in her proud demeanor stopped him.

He felt like an oaf. "I've offended you."

"No. You haven't. But that reminds me. Would you please fetch my cane from beneath the seat?"

It was the same wooden cane he'd seen propped by her desk yesterday in the study. He felt like a fool for not having guessed.

Wordlessly he handed it to her. Their hands barely brushed. She withdrew hers quickly, as if she couldn't bear to touch him—and little wonder. He'd hardly endeared himself to her just now. She resumed her pace, her carriage almost painfully erect.

She was amicable and gracious as she showed him through the cluster of buildings, and they spoke with the workmen there. He had to force his mind to the business at hand, for a dozen questions circled through his mind again and again. Why did she limp? Had she been born with some deformity of the leg? Or had she suffered some injury long ago?

He felt foolish for blundering so, yet he reminded himself that he couldn't have known. Of course he couldn't blame Heather. It wasn't the sort of thing one blurted out. Still, it didn't make the next few hours any easier—for either of them, he suspected.

She was a cripple. Lame. He pitied her; he couldn't help it. But pity was the last thing he wanted to feel for her. He couldn't allow such emotions to cloud his purpose, to color his judgment in any way, nor could he let it sway him from his course.

On another, far different level, he couldn't help but be impressed, for it seemed Lockhaven was both self-sufficient and profitable. The villagers greeted her with genuine warmth and the utmost respect, and so did her tenants. She embraced the latest developments in farming technology and encouraged her tenants to do so as well. Pride laced her tone as they traveled through the estate—and indeed, Damien could not blame her, for there was much here to be proud of. They passed ploughmen guiding teams of oxen over wide, rolling fields, split here and there by hedges as solid and stout as walls. Plump, woolly sheep meandered across the land, while fat, lazy cows dotted the pastures.

No, he thought slowly. Nothing about her was as he expected.

Just then she turned down a narrow, dusty lane lined with juniper bushes and fruit trees. It ended before a low-slung cottage with a steep, thatched roof. A hound stretched out beside the garden lifted his long nose high in the air. His nostrils twitched as he caught a familiar scent— and an unfamiliar one as well.

Beside him, Heather tugged gently at the reins; the curricle rolled to a halt. Damien jumped down and reached back to assist her. She did not disdain his touch, yet neither did she speak. The dog rose and loped over. She called him by name, reaching down to scratch his mangy coat.

"Hello there, Samuel. Where is your mistress?"

The mutt's mistress had just appeared in the cottage doorway, shielding her eyes against the glare of the sun. When she saw the curricle, she gave a cry of delight.

"Miss Heather! Whatever brings you here?"

The woman was big and rawboned, older than Heather by a number of years—and heavy with child.

Damien remained where he was as the two women embraced heartily. "I told you I'd stop by to check on you this week, Bridget." Heather chuckled, then glanced at Damien. "Bridget and

her husband, Robert MacTavish, farm this sec-
tion of land," she told him. "Bridget, this is
Damien Lewis, my new estate manager."

Bridget dropped into a clumsy curtsey. "It's
pleased I am to meet you, sir. I only wish my
husband, Robert, were here to meet you as well,
but he's helping out at the blacksmith's shop in
the village."

Damien inclined his head. "Then perhaps I'll
see him yet today, Mistress MacTavish."

In the meantime, Heather had turned back to
the curricle. "I have something for you, Bridget,"
she said over her shoulder. As she spoke, she
tugged two large baskets from beneath the seat.
Damien quickly stepped back to lend a hand.
She slanted him a glance from beneath silky,
dark lashes.

"Would you be so kind as to take these inside
the cottage for Bridget?"

"Certainly." He lifted the basket from the
curricle and stepped toward the doorway. "Mistress MacTavish, if you'll just mind the door for
me . . ."

Bridget hurried to oblige. Heather trailed behind them. Inside the cottage, Damien set the
baskets on a small worktable in the kitchen.

"Oh, my," Bridget breathed. "What is this,
Miss Heather?" Bridget scurried forward. She
reached out to flip aside white linen napkins, one
after the other. "Cheese and bread . . . a ham—
oh, and bacon, too! Oh, we'll be feasting for
weeks!"

"And I didn't forget your favorite—two jars of

Cook's strawberry jam from last harvest." Heather's eyes were twinkling.

"Oh, Miss Heather, you shouldn't have." She dabbed at her eyes with a corner of her apron. "It may be some while before Robert and I can repay you—"

Heather shook her head. Her hands clasped the older woman's. "Don't fret about that, Bridget. All that matters right now is that you take care of yourself and give birth to a healthy babe. Then, when you're ready, your position at the manor house will be waiting for you. Now tell me, are you doing as I asked? Are you resting for a time every morning and afternoon?"

Bridget's head bobbed up and down. "Oh, yes, ma'am. Twice a day, regular as clockwork."

"And are you able to put your feet up on a pillow? It will help when you sit as well, Bridget."

"I am, Miss Heather. And do you know, my ankles have not been nearly so puffy."

"That's good, Bridget."

"But my back . . . oh, it pains me somethin' awful at times."

Heather's features were compassionate. "I know, Bridget. But it'll soon be over, and, I daresay, it'll be worth all the discomfort." She squeezed Bridget's hands. "It's time we were on our way. I'll come see you again next week, I promise." She patted the woman's swollen belly. "Now take care of yourself and that little one."

Outside, Bridget reached out and hugged Heather fiercely. "Miss Heather, I pray nightly that this babe will be a girl! For if it is, I've

already told Robert we'll name it after you—
she'll be called Heather, and I hope she'll grow to
be as kind and generous as you!"

Heather blinked in surprise. "You'd name
your daughter after me? Really?" Her soft mouth
curved into a smile. "I'd like that, Bridget. I'd
like that very much." She leaned forward and
kissed the other woman's cheek. Damien could
have sworn there was a sheen of tears in those
brilliant violet eyes.

She was still smiling when she turned from the
lane several minutes later. Damien tipped his
head to the side and looked at her. "Bridget
works at the manor house?"

Heather nodded. "She's worked as an upstairs
maid for nearly four years now. But she's due in
less than two months, and last week it simply
became too much for her."

He continued to study her. "Are you a midwife?"

She seemed embarrassed. "Oh, no! Though
I've assisted at a number of births alongside the
midwife. She lives in the village just north of
here." Her eyes seemed to turn cloudy. "I only
hope she's able to come when Bridget delivers."

Damien raised a brow. "She trusts you," he
commented quietly. "Somehow I almost think
she'd prefer that you attend her."

Heather's expression was troubled. "Nearly
twenty years they've waited for a babe, and none
to come until now. Bridget was certain she was
barren. Unfortunately, it's been a difficult preg-
nancy. She belongs in the midwife's capable
hands, not mine." She smiled slightly. "You

should have seen Bridget when she learned she was with child. I swear everyone in the neighboring shire heard her shriek with happiness. I fancy this babe will be spoilt as no other."

As if on cue, there indeed came an excited cry from behind the curricle. Damien twisted around to see two small figures on horseback racing down the road toward them.

"Heather!"

"Heather, wait!"

Heather had turned as well. Raising a hand to her brow, she shielded her eyes against the sun's glare. "It's my brother and sister," she said. Both surprise and pleasure laced her voice. "There's Mama," she murmured. "Oh, and Beatrice." She pointed to where two figures had just come over the rise in the road. "Another sister," she added. Snapping the reins, she turned the curricle around to await them.

The children halted amidst a cloud of dust—a boy and a girl. They were young, he saw. The girl was perhaps thirteen or so. He judged the boy to be eight or nine years of age. Since he'd already alighted from the curricle, he stepped forward to help them from their mounts.

The girl, a pale blonde with an elfish face, thanked him shyly, then spun toward the curricle. The boy flashed a wide, unabashed smile and did the same. By the time he turned, they had both flanked Heather on the seat.

"You haven't visited in days," the girl was saying. "We've missed you, Heather."

Heather gave her a quick hug. "You could have come to visit me," she teased.

"We were," the girl said promptly.

Just then the boy piped up. He stabbed a finger at Damien. "Who are you?" he asked cheerfully. "Are you Heather's beau? Mama says she should have a beau."

Two spots of rose immediately flared high and bright in Heather's cheeks. Damien found himself possessed of the oddest urge to chuckle. Instead he came to her rescue.

He clicked his heels and gave a mock salute. "Damien Lewis at your service, young sir. I am your sister's new estate manager."

Heather had slipped her arms around the youngsters. "My sister Christina, Mr. Lewis, and my brother, Arthur—who has apparently forgotten that he does have the good manners not to point."

"And I," a sweet feminine voice chimed in, "am Heather's mother, Victoria Grayson. And this is my daughter Beatrice." The young girl beside her gave a beaming, vivacious smile. He inclined his head in acknowledgment.

Victoria had extended one gloved hand toward him. "I'm so glad that Heather has finally engaged a new estate manager," she was saying. "I'm sure you'll do a fine job."

Lady Victoria Grayson, clad in a fashionable riding habit, sat atop a spotted white mare, her hat perched at a jaunty angle on her bright blond curls. She was slender and petite, her waist as narrow as that of a woman twenty years her junior. Her daughter Beatrice had inherited the same blond hair, wide-set blue eyes and heart-shaped face.

Briefly he shook her hand. "I shall certainly try, my lady, though I've discovered today it will be quite a task stepping into Robin's shoes."

Victoria Grayson laughed. "Oh, I shouldn't worry if I were you, Mr. Lewis. Heather would never have engaged you if she didn't have every confidence in you." She turned her attention to Heather. "As for you, young lady, I'm almost inclined to believe you've forgotten you have a family." Though her tone was mildly reproving, her expression was soft.

Heather bit her lip, her eyes conveying a silent apology. "It's been a busy week, Mama."

"So I see, dear. But since we're so near Stonehurst, why don't you stop for a bit? I fear your father will never forgive either of us if you don't stop to say hello, at the very least. Better yet, stay for tea. And of course we'd love to have you, too, Mr. Lewis." She cocked her head to the side. "Can you spare an hour?"

"Of course I don't mind, Mama." Heather's gaze slid to Damien. "Unless it's an inconvenience for you, Mr. Lewis?"

Damien shook his head. "Not at all."

Indeed, he had to smother his satisfaction. Tea with Miles and Victoria Grayson. It couldn't have worked out better had he planned it himself. . . .

Half an hour's time found all of them seated in the huge, sumptuously furnished drawing room at Lyndermere Park, the country residence of the Earl and Countess of Stonehurst. Miles and Victoria occupied a settee across from the fireplace. The girl Beatrice sat to their right. Heather was in a velvet wing chair, her cane propped against the arm; Christina sat next to Heather, her head against Heather's shoulder. Arthur had devoured his poppyseed tea cakes and was off to the kitchen to beg for more.

Miles Grayson was a tall, dark-haired man with a spare, lean build and a commanding presence. His hair was sprinkled with gray and faint grooves lined his mouth, but like his wife, there was an air of youthful vitality about him. Damien was well aware that many a highbrowed aristocrat would never have invited him—for he was, at the moment, a mere employee of his daughter—into his house, let alone his drawing room. But they did not stand on formality; Miles Grayson appeared as gracious and hospitable as his wife, Victoria, totally without pretension.

Just a few short minutes with this family had revealed much. The bond Heather Duval shared with the Graysons was not one of blood . . .

But one of love.

A bitter darkness seeped into his soul. He envied them, all of them. The Graysons. Heather Duval . . . and yet he almost hated them. For this was a setting that he and Giles would never share. They would never sit together as brothers, with their families gathered close around the hearth, laughter and voices surrounding them. . . .

Giles had been robbed of this . . . as he had been robbed of his brother.

"Well, Mr. Lewis, what do you think of Lockhaven so far?" This came from the earl.

Damien shook aside his moodiness. "I'm very

impressed. It seems an extremely well-run estate."

"You should have seen Lockhaven four years ago. Oh, the house was in fairly decent repair. But the previous owner was far more interested in leaving his money at the gaming tables in London. Fields lay fallow, and most of the tenants had moved away." His gaze flickered to Heather. "I must say, Heather has done wonders. And, much to my wounded pride, all without my help."

"Well, you certainly tried hard enough." His wife frowned at him good-naturedly. "You were constantly looking over her shoulder—and trying desperately not to let her know it."

"Oh, she knew it," Heather injected dryly.

They all laughed, while Miles smiled feebly. "What can I say? I taught her well."

The incredible blue of Heather's eyes softened to a haze of violet. "That you did, Papa. That you did."

From the mantle, a mahogany clock tolled the passing of another hour. Victoria glanced between Beatrice and Christina. "Christina, it's time to study for your Latin examination tomorrow. Bea, the dance master will be here shortly. You'd best see that all is ready in the music room."

Christina immediately rose, but the older girl's full lips pouted. "Oh, Mama, must I? Please, let me stay."

Victoria arched a brow. "No, love."

"But he says I will never learn, that I have two left feet."

"Ah," Victoria said lightly. "All the more reason to practice, practice, practice."

Beatrice sighed and murmured her good-byes. Damien smiled politely, but all the while his attention remained on Heather.

The French doors behind her were slightly ajar. The breeze blew a wisp of hair across the curve of one cheek. He knew that, if he were to touch it, it would be as velvety-soft as the petal of a rose . . . he could almost feel it tickling against his skin. She raised a hand to brush it aside. He remembered the feel of her hand within his, small and dainty. A heaviness settled in his loins. God help him, he wanted to make love to her even more than he had yesterday morning. . . .

But what was this? He was immediately irritated with himself. He was acting like a green youth, as if he were smitten with the chit! Perhaps he'd been wrong last night. Perhaps he needed a woman after all. Maybe he should have taken that buxom, eager wench at the tavern. Perhaps then this fire in his blood would be quenched. . . .

Dimly he heard Victoria speaking. "Cook was telling me the spice peddler stopped by today. It seems there's a traveling fair passing through the shire. It's expected any day now. I remember, Heather, you always loved the jugglers when you were a child. Will you attend, do you think?"

Damien scarcely heard her reply. The talk turned to other matters, but it wasn't long before Heather reached for her cane. Damien wasted no time getting to his feet as well. The heat in his loins had cooled, but the darkness in his heart had yet to lighten.

Miles and Victoria accompanied them outside. While Miles handed Heather into the curricle, Damien resumed his place beside her.

She picked up the reins, her regard on Miles. "What would you like for your birthday, Papa?"

"Your prize ram," he said promptly.

Miles missed the wink that passed between Heather and Victoria, but Damien didn't. When Heather laughed, a tinkling, musical sound, he felt as if he would splinter into a thousand pieces.

"Think of something else, Papa." With a final wave, they were off.

Both were unaware of Victoria Grayson's lingering gaze as the curricle sped away.

She linked her arm through her husband's. "Mr. Lewis seems a very nice young man, doesn't he?"

"Hmmm."

Together they strolled back inside. "Intelligent, too, wouldn't you say?"

"Most certainly. Heather's made an excellent choice, if I do say so myself."

Victoria's tone was innocence itself. "Bea had confided to me that Mr. Lewis was quite the handsomest man in all England. Do you suppose Heather thinks so, too?"

Miles stopped short. "I beg your pardon?"

Victoria chuckled.

He blinked. "Heather, you say?"

She reached up to touch his nose. Her tone was

airy. "Heather is a woman full-grown, my love—
and she is *not* blind. But do you know, I do
believe Bea is right."

   She left Miles staring in dumbfounded amazement after her.

Four

Heather cast a furtive glance beneath her lashes at her companion. Before she'd left for her dance lesson, Beatrice had scarcely taken her eyes off him, from the instant she'd entered the drawing room. Had anyone noticed . . . had *he*? Her mind raced on. He must be used to such attention from pretty females. Heather, however, couldn't help feeling vastly perturbed with Bea—and with herself for taking note of her sister's obvious preoccupation!

But, with forced gaiety, she displayed no sign of it as she addressed him. "Well," she said lightly, "I do believe you've passed muster."

He turned his head. "I beg your pardon?"

"I'm not complaining, mind you. But when Robin died and I began searching for a new estate manager, I suspect Papa would have dearly loved it if I'd asked him to assist me in finding a replacement."

"And you didn't?"

She shook her head.

"Are you saying the two of you tend to cross swords?"

"Oh, no, not in the least! But, you see, my sister Bea visited yesterday after I engaged you, and I've no doubt the subject came up at dinner last night. So I suspect Papa has been chafing ever since, wondering whom I'd hired, if I'd made the right choice. . . ."

"Hmmm," he said dryly. "Then perhaps I should be glad I've gained Papa's approval. I'd not want the Earl of Stonehurst after my hide."

Heather laughed.

"But," he went on, "even though you are of age, and an immensely capable woman, I think it's only natural that your parents show such concern."

His praise was oddly pleasing. "They are my family," she said simply. "I consider myself very lucky to have them."

"It's obvious they feel the same."

Heather's expression grew soft. "Thank you," she said quietly.

For a moment the only sound was that of hoofbeats clopping down the road. Beside her, Damien spoke. "I hope you do not think me rude or presumptuous, but I confess I'm curious . . . I couldn't help but note that you carry a different surname than your parents, yet you told me you have no husband. Perhaps I misunderstood . . . ?"

"No," she said quickly. "My surname is Duval—I'm the daughter of Bernard and Justine Duval. When I was very young, we were victims

of a carriage accident not far from here. I was the
only survivor. You see, my parents were on their
way to visit Miles Grayson; they'd met him in
Paris years earlier. My father was a French
aristocrat; my mother, an English lady. Unfortunately, my father made some ill-timed invest-
ments and was impoverished. They had come to
England to begin their life anew."

Liar! Damien longed to shout. *Your father is
James Elliot, a murdering bastard, not Bernard
Duval. And your mother was from London, but
she was no lady.*

"After the accident," she went on, "I became
Miles's ward. I believe I was about four years of
age. I was eight when he married Victoria."
There was a tiny pause. "I'm sorry," she said
softly. "I didn't mean to confuse you. But it's
just that I think of Miles and Victoria as my
parents, and Beatrice and Christina and Arthur
as my sisters and brother."

Damien's smile would surely crack his face. "I
can see why."

He said no more, but Heather had a distinct
sense that all was not right. Perhaps the subject
of family was one that distressed him; after all,
she really knew nothing about his private life.
She was suddenly intensely curious about his
own background, yet there was something about
his stoic profile that stopped her from inquiring.
Puzzled, she turned her attention to her driving.

The rest of the journey back to Lockhaven
passed in silence. At the stables, he leaped down,

then turned to lift her to the ground. Heather stood while he handed her her cane, feeling awkward without quite knowing why.

"There are some bookwork and maps you should review as well, Mr. Lewis. If you'd like, I'll leave them on the desk in my study tomorrow morning. You can pick them up at your convenience."

"I'll do that, Miss Duval." He inclined his head. "Good day."

Several minutes later, she stood near the window in her room, watching him ride off in a cloud of dust. With a sigh, she allowed the dainty lace curtain to slip back into place.

Her gaited step took her across a delicately muted carpet of blue and gold, with a border of laurel leaves. She halted before a low mahogany chest of drawers fronted with rosewood accents. Occupying a place of honor atop the chest was a silver, claw-footed jewel case. Raised, polished scrollwork edged the side corners and top. Mother-of-pearl glistened as the lid caught the last fading rays of the sun. With a fingertip she traced the lettering etched within a small oval.

Her eyes grew tender. "Beloved," she murmured aloud, then smiled wistfully. This jewel case was all she had left of her mother, Justine Duval. Miles had told her he'd always regretted that everything else had been smashed to smithereens in the accident—but for Heather, it was enough. She would treasure it always.

Yet in the next instant, her eyes grew cloudy. Feeling almost guilty, she raised the lid. Her fingers dipped within. But it was neither pearls or jewels that she withdrew from the velvet-lined compartment.

It was the sketch of Damien Lewis.

Someday, she thought vaguely, she would like to paint him. . . .

She studied the drawing, drawn to it by a force she couldn't deny. She hadn't been wrong. She could feel it in her heart, in every part of her. This was a man who had known pain, a man who knew it still. . . .

A man with secrets?

Where the thought came from, she didn't know. Disquieted by the notion, she bit her lip. The memory of the hour spent at Stonehurst flooded her mind.

He hadn't seemed out of place at all, she realized. His manners were impeccable, his speech cultured. Certainly he was well-educated. Was he the son of some wealthy merchant? When he'd left this evening, he'd been so quiet. Almost brooding . . . Slowly she released her breath, stung by the feeling that all was not as it should be. . . . Who was he? Why was he here? He'd said he'd managed a plantation in Virginia. Was it true? Or did he have some hidden reason for coming to Lancashire—more precisely, to Lockhaven?

But that was preposterous. She was tired. The day had been a long one. That was all, for it wasn't her nature to let her imagination run wild. No, she would not succumb to such whimsical musings. She would leave that to Beatrice.

After dinner, she went straight to bed. Sleep came soon and easily. But then she began to

dream . . . only it was not a dream of all things
pleasant and restful and soothing.

*She lay huddled in the dark, afraid to move,
afraid of making the slightest sound . . . afraid of
something, but she knew not what.*

*She knew only that she must be quiet, for if she
was not, she would be punished. And above all,
she did not want that.*

*Only it was so cold. A thin, tattered blanket was
her only covering. The meager fire in the grate
was almost out. And the floor was so hard. Dampness seeped through the floor so that she could
barely stop shaking.*

*Rolling to her side, she drew her knees to her
chest. A tiny half-sob escaped. And then it was too
late. . . .*

He'd heard her.

*Her eyes flew wide as he rose from the corner, a
huge, hulking figure.*

*She stifled her cry, for she knew she'd made him
angry again . . . he was always angry. Terror iced
her veins as he came to stand directly over her.
Her heart pounded with fear. She wanted desperately to get up, to run, but there was nowhere to
go. Nowhere to run. She tensed, for she dared not
make a sound, not even the veriest peep. Perhaps
if she lay there unmoving, he would leave her be.*

*"Bitch," came his raspy voice. "God, but I curse
the day you were born." Her eyes snapped open.
She saw him then as he raised his fist high. In the
glow of the firelight, his face was a twisted mask of
rage. . . .*

She bolted upright in her bed. Her breath
rushed from her lungs. Vivid in her mind was

that face . . . *his* face. In the dream, she couldn't tell the color of his hair, yet she had the oddest feeling it was dark . . . but his eyes were gleaming pools of hatred. . . . In the dream, she knew that face—knew it and feared it.

She shuddered. It came to her at times when she was troubled, this dream. It had come to her often when she was younger, away at the school for ladies, which she'd so hated.

She wiped her palms on the counterpane. They were ice-cold and clammy. That terrible man in the dream . . . who was he? Was he someone she had seen before? How she wished she knew!—or did she? Perhaps it was better this way. Perhaps she was better off not knowing.

A shiver shook her slender form. She lay back down again, but this time she didn't sleep . . .

For fear of dreaming.

Heather was not the only one to spend a restless night. Damien lay awake for ages; with a grimace, he finally rose from the bed. He shrugged into a robe, then poured a generous amount of brandy into a glass and moved to sit in a wing chair near the hearth.

But he drank only sparingly. For the most part he stared into the amber liquid, his mind twisting and turning. The darkness in his heart lent him no ease; the somber mood that had slipped over him at the Graysons' persisted.

The day had been a revealing one, yet not in any way he might have foreseen. Indeed, he decided blackly, perhaps by now he should have begun to expect the *un*expected.

Perhaps it was small of him. Perhaps it was petty. But he couldn't help but think most men would have been repelled by Heather's lameness.

His mouth twisted. Hah! If only he were!

But there was something else as well, something he'd never bargained for, not in a hundred years. Respect for all she had accomplished in her young life. Admiration for her tenacity and ability to succeed despite her lameness.

He was reminded of Bridget—Heather's concern for the elder woman's well-being, her empathy for Bridget's childless state these many years. Unless he was mistaken, such was not an idle case. Indeed, he thought slowly, it seemed that Heather possessed a goodness, a sweetness of spirit, that extended to all those she knew and cared for.

These things were real. As real as the love she bore for her family—the love they returned in full measure.

It was inevitable, perhaps. But Damien couldn't help but think of what lay ahead for him. . . .

A goodly portion of his voyage to England had been spent contemplating exactly that—his future. He'd spent his first ten years in Virginia devoting nearly all of his attention and efforts to Bayberry—to seeing the fruits of his labor realized. Women had been a pleasant diversion during that time, but he'd never contemplated marriage with any degree of seriousness, for no woman had captured his fancy to such an extent.

Bayberry had indeed prospered, and all he sought lay within his grasp. But it was only recently that he'd come to a sense of his own limitations—another dimension of his deepest ambitions. He had no wish to see Bayberry—all he had worked for—pass into the hands of a stranger when he was gone. It was time he considered a family—a wife at his side. Children at his feet . . .

But Giles's death had changed everything, he thought bleakly. And in that moment, Damien felt alone as never before. He hadn't planned on inheriting the earldom; he didn't *want* either the title or the responsibility. He'd much rather have Giles back. . . .

But that could never be.

With a sigh, Damien set aside his glass. When this was over—when he'd found James Elliot—he must make a choice. A choice to return to Bayberry . . . or remain in England.

The fair Victoria had spoken of arrived several days later. Everyone in the manor house was abuzz with the news. Later that evening, Heather decided to pay a visit to the village. She enjoyed browsing among the goods brought by the various vendors. But most of all she enjoyed the gaiety and high spirits it wrought, as she had since she was a child.

The fair had been set up in the grassy meadow next to the bakery. Near the rectory, she left the pony and cart she used when she traveled alone then headed toward the meadow. She passed a cartload of fresh fish and wrinkled her nose at another of pale, sour oranges.

"Oh, come now," shouted the vendor.

"They're full o'goodness inside, I tell ye!" Heather merely shook her head, smiled and moved on.

"Look at this china, madam! Thin as air, mind you. Why, you can even see through it! Came straight from the tables of the Duke o'York, it did!"

She passed a tinker with braziers and grindstones, and a cart filled with crockery, then stopped to buy a dozen ells of satin hair ribbon, and spices for the kitchen. She gawked in amazement at the juggler and laughed with a group of children watching an organ grinder and his tiny monkey.

The next vendor, a tall, thin man clad in a stiff wool suit, had set out his display atop several large tables. Heather stopped curiously, for there were bottles and crocks of all shapes and sizes.

"Here's a bargain for all you ladies, a lotion that will whiten your skin so's it's as fair as any beauty's in London! You can have it for a crown—a tremendous sacrifice!"

"A crown!" one woman shouted back. "I vow it's not worth a shilling, but that's what I'll offer!"

"A shilling! Why, that's robbery! It cost more than that to make, but I'll tell ye what. Half a crown and no less!"

The woman rolled her eyes.

He held a different, dark-colored bottle high. "How 'bout this? It'll cure most any ailment from toothache to palsy."

The woman walked away. Heather was about to do the same, but all at once her elbow was seized in a steely grip.

It was the vendor. "Wait, m'lady." Gleaming eyes swept the length of her. "I saw ye come near, and I've a special salve, just for you. It'll heal that leg o'yours, or my name's not Peter Lennox."

Something inside her seemed to shrivel. She shook her head.

"Oh, come now." He pointed at her leg. "Ye can't enjoy bein' lame. Why, I used this salve on my crippled nephew, and he walks as straight as an arrow now."

The crowd had moved on, and no one was watching. She tried to pull back, but the man's grip was unrelenting.

"No," she told him, her voice very low. The last thing she wanted was to make a scene.

He persisted. "But it works miracles, I tell ye." He tugged at her arm, his fingers biting deep into her flesh. "Come, just let me show ye."

Panic swelled in her breast. Heather shook her head and tried to twist away, but he was too strong.

Before her there was a flash of movement. A lean, dark hand curled around the man's wrist. "The lady declined," said a quiet male voice. "Leave her be."

It was he—Damien Lewis. The vendor needed no further urging. His fingers fell away from her arm.

"Just tryin' to help the lady," he muttered gruffly. "If she doesn't mind bein' a cripple, so be it." He hunched his shoulders, then spun away toward his cart and began loading his goods inside.

Heather stood motionless. *Lame. Crippled.* The words stabbed at her. Her face burned painfully. Her heart cried out. *I'm not lame. I'm not a cripple.* But you are, whispered a voice in her head.

Damien had yet to move as well. Mortified beyond words, she could feel the weight of his regard. Sheer dint of will made her square her shoulders and tip her chin upward. She was suddenly smarting. What was he waiting for? Did he expect her to gush like a simpering, helpless female? Well, she was not. She had relied on no one but herself for a number of years. That was how she wanted it, and how it would stay.

"Thank you, Mr. Lewis." Her tone was as frigid as her gaze. "But I assure you, that wasn't necessary. I was hardly in need of rescuing."

A dark brow slashed high. "Indeed," he said, and his voice was as cold as a winter wind. "My apologies, then."

They each turned away and marched in opposite directions, unaware that the scene had been witnessed by someone else. Damien hadn't gone more than several footsteps before a hand claimed his arm. He whirled around, his eyes flaming as if he expected to do battle.

He faced Miles and Victoria Grayson.

Victoria spoke first, in obvious distress. "Mr. Lewis. May we have a word with you?"

Damien hesitated.

Miles glanced at Victoria, his expression uncomfortable. "Victoria, I'm not certain this is wise—"

"Perhaps not, dear. But I—I believe this should be said." Her plea quelled her husband's objection. A silent message passed between them; then he shifted his gaze to Damien. "A moment of your time, if you please, Mr. Lewis." The earl's tone was very quiet.

Damien decided there was little point in arguing. He followed them around the corner of the butcher's shop, where it was quieter.

"We truly do not mean to interfere in your affairs, either yours or Heather's." Victoria spoke quickly. "But we saw what just happened and . . . oh, Heather would never forgive us if she knew we championed her right now, but I should like to—to explain, if you will."

Damien shook his head. "There's no need," he began.

"Oh, but there is! Heather should not have spoken as she did. It truly is not like her to be so—so biting, I assure you. And I should like to explain, only . . . I'm not certain that I can!" Wringing her hands, she cast a pleading glance at her husband.

"I believe what my wife is trying to say is this, Mr. Lewis. Heather has always been very self-conscious about her limp, though I daresay she would be the first to deny it."

"That's understandable."

"We have tried not to let it handicap her in any way, but none of us must live with what Heather must live with. Please try not to take this incident as an affront against you, Mr. Lewis."

Damien gave the pair a long, searching look. "Why does it matter to you?"

Victoria answered straightaway. "Because we think you are an exceptional young man, and we should hate for you to leave your employment because of this unfortunate incident."

He quelled a bitter laugh. *Oh, I'm not going anywhere,* he thought. *Not just yet.*

"Because of her limp, Heather was always different from other children," Victoria went on. "But we did not want her to feel that she was inferior—for indeed she is not!—and so we raised her to think for herself, to *do* for herself."

"No doubt you considered it odd that an estate the size of Lockhaven should be in the hands of an unmarried woman," Miles said.

Damien hesitated. What was he to say to that? His thoughts must have shown, for Miles smiled briefly and clapped him on the shoulder. "Don't be ashamed of it, lad."

Lad. Some strange emotion squeezed his heart. His father had called him that, so long ago the memory was nearly forgotten. A part of him argued that Miles Grayson had no right to assume such familiarity; he didn't even want to like Miles and Victoria Grayson. Yet, God help him, he did.

The ghost of a smile lifted his mouth. "I admit it crossed my mind."

Miles nodded. "From the time she was very young, we knew Heather did not want to be a burden on us—or anyone. That's what led us to purchase Lockhaven for her on her twenty-first birthday. It was a way of assuring her future—"

"And a way of preserving her pride and dignity, while allowing her to fend for herself." Not until it was out did Damien realize what he'd said.

Victoria flashed a smile. "You do understand," she said happily. She slipped her hand into her husband's elbow.

The look he gave the pair was unflinchingly direct. "You care for her very much, don't you?"

Miles and Victoria glanced at each other. "You know she wasn't born to us." It was a statement, not a question.

He nodded. "She said she was your ward, that her parents were killed in a carriage accident—that her father was a French aristocrat married to an Englishwoman." Damien held his breath, his entire being suddenly awash in anticipation. A dozen questions whirled through his mind.

Would Miles contradict Heather? Was he aware that James Elliot was her father? That he'd spent the last twenty years in Newgate? Was that why he'd raised Heather as his ward? Did he know Elliot was still alive? Did he know where he was?

If he did, he gave no sign of it. "Yes," he said, his features grave. His voice echoed his fervent intensity. "But that has never made any difference, not to either of us. I loved Heather the moment she came into my home, so young and helpless, barely alive. Victoria felt the same the instant she set eyes on her, when Heather was just a child of eight. We held her in our arms when she was sick. We nurtured her and watched her grow into the beautiful young woman she is today, and that is a bond that can never be taken from us."

His hand came out to cover his wife's; he gave it a little squeeze.

"Heather is no different than our other children. She is our eldest daughter, and that is something that will never change."

It was a moment before Damien said anything. "I think Heather is very lucky to have you," he said quietly. "And you have my word this conversation will go no further."

Victoria's smile was blinding. She surprised him by taking his hand within hers. "I knew you were a good man," she said simply.

They parted company then. Damien didn't linger in the village, but found Zeus and started for home.

Home. The word left a bitter taste on his tongue. He had no home, not at the moment. He couldn't return to Yorkshire, nor could he return to Bayberry.

His thoughts were a mad jumble. God, why couldn't this be easier? He had so many questions—and no answers. That business about Heather's father being a French aristocrat . . . where had that come from? It was a lie; it had to be, yet Miles—and Heather, too—were so sincere! He felt almost guilty for deceiving them, yet he couldn't reveal himself. Not yet. It was far too soon. No, he thought. He must do as he'd planned. He must bide his time and wait. . . .

He wanted to gnash his teeth in fury and frustration.

So engrossed in his musings was he that he was almost upon the low-slung fence that fronted his

house before he realized someone was sitting on
the vine-covered porch. . . .
 It was Heather.

Five

The night was clear and bright and warm, the sky brilliantly studded with dozens of stars. She heard the sound of his horse long before she saw him.

When he came into view, her heart tumbled in her chest, as if in slow motion. Through the silvery moonlight, his shoulders seemed wider than ever. Seated as he was, high upon his saddle, his form immensely strong and powerful, it was as if he were some ancient god sent from on high.

She couldn't see his face, yet she knew the instant he sensed her presence. The hoofbeats stopped. All was silent, as if the very heavens held their breath.

Then he nudged his horse forward, halted a dozen paces from the house and dismounted. There was a wooden bench next to the door, and it was there she'd been sitting until she now pushed herself clumsily to her feet. Her palms were damp; she wiped them on her skirt as he approached.

He stopped before her. Through the darkness his eyes were but a glimmer of silver.

"Well," he said softly. "Have you come to send me on my way?"

She shook her head and tried to smile, but failed abominably. "I should never have snapped at you as I did, Mr. Lewis. I knew as soon as I left how rude I'd been."

"You were," he agreed.

Her eyes clung to his. "I—I do hope you'll accept my apology."

"Done," he said lightly. He swept a hand toward the bench. "May I suggest we sit down?"

Heather glanced at the small bench and shuddered inwardly as they sat. Their shoulders touched; there was no way to avoid it.

"I owe you an apology as well, Miss Duval. I was quite forward when I saw you sketching the other day."

Heather smothered a pang of distress. Did he trifle with her? She was unused to such directness—and such attention. She didn't know what to say, and so she said nothing.

"Why did you tell me your name was Alice?"

It was disconcerting to be so close to him. He was so big, he made her feel small in a way she wasn't quite sure she liked.

She quelled an irrational panic. He unnerved her . . . he disturbed her.

He also fascinated her.

"We don't have many strangers pass through

this area of Lancashire." It was the only excuse she could think of at the moment.

"Were you afraid of me?"

If only he would stop looking at her! "A—a little."

Mercy, she still was!—though not in the way he thought. Never in her life had she been so aware of a man as she was of Damien Lewis. Little wonder, that—for indeed, her experience with men was nil. She had convinced Mama and Papa she didn't want—or need—a London Season. Thus, most of the men she had known were aging farmers, beaming new husbands or fathers, or men she'd known throughout most of her life.

His tone was as soft as velvet. "There was no reason to be frightened."

The silence ripened. She stared up where the stars filled the heavens. She was not as composed as he; her thoughts skipped wildly from one to another. Whatever had possessed her to come here? She should leave, this instant.

"Yes" —her laugh was a trifle breathless— "I suppose you're right."

His regard had yet to leave her. It was as if he sought to commit her every feature to memory . . . but that was ridiculous.

"May I ask you something?"

"Certainly."

"The accident you mentioned, the one in which your parents were killed? Is that when your leg was injured?"

Everything seemed to freeze inside her. She had to stop her hand from moving to the knotted, misshapen lump of flesh that was her knee.

Wordlessly she shook her head.

"I see," he murmured. "So it was something you were born with?"

The silence dragged on endlessly. More than ever, she wished she had never come.

What was he thinking? Did he pity her? Did he secretly scorn her and hold her in disdain?

Darkness stole through her. He couldn't know, she thought painfully. He couldn't know the ache hidden deep in her heart. She hated the whispers she had always endured, the shocked stares. . . . Scarcely a day had gone by that she hadn't wished she weren't lame, that she hadn't wished she could change what she was—a cripple. She wanted to be like everyone else. To run. To jump. When Mama and Papa had sent her away to that horrid school—Miss Havesham's School for Young Ladies—she'd never been judged for her manners or her looks, her decorum or her wit.

Her mind spun, and all at once she felt herself hurtling back in time. She cringed, for once again she could heard those terrible taunts. . . .

Did you really think we liked you, Heather? Well, no one does. No one wants to be near you.

There was more childish laughter tinged with malice.

You're not like us, Heather Duval. You can't run. You can't walk like the rest of us. You can't dance. You can't even ride—and every lady of good breeding can ride. You're lame. A cripple.

Always, she thought with a pang. Always she was judged by something she could never change . . .

Her limp.

The breath she drew was deep and uneven. "Must we talk about this?"

He had turned to face her. "It makes you uncomfortable?"

"Yes. Yes, it does."

His tone was very quiet. "I don't mean to embarrass you."

Then don't ask me such questions! The retort nearly sprang from her lips. Somehow she stopped it.

With one hand she made a vague, short gesture. "May we talk of something else?"

"Of course."

With relief she expelled a long, pent-up breath. "Good," she murmured, "because it occurs to me we've done a good bit of talking about me and very little about you."

Beside her, he tensed . . . or did she only imagine it?

"I find I'm curious as well, Mr. Lewis. Why did you wish to stay in Lancashire?"

His brows shot upward. "Do you think there's a reason other than what I've stated?"

"Ah," she said lightly, "but you did not state why you chose to remain in Lancashire."

He said nothing; Heather had the strangest sensation that this time she was the one who'd caught him off guard.

"I dislike London," he said at last. "I prefer the country."

She smiled. "So do I. My father feels the same. He doesn't care for the city, but my mother adores it, and so they visit their town house there several times a year. My sister Beatrice is like Mama—she thrives on it. But Christina is more like me, a country girl at heart, I think."

"And Arthur?"

His tone was cool, almost detached, as if he posed the question out of politeness.

"Arthur has yet to make up his mind, I fear. He is happy wherever he is."

Through the darkness, she searched his face. "Do you have family? Brothers and sisters, perhaps?"

A mask seemed to descend over his features. Every muscle in his face tightened. His features were taut, almost harsh. "No." A single word was all he voiced.

In one swift movement, he rose and strode forward. The pasture yawned before the cottage, and it was there near the fence that he stopped, some ten paces distant. She was certain she'd said something very, very wrong. . . .

She moved toward him, quite without knowing it. She stood slightly behind him, her lips parted, almost too afraid to speak.

"I'm sorry, Mr. Lewis. I didn't mean to offend you, or to remind you of something you would obviously prefer not to discuss."

He said nothing. The set of his shoulders was tense, so very tense. The need to stretch out a hand, to touch him, to comfort him was almost overwhelming . . . why it was so, Heather didn't know. She only knew in that moment, he seemed so very alone . . . as she had so often been alone. . . .

There was a low whinny at his elbow. Heather
saw that his horse had come up to the fence to
nudge his master's shoulder. Slowly Damien
brought his hand up. With his knuckles he
rubbed the sleek black skin of the huge beast's
finely muscled neck. The animal responded by
dipping his nose into Damien's hand.

His profile was etched in the silver glow of the
moon. Her eyes moved slowly over his features,
one by one—the wicked slash of heavy, dark
brows, the slant of his cheekbones, the chiseled
squareness of his jaw, the sensuous smoothness
of his mouth . . .

"He's beautiful," she heard herself say. Her
stomach quivered oddly. And she knew it wasn't
just the horse she meant, but his master. . . .

"His name is Zeus," he said softly.

Heather smiled slightly. "He's beautiful," she
said again.

Softer still, so soft she had to strain to hear
him, he said, "He belonged to my brother."

Heather knew then . . . she *knew*.

His brother was dead.

It was what had drawn her to him . . . she had
found in him a secret torment that matched her
own. A kindred spirit . . .

Her fingertips were on his forearm; it happened unthinkingly. It was but a touch—a fleeting touch, at that—to convey her sympathy.
Silence drifted between them, yet it was not as
before. She needed no words . . .

. . . nor did he.

Withdrawing her hand, she smiled slightly.

"Odd that his name is Zeus. My father has a stallion named Apollo whom he plans to put out to pasture soon." She paused. "Indeed, since Papa's birthday is in just over a fortnight, I'd thought of buying him another as his gift. Robin often spoke of a breeder in Cumberland named Ferguson, and I'd hoped to travel there to look." She gave a little laugh. "Unfortunately, I know very little about horses, and I should hate to bring home a nag."

White teeth flashed in the darkness. "Oh, I doubt you'd do that," he teased. "But at the risk of sounding quite arrogant, I do happen to know a prime bit of horseflesh when I see it. If you'd like, I'd be happy to accompany you."

Heather's eyes lit up. "You would? Oh, that would be wonderful! I would so love to surprise Papa."

"Then so be it. How near to the Scottish border is it?"

Heather was thrilled. She'd been at a loss as to what gift to make her father, but this was perfect! She nodded. "Not far. 'Tis a journey that will take a day each way by carriage, I believe."

"When would you like to leave?"

It took but an instant to decide. "The Friday after next, I think, provided that meets with Mr. Ferguson's approval." She searched the hazy outline of his features. "Tell me true, Mr. Lewis. You really don't mind?"

"Not in the least."

Happiness bubbled all through her. She smiled . . . and their eyes collided. Then something changed . . . *everything* changed. He held her gaze in what was surely the longest moment in all her days. His hand came up. And it was as if something passed between them. Her breath caught raggedly. Heather was certain he would touch her—her cheek, her hair . . . God, but it didn't matter, for shivers of excitement leaped in her breast. She didn't know if Bea was right—if Damien Lewis was the handsomest man in all England. But he was certainly the most handsome man *she* had ever seen. . . .

But suddenly she *was* afraid. Oh, not of him, but of the confused longing that swelled within her like a raging tide. And all at once the silence was no longer dark and intimate, but glaring and awkward.

She was a fool, she realized. A fool to allow her emotions to run away with her so. Damien Lewis would want nothing to do with a woman like her. Of course he would never think of her in . . . in *that* way. To him, she was his employer. No more, no less.

Besides, whispered a hated little voice in her mind. *He could have any woman he wanted, a woman who is whole and hearty and beautiful. He would never look twice at a woman who is maimed. . . .*

She grabbed at her skirts. "It's late. I—I must go." Her voice was shaky and tremulous; it sounded nothing at all like her own.

"Let me take you back to the house."

"No." Her denial was breathless but firm. "It's not necessary. It's quite safe, really."

Nonetheless, he was there beside her as she turned and moved toward her cart. Without a by-your-leave, he set his hands upon her waist. She drew a sharp breath; her spine went utterly straight. If he noticed, he gave no sign of it as he lifted her into the cart. Her lips feeling wooden, she thanked him and bid him good night.

Later . . . later she would wonder whatever possessed her to stop the cart and twist around to face him.

"Mr. Lewis?"

He hadn't moved from where she'd left him. Booted feet braced wide apart, his form was a stark, powerful outline in the moonlight.

"Yes?" His eyes glimmered like silver.

"I—I limp because of my knee. It's . . . I'm . . . I'm maimed." God, how she hated that word! "I—I don't know how it happened. It's been like this as long as I can remember."

Heather didn't await his response. Her feeble courage deserted her. With a jangle of the harness, she disappeared into the darkness.

It was Damien who remained unmoving for the longest time. Oddly, he knew what her admission cost her; she had bared a part of herself she guarded closely, a secret she would not divulge to just anyone. She had released to him a corner of her soul. . . .

Guilt ate into him like acid. He didn't deserve it. She would never have confided in him if she knew who he really was—why he was really here. Yet even while he despised himself for his deceit, he knew there was no other way.

A scathing curse blistered the air. He didn't want to feel this way about her. He didn't want to feel anything! Not sympathy. Not compassion. Most certainly not this damnable attraction to her—most especially not that!

He was drawn to her as strongly as ever; that was something that had not waned, not since that very first day. He wanted her as much as ever. *More.* His little gypsy . . .

He had to grit his teeth to keep from going after her. From dragging her into his arms, smothering that rose-hued mouth with his own—and to hell with the world.

But he couldn't. He *wouldn't*, for those were feelings that had no part in his mission here.

His jaw clenched tight, he spun around and strode toward the house, but one thought high in his mind.

He must find a way to conquer this hellish desire for her . . . and soon.

Heather spent the next week feeling torn as never before. Something was happening. Something she could not stop. Something she could not control. It was as if all the composure she'd ever known were spinning away, beyond reach, and she knew not how to recapture it. Her well-ordered life had been tipped on end. . . .

As a child, she had grown to accept herself as she was. She could not *do* as other children did. She could not *walk* as other children walked. Ah, yes, she had accepted it . . . and hated it.

Deep in her secret heart, she had often longed

to be the beauty everyone envied, the darling of the celebration, the most graceful dancer on the ballroom floor, the fastest rider on the hunt. But she couldn't ride, because her knee pained her. She couldn't dance, because her clumsiness forbade it, and she refused to look even more the fool.

She'd never received an offer for her hand—nor would she! In five-and-twenty years, she'd never even been kissed. Always . . . always she had known she would never marry, though Mama and Papa had assured her that in time, some dashing young man would fall madly in love with her. But Heather knew differently. What did it matter that she was kind and generous and sweet-natured? She was lame, and that was something others never forgot . . .

Nor did she.

But she had learned to appreciate what she had—her resourcefulness and her wit. She had learned to appreciate her pleasures, simple though they were—the loveliness of the meadow where the dog roses bloomed, the sound of the sweetly pure concerto of a thrush, chuckling as a dog cut sheep from the flock. She was content with her life . . .

But no more.

No more, for now her days were often plagued with a restless dissatisfaction. It was as if some blight had been cast upon her soul.

All because of him . . . Damien Lewis.

He performed his duties exceedingly well, of that there was no question. She did not regret hiring him, for he was without a doubt the best man for the job. On matters of the estate, the two of them dealt extremely well together. Indeed, she saw him nearly every day. Outwardly she was calm and composed, but inside was a world of turmoil. If only she were not so—so damnably aware of everything about him. . . .

Only yesterday they'd sat together in her study, reconciling ledgers. But her mind—and her eyes—displayed a most shocking tendency to stray from the figures in the ledger . . . to the figure of the man sitting beside her! He smelled of some woodsy, spicy scent that was infinitely pleasant. His fingers curled lean and brown and strong against the delicate china of his teacup. He'd rolled up the sleeves of his shirt, baring muscular forearms liberally coated with fine, dark, masculine hair. And when he bent his head down low, her gaze returned in fascination again and again to the way his hair curled just so against the bronzed column of his nape.

He had only to walk into view and she felt scattered in every direction. Her stomach felt peculiarly weightless. Her heart would flutter.

She resented him, resented him fiercely! All her secret yearnings had returned, stronger than ever . . . stronger than she remembered. At night she tossed and turned, as she had in those long-ago days of budding desires and senses, when she was of an age with Bea. She fell asleep wondering what it was like to be kissed by a man, to feel his lips against hers. Would they be warm and dry? Moist and cool? What was it like to be held tight against a man's chest? Visions flashed in her brain, only now there was a face attached to those visions. . . .

Yet she longed to discover those mysteries for herself. Just once. *Just once . . .*

She arose one morning feeling tired and irritable. With a weary sigh, she stripped off her nightgown. She turned, only to confront her naked body in the cheval glass that stood in the corner. In truth, she'd never been one to pamper her body with lotions and perfumes; indeed, she'd paid scant attention to it, always dressing and bathing with an economy of effort.

Now, she examined her naked limbs with an almost critical detachment. Her hair tumbled over one bare breast in sensuous abandon. Her breasts were high and full, yet not too heavy for her small frame. Small coral nipples tipped those ripe, firm mounds. Her belly was flat, concave between the span of her hipbones. She frowned. Had she dropped a bit of weight recently? Still, the curve of her hips flared out from her waist, narrow but feminine and not at all boyish. Unbidden, her fingertips stroked the curved underside of one breast. No, she thought wonderingly, her body was not so unpleasant to look upon. . . .

Her gaze fell to her right knee, to that knotted, misshapen joint that turned inward. Her satisfaction withered, until all that was left was a hollow emptiness that echoed all through her.

Later that day, she absently rubbed her knee. It ached abominably; even the long, hot soak in the tub this morning hadn't helped, as it usually did.

Just then Bea burst into her study. "Heather! Oh, Heather, come quickly. You'll play the piano for me, won't you? Mr. Lewis is quite the dancer, and he's promised to teach me the waltz! And later he's promised to teach me something called the Virginia reel!"

Heather laid aside her quill. "Bea, I'm really quite busy——"

"Oh, but you can spare a moment, can't you?" Her sister pleaded prettily, the picture of blond enchantment in a gay white flowered dress and matching slippers. "Heather, love, please! It won't take long. I know Mama is disappointed in me, but Pierre is so rigid and impatient——I get so flustered I can never get it right with him!"

She sighed. "All right, Bea." She arose and picked up her cane from the side of the desk.

Bea was ecstatic. "Here she is!" She bounced inside the music room with a flourish. Damien stood in the center of the polished wooden floor, his hands behind his back. At their entrance, he inclined his head. His gaze briefly touched Heather's. She gave a cursory nod and limped toward the piano in the far corner.

"I vow Heather plays quite divinely, but you'll see for yourself. Oh, and she's quite talented with watercolors, too, Mr. Lewis." She chatted on gaily. "Why, she's done nearly all of the paintings here in the house."

Dark brows shot up. His gaze encompassed several on the nearest wall, one of a harp and pianoforte, the other a pastoral scene of livestock grazing in the fields.

"Very impressive," he said. "And do you sketch as well, Miss Duval?"

Heather had just sat at the piano bench. Her jaw closed with a snap. She shot him a blistering glance, but his eyes were twinkling. With a sweetness she was far from feeling, she asked, " 'Tis a waltz you want, is it not?"

"Yes. Yes, please." Breathlessly, Bea stepped up before Damien. Shyly she placed one small hand on his shoulder. With a faint smile, Damien clasped her fingers lightly within his and settled his hand on her waist.

Tearing her gaze away, Heather launched into a light, merry tune. But while her fingers skimmed the familiar notes, her eyes skipped back to the couple again and again.

Bea was right. Her waltzing was inexpert and stiff.

Damien said nothing until they were midway through the second song. "Relax," Heather heard him say as they passed by. "Forget who you are—where you are. You are a billowing young willow, and your limbs are flowing with the softness of a gentle spring breeze. And remember—your feet are not platforms, Beatrice. They are light as air, never touching the earth."

They whirled across the floor. Again . . . and yet again.

"Yes. Yes, Beatrice . . . that's much better. . . ."

Around and around they dipped and swirled. Before long, Bea was waltzing as if she'd been born to it.

Some unfamiliar emotion inside Heather wouldn't allow her to look away. Her fingers moved across the keys, but the lilting melody was an endless blur in her ears. There was a fist curled tight in her chest, heavy and hard. She felt as if her heart were encased in chains. The pair on the floor were no longer two, but one. Their steps matched perfectly, spinning and graceful and fluid, their movements supple and elegant.

Arching her neck, Bea laughed up at her partner, one arm raised swan-like about his shoulder as their steps skimmed across the floor. . . . The pain in Heather's heart was tortuous. To them it was such a simple thing, to move their feet just so to the music, something they both took for granted. On and on they danced, caught up in the melody, the lighthearted mood of the music . . . and each other.

The song ended. Laughing, Bea gave a deep curtsey while her partner bowed in return. Rising upright, she clasped her hands together. Her eyes were shining like the moon in a starlit sky.

"Oh, that was marvelous!" she beamed. "I didn't know waltzing could be so—so wonderful!"

Damien took her hand and bowed low. "My pleasure, mademoiselle."

Heather slipped from the music room. They never even noticed.

It was some thirty minutes later when she emerged from her study again. She had just entered the drawing room when the sound of voices caught her ears. The beveled French doors to the terrace were open, and it was toward them that she directed herself.

The voices were louder. Heather paused, just inside the threshold.

"Do you truly think me pretty, Mr. Lewis?"

Heather's spine went rigid. Soft lips thinned to a straight line. It was Bea—and Damien.

The two came into view, strolling up the flagstone path. "Of course you are, Beatrice. When you come out next year I have no doubt you'll have dozens of handsome young bucks vying for your favors."

Bea gave a trilling little laugh, fluttering her lashes. "Oh, but one is quite enough," she proclaimed airily. "Indeed, one is more than enough when he is the *right* one."

Heather gripped the head of her cane with both hands; it rapped sharply on the floor.

Bea glanced up. "Heather, there you are! Mr. Lewis has promised another lesson soon. You'll play for us, won't you? But of course you will, you're such a dear."

Heather made no reply. "Walk with me, Bea," was all she said. Ignoring Damien, who had stepped aside, she took her sister's arm. She could feel his eyes burning into her back as she and Bea turned away from him, but she paid no heed. She was simmering inside, and she didn't particularly care if he knew it or not!

They hadn't gone far before Bea frowned over at her. "Whatever is wrong, Heather?"

Heather stopped short. Taking a deep breath, she rounded on her sister.

"You are not a ninny, Bea." She did not mince words. "You know full well what you are doing."

Beatrice blinked. "What! Surely you're not angry because Mr. Lewis and I were walking in the garden! We—were looking for you." It was an excuse, a feeble one at that.

"I was in my study," Heather snapped. "Had you looked for me there, you would have found me. Furthermore, I think you *wanted* to be alone with Mr. Lewis. Frankly, Bea, I am appalled at your lack of decorum."

Bea pouted. "Oh, come. This isn't London. I hardly need a chaperone."

"I beg to differ with you. It appears you do."

Bea's eyes flashed. "And I beg to differ with *you*, Heather. I do not need a chaperone—not you or any other!"

"You're smitten with him, Bea, a man nearly twice your age. Heavens, what were you thinking—cavorting in the garden with him?"

"Cavorting in the garden! Why, I did no such thing!"

"Then what would you call it?"

Bea's face went fiery red. Heather knew then that she was right—Bea just wouldn't admit it.

"You were the one who left us alone," Bea accused.

"I did, and I see now it was a mistake, but I never realized you'd hang onto him like a leech. I'm ashamed of you, Bea! What do you think Mama and Papa would say?"

"Oh!" Beatrice gave an indignant cry. "And I suppose you'll hurry and tell them as soon as you are able, won't you?"

"You were making a fool of yourself, Bea, and you don't have the sense to realize it! Asking him to teach you to waltz . . . walking in the garden alone . . . and I heard you ask if he thought you were pretty. You were flirting quite shamelessly! Well, I warn you, Bea." Her tone was severe. "I'll have no more of these little trysts with Mr. Lewis. I won't have my sister acting like a hoyden."

Bea's jaw had dropped open. "You—you're jealous, Heather. You're jealous because he thinks I'm pretty, because he—he likes me. You're jealous because I can dance and you can't!" Her beautiful blue eyes were swimming with tears, but the tip of her chin was mutinous. "And you have no right to tell me what to do, Heather. You're just an old cripple. You—you're not even my sister!"

Heather flinched as if she'd been slapped across the face. As Bea whirled around and ran down the path, she could only stand there frozen and motionless, as if she'd been cast in stone. The sound of muffled sobs hung in the air.

You're jealous, Heather. You're jealous because he thinks I'm pretty, because he—he likes me. You're jealous because I can dance and you can't!

A riot of confusion gripped her soul. No! she thought wildly. No, that wasn't right! She was glad that Bea was young and lovely, that she would someday have the world at her feet. She neither envied her youthful beauty nor resented her lithe, supple grace. She wasn't jealous of Bea, she wasn't!

You have no right to tell me what to do,

Heather. You're just an old cripple. You—you're not even my sister!

Her heart constricted. Her head bowed low. *Bea*, she thought wrenchingly. *Oh, Bea, how could you say that to me?* If she'd wanted to wound her, she'd succeeded quite admirably.

She should go after her. She really should . . .

Heather's head came up. Damien had presented himself before her. With the sun at his back, the span of his shoulders broad as the wheat fields, he was a figure both powerful and formidable.

She wasn't up to this, she thought vaguely. Not now. Her control was tenuous; it was as if she were coming apart inside.

"Well, that went well."

So he'd heard. Even as a burning shame scalded her veins, she managed to summon an icy strength.

A slender, black brow arched high. "Eavesdropping, Mr. Lewis? I'm disappointed. Somehow I'd thought better of you."

"It was difficult not to hear, Miss Duval." Disapproval resided in the coolness of his tone.

Heather's eyes narrowed. "If you think to censure me, Mr. Lewis, please think again."

Damien stood his ground. "Oh, I know it's none of my affair. But I wonder . . . weren't you a bit hard on your sister? She is, after all, barely out of the schoolroom."

"Oh, forgive me, Mr. Lewis"—though her tone was sweet, it cut like a blade—"I didn't realize you'd noticed."

His jaw clenched. His eyes flickered like lightning, warning her she'd hit a nerve. But Heather cared not, for by now she had warmed to her ire.

"What, Mr. Lewis. Nothing to say? Well, I've plenty to say. I'm furious that you dare to criticize me, when it's because of you this happened. Bea is quite taken with you. Surely you've noticed."

He sighed, a sound of indulgence. "Of course I did. But she's also very young—"

"Young, yes. And beautiful. And tempting, Mr. Lewis?"

His jaw clamped shut. She sensed he restrained his temper with difficulty. But then he smiled, a crooked smile that lifted one side of his mouth. "Your imagination is quite vivid," he said easily. "I assure you, I'm not one to rob the cradle. As for your sister, 'tis my belief she was merely testing her charms."

So now he would ridicule her? Heather's nails dug into her palms. "You find it amusing, do you, Mr. Lewis? Well, I won't have it, do you hear? I won't have you encouraging her!"

His smile vanished. "I'm quite aware of your sister's feelings. But unlike you, I feel a bit of diplomacy is in order. I have no interest in her, save that she is a charming young girl who will no doubt catch the fancy of some handsome young buck one day. But rather than crush her like a bug, I think it better to let her down gently."

"Gently?" It was an outright scoff. "By lavishing your attention on her, Mr. Lewis?"

He bristled. "I showed her how to waltz, Miss

Duval, and she enjoyed it immensely. Yet you make it sound as if we committed some grievous offense. One might almost believe you were envious of her."

Heather glared at him. Why must he sound so blasted logical?

White teeth flashed in that tanned face. "But it occurs to me that you never allow yourself to laugh and savor those lighthearted times which come our way, Miss Duval. And perhaps because *you* do not, you don't want your sister to enjoy herself, either."

All at once the battle had shifted to different ground. He made her sound like a shrew from the furthest reaches of hell. But she wasn't. She wasn't . . . *or was she?*

Guilt arrowed straight to her heart. She'd made Bea cry. Never in her life had she made anyone cry. And Bea was her sister—no matter Bea's angry denial. They were still sisters. . . .

But who was he to criticize her like this? A smoldering resentment simmered in her veins. "You don't know what you're talking about, Mr. Lewis. You don't know *me*—"

"On the contrary, Miss Duval. You're a bitter young woman who feels sorry for herself. You're a coward who shields herself from life. You hide here at Lockhaven rather than face the world head-on."

His arrogant half-smile was maddening. She longed to slap his face.

But all at once there was a huge lump in her throat. Her control was fragile, though she'd be damned if she'd let him know it. She wouldn't give him the satisfaction of knowing he'd rattled her . . .

. . . of knowing he was right.

"That's not true," she denied. "I lead a full, rewarding life, and I'm immensely content with it."

But she wasn't. Not since *he* had come into it. . . .

"Are you? I've seen your paintings, Miss Duval, and not all are tranquil and serene. What about the one in your study, the hunchback with no face? He stands upon a hilltop, surrounded by masses of black, roiling clouds."

It was frightening . . . *he* was frightening, for it was as if he had seen into her very soul.

"Stop it," she cried. "Stop it!" Her cane fell to the ground. She clapped her hands over her ears to shut out the sound of his voice.

He wouldn't allow it. He dragged her hands back to her sides and held them there.

"Do you think I don't see it? The hunchback is alone, Heather, as you are alone. Disfigured . . ."

She groped for anger—for pride—and could find neither. Desperate, she was convinced that retreat was her only hope. She struggled against his hold, to no avail. The hands around her wrists were like manacles.

"Let me go!" she nearly screamed. "I want to leave!"

"What! Will you run away again?" Mocking gray eyes glittered down at her. "Well, not yet, Heather. Not just yet."

She managed to wrench free. Then it happened. He snared her elbow and spun her around . . .

Straight into his arms.

Six

One single, startled breath was all she drew . . . and then his mouth came down on hers, swallowing her cry of surprise.

It happened so fast. . . . She caught a mind-teetering glimpse of his eyes—ah, but what she saw there nearly made her cry out. His gaze was blistering, a reflection of the storm that raged between them.

A tremor of shock went through her. Yet for all the fierceness of his expression, he didn't hurt her. His hold was demanding, yet not rough. His arms were hard about her back; drawn full and tight against him, there was no part of him she couldn't feel! She was searingly conscious of the breadth of his chest against the softness of her breasts. His thighs were like pillars of rock forged against her own.

Her fanciful daydreams had ill prepared her. In all her days, she'd never imagined a kiss would be like this. He did not plunder, but took possession of her mouth with a stark, bold mastery that left no room for denial.

And yet . . . God above, that was the last thing on Heather's mind. His lips were hotly passionate, utterly persuasive, sweet beyond reason . . . beyond all measure. There was a vague, distant pounding in her ears—her heart, she realized. Seized by a strange, inner trembling, her lips parted instinctively. A jolt shook her as the tip of his tongue touched hers, yet she didn't retreat. Instead, she let him explore as he would . . . as, indeed, he did. . . .

The very earth seemed to move beneath her feet. His breath was a warm rush in the back of her throat. Odd, but she didn't feel his kiss only against her lips. It flamed all through her, to parts she'd never imagined. She could feel the slight roughness of his beard against her own silken smoothness. The touch of his hands on her waist was like a heated brand; it was as if it burned through her clothing to her skin. Even as her breath grew quick and ragged, her limbs grew weak, like melted butter. Her hands crept upward. Her fingers uncurled in the folds of his shirt.

Damien nearly groaned aloud. She'd never been kissed before. He'd never been more certain of anything in his life. Always before, he'd been a man who preferred a woman with experience, who could pleasure him as he pleasured her.

Yet Heather was different. She was untouched, wholly and completely, and the knowledge went through him like wildfire. He yearned to turn her cool innocence into fiery awakening. Lord, why bother to lie to himself? In truth, this was but an excuse to do what he'd been longing to do all along. She had stirred his temper, aye—and heated his blood to a raging boil. Blood gathered between his thighs, swelling his manhood to an almost painful erectness. It was all he could do not to lay her down, strip away the confining strictures of their clothing and plunge deep within her satin cleft.

His fingers dug almost convulsively into the narrow curve of her waist. For a moment he swung perilously between heaven and hell. He thought blackly that he was damned no matter which he chose. . . .

But it seemed the choice was not his at all, for at that very instant Heather wrenched herself free. She stumbled back, nearly losing her balance. She caught herself just in time.

She swallowed. Her gaze trekked slowly up the strong, corded column of his neck, past lips that all at once seemed hard as stone, to collide with his gaze, which was dark and unreadable. He betrayed no hint of expression, neither pleasure nor displeasure. As always, his thoughts were a mystery.

Slowly she raised a trembling hand to touch her mouth. She confronted him, her voice both accusing and confused. "You—you're mad!" she whispered. She sought very hard to keep her voice from shaking.

One broad shoulder lifted in an indolent shrug. "Perhaps."

"I—I could dismiss you!"

And probably should, he thought. His gaze wandered downward, back up to tremulous lips. Desire cut through him, so intense it was a physical pain. Christ, her mouth was incredible. Soft and pink, still dewy-wet from the eager glide of his tongue. . . .

Two bright spots of color appeared high on her cheeks. Her eyes were huge. "Wh-why are you staring at me like that?"

Caution flared high and bright within him. He dismissed the idea just as quickly. With soft deliberation he said, "Because I'm thinking I'd very much like to kiss you again, Miss Heather Duval."

Did he mock her? Her thoughts—her very emotions—were a wild scramble in her breast. She didn't know. Indeed, she scarcely knew her own name at this instant.

He moved so abruptly she jumped. But he merely bent to retrieve her cane from the pathway. He extended it toward her, a wordless challenge inherent in his features until she gingerly stretched out a hand to accept it.

Only then did he deign to speak. "But you needn't worry. Though it will cost me dearly, I will restrain myself."

Now she knew for certain that he mocked her. Though she longed for some ready retort, none sprang to her lips. She could only watch as he turned and strode from the terrace, whistling a merry tune as if he hadn't a care in the world. It passed through her mind that she had just experienced the most exhilarating, wondrous moment of her life . . .

Yet it was also the most despairing.

She'd finally discovered what it was like to be held close in strong male arms. To be kissed . . .

And now she knew what she'd been missing.

Heather arose rather late the next morning. She had slept little, if at all. All through the night, she'd relived that scene in the garden with Damien. She resented him fiercely for what he had done—oh, it wasn't that he had kissed her. But he had turned her inside out. She was uncertain of herself as she'd not been in a long, long time, and she despised him for it . . . though she despised herself no less for her weakness.

Nor could she forget . . . he'd called her Heather. Never before had he done so, and it made what had passed between them all the more intimate.

Then there was that awful business with Bea. She'd been a hypocrite to accuse Bea of being smitten. Indeed, that very same phrase might well apply to herself . . . she would have to go see her, and soon. This evening, she decided.

Though she was not one to laze abed, she was sorely tempted to remain there the rest of the day. But he had accused her of hiding from the world, and she'd not give him the satisfaction.

Still, throughout the morning, she stayed in the house. Not until afternoon did she garner the courage to venture without. She had tea with the vicar every Thursday afternoon, and she vowed that this particular afternoon would be no different. So it was that she spent an unremarkable hour or so with the vicar and his wife. Yet all the way to and from the village, she prayed she wouldn't encounter Damien Lewis.

Once she was home, she considered going to the conservatory to paint, but her nerves were too unsettled. And she couldn't help but think of what he'd said about her paintings.

Yet another reminder she could have done without.

At home she struggled up the stairs, feeling as if she were one hundred and twenty-five instead of twenty-five. One day, she thought absently, she would establish her bedchamber on the lower floor.

Upstairs in her room, she dropped her bonnet next to her jewel case. As she had a hundred times before, she stopped to trace the word engraved on the lid—*Beloved*. Usually, the ritual act evoked comfort in her breast at those times she chanced to need it, yet it eluded her this day. With a sigh she dropped her hand to her side and moved over to the bed to sit.

There was a light rap upon the door. Before Heather could respond, it opened.

Beatrice stepped inside.

Heather had no time to rise. Startled, she stared at Bea, whose eyes were as wide and wary as surely her own must be.

Linked before her waist, Bea's fingers pulled at each other. "May I come in, Heather?"

Her voice was uncharacteristically tenuous. Heather's heart went out to her. Wordlessly she patted the space beside her.

Bea didn't hesitate, but closed the door behind

her. Once she was seated on the bed, Heather slanted her a faint smile.

"I'm glad you're here, Bea. You spared me a trip to Lyndermere this evening to see you."

"You were coming to see me?"

Heather's features were grave, her voice very gentle. "I have no desire to leave things as they were when last we saw each other, Bea."

"I—I know," the younger girl said quickly. "That's why I'm here." She gazed down at her knotted hands. "Oh, Heather," she burst out. "I'm sorry. I'm so sorry. You were right—I shouldn't have been so forward with Mr. Lewis. But I—I didn't mean what I said, truly! I should never have said you weren't my sister." Tears pooled in her eyes. "I didn't mean to hurt you, and I knew I had, as soon as it was out. And then I was so afraid you'd be angry with me forever."

Heather's arm had slid around her shoulders. "Shhh, Bea," she soothed, drawing her close. "We all do things we regret, love. I was horrid, too. I made you cry, and then I felt terrible for being so mean."

Bea sniffed and raised her face. "Then you'll forgive me?"

"If you'll forgive me, love." She brushed a damp blond tendril from Bea's cheek. "We're sisters in every way that matters, Bea. That's all that's important."

Bea's smile was watery. "That's what Mama said, too."

Heather gave a dry chuckle. "A wise woman, our mother," she teased. She tipped her head to the side. "Do you think it's something she eats?"

They were both still laughing when Bea left a short while later. Heather felt as if a very great weight had been lifted from her shoulders—and her heart. She was even humming a little as she entered her study.

But someone was already there. A figure was bent over her desk—Damien. The fabric of his shirt stretched tight across his back, clearly outlining every muscle. The artist in her leaped to the fore—how she would love to capture that lean male form in primal, naked glory.

She would have fled without a sound, had she possessed the ability to do so. As it was, he'd already discerned her presence. Straightening, he turned to face her. All at once her mouth was as dry as dust.

"Miss Duval. Marcus told me you were with your sister and I didn't want to interrupt, so I was just leaving you a note."

Miss Duval. Heather inwardly cringed. That sounded so icily remote after what had happened between them last night. But his expression was calm, his manner utterly indifferent. It might never have happened. No doubt he'd put it from his mind. Forgotten it completely.

But she wouldn't forget. She would *never* forget.

Her heart was pounding so hard she could feel it against her ribs. Nervously she moistened her lips with the tip of her tongue. "Was there something you wished to discuss with me?"

"Yes. I was out near the Tucker farm this morning. The pilings on the bridge over the stream there have begun to rot. Should the waters chance to rise with a heavy rain, I suspect it may wash out. I wondered if you wished to have it repaired now."

Her nod was jerky. "I see no point in waiting until it's too late. If the bridge washed out, the Tuckers would be isolated."

"Good. I'll see to it, then." He closed the distance between them as he spoke. But he didn't exit the study, as she thought he would. Instead he stopped before her.

Her gaze climbed high . . . higher still. Lord, but he was tall! He made her feel small and helpless, and she liked it not a whit!

"I also wanted to make certain you'd not changed your mind about our trip to Cumberland tomorrow."

Cumberland. With all the uproar of the last twenty-four hours, it had slipped from her mind like water through a sieve. But she wasn't about to let him know it.

She raised her chin slightly. "I cannot think why," she stated succinctly.

"Nor can I, Miss Duval. Nor can I." His gaze dropped fleetingly to her lips. His smile was a thin disguise. "Shall we meet at the stables in the morning at . . . ?" His brows rose as he waited for her to finish.

"Eight o'clock will be fine, Mr. Lewis." Their eyes locked. Had she not been so furious, she might have recognized a glimmer of admiration in his. As it was, her gaze drilled into his back as he left.

More than anything, she'd have liked to cancel their trip. But he would have called her a coward again. Indeed, she thought angrily, he'd expected her to wilt like a fallen blossom, and she wasn't about to prove him right. He'd called her bluff—and won, damn his hide!

Slowly she released a long, uneven sigh. She was most definitely not looking forward to this journey.

Smoke curled eerily upward into the dead of the London night. It was well after midnight, and few were about at such an hour. An old crone, huddled into a niche in the chipped stone wall, half rose and stretched out a scrawny, gnarled hand.

"Please, sir," she called in a scratchy, quavering voice. "Have ye a coin for an old woman?"

A knotted fist sliced through the air. The blow knocked the woman off her feet and sent her sprawling headlong on the muddied ground.

"Away with ye, bitch!" came the angry mutter.

The tall, burly figure crossed the cobbled streets and into a dark alley behind the public house. His footsteps trod heavily on the wooden beams as he made his way up the back staircase and into a tiny room directly above the taproom.

There James Elliot lit the remains of a stubby candle, then began to empty his pockets of the night's work. Several gold rings rolled in wobbly circles. Two fat purses stuffed with coin dropped onto the table. His eyes gleamed as he dangled a highly polished pocket watch suspended on a fancy, glittering chain. On impulse he stuffed it back into his pocket. He'd taken a fancy to the piece—perhaps he would keep it.

Grabbing a dirt-crusted bottle from the table, he tipped it to his lips. He gulped the whole of its contents and wiped his mouth with the back of his hand. His gaze swung around the room, to the straw mattress humped in the corner, the chair propped against a yellowed wall. His lodgings were dingy and crude. After twenty years in Newgate, he'd merely exchanged one hellhole for another.

His mood was suddenly vile. He swung the bottle to the table with a force that nearly snapped the flimsy wooden table in two. What did it matter that he was free? Twenty years he'd waited patiently. Planning. Scheming. Dreaming of the day he'd be free . . . the day he'd be rich. It was all that had sustained him during those infernal years in prison.

His eyes half closed. He could see the silver, claw-footed jewel case in his mind, the image as vivid as it had been the day the Earl of Deverell met his Maker.

Hidden within the case is my legacy to my wife, a treasure I pray she will find beyond price. She will know how to find it, for she alone knows the secret . . .

Mad, Thomas the jailer had called him when he'd boasted of the treasure that awaited him once he was free. But he wasn't mad. It was his prize. His salvation. By God, he'd earned it.

His lips curled back over yellowed teeth. If only Justine hadn't stolen it, all would have been so different! But the case hadn't been with her at the site of the accident. He'd reached there within the week, and bits of clothing were still strewn all about. But the jewel case was nowhere to be found.

Of his young daughter, he gave but momentary consideration. Apparently the accident had spared her life—what a pity! If she ended up in an orphan house, it made no matter to him. Certainly he had no intention of presenting himself as her father. Nay, not when he was at last well rid of the burden of his crippled bratling!

His gaze strayed to the stump of his thumb. A snarl twisted his features. The little bitch had maimed him for life, and he'd never forgiven her. Aye, he thought viciously. It would have been better had the sniveling little bitch died. . . .

He hoped she had.

His mind returned to the jewel case—to more important matters.

Not long after he'd been imprisoned, he'd learned that the earl's wife had died . . . and the secret of the jewel case along with her. James had pondered on this long and hard, night after night, for God knew there was little else to think about in that wretched hole; it was this that had given him renewed hope, all that had sustained him through those long, hellish years. . . . What if the jewel case had found its way back into the Deverell family?

No one else knew of the secret compartment. *No one.* He had only to find it, and the secret would be forever his. . . .

And so he'd gone to the Earl of Deverell's family estate in Yorkshire, to the home of Giles Tremayne. Only the jewel case was nowhere to be

found. And the fool Tremayne declared he knew
nothing of it—or the treasure within! The memory of his rage scalded his veins anew. Of course
he'd been livid—what man wouldn't be? If Giles
Tremayne wouldn't give over the jewel case, what
use was he? Besides, he thought furiously, Tremayne was a liar, and deserved to die.

But the jewel case was still lost to him.

He stared off into the shadows. It had to be
somewhere, he thought broodingly. And
someday . . . someday he would find it.

Seven

The carriage sped toward Cumberland, climbing rolling hills that took them steadily northward, cutting past glittering lakes of deepest sapphire. Sheep grazed in placid green valleys, occasionally lifting their heads to gaze at the conveyance that interrupted their peace.

Inside the small, cramped interior of the coach, Heather's companion looked totally at ease. His long, booted legs stretched out before him, his arms crossed over his broad chest in contented repose. With his eyes peacefully shut, his lashes lay like ink-black fans upon the high plateau of his cheekbones.

Such tranquility was not the case for Heather. The journey progressed in silence. Neither of them was disposed to idle conversation. She could have screamed, for the trip was as endless as she had feared. The tension wound in her breast was almost unbearable. His nearness was overwhelming. So close to him like this, it was all she could do to take in enough air to fill her lungs. In those moments where their eyes chanced to collide, she felt the biting touch of his gaze like the lash of a whip.

They stopped for luncheon at a tiny tavern, and it was a welcome respite. It was with an icy dread that Heather climbed back inside the coach. Yet it wasn't long before her limbs grew heavy. Her senses were lulled by the creak of the springs and the sway and bounce of the vehicle; her neck began to loll. Her breathing began to deepen. Hard as she tried, she couldn't keep her eyes open.

The next thing she knew, she felt absurdly warm, yet wonderfully so. Her cheek rested on soft, fragrant wool that carried a familiar scent. Her senses warm and sleep-shrouded, she nestled against what she knew instinctively was a warm male shoulder. It really was a most comfortable place to rest. . . .

She bolted upright, eyes wide in appalling chagrin. One small hand flew to her breast. She scrambled back against the cushions as if he were the very plague.

"What are you doing over here?" she gasped.

Beside her, Damien gazed down at her, as calm as she was unsettled. "Your posture was most awkward, Miss Duval. Your head was bent sideways, like a frail stem about to snap. I merely thought to save you a few aches and pains tonight."

Heather's mouth opened and closed. She could hardly chastise him for being considerate, now could she?

He removed himself to the other side of the

coach. Gray eyes held her in watchful regard, cool and inquisitive. "As I recall, you once said your parents were French, did you not, Miss Duval?"

"My father was," she said quickly. "My mother was English."

"And what were their names?"

Heather hesitated. A curious foreboding had knotted her stomach, yet for the life of her, she couldn't have said why. "Bernard and Justine Duval," she supplied after a moment.

"Where are they buried?"

"In the cemetery outside the church in Lyndermere."

"I see." He paused. "One would have thought the Earl of Stonehurst might have sent them home to be buried."

"Ah, but they had no home. Didn't I tell you that, Mr. Lewis?" She had. She was certain of it. With her head angled to the side, she studied him. Her unease hadn't lessened. "That they had just come to England in order to make a new life for themselves?"

"I'd forgotten," he said smoothly . . . almost too smoothly?

She couldn't quell the notion, but there was no time for further speculation, for he was speaking again.

"Your mother Justine . . . what sort of woman was she?"

Her eyes narrowed. "And what sort of question is that?"

His eyes flickered. "I meant no harm, Miss Duval. I merely wondered if you resemble her."

"I . . . I couldn't say." She paused, then said slowly, "My mother didn't linger long after the accident. But Papa knew her well and said she was a kind, sweet soul whose only thought at the end was of my well-being." Her expression was one of wistful yearning. "That's the one thing I'll always regret. That I never knew my mother."

"You don't remember her?"

She shook her head.

"And your father? Do you remember him?"

"No, but I—I think I resemble him. His hair was dark like mine." The statement came from nowhere. The memory came as if plucked from somewhere deep in her being, from some place she hadn't known existed, even as the image of a tall, black-haired man flashed through her brain.

Heather looked at him, stunned. "Good heavens," she said aloud. "How odd . . . I—I've never before recalled what he looked like."

Damien's regard sharpened. He echoed the sentiment. How odd indeed, for Corinne had stated that the man who killed Giles had grimy black hair. All at once he wondered if Heather weren't lying. Perhaps Elliot had already come to Lockhaven. Perhaps she knew where he was. And yet, her surprise seemed genuine.

Dammit, he didn't know what to think anymore! With an effort, he curbed his frustration. "It's possible you remember more than you think," he suggested. "Indeed, sometimes one memory may trigger another. Do you remember anything else about him?"

It was her turn to gaze at him sharply. Why all these questions from Damien? *Damien.* Even as

it struck her that she no longer thought of him as
Mr. Lewis, a vague disquietude nagged within
her. It struck her that there had been times when
she'd been made uneasy by his prolonged stare.
It was as if he searched for something . . . but
what?

"And I find your questions most curious, Mr.
Lewis. Frankly, I do not understand your interest
in my background—in particular, in my father."

His gaze flickered. "There's no need to be so
defensive, Miss Duval. It was more an observation than anything else, I assure you." He
shrugged. "You seemed distressed. I was merely
trying to be helpful."

Heather made no reply. Had she been defensive? She wasn't certain.

"If you have no objection, Miss Duval, I think
I'll ride with the driver for a while."

"Certainly, Mr. Lewis." She gave a nod of
assent, in all honesty relieved to be spared his
presence. She watched as he rapped on the hatch
behind the driver's seat. The portal opened, and
he voiced his intent. Within seconds, they'd
rolled to a halt. With nary a backward glance, he
leaped down and left her alone.

Heather's gaze remained fixed on the door
he'd just passed through. Despite his glib response, his questions disturbed her. Not for the
first time, she wondered who Damien Lewis
really was. Oh, she knew what he said. But was it
the truth? She disliked the doubts that suddenly
leaped in her breast, yet they were not so easily
subdued.

With a sigh she turned her attention to the
greenery passing by outside. Soon the road

wound in and out of a verdant woodland. When dusk began to drop its gauzy folds on the hilltops, they stopped at an inn for the night, a rambling stone building partially hidden in a copse of trees.

She alighted from the carriage to discover Damien had already gone inside without waiting for her. She pressed her lips together. Glancing around, she noticed a meandering brook that sneaked through the grass nearby. Several ducklings darted and twisted to and fro. Tiny flies buzzed in the air above the bushes. All around, spring was a warm, vibrant celebration, but for once Heather paid little heed. The afternoon's turbulent musings of her mind had spoiled all else for her.

It was several minutes before Damien emerged.

"We're in luck," he said, striding toward her and Morton, the driver. "I was able to get the last two rooms for the night, and there's room in the carriage house."

He offered his arm. Heather waited a heartbeat, then lightly placed her fingertips on his sleeve, unaware of the tightening of his lips at her telltale reluctance. He guided her to the far side of the inn where the main entrance was, but there she stopped short. She gazed in mute distress at the high, wooden steps that angled toward the doorway.

The next thing she knew she was whisked from her feet and swung high into the air. Firmly ensnaring her in strong male arms, he carried her bodily—aye, and boldly!—up the stairs.

Heather was bristling by the time he set her on
her feet. She should be grateful, she knew, for the
cramped hours in the carriage had left her knee
aching and stiff. Yet her pride wouldn't let her
yield even that to him.

She inhaled a stinging lungful of air. He might
regard her as a cripple, but she was not helpless,
and it was time he knew it. Nor did she wish to
draw attention to herself, and he had just embarrassed her beyond words!

"I do not recall asking for help, sir," she said
in low, clipped tones. Her chin climbed high
aloft. "I realize I am hardly a picture of grace,
but I assure you I am fully capable of negotiating
a flight of stairs on my own. I've been doing so
for quite some years now—why, fully all of my
life!" The sharp rapping of her cane as she
crossed the wooden floor conveyed her displeasure quite well.

Neither one said a word to each other as the
innkeeper's wife showed them to their rooms.

Heather was still smarting when he joined her
in the common room a short time later. With a
cursory nod, he took the chair across from her.

His hand smoothing his chin, he scanned the
room. Loud, raucous laughter and boisterous
voices rang throughout. He judged the crowd to
be a mix of merchant and farmer alike, but he
disliked the look of the two gentlemen who sat
on a bench against the far wall. One wore a
jaunty hat pushed back on his head. The other
had curling blond hair that swept across his
forehead. With their eyes they prowled the room
like hungry cats in search of a meal.

He frowned. "The crowd seems a bit rough," he said. "Perhaps we should dine in our rooms."

Heather shook out her napkin and placed it on her lap. "Do what you like, Mr. Lewis"—she didn't look at him as she spoke—"but I would like to remain here."

Damien tensed his jaw. "Then I'd better stay," he said brusquely.

Her head came up, her eyes ablaze like gems. "I'm well aware that you'd rather not, so please do not bother."

"But a woman alone—"

She cut him off abruptly. "As you should know, I'm quite capable of fending for myself."

Damien's chair skittered backward. God, but the woman was stubborn.

He took his meal at a small table in the far corner. A glass of ale in hand, he turned and surveyed with burning eyes the woman who so tormented him. For all that she was the most intelligent, level-headed young woman he'd ever met, she was also the most irritating. Oh, he knew what she was doing. He'd meant no affront when he carried her up the stairs, but she'd taken it as such and now she was taunting him. Punishing him. Defying him, for undoubtedly she thought it wasn't his place to object to her behavior—or to intervene.

His mood was suddenly anything but easy. Needing a breath of fresh air, he surged to his feet, leaving his ale on the table. Four long strides took him to the doorway, yet at the last instant something stopped him from leaving.

He glanced back over his shoulder. The two

gentlemen on the bench were whispering; their
backs were to him. Apparently they were under
the impression he'd gone; they had fixed greedy
eyes upon Heather. Even as Damien watched,
they rose and approached her table. Her expression was one of startled surprise when the pair
presented themselves before her and bowed low.
She started to cast a fleeting, sidelong glance
toward the table where he'd been sitting, then
chanced to see him near the doorway.

Their eyes met and held for the space of a
heartbeat.

Then, with a faint lift of her chin, she turned
back to the pair. She was smiling, waving a
graceful hand toward the vacant chairs across
from her.

The pair immediately sat.

Damien seethed. The stupid little fool! What
did she think she was doing?

Before long the blond laid his hand across hers
where it rested on the table. Every muscle in
Damien's body went stiff. Heather tried to with-
draw, but the man's hand now clamped the
delicate span of her wrist. Alarm flashed across
her features.

Damien was halfway across the room within
the span of a second.

The pair had pulled Heather to her feet. She
gave a stricken cry, only to have her face jammed
into the blond man's shoulder. They flanked her
on either side. One small wrist was still imprisoned; his hand on her waist, he started to turn
her bodily toward the stairs.

Damien blocked their way.

"Good evening, gentlemen." His tone was ever so mild.

His expression was murderous.

The man in the hat went pale. Another time, it might have been gratifying, but not now.

The blond was not so cautious. Straightening himself to his full height, he squared around to face Damien. "Move aside," he ordered harshly.

Damien inclined his head. "Not until you release the lady."

"The lady is coming with us!"

"The lady," he said with soft deliberation, "may have something to say about that." He looked at her. "Heather?"

Heather's eyes were huge, the shade of darkest purple, filled with sheer terror. She tore her elbow from the stranger's grasp. Three small steps brought her to his side. He could feel her quaking against him. His hands curled into fists as he struggled against the urge to draw her close against his side. Dammit, she'd brought this on herself, and it was time she realized it!

But it wasn't over. Muttering a vile curse, the blond clapped a heavy hand on Damien's shoulder. "Now see here—"

He got no further. Damien whirled. A lean fist shot out, crashing into the blond man's jaw.

The wretch slumped to the floor without a sound.

The man in the hat held up both hands. "Easy, man." Slowly he began to back away. "She's yours, I can see that. Let's just leave it at that, shall we?" He whirled and bolted toward the outside entrance.

Stunned, Heather stared up at him. "Dear God," she said faintly. "You—you probably broke his jaw."

"Quite likely." He spoke from between his teeth.

Grasping her arm, he steered her toward the stairway. His features were a mask of unrelenting purpose. The gaping onlookers, who'd gone silent during the episode, parted like the sea before Moses. With a finger, he flicked a silver coin to the proprietor.

Upstairs in the narrow hallway, he strode straight to her room. His was the next door down. Flinging open the door, he pushed her across the threshold, then stepped inside. With the flat of his hand he slammed the door closed. Snatching a candle from the stand, he lit it from the fireplace, then jammed it into the candlestick on the table.

She hadn't moved. Indeed, she still stared at him as if he were a madman. With a shake of her head, she spoke his name.

"Damien—"

He was in no mood for another scathing denunciation. "Spare me the remonstration," he said bitingly. "Like it or not, this time you *did* need rescuing."

"But—"

He lashed out at her furiously. "Perhaps you're more like Beatrice than you know, Heather. Were you testing your power as a woman? Well, you were a rousing success, love. They wanted you. They wanted to rip your clothes off. Touch your naked body. Stuff you like a sausage between those lovely legs of yours."

She flushed at his vulgarity.

"And if I hadn't been there, that's what they would have done. No doubt they would have taken turns—"

"Stop!" she cried.

Two steps brought him before her so they stood toe to toe. "No, Heather." He grasped her shoulders and gave her a little shake. Dazed, she let her head fall back. She gazed up at him, her eyes like saucers. "You'll listen, by God. It's time you came off your tower. It's time you learned what the world is like. You can't bait men like that and not expect to pay the consequences."

"I—I wasn't baiting them!"

"You were," he said fiercely. "Every slow, sweet smile was a temptation. Every coy sweep of your lashes over your eyes, an invitation."

A hand swooped down to clamp the fullness of her breast. She cried out at the suddenness of his movement.

His breath grated past her ear. "That's what they would have done, Heather." His hands fell to her hips. Dragging her forward, he ground his loins against the hollow of her belly. "And this is what they wanted."

She shuddered with revulsion. His words painted a stark picture in her mind, black and cold. The very thought of those two men touching her like that made her sick inside. To her shame, she felt the stinging ache of tears in her throat. The breath she drew was deep and wavering.

Her chin quivered as she tried to speak. "I—I didn't know," she said brokenly. "I'm sorry. I—I didn't know!"

His features tightened. "Yes, you did. Tell me, which one did you fancy?"

"N-neither of them," she cried. "I don't know why I did it. It—it wasn't them. It was you. Oh, don't you see . . . it was you and I—I just wanted to make you . . ." All at once she blanched, as if she'd said too much.

His eyes narrowed. "What, Heather? Were you trying to make me jealous?"

Indeed, Heather didn't know what devil's spell had come over her. She had felt reckless—and strangely out of control. But now his anger blazed all through her, and she wished with all her heart that she hadn't been so foolish.

Her composure was shattered. She couldn't say a word.

The silence heightened to a screaming pitch.

Above her, there was a muffled exclamation of disgust. She felt him tense, and she sensed that he was about to spin around and leave.

A startled, unbidden cry sprang from her lips. "Wait!"

Her fingers came out to clutch at his jacket. At the contact, she felt Damien's body go stiff. He searched her face and saw the tears she fought to control. Everything inside went utterly still, for he felt the conflict raging within her as if it were his own.

His anger had passed. Her fear had fled. And now a maelstrom of emotion churned inside them both.

"What, Heather?" His tone was low and intense. "What do you want?"

Their eyes locked. Heather's heart thundered painfully. She was trembling from head to foot. Yearning and fear and an agony of longing whirled like a tempest in her breast. She just wanted to be held. To feel safe and comforted, only she couldn't tell him. He couldn't know what it was like to feel so alone, she thought with a pang. To need so desperately the heat and shelter of another body, to drive away the chill of loneliness. . . . But she couldn't tell him. Not *him* . . .

Something broke inside her. Her fingers curled and uncurled against his chest. "I don't know," she cried helplessly. "I—I just don't know!"

His eyes darkened. "Well, I do, Heather. *I do.*"

Eight

God in heaven, he *did* . . . and it was all she wanted. Everything she needed.

His lips on hers were impossibly warm . . . impossibly sweet. He kissed her slowly, leisurely, a kiss that turned her inside out. His arms were strong about her back, and she melted against him as if her limbs were made of pudding.

Her breath quickened, as if she'd been running uphill. Heat gathered low in her belly, slowly radiating outward. She felt as if some powerful force had taken over her body. Her head fell back. She offered the honey of her mouth with an abandon she hadn't known she possessed. With a tiny growl deep in his throat, he tugged the center of her lower lip between his own, the contact incredibly erotic.

Pleasure swirled all about her, heady and divine. There were only the two of them, caught up in a world where nothing else existed save the wonder of this moment. Sensation unfurled within her, like the curling strands of a ribbon that rippled through every part of her.

Slowly he released her mouth.

Her eyes fluttered open, heavy-lidded and drowsy. He was staring down at her, his own eyes dark and fathomless.

"Again," she heard herself whisper.

To her surprise, one corner of that hard mouth turned upward. A teasing glint had appeared in his eyes. "Why, Miss Duval," he murmured. "Have you never been kissed before?"

His features were caught in the flickering glow of the candlelight. His cheeks and chin carried the faint shadow of his beard; she had felt that slight roughness against the softness of her skin and thrilled to the intensely masculine feel of it. Her gaze traced the bold, dark slash of his brows, his thin, straight nose, the sharp plane of his jaw. Her stomach tightened. He was so handsome he stole her very breath.

She couldn't help but respond in kind. "Well," she said lightly. "There was one other time . . ." She let the sentence trail off provocatively.

"I see. And did you like it?"

The glimmer of a smile touched her lips. "'Twas heaven," she said simply.

All trace of laughter fled his face. His eyes seemed to blaze with the heat of a tropical sun. "Then I'll do so with pleasure," he muttered just before his head came down.

This time there was fire in his kiss—it deepened to an intimacy only hinted at before. Inexperienced as she was, she could taste the hunger in him and reveled in it. Marveling at her daring, she buried her fingers in the dark hair that grew low on his nape. It curled around her fingers, springy and sleek, with a life of its own.

She grew bolder. The tip of her tongue danced lightly against his. Once, and then again. A tremendous shudder wracked his body. He groaned. His arms tightened around her back, his hold so fiercely urgent that her toes left the ground. And they were close—so close—she could feel the raging thunder of his heart as if it were her own.

Heaven. The thought burned through her once again. Sheer heaven . . . In all her days, nothing had felt so good. *Nothing.*

Lightly they spun. For one brief, never-ending moment, they stood at the edge of the bed. Her senses whirling giddily, she was only half aware of deft fingers dealing with the hooks and eyes at the back of her gown.

In the very next breath, it lay pooled about her ankles. Her shoes were disposed of just as quickly, and then she was lying on the bed, clad only in her chemise and petticoats.

"Oh, God." The words caught in her throat as she realized her state of dishabille. And then even that realization was forestalled as she saw Damien's shirt whisked over his head and dropped to the pile at his feet. For a spellbinding heartbeat, he stood there, wearing only his breeches, naked from the waist up.

All else was forgotten. Her mouth grew dry. He was . . . magnificent. There were no other words to describe him. His shoulders were wide and sinewy, gleaming bronze and gold in the candle-light. The muscles of his arms were sharply defined and bulging. She could see the veins that traced beneath his skin. But it was the wide expanse of his chest that drew her gaze in endless fascination—dense, dark hair grew in a curly forest that disappeared beneath the waistband of his breeches. She wondered vaguely if it extended further, clear to the place that proclaimed his manhood. . . .

Her palms grew damp. She longed to touch him, to skim her hands along the taut, sleek lines of his arms. She wanted to slide her fingers through the pelt on his chest, to feel it against her palm. The very thought was exciting . . . dangerous. Forbidden.

Time stood still as he watched her . . . watched her watch *him*.

"Heather."

The sound of her name sent her attention flying to his face. She was glad the darkness hid her embarrassment—at both her unabashed perusal of him and her own state of undress—for she knew her face was flaming. She was unaware that she had risen to a half-sitting position until he sat on the edge of the bed.

He wasn't content to stop there. Slowly, he extended a hand toward her breast but didn't allow it to fall. Panic burgeoned swiftly within her. She knew what he wanted. But no man had ever touched her. No man had ever *seen* her. She was no beauty. She had an unreasoning fear that he would be profoundly disappointed.

"Wait!"

The cry surfaced without warning. Her hand clamped his where it was poised at the ribbon that closed her chemise.

Slowly he raised his head.

"Let me, Heather." His tone washed over her, soft as silk. His fingers beneath her chin, he guided her eyes to his. "Let me. Please."

Please. The air between them grew close and heated. Heather was certain her heart would burst the bounds of her chest at any second. Yet she couldn't deny him. Heaven above, she *couldn't.*

His fingers touched the ribbon that held her chemise closed. She nearly jumped out of her skin.

Damien smothered a laugh. "Easy," he soothed. "I won't hurt you. I promise, I won't hurt you."

Her eyes clung to his. His knuckles grazed the harbor between her breasts. A flick of the wrist and she was completely bared to him. . . .

He gazed at her. She looked away. Yet still she could feel his eyes, scouring her nakedness. Leaving no part of her untouched.

Time stood still. There was no sound but the thin trickle of her breathing.

"Pretty," he murmured, just when she'd decided she could stand it no longer. There was a note in his voice she'd never heard before. "So pretty . . ."

His praise was like warm rain upon arid earth. Heather could have wept.

A fingertip traced the sweep of her collarbone. Delicious shivers played all through her. That lean dark hand swept lower . . . ever lower. Heather held her breath. Her breasts were tingling. Aching. For what, she knew not. . . .

His touch eroded her fears. Somewhere deep in the depths of her being, a stranger fluttered to life. In her ears she could hear the ragged tremor of her breath.

He cupped the underside of her breasts in his hands. With his thumbs he traced tiny circles around and around her nipples, coming close, yet never quite touching the dark, straining peaks, driving her half-mad with need.

At last he brushed his thumbs across the tips, again and again. Pleasure shot through her, like a streak of lightning. To her shock, she couldn't tear her eyes from the sight of her rounded softness filling his hands.

Then his mouth was on hers again. With naught but the pressure of his chest, he eased her to her back. Heather clung to his shoulders, without care, without shame. The skin beneath her fingertips was startlingly smooth and hard. She longed for the courage to explore as he explored, but alas! it deserted her.

But there was more.

Warm lips slid down the fragile arch of her throat. Heather couldn't tear her eyes from the sight of his dark head hovering over the jutting mounds of her breasts. Her nipples burned like twin peaks of fire. God above, what was happening?

Her breath emerged in a rush. Surely he would not . . .

He did.

His tongue touched her first. Pure sensation bolted through her, swift and unremitting. Her body twisted, instinctively seeking more.

And again he knew her body better than she herself. With the lash of his tongue he circled and teased one ripe, quivering peak, then the other. She stared down at herself, at her nipples, wet and glistening from his taunting play. Later she might hate herself. But not now. Dear God, not now. She prayed the delicious torment might never end. He took the tight, straining center deep into his mouth. Licking. Sucking. Drawing and pulling until at last a flood of sensation broke free within her and she bit back a cry. Excitement shot down to that secret, forbidden place, there between her thighs.

It couldn't really be happening. It seemed a part of her most cherished dream. Her most fevered fantasy . . .

He moved so that they lay on their sides, facing each other. Strong hands slid down to clasp her buttocks, urging her against him. In shock she felt the rigid length of his manhood, massive and taut against her belly.

The waistband of her silk drawers was but a feeble barrier; the flimsy tapes were thrust aside. She felt his knuckles skim the hollow of her belly. Those daring fingers trespassed further, tangling in the fleece that guarded the cove of her womanhood.

Her legs slammed shut. Her breath left her in a scalding rush. She tore her mouth from his. Her fingers convulsed around the hardness of his arms. "Please." All that emerged was a half-strangled sob. *"Please."*

The sound was a cold slap of awareness—it went through Damien like the tip of a knife. His rod pulsed hotly, straining to be free of the barrier of his breeches. The vibrant promise of her body so near his was almost more temptation than he could stand. He longed to be naked. Against her. Inside her. Driving deep and hard and filling her until there was no more of him to give. . . .

He gritted his teeth against the desire churning in his gut. She wasn't ready for this. They both knew it. No matter how much the heavy fullness in his loins urged otherwise—demanding fulfillment—he couldn't take her. Not now. Not like this.

Cursing inwardly, he rolled from her. His mouth drawn into a grim line, he stared at the shadows dancing on the ceiling.

The instant she was free, she curled into a tight little ball. Though she made not a sound, her shoulders were shaking. Damien turned his head to peer at her.

"Heather." His voice stole through the darkness. "Heather, look at me."

She refused. Instead she sat up, confusion, desperation and shame a soft haze in her eyes. She tried to tie the ribbons of her chemise, but her hands were shaking so badly she couldn't manage it.

Damien peremptorily pushed her fingers aside, doing up the ribbons as deftly as he'd untied them. When he'd finished, he grasped her shoulders, leaning back so he could see her.

"Nothing happened, Heather," he said firmly. "Do you hear me? *Nothing happened.*"

Her mouth quivered. Her lovely eyes shimmered with betraying moisture. She looked utterly stricken.

"I'm sorry," she said in a quavering voice. "I'm sorry. I—I know you must be angry—"

"I'm not." God, if only he could be. It would have been so much easier. . . .

She drew a long, shuddering breath. "It's just that I—I don't know what's happening to me."

But Damien did. The pangs of sensual awakening had come to life inside her, and the knowledge drove him half-wild. His belly knotted. He longed to show her all she craved, all she didn't know. He gritted his teeth against the driving need to strip away her clothes and feast his eyes on pink, satin flesh that had been hidden away until now.

Slowly, as if the movement pained him, his arms closed around her. He eased to his back, taking her along with him, then tugged the counterpane up around them to shield her nakedness.

With a breathy little sigh she turned her face into his shoulder.

Something caught at his heart. The realization washed over him then—when she was Heather Duval, mistress of Lockhaven, she was on sure footing. Strong. Confident. Independent as any man. But when it came to being a woman . . .

"This—isn't very proper." Her whisper pierced the darkness.

"To hell with proper." Damien was in no mood for propriety just now.

"I—I think my mother would be quite shocked."

"Are you?" He posed the question pointedly.

Her cheek was downy soft against his shoulder. "I suppose I should be." Her voice conveyed her hesitation. "But I—I'm not," she finished breathlessly.

"Then that's all that matters."

Silence drifted between them, both immersed in their own thoughts.

"Damien?"

He liked the sound of his name on her lips. But deep inside, he was consumed with the need to hear her cry it in a scream of ecstasy, a tender whisper of yearning, a mindless, frenzied plea of passion.

"The other day when I was angry with you and Bea . . ." Her voice came haltingly. "You were right. I was jealous of Bea. Because she's graceful. Because she can dance. Because she can ride. And"—he had to strain to hear—"because of you."

Because of you.

Even as triumph surged high in his blood, a bitter shadow crept through him.

Don't! his mind screamed. Don't say any more. This shouldn't be happening. Not with her. Anyone but her . . .

He could feel the warm trickle of her breath

across his skin. "No doubt you think me petty and mean." Her voice was thready and small.

He kissed the smoothness of her temple. "We all succumb to envy at some time or another," he said quietly. "But that does not make you petty and mean, and I most certainly do not think you so."

The top of her head brushed his chin as she looked up at him. Her moods were like her eyes, he thought, by turn light, then dark. "Truly?" she whispered.

His arms tightened. "Truly."

The glimmer of a smile rimmed the lovely curve of her mouth. She ducked her head down and sighed, a sound of relief and contentment.

He'd thought she'd grown up pampered and spoiled. The little girl who had everything. But that was before he'd considered what she'd had to endure—the jeering mockery, the horrified stares—what she *still* endured. Oh, she tried not to let it show. She was staunch and steadfast. But he had glimpsed the pain she tried to hide—the hurt—and her vulnerability speared his heart.

He stroked the shallow groove of her spine, a soothing, monotonous motion. It wasn't long before the rise and fall of her chest became deep and even. She slept.

But Damien's mind was anything but idle. He felt protective of her. Possessive. Yet a voice within whispered that such emotion had no part in his plans here. . . .

A curious tightness settled about his heart. His lip curled with self-disgust. She had no idea who he was . . . why he was here. She trusted him.

She *trusted* him as she had trusted no other man. He knew it instinctively. She no longer flinched from him, as she had when they'd first met. He'd touched her as no other had touched her. . . .

This was dangerous, in a way he hadn't anticipated, for reasons he hadn't anticipated. *She* wasn't what he anticipated. Her father was a murderer, and, somehow, he'd expected that same evil to be revealed in her.

She knew nothing of her father—of James Elliot. He was becoming more and more convinced of it.

She shifted, nestling the entire sweet length of her form against him. Damien froze. He could feel the plumpness of her breast ripe against his side, the hollow of her belly flush against the jutting plane of his hip.

Her body—what he'd seen of it—was enchanting. He gritted his teeth. The gleaming slope of her shoulder peeped above the counterpane, tempting him unbearably. Unable to stop himself, he lifted a corner of the counterpane to gaze at her.

Her hair was glorious, spilling about her like a waterfall of shining, black silk. She was delicately made, her limbs small and dainty, her skin as smooth as Devonshire cream. He knew that, if he were to try, his thumbs would meet as he encircled her waist with his hands. Her breasts were small, like the rest of her, yet lushly ripe and made to fit perfectly into the palm of his hands. Strawberry-sweet nipples thrust against the thin white lawn of her chemise, tantalizing fruit just waiting to be plucked.

A blaze ignited in his veins. His insides wound into a knot, coiled tight and hard. His body, already seized with a near-painful heat, needed little provocation. His senses blazed like white-hot fire. He steeled himself against the urge to roll over, to kiss her into drowsy wakefulness, thrust his shaft long and hard within her velvet channel and feel her tight, clinging sheath clamped around the part of him that echoed the throb of his heart.

He'd wanted her from the start. He wanted her now.

She shifted, drawing his attention to her right leg. His scrutiny sharpened—as did his curiosity. His eyes narrowed. He considered baring her knee, to see for himself what he knew she would hide most insistently if she knew his intention. Yet in the end, he decided against it. It would have been almost a . . . a violation.

Darkness stole through him, searing his lungs so that he could hardly breathe. Something bitterly dark and ominous cast its shadow over him.

This was madness. He was mad. He cursed himself for giving in—to her. To the desire that reigned unchecked. He didn't want to feel this way. He wanted to feel nothing for her. Not sympathy for her limp. Not admiration for her spirit and determination. Certainly not this gut-churning desire that would not die.

He should never have touched her. But he had, and now they must both pay the price.

He should leave, he told himself blackly. Now. Before it was too late, for both of them.

Careful not to wake her, he slipped from the

bed. Noiseless footsteps carried him to the narrow window that looked down upon the forest. He stared bleakly into the stark blackness of the night.

No, he thought. He couldn't leave. The die had been cast, the game begun. He must stay and see it through. Whatever it took. Whatever the cost. To him . . .

Or to her.

Nine

Morning bloomed with buttercup-yellow hues that streamed through the shutters, lighting every corner of the room with splashes of sunshine, drawing Heather from slumber.

She lay very still, her eyes closed, the smoothness of her brow puckered. Something vague touched the fringes of her mind. She stretched and sat up slowly, then started to push away the counterpane.

Her eyes widened. Why, she'd slept in her underclothes . . . .

She'd slept in his arms . . . in *Damien's* arms.

Memory rushed back in scalding vividness. The beat of her heart grew wild and stormy. Her fingers fell to the swell of one breast. She stared in mingled horror and fascination. He had seen her. He had *touched* her. Her stomach knotted. Once again, she could feel the heated strength of his fingers sliding over her skin, the hot, wet suction of his mouth on her nipple . . . .

Her eyes squeezed shut. No lady would allow

him to do what he had done. Was she wanton? Wicked? She wondered anew about her parents. Papa had said her mother was kind and good. But what if she wasn't? What if he was wrong? Was her blood tainted, that she could behave so shamelessly?

She pressed the back of her hand to her forehead to stop the turmoil roiling in her breast. Her heart cried out. What was wrong with her? Why these sudden doubts? Was it the questions Damien had asked of her? The questions for which she had no answers?

Slowly she rose and dressed. She was suddenly anxious to have their business here concluded— but she was not looking forward to the long journey home.

Damien was already seated in the common room when she descended the stairs. He spotted her immediately and came across to escort her.

"Good morning." His voice rang out clear and strong.

Heather gripped her cane and awaited him nervously. "Good morning," she murmured. Meeting his regard was the hardest thing she'd ever done. His gaze was as calm and steady as the man himself. His features conveyed no hint of what had passed between them last night. Heather was grateful—and only too willing to take her cue from him.

The innkeeper, a heavyset man with a bulbous nose, brought their breakfast—great, heaping platters of ham, eggs and cold fowl. "No harm done last night, eh? Everyone has a tiff now and then"—he gave a throaty chuckle—"me and m'wife more'n most." He nudged Damien with an elbow. "Besides, she's a lovely one, eh? Any man can see why you'd be protective of her."

Damien's eyes never left her face as he spoke. "She is beautiful, isn't she?"

Heather stared at where her hands lay clenched in her lap. She couldn't look at them, either of them. Her cheeks were flaming by the time the innkeeper hurried to the next table.

Reaching deep inside for a courage that was proving vastly elusive, she dragged her eyes upward. "Why did you say that?" she asked levelly.

He had leaned back in his chair. "Because it happens to be true. Has no one ever told you so?"

She inhaled sharply and looked at him fully. "Do you mock me, sir?"

"Not at all." When she said nothing, he persisted. "You haven't answered me, Heather. Has no one ever told you how lovely you are?"

She averted her eyes. "Of course my parents have." Her tone was very low. "But no . . . ," she faltered, ". . . no gentleman has ever done so."

His tone was very quiet. "Then I consider it a privilege to be the first."

He was unsmiling. It struck her that he seemed very . . . somber. Did he really think she was beautiful? Flustered but determined not to show it, Heather picked up her fork. But all throughout the meal she felt the probe of his eyes on her profile. It was unsettling and disturbing . . . and exciting as well.

Her emotions were scattered a hundred different ways. What was he thinking? Did he regret kissing her last night? Had he found her inexperience distasteful? All at once she yearned to be a woman of the world, knowledgeable in the ways of men, in the art of seduction and flirtation. Was that what men wanted? Was that what *he* wanted?

If only she knew. If only . . .

She was only too glad when the meal ended and they could be on their way again. It was but a short ride to the home of John Ferguson, a portly, bewhiskered gentleman with a rolling belly laugh. Heather liked him on sight. They chatted briefly; then he took them to the paddock, where they met his stable master, an aging Scotsman named Angus.

Ferguson clapped the Scotsman's shoulder. "Any questions, m'lady, he's the man to ask. Knows more about these fine animals than I could ever hope to."

Damien had moved to the fence. In the pasture, a number of horses grazed lazily—a big black, a dainty roan mare, several geldings. But as Heather stepped up beside him, one in particular caught her eye—a towering gray stallion.

Her breath caught. "The gray . . . why, he's gorgeous!"

The animal had snared Damien's attention as well. "That he is," he murmured. A faint smile curled his mouth. "Just look at him. He knows it, too."

It was true. As if he sensed their scrutiny, the gray reared back and pawed the air with flashing hooves. He then pranced proudly across the grassy field, tossing his head high, as if he were strutting and preening.

Heather gave a bubbly laugh. "You're right. He does know it!" She turned to Angus. "The gray. Is he for sale?"

Angus stroked his drooping mustache. "Oh, you don't want that one, mum. Too spirited for a lady."

Two bright spots of color appeared on Heather's cheeks. Her smile slipped a notch. "Oh, he's not for me," she said quickly. "I'm looking for my father, who happens to be a superb horseman."

Angus nodded. "He's a youngster, just over two years old. Mr. Ferguson bought him for the missus, but he's proven too much for her to handle. Would ye like to see 'im?"

"Very much."

Both she and Damien answered in unison. When he slanted her a lopsided smile, her heart skipped a beat. He was so very handsome . . . .

It was several minutes before Angus was able to catch the stallion. He led the old man a merry chase, ducking and swerving. Watching Angus run bowlegged after the stallion, Heather couldn't withhold a mirthful laugh.

Finally he led the gray through the gate to where they waited. "Ye see?" Angus shook his head. "He's a bit wild at times. Needs a firm, strong hand to let 'im know who's master, and that's what the missus didn't have."

The gray tossed his head, his nostrils flared, his ears pricked high. His broad head, huge, expressive eyes, gracefully arched neck and powerful shoulders confirmed his noble bloodlines. His coat was like molten steel, shiny and sleek, gleaming with every move of his body. He stood with quivering skin, his sleek, powerful muscles bunched.

Damien slowly extended a hand. The gray snorted, straining restlessly against the halter.

Angus's hand tightened on the strap. "He's a bit stiff with strangers." His tone was apologetic.

Damien stepped closer. "Not with me," he murmured. He edged closer, running his knuckles along the gray's neck. "That's the way, boy."

He continued to speak in low, soothing tones. Heather watched in fascination as that strong, brown hand stroked the quivering sides over and over, calming the animal . . . as Damien had calmed her. The animal quieted beneath his touch and became still. He thrust his muzzle familiarly into Damien's shoulder.

Angus gave a blustering laugh. "Well, saints be . . . I can see ye don't need me, so I'll just leave the three of ye alone fer a bit. If ye need me, I'll be in the stables. Just give a whistle." With a wave he went his way.

Up until now, Heather had remained a fair distance from the stallion. Now Damien cast her a curious glance.

"Don't you want a closer look?"

Heather took a deep breath and edged forward. Her heart was pounding like a drum. Still several feet away, she started to raise a hand, but the gray snorted and sidestepped skittishly.

Heather started abruptly.

One hand on the gray's halter, Damien extended the other.

"Come," he said softly.

Heather's gaze skipped from his hand, to eyes the color of pure silver, and back again. Wetting her lips, she put out her arm.

His hand closed around hers, his grip warm and strong. Lightly he squeezed her fingers, gently tugging her forward. "There's nothing to be afraid of."

Heather's laugh was weak. "Does it show? I'm afraid I don't have much experience with horses. One of the stableboys always hitches up my cart."

Her hand still clasped within his, he guided her fingers to the gray's muzzle. Tentatively, she stroked the long, velvet nose. "Easy," he murmured. "That's the way. Slow and easy. Let him feel your touch. Let him smell your scent. Let him know you won't hurt him."

His hand released hers. Heather rubbed the graceful line of the gray's powerful neck. She trembled anew, though not from fear. She could feel the unyielding breadth of Damien's chest against her back. His nearness was like a spell that wrapped itself around her, an invisible web from which there was no escape. She ached with the need to turn into his embrace, to surrender her mouth for the blazing rapture of his kiss.

But all at once she *was* afraid—terrified that if she did what she dared not do, he would not want her . . . not the way she wanted him.

The gray nickered, a sound of satisfaction.

"There. You see?" His breath slid past her ear, cool and fragrant. "He knows he can trust you."

Trust. Trust was a fragile, infinitely precious emotion, one that Heather had learned very early was never to be given lightly. Did she dare trust Damien with these newfound, tremulous feelings that blossomed in her breast? The thought progressed further . . .

Could she trust him with her heart?

He withdrew a step, and the turmoil inside her eased a bit. She glanced at him, warming as she saw his approval.

She scratched the gray's coat with her nails. "He's so big," she murmured with a faint smile.

"Sixteen hands, I would say." There was a small pause. "Why don't you ride, Heather?"

Her smile withered. Her gaze shied away from his. "I can't," she said quietly. "I tried when I was younger, but it pains my knee."

His gaze sharpened. She sensed he was about to say more, but just then Mr. Ferguson reappeared, rubbing his hands together.

"Angus tells me you're interested in the gray here. A fine animal, as you can see. My wife had planned to keep him for herself, but, as Angus no doubt told you, he's a tad too energetic for her."

Heather turned, grateful for his timely intervention, for it saved her from further awkward questions.

"I'm most interested, Mr. Ferguson, provided we can agree on a price."

A bit of haggling, and the deal was done. They made plans for Damien to ride the gray back to Lockhaven, while Heather traveled back in the

carriage. She was secretly glad, for the prospect
of being alone with Damien was one she would
rather not face. A little voice inside chided her
for being so spineless, but she couldn't help it.
When Damien Lewis was near, it seemed she
knew herself not at all . . . .

But it was during the long journey home that a
steadfast resolve crystallized in her breast.

What had happened last night . . . must never
happen again.

She'd been kissed and touched, and she would
hold those cherished, heart-stirring memories
inside her forever—her every wish fulfilled. A
bitter ache tightened her throat, but she pushed
it aside. She had learned life's lessons only too
well, and at an early age. And thus, she had
learned to be true to herself. She would not lie to
herself about the future, for to do so would only
lead to bitter, deflating disappointment.

And so she would never know what it was like
to be truly loved by a man, in every way . . . in
the way that really mattered.

The risk was too great, the price too steep.

A tight band seemed to creep around her chest
and squeeze. No, she thought with a pang. She
couldn't let Damien close. She couldn't allow
him to touch her again, to kiss her. Because when
he did, somehow it seemed she always lost her
head . . . .

The next time might well be her heart.

It was better this way, she reminded herself
over and over. Better . . .

But much more painful.

Ten

Papa's birthday fete was a rousing success. The gathering was small but intimate, attended by family and neighboring friends. Heather watched her mother slip an arm through her father's elbow. Laughing, Miles clasped his hand over hers, then bent low and brushed her lips with his.

For an instant, sheer, stark pain clutched Heather's heart. Such displays were hardly unusual, for her parents had never been shy about letting their feelings be known. But today—today was different.

She envied their closeness. Their ease with each other. She envied the love they shared . . .

And despised herself in the bargain.

The celebration lasted most of the afternoon on the south lawn. The guests had departed when Victoria made her way to where Heather sat, enjoying the warmth of the sun on her face and the fragrant scent of the breeze.

Victoria dropped a kiss on her cheek and

collapsed into the chair next to her daughter. "Finally, a chance to rest." Her tone turned anxious. "Did it go well, do you think?"

Heather smiled. "Your parties always turn out smashing, Mama. You always fret for no reason."

Victoria sighed. "A mother's lot, it seems."

Heather's smile remained in place, but something inside her twisted. Her heart throbbed wistfully, for that was something she would never know . . . .

"At any rate, I'm glad it's over." Dressed in a pale blue frock that matched the color of her eyes, Victoria appeared as youthful as ever. She fixed those incredibly blue eyes on her daughter. "It seems like ages since we've had the chance to talk," she said lightly. "Indeed, it seems we've hardly seen you of late. It's not because of that incident with Bea, is it?"

Heather blinked. Oh, but she should have known, for Mama was not one to mince words.

Heather glanced down to where her hands were folded in her lap. "I thought her too forward. Was I wrong, Mama?"

"Heather, I know of no one with a steadier head than you, sweet." She gave a tinkling laugh. "Why, many was the time when I first married your father that I considered coming to you for advice—and you but a child of eight! Besides, Bea is fanciful and headstrong and must learn she cannot always have her way."

"I was harsh with her, Mama."

Victoria's gaze softened. "So are we all at one time or another, love."

"But I made her cry. And I cannot remember a time when you or Papa ever made *me* cry."

"And now I think you are too harsh on yourself. But that's your nature, I think—you expect much of yourself. At times too much, I fear." Suddenly she reached out and touched Heather's cheek. "You look tired, dear."

Heather avoided her gaze. "I'm fine, Mama. I just didn't sleep particularly well last night."

It was an excuse; they were both aware of it. But in that special way she had, Victoria knew when to press and when to leave well enough alone.

But she did reach out and take both of Heather's hands within hers. "Love, if you ever wish to talk—oh, about anything, anything at all!—you know you can come to me, don't you?"

Heather went still. Mama knew. Somehow Mama knew there was something between her and Damien . . . but she couldn't tell her—she couldn't tell anyone!

She summoned a wisp of a smile. "I know, Mama."

Victoria stared at her for several seconds, then lightly steered the conversation elsewhere.

A short time later, when Victoria went inside to check on dinner, Heather rose and made her way to her father. He was leaning on the fence near the pasture, a half-smile on his face as he watched the gray stallion race across the field.

He slanted her a slight smile as she stopped beside him. "He's as fleet as the wind, isn't he," he murmured, then paused. "Wait! That's what

I'll call him . . . Pegasus! What do you think, Heather?"

"I think it a fitting name indeed, Papa."

The satisfaction in her tone made him laugh. He turned an eye upon his eldest daughter. "So. You're feeling rather pleased with yourself, are you, poppet?"

Poppet. It was the pet name he'd called her as far back as she could remember. Heather chuckled. "With good reason, I suspect. But now I'd ask the same of you, Papa. Are you pleased with your gift? Or would you have preferred my prize ram?"

"Ah, but your prize ram would not carry me with such speed," he stated blithely.

She eyed his tall, imposing form up and down. "My prize ram would not carry you at all!"

It was his turn to chuckle at her teasing. His mirth subsided, and he glanced at her. "I never suspected—nor did I realize you were such an excellent judge of horses. Where did you find him?"

"Actually, Da—" She caught herself just in time. "Mr. Lewis accompanied me to a breeder in Cumberland by the name of Ferguson."

"Ferguson? Outstanding! His horses are coveted from here to Paris." He cocked a brow at her. "I do hope he gave you a fair price."

"He did indeed. I learned to bargain from a master, remember?" They chatted on for several minutes, but soon Heather fell silent.

Miles reached out to touch the faint lines etched between finely arched black brows. "What's on your mind, poppet?" he asked softly.

Heather took a deep breath. Her gaze was unerringly direct. "Papa, what did my father look like?"

Shock rendered Miles immobile. Somehow he managed to quell it. Before he could respond, she went on.

"Was he a tall man with black hair?"

Miles gave her an odd look. "Yes. Yes, he was, pet."

"You're quite certain?"

The merest hesitation. "Quite."

She didn't seem to notice, thank heaven. "Yes. Yes, of course you would be." She spoke as if to herself. "After all, you knew him well . . . ."

"Your mother was petite like you, Heather, only with chestnut hair. But you have her eyes." He held his breath. This, at least, he knew to be true . . . .

She let out a long, pent-up breath. "I'm sorry, Papa. I didn't mean to snap at you."

"No harm done." His tone was light. "But why that particular question, poppet? It's been quite some time—years, I believe—since you've asked after your parents."

She gave a tiny, rueful shake of her head. "It's just that I suddenly recalled the memory of a tall, black-haired man, and I had the most bizarre certainty that he must have been my father. It's rather odd, don't you think?"

Miles disguised his uneasiness with a smile. "I really couldn't say, sweet. But certainly it's nothing to worry about."

"Yes. Yes, of course you're right."

Later that night, Victoria sat before the dressing table in their bedchamber, pulling a brush through wavy, blond curls, her expression preoccupied. Finally she laid the brush aside and glanced at Miles. Clad in a rich burgundy dressing gown, he stood at the window, gazing out into the night.

"Heather looked tired today, don't you think?"

So immersed in thought was he that she had to repeat her question.

"I'm afraid I didn't notice." He turned back to the window.

Victoria frowned. Heather wasn't the only one acting strangely today. His posture was rigid and tense. For a man who'd been riding the cusp of happiness throughout the day, his sudden quiet tonight concerned her grievously. Rising, she crossed to him and laid gentle fingertips on his shoulder.

"What's wrong, Miles?" she asked softly.

His voice was low and strained. "She asked about her father, Victoria. She asked what he looked like."

Victoria's lips parted. "No. Oh, no. Oh, Miles, what did you say?"

He turned to her. "Christ, I—I didn't know what to say. She's made no mention of them for years. . . . Before I could answer, she asked if he was a tall, black-haired man."

"Was he?"

His features were drawn. "I told her he was, but I—I don't know for certain, Victoria. It was dark and raining the night of the accident. He was already dead. I was trying to save Heather and her mother." He paused.

"But as I stood there with Heather today, the strangest thing happened. I began to wonder . . . what if the man with Justine was not her husband? What if he was not Heather's father?" He pressed taut fingers to his forehead, then sought her gaze. "Victoria, it's all I've been able to think of since! What if he was not her father?"

A tiny frown lined Victoria's brow. "Miles, you have no reason to believe he was *not* her father."

"Not then. Don't you see, not then!"

"They were traveling together, weren't they? The three of them?"

"Yes. I assumed he was her father. And Justine asked after him. 'How is Bernard?' she asked over and over. 'Tell me he is well,' she pleaded again and again." Miles began to pace. "He had come with her, and I was so certain he was her husband."

"Miles, I would have been just as convinced," Victoria pointed out.

"But what if I was wrong? I made no inquiries, Victoria—at first because I believed they were a family; later because I didn't want to know. I didn't want anyone to know! I wanted nothing to jeopardize my chances of being granted wardship of Heather—the less known about her parents, the better, or so I thought."

He stopped in the middle of their room. In all her days, Victoria had never seen him so agitated.

The veins stood out in his neck. "God, but I pray she remembers no more! I shudder to think of it, for not once did Justine ask about Heather—if I had not told her, she'd never have known whether the child lived or died!"

Victoria went to him. She slipped her arms around his waist. "Miles, calm yourself." She gazed up at him. "The man with Justine was her husband—Heather's father. It has to be."

His arms came around her slowly. He rested his chin on her head. "You're probably right. But Heather's questions trouble me. Victoria, if she should find out the truth . . . that I never laid eyes upon them before that night . . . she would be devastated. And I could never tell her what a vile woman her mother really was. As she lay dying, she cursed her—cursed her daughter for living! Victoria, if you'd heard her . . ."

The anguish in his tone tore at her. She sensed in him a fear she'd never seen before.

Seeing him like this was like a knife in her heart. Victoria's throat grew achingly tight. She rubbed her cheek against the satin of his dressing gown. "I know, love," she whispered. "I know."

His arms tightened around her. She could feel the desperation in his hold.

"All these years, I've told myself I did the right thing. But now—"

"Miles, do not agonize so! You did what was right! You loved her, and you sought to protect her in the only way there was! Why, Heather might have gone to an orphan house if you hadn't. And you know those poor children receive no care, and especially a child like her. She would have been left in a corner with no one to tend her—no one to care!" Tears started in her eyes. "I cannot bear to think that Heather might have grown up so cruelly!"

"I know, sweet. I know. I cannot bear it, either." He pressed her cheek against his chest. Now it was he who comforted her.

They remained there, wrapped in each other's arms. But there was no ease for his mind, no respite for the restless nagging at his heart.

For the chilling suspicion encumbered his mind as never before . . . what if he had made a terrible mistake?

What if the man killed in the accident with Justine was not Heather's father? If he was not . . .

Miles's skin prickled eerily. A chill seemed to touch his very bones.

. . . then who was?

Heather left Lyndermere far behind, lost behind a tall stand of green-leafed maple trees. Small, gloved hands were loose on the reins. She paid no heed as the cart bounced and jostled down the road. The trip back to Lockhaven was one her pony had made a hundred times before, and she gave him his head; he knew the way as well as she.

Before she knew it, she was back at Lockhaven. Daniel, one of the stableboys, ducked out from the stable. "Good evening, mum," he greeted. "I trust you had a pleasant day?" He reached out to take the pony's bridle.

"I did indeed," Heather began. All at once

there was a thunder of hoofbeats. They both looked up to see Damien bearing toward them.

One look at the urgency on his features and Heather knew something was very wrong.

She half rose from the seat. Dread curled her insides. "What?" she cried. "What is it?"

He barreled from the saddle. "I just met Robert MacTavish on the road. He went to fetch the midwife for Bridget, but she's gone to visit her daughter in Somerset and not due back until tomorrow. She needs you, Heather."

Heather's breath caught. "She's in labor?"

He nodded.

She gave a sharp cry. "But it's too early—she's not due for another month."

Hands on her waist, Damien had already plucked her from the seat.

"We have to hurry," he said tersely. "Robert says she's in a bad way." He glanced at Zeus. "Can you ride with me? It'll be quicker."

Heather nodded.

A moment later she was up in the saddle in front of him.

The position was shockingly intimate. Her good leg was braced against the entire length of his thigh—she could feel the iron-thewed hardness even through the thickness of her skirts. He hugged her hips with his own. Her bottom was nestled against the notch between his legs—yet another place that was brazenly hard . . . .

His arms locked fast around her. "All right?"

"Yes."

His breath rushed past her ear. "Your knee—"

"I'm fine. Please, Damien. Hurry."

It was a wild ride, yet by the time they alighted at the MacTavish cottage she remembered little of it. Robert, a thin, wiry man, met them at the door. His dark eyes were frantic. His fair hair stood on end, as if he'd thrust his fingers through it repeatedly.

"Miss Heather," he said fervently. "Praise God you could come. Bridget's been asking for you."

Heather entered the bedroom, where Bridget lay on the bed against the far wall. Her hair lay over her shoulders, lank and damp with sweat. A light blanket was drawn up over the mound of her belly. Her eyes were huge and filled with terror.

"Hello, Bridget," she murmured. She sat on the edge of the bed and took Bridget's hand. "When did your pains start?"

"My water broke at dawn." Her voice was thin. "The pains started not long after."

"Are they close together?"

Bridget hesitated. "Sometimes." She clutched at Heather's hand. Her chest rose and fell in quick, shallow breaths. "I—I'm so afraid! Miss Heather, I—I don't think I felt the babe move since last eve. And now the pains come, but no babe."

"It may be that you don't feel anything because of the pains. And I know it's little comfort, but first births sometimes take quite some time." Heather spoke softly. Soothingly.

Even as Heather slipped her hands beneath the

blanket onto the mound of her belly, another contraction began, drawing and tightening beneath her fingers.

"There, now. It's over. Breathe long and deep, Bridget."

Bridget's smile was but a grimace, but it was a smile nonetheless. "I . . . it's not so bad now that you're here."

Her fingers gentle, she examined Bridget more fully. Withdrawing her hands, she slanted Bridget a glance of wordless reassurance. Turning her head, she saw Robert at the foot of the bed. From the corner of her eye she saw Damien in the other room. Giving Robert a sign, she motioned him to the doorway.

"How is she, Miss Heather, she and the little one? Is she all right?"

Heather's tone was hushed. "I think so. The babe is in the proper position, but she said she hasn't felt him move since yesterday."

"I know. Is that bad?"

Heather hesitated. "It may be," she admitted. "I don't want to alarm Bridget, but I must tell you true, Robert. I was with the midwife once during a similar birth"—she hesitated— "Robert, it's possible the babe may already be lost."

Robert swallowed bravely. "I know you'll do what you can, Miss Heather. But I"—his voice cracked—"I don't know what I'd do if I lost Bridget."

Heather squeezed his arm. "I think she'll be fine, Robert. But if the worst comes to pass, it's then that she'll need your love and strength." A silent message passed between them. His eyes were suspiciously moist, but he nodded.

"Good. Now I need your help, Robert. Can you fetch me a basin of cool water and a cloth? Later I'll need hot water, so can you put a kettle on to boil?"

He nodded and dashed away, anxious to be of assistance.

Heather soon returned to the bedside, basin in hand. Wringing the water from the linen cloth, she wiped Bridget's pale brow.

"Try to rest when you can," she urged. "Save your strength for later."

Time crept by slowly. The hours passed.

Bridget's belly heaved and knotted. She writhed and twisted on the bed. As she labored to bring her child into the world, her pains fast and furious, Heather's hopes plummeted. The signs were not good, but she let none of her concerns show to this poor, frightened woman.

At last it was time. Bridget's strident screams had given way to feeble moans. She lay with her knees drawn up, panting and weak.

Heather was at the foot of the bed. "One more time, Bridget," she encouraged. "You're almost there. One more time and it will all be over. . . ."

With a massive effort, Bridget raised up on her elbows. Her face contorted as she struggled to push the child from its berth within her body. She groaned, a long, low sound of agony.

A small, wet body slid into the clean white cloth in Heather's hands. Her cry of joy curdled in her throat.

She stared into the miniature, wrinkled face,

its paper-thin eyelids screwed shut. The babe made not a sound. Nor did it move.

She blinked, praying her eyes deceived her. Willing the infant in her hands to live. . . .

She prayed in vain.

An unseen hand clamped tight around her heart. Heather silently screamed her outrage. The babe was a girl. So very small, but perfectly, beautifully formed.

The cord was coiled tight around the tiny neck.

Bridget peered up at her. "Miss Heather," she said weakly. "My babe . . . a boy or girl?"

Struggling against the burning threat of tears, Heather covered the child's face with the end of the cloth. Her voice was raw. "A girl."

"A girl! And is she well?"

Heather raised her head. Bridget looked up at her and gave a stricken cry. "No. No!"

Laying aside the babe, Heather moved to her side and held her close. "Bridget," she whispered, touching her shoulder. "I'm so sorry . . . I know it's hard. But there can be others—"

Bridget clung to her. "There'll be no others," she choked out. "In all these years, there've been no others."

The door burst open and Robert appeared. His eyes sought Heather's.

She shook her head. She rose as Robert charged forward. Grasping her cane, she left the room, closing her ears to the sound of Bridget sobbing her heart out against her husband's shoulders.

Despair wrenched at her. She felt sick. Sick at heart. Sick to the depths of her soul. Her steps carried her blindly forward. She flung open the door and rushed out into the blackness of the night.

"Heather!"

But she was beyond seeing. Beyond hearing, heedless of the call of her name, the figure that appeared from the shadows.

Footsteps pounded behind her, shrinking the distance between them. Her steps quickened awkwardly. She forged ahead, running as best she was able, paying no mind to the damp earth beneath her slippers, the brambles that caught the hem of her gown.

"Heather, don't!"

Damien's heart lodged in his throat when she stumbled, lurching forward onto her hands and knees. He dropped down beside her. Strong hands clamped onto the narrow bridge of her shoulders.

"Heather, in God's name!"

Her arms crept around her chest, a pose of utter bleakness. It stabbed at his chest like a blade. Her head was bowed low, but her hair had come loose. It spilled like a raven's wing around her form, shielding her like a shimmering, midnight waterfall. She quivered in his hands like a leaf in a storm.

With one hand he brushed the tangled cloud of hair from the delicate line of her jaw so he could see her. Dampness glistened on the pale curve of her cheeks. She was crying, he realized numbly, though she made not a sound.

He inhaled harshly. Stunned, he stared at her, his heart twisting. "Heather," he said hoarsely.

Her lashes fluttered. Her lips trembled. Slowly she raised the narrow oval of her face to his, her eyes huge and wounded. Bending his head low, he waited for her to speak.

"They were going to name her for me," she said faintly. "They were going to call her Heather. . . ."

Eleven

Her voice wooden, she told him how the babe had been born dead, the cord coiled tight around its neck.

Then she spoke no more.

Instead she lay huddled against his chest, limp and listless, all the way back to Lockhaven. Her desolation tore at his insides. His arms engulfed her, his embrace protective—and possessive. A storm of grief blustered inside her, but she refused to release it. He wished she would sob out loud, vent her rage at fate's injustice . . . anything but this damnable, endless silence.

In the stableyard at Lockhaven, Zeus nickered softly. A sleepy stableboy appeared, yawning hugely. But his eyes nearly popped out of his head at the sight of his mistress in Damien's arms.

Damien tossed him the reins. "There's five shillings in it for you if you rub him down now and give him an extra handful of oats."

The boy snapped to attention. "That I will, sir."

Damien slid from the saddle, his burden still cradled against him. Long strides quickly carried him to the house. A loud bang on the brass knocker brought Marcus scrambling to the door, wearing a voluminous dressing gown, barefooted and spindle-legged.

His reaction was the same as the stableboy's. "Mr. Lewis!"

Damien moved swiftly past him. "Good night, Marcus," he said calmly. He didn't miss a stride down the long hallway and all the way up the curving staircase. He didn't pause until he reached the landing.

His breath stirred the baby-fine hairs at her temple. "Your room," he said succinctly. "Where?"

"To the left. The double doors at the end." She gave a tiny sigh and turned her face into the warm crease of his neck.

He set her on her feet, then went in search of a candle. Yellow light flared as he lit one atop a cherrywood writing desk. A cursory glance revealed pale blue satin hanging from the canopied bed. Matching draperies were at the windows. The furnishings were much like the woman herself—understated, yet tasteful and feminine. There was a watercolor framed on the far wall— a field of wheat billowing in the wind beneath fair summer skies. Another of her efforts, he suspected.

Frowning, his eyes returned to her. Her lovely

features were distant and bleak. She had yet to move.

He crossed to her. "Heather."

It was as if she didn't even hear. As if she'd retreated to a place where no one could reach her.

Concerned, he reached out and gave her a little shake. "Heather, stop this!"

Dazed, she looked at him.

"Listen to me. What happened is not your fault."

Her eyes were two endless pools of pain. "You're wrong," she whispered. "It is my fault. Bridget's babe died because of me. If the midwife—"

"But she wasn't. Besides, it would have made no difference."

She shook her head, over and over. "No. No, you're wrong—"

"I was there, remember? No, not in that room. But I was there, and I know what happened. I know *you*, Heather. You did what you could. You did *all* you could."

Her cry was jagged. "But it wasn't enough. Don't you see, it wasn't enough! I should have been able to save her babe—her daughter!"

Damien understood her helplessness, the injustice. "I know how you feel. I know it's not fair, but sometimes life is not fair! I felt that way when my father died, when I was just a boy. And my mother, too. I felt that way when my brother, Giles, was m"—he caught himself just in time—"when I found out he was dead. I was less than a week out to sea, on my way home, when it happened, Heather. When I arrived in Yorkshire, he was gone. I kept thinking, if only I'd left earlier, he might still be alive. I know it's hard—for everyone. For Bridget and Robert. But they must accept it and go on. If they're lucky, perhaps there will soon be another."

"No. There won't."

He gestured vaguely. "You can't know that, Heather. They're still young and—"

"And they've already waited years for this babe!" Her anguish rose in her like a kettle about to boil.

Her eyes were suddenly blazing. "Don't look at me like that! Don't you understand? Bridget's chance is gone. She'll never hold her baby. She'll never feel her warm and soft and alive against her breast . . . never! Her arms are empty . . . they'll always be empty. Just like mine. Just like mine . . ." Her voice broke.

And so did she.

Tears ran in rivers down her face. Her shoulders shook as the dam inside her burst.

Damien wrapped his arms around her. Her words made no sense to him, but he couldn't stand to see her like this. His hand swept up and down her spine.

Yet still she fought him, her eyes wild. She raised her hands between them and tried to push herself away. "Don't!" she cried. "Don't pity me!"

"I don't."

"You do! You pity me! I felt it that first day at

the dairy. I could feel you staring at me because I—I limped. I felt your—your pity!"

"Perhaps then, Heather. But not now." He captured the point of her chin between his thumb and forefinger and forced her face up to his. "You're the most independent, capable woman I've ever known. Indeed, you're the most exceptional woman I've ever known. And quite probably the most beautiful—"

"Now I know you're lying! I'm not beautiful . . . I . . . I'm . . ." Her eyes squeezed shut. Her voice shook. Tears leaked from beneath her closed lids. "I'm . . . deformed. If it were not for Mama and Papa, I—I would be hidden away where no one would have to look at me. I'm . . . deformed," she said again, such raw pain in the word that he felt pierced to the quick.

His jaw clamped tight. "No." He spoke the word like a condemnation.

"Yes," she whispered. "*Yes.*"

She turned her face aside. A dry, jagged sob escaped, a sound pulled from deep in her breast, then another. Her spine seemed to wilt. She would have collapsed if he hadn't caught her.

He bent and carried her to the overstuffed chair near the fireplace. He held her while she purged herself of her grief. She cried for Bridget. She cried for the baby.

She cried for herself.

All the while he cradled her near, smoothing her hair, murmuring against her temple.

Bridget's arms are empty . . . they'll always be empty. Just like mine. Just like mine . . .

His heart squeezed.

You pity me! I felt it that first day at the dairy. I could feel you staring at me because I—I limped.

Suddenly he understood—God, but he wished he didn't! This beautiful, young creature who had spent her life apart—pushed away from society because she was different—was certain she was doomed to a life of lonely solitude.

What would happen to her when he was gone? He shouldn't allow himself to care . . .

He couldn't stop himself, either.

He had no intention of leaving her tonight. Whether she approved or not, he resolved to stay. She was simply too vulnerable to be alone tonight.

In time her weeping ceased. She lay against him, warm and pliant. After a moment, she stirred restlessly. A hand came out to twitch at her skirt.

A grim smile touched his lips. No doubt she wouldn't thank him tomorrow, but he wasn't going to allow either of them to sleep fully clothed. Sitting up, he rose and gently set her on her feet beside the bed.

Her eyes were open, her expression faintly confused. "What are you doing?"

His hands were already on the back of her gown. "Putting you to bed." With a detached efficiency he was far from feeling, he pushed the gown from her shoulders. It slipped to the floor. She stepped obligingly from the puddle of folds.

She regarded him with a mixture of wariness and bemused expectation. Her arms came up to cross over her breasts, and Damien nearly groaned. The movement merely made those sweetly rounded mounds swell ripe and full and inviting above the lace edge of her chemise. A shaft of longing cut through him. It was swiftly buried.

He stepped to the bed and swept the covers aside, then turned and waited, one dark brow aslant.

She remained unmoving. Instead her littlest finger came out to catch his. Her eyes grazed his.

"Are you leaving?" The words were but a breath of sound.

His pulse seemed to stop. He bent and kissed her lips, checking his hunger but not his intent. "I won't leave you alone tonight, Heather."

Her tremulous smile made his heart catch.

He could feel her eyes on him as he stripped down to his breeches, chafing at the restriction as he slid into bed beside her. He'd have liked nothing better than to hold her tight with nothing between them, but he didn't want to frighten her again.

She burrowed into his arms as if she would slip into his very skin. Nestling against the sleek skin of his shoulder, she let out a long, uneven sigh, the mist of her breath cool against his naked flesh. Damien's heart contracted. He could have screamed aloud, for somehow . . . somehow her pain had become his own. He shouldn't have let it happen. He should never have allowed himself to grow close to her. Now it was too late.

For both of them.

His spirit bleak, he held her, his embrace loosely comforting, sifting his fingers through the silken tangle of her hair.

His descent into the haven of slumber was mercifully swift.

Heather was exhausted, drained and numb. Sleep was a healing sanctuary where the absence of pain was blessedly welcome. But deep in the murky void where reality fell away, the darkness was fraught with shadows. The refuge she sought was simply not to be. . . .

She'd been sent to bed without dinner. She curled up in the dark, trying to forget her hunger. But sharp pains stabbed in her belly, for she'd had precious little to eat that day. She'd been alone most of the day. . . . She was always alone, it seemed.

A tiny whimper escaped. Though she knew better, she was unable to stifle it. . . .

From the corner came a vicious snarl. "Stop that whining!"

She froze, not daring to move, scarcely daring to breathe. She'd angered him again. She stuffed a fist into her mouth to stop the half-sob that caught in her throat, but it was too late.

He leaped from the corner and came to stand just above her. He towered over her, huge and menacing, his features dark and indistinct.

"God, what I wouldn't give to be rid of you!"

Her heart beat so fast she could hardly breathe. Fear clogged her veins as she stared up at him. "Pl-please," she stammered.

She should never have looked at him. She should never have made a sound.

"Shut up, brat!" *He whirled and snatched something from across the room, returning to stand above her.*

For one single frozen moment, their eyes collided. He raised his left hand to his chin . . . there was something odd about that hand—if only she could see it. . . .

He smiled, his eyes gleaming. It was a smile she struggled to return, but it was so very hard, for she was so frightened. . . . In a blur of movement, his arm swept high above his head. . . .

Blinding pain sheared through her.

She cowered, huddling into a tight little ball. The world fell away as pain ripped through her again. A shrill, high-pitched scream shattered the air, but she was only half aware of it. Distantly she heard it again and again. . . .

Strong hands curled around her shoulders. "Heather!" She lurched upright with a stricken cry, struggling to be free of the pain—of the nameless, horrible man that haunted her dreams. She had to get away . . .

"Heather, it's all right. Open your eyes, sweet. Open your eyes!"

She knew that voice. She clung to it, and to him, letting it guide her through the void to wakefulness.

Her lashes flickered open. Damien was next to her, his features etched with grim concern. His hands cupped her bare arms. Candlelight wavered at the bedside. She inhaled deeply, a stinging rush of air.

Damien surveyed her closely. The sheer terror
in her eyes speared his heart, but gradually it
began to ease. What devils occupied her dreams,
he wondered, that she would scream so—
screams that chilled him to the bone?

He watched as reality crept into her eyes little
by little. Her fingers clenched and unclenched.
When he pulled her close, Heather sagged
against him, for within the binding circle of his
embrace, he offered her a harbor of shelter and
safety.

At length he drew back slightly so he could see
her face. With the pad of his thumb, he brushed
damp strands of ebony silk from the downy
softness of her cheek.

"Better now?" His tone was very quiet.

"Y-yes." Her tone was faint, her voice still
shaky.

He lay back down, bringing her with him. She
lay cuddled against his side, one small hand
curled atop the middle of his chest, her fingertips
teased by the crisp dark mat of hair that grew so
thickly upon it.

"Tell me about this dream," he said suddenly.

Tension immediately invaded her body. He
expected a long, empty silence, and she didn't
disappoint him.

"Tell me," he murmured.

"Must I?" The question was muffled. She
buried her face against the bronzed column of
his neck.

His hand had been tracing an idle pattern
upon her nape. Shaping his fingers against her
scalp, he gave a gentle tug that had the desired

effect of bringing her eyes to his—albeit reluctantly.

"No," he said dryly. "But since I've been cast in the role of rescuer once again, I would very much like to know."

When she said nothing, he persisted, his gaze unerringly direct. "It's not the first time you've had this dream, is it?"

Heather's eyes skipped away, then returned. She sighed. If she refused to answer, he would accuse her of running away. Besides, what did it matter that he knew?

"No," she admitted, her tone very low. "I've had it since I was a child, though sometimes not for many years."

"Is it always the same?"

She hesitated. "Not always the same, but . . . similar."

"How does it start?"

She considered. "I'm just a child," she began at last. "It's always dark, and I—I'm lying on a hard pallet in the corner. I—I always have the feeling I've been very bad. Sometimes I'm cold. Sometimes I'm hungry."

His fingers threaded through hers where they lay upon his belly. "Go on," he said softly.

"I—I cry at night, so no one will hear. I—I try to be quiet, because I know what will happen if I am not. . . ."

She shivered. He felt the fear in her and sought to reassure her. "There's no one here, Heather. No one but you and I."

"I—I know. But in the dream, *he* is always there. . . ."

"Who, Heather? Who is always there?"

She shuddered. "A man. A cruel, terrible man—"

Damien had to force himself not to tense. "Who is he?"

Her agitation deepened. "I don't know," she said wildly. "I only know that if I make a sound, he'll punish me. He'll hurt me."

A half-formed idea buzzed in Damien's head. Perhaps this was no dream, he thought furiously. Perhaps it was a memory, torn from some place hidden deep in her subconscious. Perhaps it had really happened.

"Is he your father, Heather?"

Shock glazed her eyes. "My father . . . no. No, of course not! My father was a good, kind man." She shook her head, as if in confusion. "Papa told me so and—and he wouldn't lie to me! Of course it's not my father!"

It flitted through Damien's mind that she was trying to convince herself more than him.

"You said you remembered your father was a tall man with black hair. The man in the dream—what does he look like?"

"I—I don't know. It's too dark—there are too many shadows." She shivered once more. "It's so strange. It's so—so real! And yet I've never been punished—I've never been struck. I—I've been cared for all of my life. I've never been hungry or cold. My bed has always been soft and warm." She couldn't hide her anxious distress. "It's like . . . like there's a part of me I don't even know."

Damien held his silence, but he couldn't quell

the notion that he might well be right. That the man in her dream might very well be her father—James Elliot.

She propped herself on an elbow and stared at him. "Why am I telling you this? I—I've never told anyone, not even Mama." Her distress lay vivid in her eyes.

She would have flounced away, but he caught her arms and brought her near, so that she was half lying atop his form. "It's nothing to be ashamed of, Heather. We all have demons, every one of us."

And what are yours, Damien? What are yours? The question burned on her lips, but her courage eluded her. Then all at once, between one instant and the next, everything changed. The air between them was suddenly charged with tension.

She was painfully aware of his body beneath hers, so hard, so strong and vital and male. And their mouths were so close . . . . A tremor tore through her, from the top of her head to the tips of her toes.

She was half afraid to speak. "Sometimes I feel I've known you forever." She squeezed her eyes shut, then opened them again. Heaven help her, but this was madness. "And sometimes I feel I know you not at all. . . ."

Like a thief in the night, his fingers found their way beneath the fall of her hair. They moved, the wispiest caress . . .

His voice stole through the quiet. "And how do you feel now, Heather?"

She longed to toss her head and moan. A restless yearning quested inside her. "I don't know," she said faintly. "I—I just don't know. . . ."

His gaze rested on her lips. "Then perhaps it's time you did."

His tone made her feel as if she were melting. She couldn't look away as he mated their fingers in a burning clasp and brought it to his lips. Her eyes locked helplessly on his face while he kissed each knuckle in turn, his mouth so unbearably gentle she nearly cried out. When he'd finished, he settled her hand on his chest and wrapped his arms around her.

And then he kissed her, a kiss that was slow and achingly sweet. Ribbons of sensation unfurled within her, like blossoms beneath a warm summer sun. She felt her senses widening. Expanding. Then all at once the tempo of the kiss caught fire. The pads of his fingers barely brushed the tips of her breast, a touch so fleeting she might have imagined it. But now her nipples were hard and tight, stiff little points that throbbed and ached. She wanted not only his hands on her breasts, but his mouth . . . the taunting play of lips and tongue, teasing and tormenting.

A treacherous heat pounded along her veins. An empty ache was spawned deep in her belly. Her fingers curled and uncurled against his chest. Nor was he unaware of her, she realized. She could feel the hunger in his kiss, in the eager sweep of his tongue against hers. And there was a potent fullness there between his thighs. She could only guess at what it meant, but instinct warned her he wanted her. . . .

The knowledge made her feel heady and reckless. It wasn't enough to kiss him, she thought dizzily. It wasn't nearly enough. She wanted more. . . . Twining her arms around his neck, she thrust up against him, wordlessly conveying her need.

He tore his mouth away. Dazed, her lashes fluttered open. He stared down at her, his features drawn in a grimace that might have been pain. He made a swift, abortive move, as if to leave her.

She wouldn't let him. She tightened her arms around him, shamelessly clinging. "You said you wouldn't leave," she cried softly. "You promised!"

"Heather, no." His voice was hard. She let him pull away, and he got to his knees. His gaze pinned hers ruthlessly. "This isn't what you want," he said harshly. "You don't know what you're asking."

Slowly she sat up. Her eyes roamed his features, the chiseled curve of his mouth, the stark, masculine beauty of his face.

A muscle twitched in his jaw. "Don't look at me like that," he said tightly. "I'm just a man, Heather. I'm not made of stone. If we don't stop now, I won't be able to. Do you understand that?"

Heather trembled with a soul-deep yearning. With longing unfulfilled. But it didn't have to be that way. . . .

"Yes." Her whisper came unbidden. God, yes . . .

"I wonder if you do." His gaze seared hotly

into hers. "I want you, Heather. I want your legs
wrapped around mine. I want to bury myself
deep and hard inside you, fill you to bursting,
sheathe myself within you until there's no more
to give. I want to kiss you all over . . . in places
you've never imagined . . . in ways you've never
imagined."

His words conjured up wanton, brazen images
of the two of them, limbs naked and entwined in
a lovers' dance as old as time. Even as she felt her
cheeks stain with the heat of a blush, her blood
flamed crimson.

He had touched her as no man had touched
her. He had seen her as no one had ever seen her,
naked and bare and vulnerable. Yet he was
different from every other man in her life. She'd
seen his patience and gentleness with her younger siblings. She'd witnessed his caring, compassion and sympathy for her tenants. He'd known,
without her saying a word, that she didn't want
to be alone tonight.

He'd called her beautiful. Not once, but twice.
He made her feel special and cherished and
lovely . . .

He made her feel like a woman.

A pang swept through her. She would never
know love, not the sweet, precious bond of desire
and faith that Mama and Papa shared.

But if passion was all that Damien could give
her, then so be it. She might forever burn in hell
for this night's sin, but she didn't care.

She wanted to know what it was like to be
loved by a man—the wild splendor of joining
body and soul. Just once. Just once, she longed to

shed all that she was—her every fear, her every doubt. She longed to surrender all to her secret desires and fantasy. . . .

She knew, with all that she possessed, that there might never be another time like tonight. He was like a painting—a painting that brought color and vibrant hues to brighten the drabness of her life.

There would never be another man like him— never.

"Listen to me, Heather. You don't really want this. Someday you'll have a husband. Would you have me take what should be his—"

"No," she said.

Her mind teetered. Her senses swelled. She'd waited her whole life for this moment. . . .

Tentatively, her heart in her throat, she laid her fingertips on his forearms. Beneath her touch, his muscles were clenched rock-hard.

"I want it to be you," she whispered. "I want it to be now."

Twelve

I want it to be you. I want it to be now.

The world seemed to stand on end. Time stretched, dark and endless. The air grew thick with the weight of the tension that arced between them.

Her plea was torture—sheer, sweet torture. A tempest of emotion blustered inside him. He wanted to haul her against him, plunder the warm satin of her mouth, feel his rod embedded tight within her sheath, the honey of her passion hot and wet around his flesh as he lost himself inside her—and to hell with the world.

Her lips hovered beneath his, tempting him mightily—oh, so tempting! The tip of her tongue came out to moisten her lips, leaving them soft and dewy and just begging to be kissed. Her eyes were huge and moist, the color of violets awash with summer rain.

He wanted her. He wanted her more than he'd ever wanted any other woman in his life. She haunted him—his dreams, his every waking moment. She was like a drug that time refused to banish.

But he tried not to think about that. He tried to think about what would come later. Why he couldn't—shouldn't!—do this. What would she say when she learned he was Damien Lewis Tremayne, Earl of Deverell, not Damien Lewis? What would she say when she discovered her father was a murderer? She would hate him for his deceit.

His hands curled and uncurled against his sides. The feelings crowding his chest were part pleasure, part pain. Lord, but this was almost laughable. His conscience battered him. His scruples twisted his insides in knots. Any other man would have taken what she offered and damned the consequences.

Yet here he was, torn by desire, riddled with guilt.

What she wanted was impossible . . . or was it merely inevitable?

Slowly levering herself upward, she ran her hands up and down his arms, around to the sleek cushion of muscle covering his shoulders. Squeezing her eyes shut, she tilted her face up to his . . . and kissed him. Her lips parted as she acquainted herself with the shape and texture of his mouth.

His body clenched. He sucked in a breath. The little witch. Why, she was seducing him! he thought in amazement.

And quite expertly, it would seem. Sheer effort of will kept his hands anchored at his sides.

She splayed her palms flat across his chest—a shy, tentative quest of exploration. He sensed her uncertainty . . . and admired her daring.

But there was more.

Her palm strayed lower. Clear past the waistband of his breeches and below . . .

Her fingers slowly uncurled.

His breath wrenched from his lungs. A jolt of sheer pleasure ripped through him. Her innocent caress inflamed him past bearing. He thought he spoke her name—or did he? A sound of pure anguish tore from between his teeth.

Her eyes shot up to his, faintly distressed. "What? Do I . . . do I hurt you?"

His features were rigid and strained. In answer his hand clamped hers tight against the turgid plane of flesh that strained to be free.

He swelled full and hard beneath her fingers.

She jerked her hand away as if she'd been burned. "Oh, my," she whispered.

Hunger roiled within him—raw, hot, greedy. His shaft was throbbing and full, painfully erect. His blood was on fire. Later there would be regrets, even anger. When the time came, he would deal with it. For now, nothing else mattered but this gut-twisting need that would not be denied.

"Heather. Oh, God . . . Heather." Her name was half laugh, half groan.

He crushed her against him, the pressure of his mouth fierce and wildly consuming as it came down on hers. And then she was melting against him, her arms wound tight around his neck as she surrendered all he sought.

His embrace was almost frighteningly strong, but Heather gloried in it. He fed on her mouth like a starving man devouring a bountiful feast. Until this moment, she hadn't been truly alive.

When that first small storm had passed, he dragged his mouth away. "I'm sorry. I didn't mean to shock you."

Her gaze climbed no higher than his chin. "You—you didn't," she quavered.

Slowly he drew back and searched her face. A blunted fingertip trailed down the line of her jaw. "There's still time to change your mind, Heather." He was quietly intent.

She shook her head.

His eyes fell to where the strap of her chemise had fallen down her arm. She flushed as she saw where his gaze rested, but she made no effort to retrieve it.

His fingers swept across the curve of her breasts where they swelled above the neck of her chemise, coming to rest with precise awareness on the harbor between, a touch that robbed her of breath.

"Remember that day in the meadow? The first time I saw you?"

She nodded. "You wanted my sketch."

One corner of his mouth turned up. "I'd forgotten that." His smile faded. "I wanted you. I wanted to take you back to my room at the inn and spend the rest of the day and night making love to you, my barefoot little gypsy. I wanted you then." There was a heartbeat of silence. "I want you now."

She touched his mouth, a touch that surprised them both. "Truly?"

"Truly." He kissed the tips of her fingers.

Her heart surely stopped in that moment. The relief that poured through her made her giddy and weak. She'd never thought to hear those words—never in her lifetime. But hearing him say it aloud made it all the more real, all the more priceless.

He lowered his head. Their lips met and clung sweetly—the urgency was gone. There was no need to hold back, for they both knew where they were headed . . . and neither wanted to turn back.

His fingers were warm against the valley between her breasts as he untied the ribbons of her chemise. Then his hands were on her shoulders, pushing the cloth aside. Her petticoats came next, falling in a heap atop her chemise.

She lay on her side, facing him. Every inch of her lay open to his gaze, feminine charms bare and unbridled. His eyes, dark and intense, pored over her, leaving no part of her untouched. His gaze lingered on the pink-tinted tips of her breasts, the downy fleece at the juncture of her thighs. Heather blushed fiercely but didn't flinch from his regard. A touch conveyed his approval. A hand settled warmly on the nip of her waist. He caressed her lightly, sliding his fingers down the curve of her hip and thigh.

He didn't stop until he reached her right knee.

Heather froze. Panic blazed in her breast. Her eyes flashed almost fearfully to his face.

He never even noticed. With infinite gentleness he explored the knotted, raised flesh, the unsightly depression on the outer plane where the bone lay hollow and distorted.

A hot ache burned her throat. She felt ugly and disfigured.

He raised his head. "Does it pain you?"

"Sometimes." She spoke haltingly. "When I sit for a long time, it's stiff when I rise. And it aches when the weather is damp and cold."

"I'm sorry." He continued to stroke her knee, his fingers immeasurably gentle despite the power of his hands. "I would heal you if I could, Heather."

"It doesn't matter," she said faintly. "But I must know . . ." The breath she drew was deep and uneven. "You don't find me"—God, but it hurt to say the word—"repulsive?"

Anger flared in his eyes. "Never say that," he told her roughly. "Never."

He moved so swiftly she nearly cried out. His mouth replaced his hand, soothing her flesh with the stroke of his tongue, a caress so achingly tender that she did give a choked little cry. . . .

Tears shimmered in her eyes. She caught his head within her hands and brought his mouth back to hers. The kiss they shared was like no other, ravenous and fierce, fiery and piercingly sweet all at once.

He lowered his forehead against hers. "You're beautiful, Heather," he said against her lips. "In all ways . . . in every way."

She beseeched him. "Show me," she whispered. "Please show me."

His eyes darkened. "With pleasure, sweet. With pleasure."

He rose to stand beside the bed. Heather couldn't tear her gaze away as his hands went to the buttons of his breeches. He bent, pushing his breeches free of his legs and kicking them aside. She was granted a heart-catching glimpse of his buttocks, tight and round and spare.

And then he turned.

Taut and free, his manhood thrust boldly out from between his thighs, rigidly erect.

Her breath came to a halt. It rushed through her mind that she could not possibly take in all of him. . . .

But the sight of him naked was mesmerizing. His limbs were long and roped with muscle. The dark shadow of hair on his chest arrowed down, growing in a dark, thick jungle at the apex of his thighs. He possessed a dark, wholly elemental magnificence that sent a quiver of excitement all through her.

His eyes held hers as he stretched out beside her. Suddenly it wasn't enough just to look. She wanted to touch him, to feel for herself if he was as hard and muscular as he looked.

She couldn't help it. She indulged herself. Her fingers crept up to trace the hollows of his cheeks, the beautifully chiseled curve of his sensuous mouth. In the candlelight his skin gleamed bronze and gold. She ran her fingers over the surging sleekness of his shoulders and arms, traced the groove of his spine, dipped a finger into the shallow of his navel, hidden amidst swirls of crisp, dark hair.

His eyes snapped open; they sheared directly into hers.

"Touch me," he said against her mouth—into it. It was a heated, silken whisper, low and vibrant with need.

His hand engulfed hers, guiding it down with unwavering intent between the crease of his hips. Down . . .

The muscles of his belly clenched. Heather quivered, anxious awareness collecting in the pit of her stomach, for she knew what he wanted. The thought of touching him *there*, with no barrier of clothing between them, was daunting—yet exciting, too.

She nearly jumped at the first, startling contact. He was so very hot! But then she needed no urging. He was enormous and thick—she could barely close her fingers about him. Indeed, she marveled in awe, her hand in no way encompassed his ridged, straining length. . . .

His eyes caught the light of the candle, flickering with the same intensity. She could see the hunger on his face, and it thrilled her to the marrow of her bones.

Her pulse thundered in her ears. Velvet and satin. Heat and fire. That was his essence. Emboldened by his sharp inhalation, her fingers grazed the smooth, arcing tip of him, light as a feather. Even as the thought tore through her mind, a single drop of silky dew emerged, an ungovernable testimony to the ardor she called forth in him.

He jerked away from her. "Enough," he said thickly, "or it'll be over far too soon."

Puzzled, drunk with sensation, Heather peered up at him. He gave an odd laugh. "You'll see," he promised.

His hands climbed the rise of her ribs. Slowly he circled the boundary of her breasts, a shattering path that took him ever closer to the throbbing peaks of her breasts. She almost cried out when at last he grazed the straining summits, the pleasure was so exquisite. Bending his head, he tugged each nipple in turn into the hot, wet suction of his mouth, leaving them rouged a deep rose, shining and wet.

Since the day he'd first kissed her, she'd lain in bed and imagined what being loved by him would be like. But his every touch turned her limbs to water. Her mind had only hinted at the feelings he aroused in her. But the reality was so much better than fantasy, so very tantalizing and enticing.

In the secret place between her legs, an empty ache had begun to throb. A lean hand drifted down, skimming the hollow of her belly. She gasped as his fingers slid through the tight nest of curls at her thighs. Her legs clamped together, an instinctive reaction.

"Easy, Heather," he breathed. "I won't hurt you, I swear."

That daring finger grew bolder yet, skimming soft, pink folds, breaching deep within to brush a tiny little bud. Sensation leaped from that tiny little pearl, a thousand flames of blistering heat. She gave a jagged little cry, her nails digging into the sleek skin of his arms.

"Yes," he murmured. "That's the way, sweet."

And it was there he now worked his magic. His fingers grazed the outer folds of her furrowed cleft. With a sound of satisfaction, he penetrated slowly, a lone finger seeking out the center of her being, a shattering prelude of what would come later. All the while, his thumb circled and swirled that ultrasensitive bud of desire, skimming hot, weeping folds. She thought she would surely go mad.

She tossed her head on the pillow. Her hair streamed wildly all around her. She began to swell and throb there in the place he possessed so fully, whimpering for deliverance from this tortuous rapture. Just when she thought she could stand no more of this delicious torture, something exploded inside her, sending her hurtling over the edge into the fringes of consciousness.

Dazed, her lids drifted open. He hovered above her, his eyes glowing like embers. His shaft was iron-hard against her thigh, scalding hot.

He crawled above her, parting her thighs with the weight of his own. For a mind-splitting instant, she lay open and vulnerable as never before.

The tip of his shaft breached damp, dark curls. With his fingers he parted soft, pink folds. Heather drew a quick, ragged breath. She flinched at the brief, stabbing pain that split the virgin barrier—her innocence was no more—and then he was inside her.

It was heaven . . . it was hell. Damien bit back a groan. A wholly male satisfaction filled him at knowing he was her first—that she belonged to him alone. He wanted to prolong the bone-deep intimacy wrought by that knowledge, even as he longed to sink inside her, hard and fast, again and again. Instead he held back, his penetration excruciatingly slow. God, it felt so good! She was hot and tight around his swollen flesh; her body accepted him as if she'd been made for him alone. His blood surged thick and molten there where he lay planted so solidly within her, so tight he nearly spilled himself.

At last he lay seated to the hilt inside her. They were both panting as if there were no more air in the world left to breathe. Heather drew a deep, shuddering breath, for he was immense, the pressure of his shaft stretching her wide and deep. Her belly pressed his, soft against hard.

Above her, he'd gone very still. His breath was harsh and scraping in her ear. It spun through her mind that he seemed on the brink of some terrible pain.

Bronzed fingers brushed a tangle of hairs from her cheek. "Are you all right?" His whisper was low and husky.

The uneven breath she drew only made her more aware of the rigid thickness of his manhood impaled deep within her. Eyes clinging to his, she nodded.

"You're certain? I'm not hurting you?"

Heather noted the concern in his voice and felt the overwhelming tension in him. The knowledge that he held back in order to spare her pain tugged at her heartstrings.

"I'm fine." Her smile was tremulous, for indeed, the stinging wrought by his invasion had ebbed. At her words, his eyes seemed to blaze. Suddenly unable to bear any distance at all between them, she tangled her hands in the rich, dark hair on his nape and brought his head down to hers.

His growl of satisfaction echoed deep in her throat. With slow, measured strokes, he began to move, withdrawing almost out of her body but not quite. He could feel her sleek, wet passage stretching to accommodate him. She was so small, so hot and tight. Little by little, his rhythm began to quicken. She gasped at the delicious friction of his skin sliding against hers . . . inside her.

For Damien, the pleasure was almost more than he could bear. The scorching desire that burned in his belly clamored for release, but he held back. His fingers dug into her hips. He braced himself above her, the muscles of his arms rigid and corded, unable to tear his eyes from the sight of his swollen rod piercing deep within pink, feminine petals of softness.

Heather felt she was burning from the inside out. Fire shimmered along her nerve endings. Her hips began to catch the meter of his thrust, lifting and circling, instinctively seeking his. Sparks flamed within her, inside and out. She could feel the thunder of her heart, certain it would burst from the bounds of her chest at any moment.

Her head thrashed wildly. "Damien!" His name was a raw, shivering plea—for what, she knew not.

At the sound of his name, something gave way inside him. His mouth took hers with an urgency that made her sing inside.

"I don't want to hurt you," he gasped. "God, Heather, I can't hold back . . . I want you too much . . . I want you too much. . . ."

Everything inside her seemed to melt. Naked emotion poured through her, mind and body and heart. With a half sob she locked her arms around him. "Oh, Damien," she cried. "I want you, too. *I want you, too.*"

Her words obliterated his last fragment of control. Engulfed in dark, desperate ecstasy, he plunged into her, torrid and driving, his thrusts almost frenzied. He gritted his teeth and rushed toward the edge, damning himself for his lack of control. It was too good. He didn't want it to end . . . not yet. Not ever . . .

Heather buried her face against his neck and clung to him blindly, caught up in the same breathless fever of passion unleashed. She wanted to feel him deep inside her, deep as her heart. Each powerful thrust of his manhood echoed in every pore of her body. Then suddenly she was splintering apart inside, the sensation so intense it was almost terrifying. She cried out, feeling the clasp of her body convulse around his again and again. Above her, he gave one last piercing lunge. She felt him shudder above her. His body tightened like a bow. She gasped as his scalding release erupted inside her, drenching her with a flooding, melting heat.

His body shifted. He propped himself on his elbows and whispered her name. As her lids drifted open, he kissed her, a lingering, gentle caress that spoke of wonder and pleasure and satisfaction, of all things tender and caring and giving.

All she'd dared not believe existed. . . .

Her every wish fulfilled.

Thirteen

❦❦❦

Time had no meaning in the hours that followed. Sleep was discarded, for indeed, the night was one of sublime discovery. Heather learned there were many faces to making love—languid and tender and achingly slow, playful and teasing, furious and primitive and wild—all wonderfully splendid.

The first faint glimmer of dawn found the pair tangled in each other's arms. Her hair spilled wildly across his chest, a silken curtain of black. A strong, possessive arm wrapped her close against his side.

"I had no idea you were such a wanton young lady at heart," Damien teased.

Heather suppressed the urge to hide her face against his shoulder. Instead she curled a finger in the dark jungle on his chest and tugged. "I heard no complaints before this, sir," she accused in mock indignation.

His arms tightened. "And you'll hear none, either. Indeed"—the timbre of his voice dropped so it was low and husky—"you've given me a night I'll not soon forget."

Startled, but pleased beyond measure, Heather peered up at him. Something flitted across his features, something strange and unfathomable, something she didn't understand. She frowned, convinced he was about to say more, but he did not.

Instead he pointed to the watercolor on the wall. "Where did you learn to paint so well?"

She considered a moment. "I learned the most rudimentary elements from my tutor when I was very young. But I suppose I would have to say Miss Havesham's School for Young Ladies in London."

"Why so modest, Heather? You're really quite talented."

One bare shoulder lifted in a shrug. He could see she was embarrassed.

"I learned what everyone else learned, or, as the inestimable Miss Havesham used to say, 'A lady must be prudent and delicate. A lady must know how to charm and be charmed. To be sweet and ever obliging; to embroider and sew, sing and play and paint like the masters—or at least make a valiant attempt to do so,'" she quoted. There was a pregnant pause. "I suppose one might say I learned some things better than others."

Damien shifted so he could see her more clearly. "Come now," he objected. "I cannot believe you weren't her prize pupil!"

"I excelled in the classics and the arts, at things that were best done with my hands. However"—her tone was falsely bright—"as you've noticed, 'tis a trifle difficult for someone with my . . . how shall I say this delicately . . . my limitations . . . to glide across the floor like a swan upon water. I could not post a trot, nor could I dance as if I were an angel with wings upon my feet. I fear I was an abysmal failure in many respects."

Too late he realized his mistake . . . Heather's gaze had lowered, stringently avoiding his. Her little wooden smile tore at his soul.

He trapped one small hand beneath his where it lay between them on the sheet.

"It doesn't matter," he said gently.

The chambers of her mind echoed with the memory of those long-ago taunts . . . and so did her heart.

You're not like us, Heather Duval . . . you're lame. You're a cripple.

Ruthlessly she pushed aside the memory. "It did then," she admitted unthinkingly. "But— not now," she added when she realized what she'd just revealed.

No matter her denial, the hurt little girl she had once been had not been forgotten. She was still there, still a part of the woman. In that instant, he knew that Heather had never had the childhood she should have had. Fate had not allowed it.

"If you were so unhappy," he said quietly, "why didn't you tell your parents? Why did you stay?" He couldn't imagine that Miles and Victoria would have forced her to do anything that would have harmed her spirit in any way.

She focused on the tangle of hairs that grew at the base of his throat. "Mama and Papa thought I should be with girls of my own age. That was why they sent me. I—I stayed because I—I didn't want to disappoint them."

He gave her a long, slow look. "You hated it, didn't you, Heather? Yes, of course you did. And they still don't know it, do they? . . ."

Heather trembled. She said nothing, nor was there any need for words. Her silence said it all.

Indeed, Damien couldn't blame her. She'd stayed on to prove to herself that she was as good as anyone else. No, Heather would never give in to defeat. She would endure, no matter the cost. Vulnerable as she was, she would rise and stand firm as any soldier, unwavering in her resolve . . . and all the while crying inside.

She was strong, he realized, far stronger than many men . . . yet he wondered if she knew it.

He came to a sudden decision. He threw off the covers and rose, heedless of his nakedness. Swiftly rolling up the carpet that covered the center of the floor, he pushed it alongside the far wall, then strode to the middle of the room.

"Come" was all he said.

She clutched the sheet to her naked breasts and stared at him as if he'd lost his senses.

"You needn't look at me like that," he stated calmly. "You've spent a lifetime wishing you knew how to dance—I think it's time you learned."

She inhaled sharply, her distress vivid in her eyes. "Damien, I've already told you, I cannot—"

"You rode Zeus tonight, didn't you?"

"Yes, but . . . with you." She faltered. "Not—not *alone*."

He held out a hand. "And you won't be alone now, will you?" he asked softly.

His tone—as well as the tenderness in his gaze—made her pulse flutter strangely. The hold of his eyes was utterly compelling. Endlessly persuasive.

She pushed the covers aside and rose. A curious sense of unreality assailed her. This was happening to someone else. It had to be . . .

She glanced nervously at the end of the bed, where her nightgown lay. "My nightgown—"

"Hardly necessary, sweet. We don't have an audience." His fingers closed around hers, strong and reassuringly warm. "Besides, you weren't so modest just moments ago."

She couldn't share his good humor. "I wasn't standing in the middle of my room n-naked just moments ago!" She was still aghast at her own temerity.

His gaze wandered the length of her. "Either way, I very much like what I see." His tone was as intimate as his perusal.

Heather blushed the color of deep red berries.

His features gentled. "Come here now." He clasped her right hand in his left. "There. Hold my hand just so." He slipped an arm around the nip of her waist and brought her close. Her fingers hovered above his shoulder, then fluttered downward.

"Very good. Now what shall we start with? A

waltz? A pity there's no music, but no matter. We can do this, I think. Just remember. One, two, three. One, two, three . . ."

Slowly he began to move. But Heather, in her anxiety to obey, stepped so quickly she nearly tripped.

She sprang from his arms. Tears sparkled in her eyes. "You see?" she cried. "This is hopeless."

He neither chided nor censured her. Pulling her into his arms, he kissed her temple, her cheeks, holding her until her trembling subsided.

"Let's try again, shall we, sweet?" His breath rushed by her ear.

Certain she would burst out crying at any instant, Heather closed her eyes and clung.

Damien spoke in low, soothing tones. "Let's go about this a bit differently, shall we? This is a waltz especially for you and me, Heather. Just remember that. There's no need to cover the entire floor, is there? We'll take tiny, tiny steps, and waltz in a very small circle."

The desperate pressure of her hand around his eased somewhat.

"That's right. Just relax and hold onto me," he coaxed. "Feel the rhythm of my body with yours, and let me guide you. Now. One, two, three. One, two, three . . ."

He was endlessly patient. Patently convincing.

"Remember, it's just you and me, Heather. Just the two of us."

Heather gave a tiny sigh and dropped her head against his shoulder. An imaginary waltz trilled in her head. Tiny, tiny, steps, she reminded herself, leaning against him. She had only to listen to his body . . . and her own picked up the tempo. She swayed to and fro. Why, it was almost like making love. All at once she felt amazingly light-headed . . . and lighthearted as well.

"Yes . . . yes! That's the way, sweet. By Jove, you've got it. . . ."

She laughed, a bubbly sound of joy. "I—I do, don't I?"

Damien's hold tightened. He made no answer, but continued to guide her in a slow circle.

She tipped her head back to gaze at him. "You know, you're quite mad."

"So I've been told."

A girlish giggle escaped. Dear heaven, she was waltzing *naked* in the middle of her room! "The waltz was once considered quite scandalous, you know." She imparted this with a dimple in her cheek. Her gaze briefly encompassed their nudity. "But I daresay no waltz has ever been quite so scandalous as this one."

Damien's laugh was full and rich. "And I can see you are quite scandalized, Miss Duval."

Heather smiled up at him. In all her days, she couldn't think when she'd been so happy. . . .

"Yes," she said cheekily, "and I can see the subject of this discussion is having a rather predictable effect on your person, Mr. Lewis." Her gaze zipped downward.

And indeed it was.

Damien's smile faded. His eyes fell to her mouth. He trailed a finger down her cheek.

"Then perhaps it's time we remedied the situation," he whispered.

The world fell away as he carried her to the bed. Mouths fused, limbs entwined, the tempest of passion flared hot and bright. She smothered a cry as he entered her. Suddenly, strong hands caught at her, skimmed the backs of her thighs. He rolled, and now she lay astride his hips. She could feel him against her furrowed cleft, erect and pulsing.

A soft cry of confusion broke from her lips. "Damien—"

His eyes were fiercely aglow. "Take me," he ordered. His voice was low and taut. He lifted her slightly, bringing her down upon him, impaling her with the thickness of his shaft.

Heather gaped in startled surprise. Never had it occurred to her that such a thing was possible. She shifted slightly, for though the position caused no pain, it was a trifle uncomfortable. . . .

He eased a pillow beneath her right knee. "Better?" His eyes cleaved directly into hers.

Heather nodded, for indeed, speech was impossible. Her body fit his like a glove; the feeling of his manhood speared deep inside was incredible.

Slowly, tentatively, her hips lifted, then tilted forward. The sensation was indescribable. Tiny shivers raced down her spine. Guided by instinct alone, her body claimed his again and again. Her breathing hastened. Her hips undulated. She began to writhe and plunge. All the while Damien filled his hands with the bounty of her breasts, plucked pouting, pink tips until she gasped her pleasure. His eyes blazed. He thrust his thumb into the down fleece, stroking and circling the sensitive nub. With a low moan, she spun high and away into a realm of sheer bliss.

That time was the best of all.

She was still smiling when Damien eased her to her side. Still smiling when he slipped from the bed. Sunlight gilded the room, and he was aware that the household would soon be stirring to life. He pressed a kiss to the curve of those sweet lips.

"I'd better leave before anyone finds me here," he murmured.

Heather rubbed her cheek against his hands. "I suppose you're right." She sighed. While he dressed, she pulled on her dressing gown. Sitting on the side of the bed, she watched him, her gaze both admiring and wistful.

Five minutes later he was ready. He was about to return for one last kiss when a corner of paper on her bureau snared his attention. His breath drew in when he saw it was the sketch they'd spoken of only last night, the sketch she'd drawn that very first day. . . .

She'd kept it. All this time, she'd kept it. . . .

A potent smile of satisfaction rimmed his lips. He crossed to the bureau, and then he saw it . . . a silver, claw-footed jewel case.

He froze.

The world seemed to blacken. Images flashed in his brain. Images sent from long ago, from a time years past. Transferred from another place, when he was just a child . . .

He shook his head, to clear it. It wasn't possible. It simply could not be. . . .

But it was. The proof was before him. He stared at the word *Beloved* etched into a small, mother-of-pearl oval upon the lid. He stared until his eyes were so dry they burned.

"Damien?"

He didn't hear the voice that queried softly. He didn't see the frown that marred the beauty of her brow. An awful storm brewed in his breast, churning and swirling like the blackest pits of hell.

He snatched the jewel case in his hands and whirled. "Where did you get this?"

Heather was shocked. It was a rough demand, a slap across the face. She felt as if a cold wind had blown across her heart. She nearly flinched at the ruthless probe of his eyes.

Something was wrong, she thought vaguely. Something was terribly, terribly wrong. The cords in his neck stood taut. His face was a mask of stone. He was angry, she realized numbly. No. Not just angry. He was furious. . . .

Two strides brought him before her. He thrust the jewel case into her lap. "Where did this come from?" he demanded again.

Her heart constricted. His lips were drawn back over his teeth, a feral snarl, lips that had so sweetly enticed. But the look in his eyes was terrible, dark and unshuttered. She felt as if she were caving in inside, for the man who confronted her now was a stranger—one she didn't know. The hours just past might never have happened.

The jewel case was flung aside. His hands shot out, hauling her to her feet. "Answer me, Heather. *Where did this come from?*"

His gaze pinned hers relentlessly. "God dammit, *tell me!*"

Stunned, she stared up at him. "It—it was my mother's," she gasped.

"You're lying," he charged flatly.

She was suddenly trembling from head to toe. Tears scalded the backs of her eyes. She felt that her lungs would burst with the effort it took to hold them back. "I—I'm not!" she cried. "Damien, what's wrong? Why are you acting this way? Why would you say such a thing?"

He released her, as if she were suddenly abhorrent. "Because I've seen it before, Heather." He spoke through lips that barely moved. "On *my* mother's dressing table."

Her lips parted. He was mad, she thought vaguely, as mad as she'd laughingly accused him of being.

"No," she said faintly. "That's not possible. I've had it since I was a child."

His gaze was frigid as ice. "There's no mistake."

"There has to be! Perhaps they're merely similar—"

"It's not. My father commissioned it expressly for my mother, on the occasion of my birth. It was her most prized possession."

"And it's *my* most prized possession. My father—Miles—gave it to me. It's all I have left of my mother—all that was left from the accident that killed her!"

Damien's mind was racing. He wasn't mistaken. It was he who had broken the hinge—his mother had been heartbroken. He'd made her cry, and it was a moment he'd never forget. His father had taken it to London to be repaired, and it was then he'd fallen ill and died. He hadn't remembered until now, but he was certain the jewel case had been missing from his father's belongings. Yes . . . yes, he was certain. He hadn't seen it since the day his father had left for London . . .

The last day he'd seen his father alive.

An eerie foreboding prickled the hairs on the back of his neck. It was so bizarre . . . his mind screamed. How had Heather—or Justine Duval—come by it? *How*?

He hated the seething undercurrent of suspicion that gnawed at him, but he couldn't help it. Had he been wrong to trust her? Perhaps it was true. Perhaps she *did* remember her father. Perhaps he'd been right, and Elliot had been here. . . .

His jaw clamped shut. "It may have been *with* her. But it wasn't hers."

"What do you imply? That my mother was a thief?"

His mouth was a grim line. "Aye," he said harshly.

"It belonged to her," she said feelingly. "And I—I won't let you besmirch her memory this way!"

His lip curled.

"No," she stated bluntly. "You're wrong, Damien. Or perhaps you're the one who's lying."

Her gaze moved over his stony features. Their eyes locked, a battle of wills. A chill trickled over her skin.

"Who are you?" she whispered. "Who are you really?"

Now it was she who confronted him, no matter that her voice was more breath than sound.

"You know who I am."

"No." She shook her head. "You're hiding something. I can see it." Her fingers curled into her palm. "I can feel it."

A mantle of silence hung in the air.

Her breath came fast, then slow. "You don't deny it. What then! Did you plan to get close to me and"—the pain in her breast bled through to her voice—"and rob me little by little? Should I check the silver, Damien? The treasures in the drawing room? Perhaps you intended to steal the jewel case, and this is just a ploy to throw me off guard. Or did you have something else in mind? Something on a larger scale?"

A sizzle of anger sparked on his face. She didn't care.

She swept an arm toward the bed. "What was this? A tender trap? Did you think to seduce me that I might turn over my estate—my money? What a fool you must have thought me! The little cripple who would never know the difference— who might be persuaded to part with any and everything . . . why, even her virtue!" Her voice rang with contempt—a contempt that encompassed them both.

"It was you who begged me to stay, Heather. Need I remind you?"

Oh, but he was cruel to taunt her so! Her reply was swift and emphatic. "But why, I ask? Because it was to your advantage? And you still haven't answered, Damien. Did you intend to steal me blind? Or have you already done so?"

Silence.

With every breath, every heartbeat, she could feel her hopes, her dreams, drifting away. . . .

She knew then . . . knew she was right. That he was not the man he said he was.

"Tell me!" she almost screamed.

His eyes flickered. "I've stolen nothing from you, Heather."

You have, she longed to cry. Her trust. Her heart . . .

The silence was painful.

She drew back her shoulders. Forced back the crushing tightness in her chest. Armed herself with dignity . . .

For what else was left?

"I want you to leave." Through some miracle, her voice never faltered. It rang out clear and unwaveringly strong.

His gaze narrowed. "Leave," he repeated. "You mean . . . leave Lockhaven?"

Pain wrenched at her insides. She steeled herself against it. "Yes," she said. "By this evening." Coolly she met his regard.

Something blazed on his face, swiftly suppressed. "Oh, you needn't worry, Miss Duval." His eyes were as cutting as his tone. "I'll be gone long before then."

He disappeared without another word. He didn't even bother to close the door in his wake.

Feeling as old as the heavens, Heather limped across to shut it. She was nearly there when her bare toe touched something. She glanced down.

It was her sketch of him.

Slowly she bent to retrieve it.

For an instant her eyes traced the outline of his profile, the proud set of his shoulders as he stared off into the distance. She remembered how she had ached for the unknown burden he carried. . . .

With a jagged cry, she ripped it to pieces. The scraps drifted to the floor.

So did the shreds of her heart.

Fourteen

"I need to see Papa."

Victoria's blue eyes lifted from her needle-work. At Heather's entrance into the drawing room, she set it aside. "Heather, what a delightful surprise!" she exclaimed. "We weren't expecting—"

"Where is Papa, Mama?"

Blond brows drawn together over her patrician nose, Victoria tipped her head to the side. She patted the space beside her. "Please, dear. Come sit—"

"Not now, Mama."

Victoria's welcoming smile vanished. She rose and moved to where Heather had stopped short, just inside the entrance. Gently she laid her fingers on the flounced sleeve of Heather's gown. "Heather, whatever is wrong?"

Heather resisted the urge to shake off her mother's touch. She was hanging on to her composure by the veriest thread. At the slightest provocation, she would fly apart.

"I do not mean to be either rude or short with you, Mama, but this concerns a matter solely between Papa and me."

Victoria's gaze searched her face. For an instant Heather was convinced she would question her further. But she only said, "He's out riding Pegasus, love. Would you like to wait in his study?"

"Thank you. I believe I shall."

She didn't have long to wait. Within minutes Miles strode in, dashing and handsome in black riding clothes and boots. Excitement flushed his cheeks, and his dark eyes were agleam.

"Heather, you should have seen Pegasus! In all my days, I've never seen a horse so fleet of foot—" One look at her face and he stopped short.

"Poppet, are you sick? You're as pale as snow!"

"I'm fine, Papa." She laced her hands together in her lap to still their trembling. "But I must ask some questions of you. Will you answer me true?"

There was a brief pause. "Of course I will, poppet. Haven't I always done my best by you?" Concerned, he sat down beside her.

"It's about the jewel case that belonged to my mother. The one you found with her after the accident. You remember it?"

"Yes. Yes, of course."

"How long had she had it?"

"I daresay I don't know, Heather."

"Where did it come from? Was it a family heirloom?"

"I really couldn't say, love."

"But you knew her well, didn't you?"

Did a hint of wariness flit across his features? Or was it merely her imagination? Yet, for a heartbeat, she could have sworn he appeared uncomfortable, and the pangs of uncertainty bit deep within her. . . .

"Yes, you already know that. But I was hardly acquainted with belongings of a personal nature." He ran a hand over his hair. "Heather, it seems an odd thing to ask about. After all these years, why her jewel case?"

Heather let out a long, uneven breath. She decided to say nothing of Damien's accusation that the jewel case was his mother's. It was too preposterous. And Papa had never lied to her—never.

All at once she felt rather foolish. "It's nothing, Papa. Please, I—I'm just being rather silly. And perhaps a bit melancholy these days." She summoned a smile. "Truly, it's nothing."

But even after she'd departed, Miles wasn't so sure.

Victoria entered almost as soon as Heather had gone. "What was that about?"

Miles turned from where he stood near the window, staring out as the breeze stirred the treetops. His expression was grave as Victoria had never seen it.

"I wish I knew," he said quietly. "She was asking about her mother's jewel case."

"Whatever for?"

"She didn't say. Or perhaps more aptly, she *wouldn't* say. She asked how long her mother had had it, if it was a family heirloom. Christ,

Victoria, what was I to say? I've no idea." He gave a slight shake of his head. "I remember Justine clutching it when I found her. I recall thinking the very devil himself couldn't have pried it from her fingers."

"It's quite gorgeous. Simple, but lovely nonetheless," Victoria said slowly. "At times I wondered how she came to be in possession of such an elegant piece."

"So did I," Miles admitted. "But it was the only thing of substance that she had, and I thought it only right that Heather should have *something* of her mother's. She's always treasured it dearly."

"And rightly so," Victoria agreed. "Indeed, without knowing anything of Justine's circumstances, we have no right to think ill of her. 'Tis possible her circumstances declined for some such reason, and that was all she had left."

Possible, though not very probable. The thought filled both their minds.

Miles's features were somber. "It bothers me, Victoria. First she came to me with questions about her father—what he looked like. And now these questions about her mother's jewel case . . . it's odd. Very odd."

"I know." Victoria hesitated. "Yet I have this—this feeling that something else is troubling her as well, Miles. I've never seen her quite like this."

He slipped his arms around his wife and rested his chin atop her shining blond hair. His gaze was pensive. "I know. But she's a grown woman, Victoria, and, much as I hate to admit it, 'tis none of our affair. If Heather needs our help—if she wishes to confide in us—then it must come from her." A crooked smile lifted a corner of his mouth. "One never stops worrying, I fear, even after they leave the fold."

Victoria pretended to pout prettily. "What! Are you saying we cannot interfere?"

A dark brow arose. "That's precisely what I'm saying. Indeed, I seem to remember your saying those very same words quite often in the days when Heather first moved to Lockhaven."

Victoria wrinkled her dainty nose good-naturedly. The conversation moved onto other matters, and, while they shelved their concern for Heather momentarily, it was most assuredly not forgotten.

Heather spent yet another sleepless night. There was no rest for her weary body, no ease for the turmoil in her soul. She tried to blot out the memory of all that had happened here, in this very bed. She squeezed her eyes shut, burning inside when she thought of all he had done . . . all *she* had done.

But that was not all. She thought of all she'd ever confessed to him. . . . She'd exposed her every fear, her every hurt, bared her very soul.

And for what? *For what*?

In his arms she'd been so certain that she had at last discovered the sweet promise of belonging. But he had deceived her, and she hated him for it . . .

But she hated herself far more for her weakness.

Yet still a hundred questions pounded at her
brain. He'd come to Lockhaven for a purpose.
But what? And why hadn't she listened to her
heart? She thought of all the times her senses had
warned that all was not right. His manners. His
speech. His cultured air. His queries about her
parents . . . She should have listened and taken
heed. Yet still the burning question remained.

Who was he . . . really?

Near dawn, two scalding tears slid down her
cheeks. She wiped them away with the backs of
her fingers, secretly bleeding inside.

They were the only tears she allowed herself to
shed.

Over the next week, Heather went about her
daily life as if nothing had changed. A halo of
pain encircled her heart, but outwardly she remained calm and composed.

Or so she thought.

"I know what's wrong with Heather."

Beatrice made this startling announcement
after Arthur and Christina had departed the
dinner table one evening.

Two pair of eyes swiveled in her direction. A
vibrating tension hummed in the air as Miles
and Victoria waited for her to speak.

Bea took a deep, fortifying breath. "I went to
visit yesterday. Heather was not at home," she
hastened to add. "But on my way out, I heard
one of the maids confide to another that Damien
Lewis was seen coming down the stairs at dawn
the other morning."

Victoria's teacup slipped from her fingers. It

clattered on the saucer, sloshing tea across the delicate lace tablecloth.

Miles leaped from his chair like a thunderbolt—and his voice clapped like one, Bea decided with a nervous inner giggle.

"I knew it all along. I knew he was a blackguard! By Jove, I'll kill the bastard!"

"Oh, but he's not there, Papa. He's gone."

Victoria paled. "Never say that has anything to do with you, Bea," she gasped.

Beatrice yelped. "Mama, how can you say such a thing?"

Victoria glanced beneath her lashes at Miles, who had resumed his seat but now glowered at both of them. "Well, dear," she murmured, "you were quite taken with him—"

"Oh, but that was eons ago! And you and Heather were right, Mama. Handsome though he is, he is quite old. Besides, it seems he's much more suited to" —she glanced at her father, who was scowling at her blackly— "to Heather," she finished weakly.

"I dislike like what you imply, Beatrice." Miles's tone was stiff and scathing. "I'll not have you insulting your sister in such a manner."

Suddenly Bea looked ready to cry. "I meant no insult! Nor am I a child any longer. If Mr. Lewis left the house at dawn, 'tis obvious where he spent the night—"

"You don't know if that's true, Beatrice." Miles glared across the table at her.

"But what if it is?" she cried. "I—I saw them together once. His head was very close to hers and—and I think they had a tendre for each other. Then suddenly he left, and Heather looks like a wounded doe . . . I am worried about her. And I wanted to help, Papa. Otherwise I wouldn't have said a word!"

"And you did the right thing, dear, though you must understand your father's need to squelch rumors that may not be true." Victoria sought to placate both of them.

"I think it's time we found out precisely what the truth *is*." Miles started to shove back his chair.

Victoria had already laid a hand on his. "No," she said softly.

Miles looked ready to explode.

"Darling," she said quietly, "Heather is aware you love her dearly. And while I realize the two of you have shared much more than many fathers and daughters, I'm not certain Heather would wish to discuss her . . . relationship with Mr. Lewis with her father." She squeezed his fingers. "It's a matter that requires a woman's touch, don't you agree?"

"Yes. Yes, I suppose you're right." Miles's tone was gruff.

Victoria smiled at him and rose. Before she left the dining room she laid a hand on Bea's shoulder. "Beatrice," she murmured, "I trust this discussion will go no further."

Bea lowered her eyes and said meekly, "Of course not, Mama."

A week after the stillborn birth of Bridget's baby, Heather returned to the MacTavish cottage. Luckily the midwife had returned the very next day; it was she who saw to Bridget's care in the days that followed. Heather was secretly glad of the midwife's return, for she dreaded facing Bridget again.

It had taken this long for Heather to gather the courage to face Bridget. Guilt ate at her insides like acid—oh, she'd come to realize the poor babe's death was not her fault. But Heather couldn't forget . . . while Bridget had been plunged into the depths of despair, mourning the death of her child, she'd been locked fast in the wanton embrace of a lover. . . .

It was an emotionally tearing visit for both of them. In each other's arms they wept anew over the loss of the babe. Physically, Bridget was doing well—she'd been up and about for several days now. But Heather was secretly heartsick. She tried to console Bridget and assure her that all was not lost. That, God willing, there might well be another babe. But Bridget had lost faith.

And so had she.

Back at Lockhaven, she passed the reins to the stableboy. It was then that she saw Mama's white mare grazing beneath the shade of a tree. Though she was in no mood for company, she knew she must try and put on a good face, or Mama would worry. It crossed her mind that she should also apologize to both Mama and Papa. She'd been curt with both of them.

In the drawing room a diminutive figure rose from the divan, both hands extended.

"Heather!" Mama's smile was as sweet as always. "How are you, love?"

Heather obligingly gave her a peck on each cheek. "I'm fine, Mama."

"Really? You look a bit peaked, dear."

Marcus entered bearing a tea tray. Heather thanked him and they sat.

The countess poured, chattering about the divine summer weather. Heather refused the jellied tart her mother placed on her plate.

Victoria frowned. "But these are your favorite, dear."

"I know, Mama. I'm just not hungry."

Victoria studied her over her teacup. "You look thinner, love. Aren't you eating?"

Heather wished she could evade her scrutiny—and her questions. At times Mama was just a little too astute. "I've not had much appetite of late."

Victoria lowered her cup and saucer to the gleaming cherrywood table. "Heather," she said quietly, "we are all aware that something is wrong—your father, Bea and I." There was a tiny pause. "Bea thinks it has something to do with Mr. Lewis. Indeed, she's convinced you and Mr. Lewis have a tendre for each other."

Heather felt as if the rug had been pulled from beneath her feet. The observation—as well as Mama's bluntness—caught her off guard.

She tried to hide her panic. She swirled her tea in her cup, staring into the murky liquid, wishing she could disappear inside it.

"I cannot think why she would say such a thing." Her voice was barely audible.

"Can't you?"

For all the softness of her tone, she could feel Mama's eyes. Probing. Searching . . .

She jerked her head aside. "Don't!" she cried. "Don't look at me!"

The outburst startled both of them. Mama's arm slid around her.

"Heather . . . oh, sweet, I do not mean to interfere. But it makes me ache inside to see you like this, and I cannot bear it! I—oh, perhaps I am wrong—but I cannot shake the feeling that Bea is right. That you might very well be in love with Mr. Lewis—"

Heather's head jerked up. A stark, wrenching pain seized her heart. It was true, she realized helplessly. She loved him.

She loved him.

Her shoulders slumped. All the life seemed to go out of her. "It doesn't matter. He's gone. I—I sent him away."

"Heather, listen to me. I've never told you before, but . . . remember the story I told you when you were a child? The story about the scandalous young miss who kissed a wicked earl in the garden?" A wispy smile curled her lips. "Sweetheart, that was me."

Heather's breath caught. Wonderingly she raised her eyes to Victoria's. "That was you?"

"It was, love."

"But . . . Papa is not wicked."

Victoria gave a breathless laugh. "Oh, but he was far from pleased—and far from pleasant— when my father forced him to wed me. And for quite some while, I was convinced your father didn't love me. And I'd convinced myself I didn't love him, either. We had a time of it, he and I. So you see, the course of true love is not always straight and true."

"True love?" Heather's eyes darkened. She couldn't tell Mama of all that had passed between her and Damien. Mama would have been shocked.

Her lips thinned. "There's no such thing, Mama. Not for me. Never for me."

"Don't say that, Heather. Sometimes, just when you think all is lost, a flicker of hope flutters to life. Perhaps Mr. Lewis is meant for you. Perhaps he's not. Why, another man might well enter your life tomorrow—"

"No."

Victoria's heart bled along with her daughter's. "Love, you cannot be certain—"

"I can." Her head bowed low. "It's different for me, Mama. *I'm* different." The words emerged haltingly, so low Victoria had to strain to hear. "Other people . . . they don't see *me* . . . they see this." She gestured to her knee.

Heather's despair rent Victoria in two. She clasped Heather's hand within hers. "Don't lose heart, love. Don't *ever* lose heart. Not yet. You're too young to be so—so old."

She squeezed Heather's fingers. "Heather, I've just had a marvelous idea. Your father and I had planned to take Bea to London the latter part of next week. We thought we'd spend a month or so. Heather, please come with us," she entreated.

Heather smiled slightly. "I fear I'd be terrible company."

"Oh, Heather, please! We can shop and attend

the theater . . . you've always loved the theater. And I've just had a letter from my friend Sophie. She and her youngest sister, Paige, will be in London as well. Do you remember Paige? She's of an age with you. I believe the two of you met several years ago—and got along quite famously, as I recall."

Heather nodded. "She was very sweet. It was just after she married"—her brow furrowed—"a Navy officer, I believe."

"Yes, the very same! Sophie writes that Paige has been rather lonely, since her husband is at sea for the next half year. Heather, please come! We could have such a grand time, the lot of us."

Heather considered. Oddly, the idea did sound tempting. She wasn't overly fond of London, but she'd been feeling so restless lately. . . . "I don't know," she murmured. "There's Lockhaven to consider—"

"Oh, pooh! Now you sound like your father. Lockhaven will still be standing when you return, I promise you."

"But I must see about engaging another estate manager—"

"Spencer can see to both estates. I'll speak to your father about it." She reached up and touched her hair. "There are times when memories tend to overwhelm us," she added softly. "Heather, a change of scenery would do you a world of good right now. Please say yes."

Heather sighed. It seemed Mama had a ready answer no matter her protest. And perhaps she was right. Perhaps a change was what she needed. . . .

Her decision made, she lifted her chin and took a deep breath. "You're right, Mama. I—I'll accompany you to London."

Fifteen

The Earl of Deverell's London residence was an impressive sight, stately and grand. Four stories tall, the entire facade was made of red Georgian brick with dozens of high, mullioned windows. Curling tendrils of ivy and roses twined around the iron gate that separated the dwelling from the street below.

Giles had purchased the mansion some ten years earlier, since their father, a family man from the earliest days of his marriage, had spent nearly all his time in Yorkshire, and so had never maintained a London residence.

When Damien had left Lockhaven, he'd ridden at a breakneck pace for London. Deliberately he kept thoughts of Heather at bay. She muddled his brain and pulled his heart in every direction; he was half afraid to put a name to the emotions roiling in his chest. It was better this way, he told himself.

Better for whom? scoffed a voice in his head. *Not for her. And certainly not for you.*

But at least his thirst for vengeance had been renewed. He'd been perilously close to losing sight of why he'd gone there in the first place. If he hadn't found his mother's jewel case, he might have lost his head completely, and put aside his quest to find James Elliot.

A day later, Damien's carriage stopped before a small building built of gray stone near Portman Square. Inside was the office of Cameron Lindsey.

Behind his desk, Cameron glanced through the draperies. He gave a nod of admiration as he spied a glossy ruby-colored coach led by four plumed and prancing black stallions. There was a gold crest emblazoned on the door, declaring its owner to be one who held both wealth and considerable rank, but it was one he didn't recognize.

It rolled to a halt before his door. Curious now, he swiveled his chair around and gave the coach-and-four his full attention.

A footman opened the door. A tall, powerful figure leaped out, splendidly garbed in the height of fashion, from the jaunty angle of his top hat to the tip of gleaming black boots.

Cameron's eyes widened. He was on his feet and at the door in a heartbeat. He ushered the newcomer inside with a faint bow.

"Lord Deverell, this is a most unexpected visit. I planned to leave tomorrow to meet you in Willoughby."

Damien was brief and to the point. "Then it's

good that I came directly to London from Lockhaven."

Cameron waved the earl to the chair across from his desk. With his thumb he indicated the coach-and-four waiting on the street. "Ah, forgive my presumption, but are you certain you wish to make your presence so conspicuous?"

Before he'd left for Lockhaven, they'd met at obscure places, in the dark, for Damien had wanted none to know of his return to England. Damien's smile held no mirth. "Precisely the point, Cameron."

Bushy gray brows shot up. "My lord?"

"Be patient, Cameron. First, tell me how things fare here in London. Has there been any change? Any sign of Elliot?"

Cameron shook his head. "He's still hidden deep as a mole, my lord." He fell silent for a moment. "Indeed, I've considered tendering my resignation, for it occurs to me you might be better served by another investigator."

"Not quite yet, Cameron. You've done a fine job. I think it's merely a matter of biding our time a bit longer."

Leaning forward, Damien briefly told him of his time at Lockhaven. Though he did not hide his involvement with her, he did not reveal the extent of their intimacy. He ended with the discovery of his mother's jewel case.

Cameron stroked his chin. "Odd," he murmured. "Very odd. But I think you're right. It merely solidifies our belief that there's some connection between Elliot and your family." He glanced across at Damien. "What about the girl? She pretends to know nothing about Elliot, I take it?"

Damien's nod was terse. "Both her parents were killed in the carriage accident, or so she says."

"Do you believe her?"

"Yes." His response was a long time in coming. Where Heather was concerned, he couldn't be objective anymore. His heart and mind were hopelessly entwined with one another, and no matter how hard he tried, he couldn't separate the two.

"I was at Lockhaven nearly six weeks, Cameron. I've discovered I cannot be so patient after all. Elliot deliberately sought out Giles at Tremayne House. So here's what I'd like to do. I take it you've been discreet in your inquiries about Elliot's whereabouts?"

"Yes." Cameron was beginning to catch on. "Perhaps too discreet, my lord."

"My thoughts exactly. Let it be known that someone is looking for him, Cameron. Let it be known that *I'm* looking for him." His eyes narrowed. "If he wanted Giles, it's possible he may want me—the last of the Tremaynes. Perhaps we can flush him out yet."

"So you propose to make your presence known in London, then."

"Yes. If London is all agog about the arrival of the Earl of Deverell, so much the better."

Cameron's expression was thoughtfully intent. "It may very well work, my lord. It may indeed."

"Hold that thought, Cameron." He slapped his gloves on his knees. "It seems Elliot has no intention of seeking out his daughter. But perhaps" —he smiled thinly— "perhaps he'll come to me."

Heather awoke to the sound of birds chirping outside her window. Since her arrival in London, she had been blessedly lazy, sleeping late, often spending the afternoons reading, sometimes going to tea or shopping with Mama and Bea, or attending the occasional garden party. Last night they had gone to the opera; Heather had leaned forward raptly in her box, for she found the music simply divine. Her days had been filled with trivial things, but it felt surprisingly good to unburden herself so. She strived very hard not to think of Damien—of that last terrible scene— and for the most part she succeeded. But occasionally thoughts of him intruded into her mind.

They were ruthlessly chased aside.

On this particular morning, Heather sat in her room at the Graysons' townhouse. Bonnets and shawls and dainty slippers were scattered on the floor. Box upon box lay stacked upon the carpet. The bed, and even the chairs, were piled high with gowns of every color and fabric. There were crisp muslin day dresses, pastel morning frocks, brightly hued evening gowns. Bea flitted from one to the other, like a butterfly from flower to flower.

"I was far too extravagant." Heather made the pronouncement with a rueful shake of her head.

"I confess, I cannot think what came over me. I shall never be able to wear all this, never in a hundred years."

Bea plucked an elegant lavender evening gown from the pile. "Heather, you must wear this to Lady Seton's ball tomorrow night," she declared, eyes shining. "It'll be simply gorgeous with your dark hair. And this color—I just love it!—will bring out the purple in your eyes."

Heather bit her lip. "Actually," she murmured, "I'm not certain yet if I'll be attending."

Bea and Paige, the youngest sister of Mama's dearest friend Sophie, stared at her, their mouths agape. Paige was sweet and demure, small of stature, with gorgeous chestnut hair. Heather had come to value her company—and her friendship—much in the few short weeks she'd been in London. It was Paige who voiced their horror aloud.

"Heather, you must! Lady Seton's balls are divine. And it's *the* event of the year. Everyone who is anyone will be there! Why, I vow you'll never see such jewels and finery as you'll see tomorrow night. It's grand fun just to—to stand back and watch everyone!"

Bea gazed at her imploringly. "Heather, please go. You rarely get out in the country. And after all"—she spread her arms wide—"this is London! Besides," she added, an impish gleam in her eyes, "Mama and Papa will be disappointed if you don't go."

This was true, Heather admitted. She'd enjoyed the opera and the theater, and the informal gatherings at the homes of Mama and Papa's friends. But a ball was a different story altogether. . . .

Bea jammed her hands on her hips. "Heather, I see here at least *two* ball gowns. You can't let them go to waste!"

A reluctant smile tugged at her lips. "I suppose you're right, Bea."

"So you'll go?"

"Yes. Yes, love, if I must."

Bea squealed and clapped her hands. "Oh, Heather, you'll have such fun!" She turned to Paige. "Do you think the Earl of Deverell will be there?"

Paige pursed her lips. "I should imagine."

Heather tipped her head to the side and glanced at Paige. "Who is the Earl of Deverell?"

Before Paige could say a word, Bea interrupted, her features animated. "He's only been in London a short while, but he's all the rage, Heather."

"It's true," Paige added. "Everyone's talking about him. I heard Lady Churchill gushing about him to Sophie at tea just yesterday afternoon. She told how she's never seen a man move quite like him—with the grace of a panther. Yes, those were her exact words, I believe! She said he has only to enter a room and his presence is such that he commands every eye turn upon him with awe."

"Especially the ladies," Bea giggled.

Heather raised a mildly reproving brow.

Paige chuckled. "'Tis said he's wickedly attractive—why, one look from those piercing gray eyes and all the ladies swoon."

Gray eyes? Heather couldn't help it. Her heart lurched.

"Indeed," she said crisply. "He must be very young, then, if this is the first Society has taken notice of him."

"Thirtyish, I believe I heard it said." This came from Paige.

"Indeed! One cannot help but wonder, then, where he's been hiding all these years."

Paige was a font of knowledge. "Oh, he's been gone from England a good many years—where, I can't recall. He inherited the earldom on the death of his elder brother and has only now returned."

Bea sank down on the only vacant spot on the bed. Her expression had gone all dreamy-eyed. "'Tis said that he's quite the handsomest man in London."

Heather shot her a warning glance. She couldn't help but remember how Bea had thought Damien the handsomest man in all England.

"Though of course he's undoubtedly too old for me," Bea hastened to add. "Still"—she sighed wistfully—"I do wish I could attend. You'll tell me about it, won't you, Heather? Every last detail?"

Heather's eyes softened. She rose and dropped a kiss on Bea's forehead. "I daresay you'll attend more than your share of balls next year, love. No doubt Lady Seton's balls will be grander than ever." She smiled. "And then you'll be the one telling me all about it."

If the truth be told, it was Bea who was far

more excited than Heather as she dressed the
following evening. Bea poured scented rose oil
into her bath and picked tiny, white roses from
the garden for the maid to weave into her hair.

Soon she was ready for the dress. She'd let Bea
choose it, and Bea had laid out the lavender
gown she'd admired so the day before. The maid
hooked her into the gown, and at last she was
ready.

Bea clasped her hands before her. "Heather,"
she breathed. "Oh, Heather, you look like a fairy
princess."

Heather laughed lightly. "Then I fear you need
spectacles, m'dear."

"Go look." Bea pushed her gently toward the
cheval glass in the corner. Gathering her courage,
Heather raised her head, and then she could only
stare.

It was beautiful. *She* was beautiful. Her sable
hair was twisted high on her crown, entwined
with the roses. Delicate, flounced lace sleeves fell
away from the tight, formfitting bodice. Bea was
right; the pale lavender set off the luminous color
of her skin and brought out the deep violet of her
eyes. But the neckline was cut scandalously deep
and daring. Her shoulders and nearly half of her
breasts were completely exposed.

Her hand fluttered upward. "I didn't realize it
was quite so low. I—I feel half naked."

"That's because it's a ball gown, goose." Bea
struck a pose, hands on her hips, her chest thrust
out. "Gentlemen love it," she added, but the
sparkle in her eyes was at complete odds with her
low, throaty tone.

"Oh, you!" Heather swatted at her playfully, then gathered her skirts in one hand, her cane in the other.

Bea accompanied her to the landing, then suddenly charged down the stairs in a most unladylike manner. "Stand aside," she yelled. "She's coming."

Miles and Victoria glanced up from where they stood in the entrance hall. At the bottom of the stairs, Bea waited. When Heather placed her slipper on the last step, Bea bowed low, then swept an arm high in an exaggerated flourish. Heather felt a laugh gurgle in her throat.

One look at Papa's face robbed her of the inclination.

He stepped up to her and took both hands in his. "Poppet," he said simply, "you are exquisite."

Victoria couldn't say a word. She was too choked up. Tears misted her eyes.

All at once Heather felt like crying as well. Much as she loved Mama and Papa, she wished Damien could have seen her as she was tonight. If only *he* had been waiting at the foot of the stairs. . . .

The Seton mansion was ablaze with lights when the carriage drew up. A footman ushered them inside, where they were soon greeted by Lady Seton, a tall, blond woman of perhaps forty, dressed in a vibrant pink gown. Heather stood beside Mama, feeling rather nervous and wondering if she shouldn't have stayed home after all. Lady Seton and Victoria exchanged familiar greetings; then Miles kissed the gloved hand she presented.

"Annabelle, you remember my ward, Heather Duval?"

Lady Seton turned to her. "Heather, yes, of course! Why, I swear you were surely a child when I last saw you."

Heather dipped a brief curtsey. "It's been some while since I last visited London."

Victoria spoke up. "Yes, she takes after Miles, I'm afraid. Heather very much prefers country life"—she slipped her arm through Miles's and leaned her head against his shoulder—"not that I'm complaining, mind you."

Lady Seton wagged a finger. "None of that, now. I swear, you and Miles are the only couple I know who are still as much in love as you were when you first married." She gave a high-pitched laugh. "'Tis as unfashionable now as it was then!"

A pang shot through Heather. Never had she envied Mama and Papa as she did now. She wanted what they had. The love they shared— and were unashamed to show before the world. Her heart cried out at the injustice, for that was something she would never have. . . .

She couldn't help feeling the outsider, but she knew she couldn't leave so soon, either. Though everyone she met was gracious and hospitable, she was relieved when Paige arrived. By then guests were milling everywhere. Servants offered tempting trays of hors d'oeuvres. Conversation and laughter filled every corner of the salon and

ballroom. Dinner was a sumptuous feast served
in the formal dining room. Heather had to
consciously stop her jaw from dropping; the
faces at the opposite end of the table were just a
blur.

Just after dinner, Mama developed a head-
ache. Miles sought Heather out and told her
they'd decided to leave early. Heather would
have left along with them, but Paige pleaded for
her to stay. Mama encouraged her as well and
said they would send the carriage back for her.
Heather decided to remain. She'd thought the
evening would be tediously boring, but so far
that hadn't been the case at all.

Paige snagged two glasses of champagne from
a tray and nodded toward two velvet chairs
against the far wall of the salon. When they were
seated, she handed one to Heather.

"Well, Heather, what do you think of Lady
Seton's ball? Was I right? Is it *the* event of the
year?"

Heather glanced around. The scent of perfume
mingled with the heady aroma of fresh flowers.
Brocades and satins shimmered beneath the light
of a thousand candles. Jewels glistened everywhere—the women were adorned in rubies and
diamonds and emeralds; the men, in finery no
less extravagant.

"That I wouldn't know," Heather chuckled. "I
do know I've never seen such an array of jewelry
and clothing in all my days!" She lowered her
voice. "Before she left, Mama pointed out the
Prime Minister."

Paige's eyes widened. "Really?"

Heather nodded. Draining her champagne, she handed the glass to a passing footman. From the corner of her eye, she noticed the majordomo announcing several latecomers.

Suddenly Paige nudged her with an elbow. "That's him!" she gasped.

Slender black brows drew together. "Who?"

"Didn't you hear? That's him, the man we were talking about yesterday . . . the Earl of Deverell!"

Heather wrinkled her nose. A mere earl, she thought loftily, wasn't nearly so impressive as the Prime Minister, no matter how handsome he might be.

Her eyes drifted toward the newcomer. Her mind registered a tall, overwhelmingly masculine form, dark hair above a devastatingly classical profile.

Suddenly she couldn't breathe. Her stomach twisted inside her. A staggering dread gripped her heart. The man who had just arrived, the Earl of Deverell . . .

. . . was none other than Damien.

Sixteen

The grasp of her mind faltered. It couldn't be. Dear God, it couldn't be. It was the champagne, she thought dizzily. Too much, too quickly.

But it wasn't. It was *him*.

The very sight of him made her knees weak. He was riveting, splendidly attired in black evening dress. Skintight pantaloons shamelessly outlined every bulging muscle in his legs. The dazzling white of his shirt brought out the bronze in his skin.

Dimly she noted that he was talking with Lady Seton. He chanced to turn his head in her direction.

Their eyes grazed . . . then collided head-on, a moment that lasted but an instant—a moment that dragged on forever. His gaze seemed to reach her very soul, yet she resented him fiercely, for while she felt she was flying apart inside, his every thought lay shuttered behind the screen of his eyes.

A slight inclination of his head, and she was dismissed.

Pain ripped through her heart like a knife.

She fought a precarious battle for control . . . fought and won.

"Heather?" Paige tugged at her sleeve. "Heather, are you all right? You look as if you've seen a ghost."

Through sheer effort of will she summoned a smile. "I'm fine, Paige. The earl merely reminded me of someone familiar, someone I met long ago at Lockhaven." But she wasn't fine. Indeed, she was seething, engulfed in fury. She wanted to march across to him and demand an explanation. What was he doing here? Why had he come to Lockhaven as Damien Lewis? What was the pretense?

Lady Seton was at his side, introducing him to those in the salon. Beside her, Paige sat up straighter. "We're actually going to meet him, Heather! Oh, won't you have a story to tell Bea tomorrow!"

Heather was burning inside. If she only knew . . .

They were next. Lady Seton had slipped a familiar hand inside his elbow. Heather wanted to rip the lovely lady's heart out.

But she had no claim over him. Dear God, she didn't even know who he was. . . .

"My lord, may I present to you Paige Winslow, younger sister to the Viscountess Wyburn. Her husband, Daniel, is a captain in His Majesty's Navy, presently away at sea. Paige, Damien Tremayne, Earl of Deverell."

Paige had risen to her feet. She dipped a quick curtsey. "My lord."

"My pleasure, madam." Damien had taken her hand and was smiling down at her. "You must find it lonely without your husband."

"I do, my lord." Paige's tone was breathless. "Indeed, I count the days until his return."

"A happy marriage, then. If I dare say so, you are lucky, madam, both you and your husband."

Paige beamed. Heather gritted her teeth.

The pair now stood before her. Heather remained where she was, her mood mutinous. By God, she'd be neither cowed nor humbled by the rogue—whoever he might be!

"My lord, Miss Heather Duval, ward of Miles Grayson, Earl of Stonehurst."

"Charmed, I'm sure." There was a slight edge to her voice. Her gaze was cool as an English wind. She did not smile or offer her hand, but kept her fingers firmly linked in her lap.

Anger kindled in his eyes. Heather was past caring.

"Miss Duval, I am honored." His tone was oh-so-pleasant.

And then they moved on. It was over. Paige chatted endlessly, but Heather scarcely heard. Indeed, she should leave. Now, for she had no desire to remain in the same house with him.

The thought had no sooner chased through her mind than he appeared directly before her. One small hand was seized without preamble. He gave her a low bow, then straightened.

"It's an enchanting night, Miss Duval. Would you care to take a turn about the garden?"

She wanted to refuse. She wanted to slap his vile face. Her chin tipped high. His fingers tightened ever so slightly around hers—a warning, she realized.

Her gaze flew to his eyes. What she saw there stripped from her the courage to defy him.

"If you wish, my lord."

She rose. Her hand still lay clasped within his; boldly he tucked it into the crook of his elbow. He bent and handed her her cane.

It was but a short distance to the French doors that led to the terrace. The night was warm, the air sweetly fragrant with the scent of roses and perfume. The lights from the house spilled through the windows, bathing the pathway in a pale shade of gold. There was a small stone bench near a tinkling fountain, and it was there that he guided her.

A dark bleakness seeped into her soul. She could imagine no setting more inviting or romantic. . . .

As soon as they stopped, she snatched her hand away as if he were a leper.

Damien couldn't blame her. She didn't realize that seeing her here was no less earth-shattering for him. But no matter . . .

He'd felt the tremor in her hands, the iciness of her skin. And now she stood there, as beautiful and frail as a flower bending in the wind. It was all there, stark and open and glaring—the bitter hurt, the angry betrayal, the wrench of despair. Yet she faced him unflinchingly. With undaunted courage. Uncertain, yet so very brave. Gripping her cane as if it were all that held her upright.

He couldn't have been more proud of her. . . .
Never had he despised himself more.

The urge to touch her was overpowering. He trailed a finger down her cheek and found that memory had not failed him. Her skin was as downy-smooth as he remembered. His gaze wandered down her form almost greedily.

He smiled slightly. "You look beautiful," he said softly.

Her eyes were huge and wounded, suspiciously moist. He saw her swallow and sensed she held back tears.

"I've missed you, Heather." His voice was softer still. "Smile for me, sweet."

Her gaze turned blistering. She bared her teeth.

His hand fell to his side.

The silence that yawned between them was as wide as the sea.

It was she who broke it. "I confess I am at a loss," she said stingingly. Flippantly. "What am I to call you? Mr. Lewis? Or Lord Deverell?"

His gaze was steady. "We're on far more intimate terms than that, Heather. Or have you forgotten?"

Her gaze slipped. His tone was so gentle, his eyes so tender. All at once she was achingly aware of him, and wishing she weren't. She couldn't look at him, fearful of revealing a hunger for him that had yet to die—a hunger she feared would *never* die.

From somewhere deep inside, she found the iron strength she needed so sorely. Slowly she raised her head. "I've forgotten nothing," she said bitingly. "And you've not answered my question, my lord . . . or is it Mr. Lewis?"

"Ride with me tomorrow in Hyde Park and I'll tell you."

She flared immediately. "I'm not going anywhere with you!"

His smile was taunting. "Well, then, you won't find out, will you?"

In that moment she hated him, hated him as she'd never hated anyone. "Tell me, Damien. Tell me who you are. Tell me what's going on!"

Several other guests had drifted onto the terrace. She watched as his gaze flickered behind her. "Now is not the time, Heather," he said quietly.

Her jaw locked tight. "I don't care. Tell me."

"I'll call for you at eleven."

"No!"

"I'll call for you," he repeated.

She took a deep, ragged breath. Weakened by doubt, by her own treacherous longing, the tears she'd been trying so valiantly to withhold struggled to the surface. She was trying so hard to be calm. Not to be angry. Yet now she felt as if the very ground beneath her feet were crumbling away. Crumbling, as she was crumbling . . .

His voice stole through the dark void surrounding her. "Trust me, Heather."

"Trust you!" She cast back her head. "Trust me, he says! Yet how can I, when he deceived me so . . . or did he? God, I"—her voice broke—"I don't even know who you are!"

Strong arms came around her. She was swept close—close!—for a mind-splitting instant. His arms were hard and tight against her back. She sagged into his chest, trapped in a haze of conflicting emotions. The beat of his heart echoed beneath her ear, reassuring and steady. His embrace was warm and comforting, all she'd longed for, everything she'd yearned for.

But was it just another lie?

Despair dragged upon her chest like a weighted stone.

A tiny sigh escaped, a sound born of a weary resignation. It was like a dagger through his breast. Slowly he drew away so he could see her. With his fingers he tucked a stray hair behind her ear, resisting the impulse to linger.

Her lips trembled. "I have to know," she whispered. "Damien, I must know . . . who you really . . . are."

He was silent. "My name is Damien Lewis Tremayne."

"So you are—the Earl of Deverell?"

He nodded, catching her hand and bringing it to his lips. "I'll explain the rest tomorrow, I promise, Heather. Please, love, just trust me."

Love. Her heart squeezed. His careless endearment was torture. He was an earl. An *earl*. He didn't love her. He would *never* love her. He cared nothing about her, or he would never have betrayed her so.

But she wouldn't let him see her hurt. Not again. Never again. She squared her shoulders and looked up at him. "It seems I have no choice, do I?" She couldn't quite hide her bitterness.

They went back inside. Paige, she noted dimly, was blessedly absent. Damien summoned the carriage and handed her inside. He squeezed her fingers lightly. She pretended not to notice. She didn't look back as the carriage lurched forward.

It was the hardest thing she'd ever done.

At home, the rest of household was already asleep. Heather was eternally grateful, for she knew she wouldn't have been able to disguise her troubled spirits. Sleep that night was slow to arrive.

She awoke late the next morning. By the time she made her way downstairs, everyone was gone but the servants.

Promptly at eleven the bell rang. Despite the fact that Heather was expecting it, she jumped. Not wishing to appear overeager, especially when she'd protested so heartily, she waited in the drawing room until Nelson, Papa's aging London butler, came to fetch her.

"A caller for you, Miss Heather—the Earl of Deverell."

Picking up her shawl from beside her, she rose. "Thank you, Nelson," she murmured. "Should anyone ask, I shall be with the earl this afternoon."

"Very good, Miss Heather."

Damien was waiting in the entrance hall. Along with his presence came a pulsating tension. He turned upon hearing the swish of her skirts.

"My lord." She was proud of her dignified manner; inside she was a jumbled mass of nerves. "I hope I didn't keep you waiting long."

His features were inscrutable, his tone faultlessly polite. "Not at all." A faint consternation crossed his face. "Damn," he murmured. "It only occurs to me now that perhaps you should have a chaperone—"

Heather's chin came up. "I've been doing business on my own for some years now without benefit of a chaperone," she said levelly. "Besides, I am twenty-five years old—in the eyes of Society, quite over the hill."

"Very well, then." He opened the door and waited for her to precede him outside.

His carriage was a sleek, ruby-red affair, built both for speed and comfort. Seated opposite each other in the richly appointed interior, they neither touched nor spoke. His pose was casual and indolent. His arms were crossed over his chest, one booted leg thrust out before him. Heather pressed her lips together. She would neither demand nor plead for the answers that so tormented her. She'd done that last evening, to no avail. He glanced out one side of the carriage. She gazed out the opposite.

But when they passed Hyde Park, she drew in a sharp breath. Her gaze cut back to him accusingly; it was disconcerting to discover those crystalline eyes already fixed upon her profile.

A dark brow rose. "I'm not kidnapping you, Heather. I merely thought a location where we can be alone would be more suitable for our discussion."

"Of course." Turning her attention to the landscape rolling by outside, she tried to force the stiffness from her shoulders.

It wasn't long before they stopped. They were just outside the city, the setting pastoral and serene. The sky above was endlessly blue and cloudless. Damien helped her alight, then went around to speak with the driver. As he turned to come back to her, the carriage rolled off.

"I asked the driver to return in several hours," he said, answering the silent question in her eyes.

Several hours! Surely what he had to tell her would not fill half that time!

His smile was grim. "Do you think you can suffer my presence that long?"

Her words were no less grim. "It appears that I shall have to."

A stream gurgled nearby, parallel to the road. There was a small stand of oak trees a short distance away, and it was there that they headed. In his hands were a small basket and blanket. He spread the blanket on the grass, then gestured for her to sit. Heather gingerly lowered herself to the ground. His movements brisk, he unpacked wine and bread, cheese and fruit. Heather forced herself to eat from the plate he handed her, but she might have been eating dust for all she knew.

Finally she set aside the plate. A genuine smile creased her lips for the first time since she'd seen him last night. "If I didn't know better," she murmured, "I might think you brought me here to seduce me."

His smile was as fleeting as hers. "I'm trying to make this as"—he seemed to be searching for the right word—"as painless as possible," he finished at last. Something that might have been regret flickered across his face. "But I'm not sure I can, Heather. So I may as well just get on with it."

Heather clasped her hands together in her lap. Her knuckles shone white. The moment she'd waited for was upon her, only now she wasn't certain she was ready for it.

He had discarded his coat and rolled up the sleeves of his shirt against the warmth of the noonday sun. One booted leg drawn up toward his chest, he rested his wrist upon his knee and stared off into the distance. His expression was brooding, and she sensed in him the same suffering and bleakness she'd captured in her sketch the first day they'd met.

"What I'm about to tell you, Heather, is not easy for me. Indeed, when I first came to Lockhaven, I never considered that I might have to. But now that I must, I find I don't know what to say." His gaze returned to her, and now it was piercingly direct. "I want you to know, Heather"—the pitch of his voice had grown very low— "I don't want to hurt you."

She gestured vaguely. "Just—just tell me the truth, Damien. It hurts more . . . not knowing."

He nodded. "Remember when I told you that Zeus belonged to my brother?"

"Yes." Her throat was so dry she could hardly speak. "He's dead, isn't he? I remember now— Paige said you inherited the earldom when your brother died."

"That's right." His features seemed to shut down from all expression. He delivered these words into a tense, waiting silence.

"But he didn't just die, Heather. He was murdered."

Heather inhaled sharply. *Murdered.* Dear God . . .

"When I came to Lockhaven, I had but one purpose. To avenge the death of my brother, Giles."

"But . . . there are no murderers at Lockhaven!" she blurted.

"No. But I thought the man who murdered Giles would come there."

"To Lockhaven?" She was aghast. "I cannot think why!"

"I thought he would come there, Heather. I thought he would come . . . because of you."

An awful dread crowded her chest. Her heart had begun to pound a bone-jarring rhythm. "Because of me," she repeated stupidly. "Why would you think he would come because of me?"

There was a screaming rush of silence. "Because you are his daughter," he said quietly.

Seventeen

❧◈❧

Heather had gone very still. Her lips parted, but no sound came forth. Several heartrending seconds passed before she could manage a word.

"No," she said faintly. "That can't be. My father is dead. He was killed in the carriage accident along with my mother—"

He cut her off abruptly. "The woman in the carriage—Justine—was indeed your mother. But the man who was killed was not your father. Your father is a man named James Elliot, Heather." Damien's tone hardened. "And he is still very much alive."

"James Elliot . . ." Her eyes seemed to blaze. "There, you see! He cannot be my father. My name is Duval—"

"Your mother's name before she married James Elliot."

She stared at him. "But my father . . . Miles . . . he knew them. I tell you he *knew* them! My father was a French aristocrat—"

"No." His face was as unrelenting as his tone.

"I hired an investigator, Heather, the best in England. He uncovered the record of their marriage, the record of your birth. You are the daughter of Justine Duval Elliot and James Elliot."

Her breath came jerkily. "That cannot be! Papa would never have lied to me—"

Damien's arms came around her from behind. "I don't know why he did, Heather. I don't know if he's aware that James Elliot is your father."

She pressed the back of her hand to her forehead. Confused, her eyes sought his. "Even if it's true"—she gave a tiny shake of her head— "I don't understand. What does this have to do with me? With Lockhaven?"

"It's a long story, Heather. You see, I planned to visit Giles at the family estate in Yorkshire in early April. But when I arrived, Giles was already dead." His voice carefully neutral, he told how he'd managed to discover that the upstairs maid, Corinne, had fled to Northumbria in the wake of his brother's death.

"At first she wouldn't say a word. I could see that she was terrified for her very life. But finally she admitted she'd heard something the night Giles was murdered. She had crept into the hall outside Giles's study. There was a terrible row going on inside between Giles and a strange man. The stranger was tearing the room apart, throwing things, screaming at Giles and ranting about how he'd spent twenty years in prison waiting for this night and he'd not be cheated. 'Where is it?' he demanded. Over and over and over."

Damien's face was granite-hard. Heather was

half afraid to say a word. "So he was after something. But what?"

His eyes grew stormy. "I don't know. I *still* don't know. But whatever it was he was after, he didn't find it. Corrine said Giles insisted he knew nothing of whatever it was the stranger wanted. He accused Giles of lying. Of trying to keep 'it' for himself. And then"—a spasm of pain twisted his lips—"he killed him. The bastard took a poker and killed him!"

Damien's face had gone pale beneath his tan. It was a moment before he went on. "Corinne fled because she was afraid the murderer would find out she had been there and kill her, too. The murderer said he'd been in prison for twenty years. I had Cameron, my investigator, go immediately to Newgate. There had been no recent escapes, but he obtained a list of prisoners who had recently been released."

She couldn't tear her eyes from his face. "And James Elliot was among them?"

"Yes."

Her lips barely moved. "But why do you think it was he? There must have been something—"

Damien's mouth twisted. "Oh, there was. Corinne claimed she didn't see his face that night. But she said he passed close enough to the door that she saw he had black hair, and a very distinctive feature—he was missing the thumb of one of his hands."

Black hair. Her dream slammed into her consciousness with the force of a wave crashing from the sea. The man in her dream had black hair. Her mind searched frantically. And there had been something—something odd about his hand. . . .

Her blood seemed to curdle in her veins. *No*, she thought. A scream bounced off the chambers of her mind. *God help her, no . . .*

Through a haze she heard Damien.

"James Elliot was missing the thumb of his left hand," he said harshly. "It was afterward that we found out he was married, that he had a daughter. Cameron managed to discover that his wife, Justine, was killed in Lancashire, and that there was a small child with her. Shortly after that incident, Elliot killed two men in a tavern and was sentenced to Newgate. But we had no luck finding him—we still haven't! After spending twenty years in prison, I thought he'd try to find his daughter. I thought he'd come back to *you*, Heather."

There was a vile taste in her mouth. "So that's why you came to Lockhaven."

"Yes. I don't know why he killed Giles. I don't know what he was trying to find that night. But I didn't want him to realize I was on his trail. That's why I used the name Damien Lewis. The fact that you needed an estate manager was a Godsend."

"So you—you took the position in order to . . . to spy on me."

She didn't see him wince. "Heather, there was nothing else I could do. For all I knew, you might have been involved. I had no idea *what* you knew. I had to find out. I *had* to."

Every breath burned like fire in her lungs. His every word burned through her brain, a litany that played over and over. Damien had used her. Her father wasn't dead. He was alive, and he was a murderer. Her father was a *murderer*.

She rocked back and forth. Her shoulders were shaking. Tears leaked from beneath closed eyelids.

"Why did you stay with me that night? To find out what I knew?"

"No!" His hands shot out. He turned her to face him. "That had nothing to do with him. That was just between us."

"Was it?" The agony in her heart bled through to her voice. "How could you stand to—to lie with the daughter of your brother's murderer?"

His eyes darkened. "Don't do this, Heather." His voice was low, vibrant and intense. "Don't belittle what we had. I swear to you, that was the most precious night of my life."

Misty violet eyes searched his face. He saw the muscles in her throat work convulsively. "I don't know what to think. God help me, I don't!"

The pad of his thumb passed over quivering lips. "Heather, I know this is a shock. I know how you must feel—"

"You don't." It was a stricken little cry. "How could you? All these years I thought I knew who I was . . . that my father was a Frenchman. . . . Why did he lie to me? Why did Papa lie?" Tears streamed down her face.

But suddenly she lurched upright, tearing herself away. "I want to go home," she announced. Her voice was high and tight.

"No, Heather. Not like this." His arms closed around her from behind. He snagged her back against his chest, aware of the awful tension strung throughout her body.

"Let me go!" she cried. "You have no right to—to keep me here!"

"Heather." He sought to calm her. "Heather, listen to me—"

She went wild then, struggling and twisting to be free of him. Damien cursed and tightened his arms. His hold was unyielding, though not hurtful, and her arms were useless, trapped against her sides by his steely forearms banding her chest.

Slowly he brought her around to face him. He didn't release her but curled his fingers around the narrow span of her wrists. She was so stiff he felt that her entire body would surely snap in two.

"Heather. Heather, please listen to me."

She spurned him, wrenching her face aside.

He cursed. "Dammit, Heather, look at me!"

She did—and in all his days, it was a look he would never forget. Her skin was almost bloodless. Her lips were tremulous, her eyes huge and wounded.

"What?" she cried. "What more do you want from me? Haven't you taken enough? Haven't you?" It was the sound of pure anguish, torn from deep in her chest. But it was as if her stricken cries took every ounce of her strength.

She swayed dizzily; her legs buckled. Damien swore and caught her up against him before she collapsed.

She turned her face into his neck and wept.

* * *

In the coach, she lay limply against his side. Her listlessness worried him. She no longer cried; perversely, he almost wished she would. She seemed so small, so young and defenseless. A pang twisted his insides. He longed to heal her wounded spirit, take her pain inside him and make it his own.

Back at the Earl of Stonehurst's town house, he opened the door and lifted her to the ground. For the space of a heartbeat, his hands rested protectively—possessively—on the narrow curve of her waist. Even as he debated whether to carry her inside, she broke from his hold.

"I can stand." Her eyes avoided his. She glanced inside the coach for her cane. Damien retrieved it and handed it to her.

Without a word she turned and started up the broad stone steps. He fell into step beside her, cupping her elbow in his hand. He thought he felt her stiffen, but stubbornly he left it where it was.

The butler admitted them. "Thank you, Nelson," she murmured. "Are Mama and Papa at home?"

"In the drawing room, Miss Heather."

Not until then did she deign to give him her full attention. Her posture stoic and proud, she turned to him. "Shall I have someone see you out?"

"Not quite yet." His tone was unyielding. "The earl will want answers. And I've some questions of my own."

Her lips thinned. Her cane rapped smartly on the marble floor as she proceeded down the corridor to the drawing room. She fairly flung the doors wide. Like a shadow, Damien was right behind her.

Miles and Victoria were in the midst of tea. Two pair of eyes widened as they recognized Damien. Heather wasted no time on subtleties. "Mama and Papa, may I present Damien Lewis *Tremayne*, Earl of Deverell."

Another time, their shock might have been humorous. Miles was on his feet in an instant, tall and imposing. Victoria's jaw had dropped, her teacup suspended above her lap.

Miles had fixed his gaze on Damien. His expression was stony and forbidding. "I trust you have an explanation for this, young man?"

Damien didn't back down from his narrowed glare. "That I do, my lord." He nodded toward the sofa. "May I suggest we sit down? This may take some time."

The atmosphere was thick with tension as Damien began to speak. In quietly measured tones, he repeated all he'd told Heather—how his brother, Giles, had been murdered, how he'd traced the murder to James Elliot. When he'd finished, a stunned silence swamped the room.

Until then, Heather had sat with her head bowed low, her hands folded in her lap. Now she raised her head and gazed steadily at Miles. "What have you to say on this, Papa?" Her voice was very quiet, but implicit in her tone was a stark demand.

Miles's skin was ashen. He didn't answer directly. Instead he looked at Damien. "How certain are you of this? How certain are you that

Heather's father is still alive? That he is this man, this . . . James Elliot."

Damien spoke gravely. "My lord, if there were any doubt in my mind, I would not be here. I don't know why he killed Giles, but I will not rest until he is found and punished."

Miles looked at Heather. His expression was anguished. Beside him, Victoria laid an imploring hand on her husband's sleeve. "It's time, love," she said softly. "It's time she knew the truth."

Miles swallowed. She was right. His eyes caught Heather's, then swung to Damien. Heavily, he said, "You'll forgive me if I ask you to leave, Lord Deverell. But this is a matter best confined to the three of us."

Damien had already determined that. He rose, then paused. "Of course, sir. But I must have the answer to just one question. The man killed in the carriage with Justine Duval—Justine Elliot—did you know he was not Heather's father?"

Miles shook his head. "I swear to you—and to you, Heather—that I knew nothing about this man, James Elliot. The coach carried but three passengers. The driver was killed, and all these years, I thought the other man who died was Heather's father. He traveled with her mother, Justine. She called him by name—Bernard. As she lay dying, she asked for him, whether he lived or died! Heather was with them. I was convinced they were man and wife. Indeed, it never occurred to me it might not be so."

Damien nodded. With that, Miles escorted

him to the entrance hall. There he spoke for
Damien's ears alone. "There's just one more
thing. What you heard here today—I'll not have
it bandied about London. It must never go
beyond this room, for I'll not have Heather
subjected to the scandal it would cause. May I
trust you in this?"

Damien extended his hand. "You have my
word of honor, my lord. It will never be
repeated—to anyone." They shook hands, and
Damien departed.

Miles returned to the drawing room, his step as
heavy as his heart. He sat, placed both hands
upon his knees and looked at Heather. "You
believe me, don't you, poppet?"

"You swore an oath; therefore, I believe you."
Her tone was flat. "But the fact remains; you said
you knew my parents well. You said you met
them in Paris!" She confronted him accusingly.
"Why did you lie, Papa? You let me believe
that—that stupid story all these years!"

Beside him, Victoria's hand slipped into his;
she squeezed his fingers encouragingly.

"I did it for you, poppet. I did it for both of us,
because I—I could not bear to let you go! After
the accident, you were too ill to be moved, and so
I kept you with me at Lyndermere. By the time
you were well, I—I loved you too much to let
you go."

Heather trembled. She remembered a time
when she was very young, memories of being
held safe and warm in a strong, comforting
embrace. That had been Papa. Somehow she'd
always known that. But she willed the memory

away, for she didn't want to remember just now . . . she was too angry. Too furious at yet another man's deceit . . .

"Both your parents were dead—or so I thought. You were an orphan. Your parents were poor; that much was obvious. But I knew that, if I were to give you up, you would likely go to an orphan house and I could not bear the thought of you in such a place!" His voice grew hoarse. "And so . . . I lied, Heather. I lied. I petitioned the courts to declare you my ward. I thought my chances would be far better if I were acquainted with your parents—with *you*. I told the magistrate your parents were my friends—your father a French aristocrat, your mother an English lady, on their way to visit me at Lyndermere and resettle in England."

For the longest time, Heather didn't say a word. Then she said tightly, "I want to know about my mother. You said she was a kind, sweet woman. Was she? Or was that another lie as well?"

Miles glanced at Victoria; she gave a tiny nod.

His tone was wooden. "Your mother was nothing like you, Heather." His eyes squeezed shut. "She was the most vile woman I have ever known, for as she lay dying, she cursed you—her own daughter—for living. And God may punish me forever, but as she breathed her last, I—I gave thanks that you were spared her presence in your life."

There was nothing more to say. Miles opened his eyes and gazed across from her, hoping . . . waiting . . . praying for some sign of forgiveness.

But the silence in the room was like a pall. Heather got up and limped slowly across the floor. Her features were drawn in harsh, bitter lines. She left without a word. Without a look.

Miles remained where he was, too stunned to move. It was left to Victoria to pick up the pieces. She rose. Her footsteps followed in Heather's wake. She stopped only to briefly catch her husband's hand in hers.

"Do not despair" was all she said.

Upstairs in her room, Heather lay upon the bed. She'd drawn the drapes against the sunshine streaming in through the windows.

Only her head moved as the door creaked open. "Please, Mama. I want to be alone."

She sounded as old as the heavens. Victoria's heart went out to her, but she remained undaunted. Her tread was noiseless as she moved to the bed.

The mattress dipped as she sat. "I won't let you do this, Heather. To him. Or to yourself." Soft as her tone was, the words verged on steel.

Heather's eyes were on her face. "You knew?" was all she said.

Victoria nodded. "Until this day, I agreed with your father that no good would come of telling you the truth, Heather."

Heather's gaze skipped away. "It's . . . it's too much, Mama." Her voice was so low Victoria had to bend near to hear. "Damien's masquerade . . . finding out my father is still alive, to say nothing of what he is . . . Papa lying to me all these years . . ." The breath she drew was deep and tremulous.

Victoria's expression was pained. With a tender hand she smoothed Heather's brow. "I know these revelations have been a shock. But what you must remember now is that in time the hurt will ease. Then you'll see that nothing has changed."

Heather stared at the ceiling. "You're wrong, Mama. Everything's changed."

"No, love. *No.*"

Heather averted her face. Thick, black lashes veiled her expression. "Yes, Mama. *Yes.* I—I feel like I don't know who I am." Her voice trembled. "I—I feel sick inside. I feel dirty. Unworthy. Like God has cast some blight upon my soul—my life."

Victoria's heart twisted. "Heather. Oh, Heather . . . you've nothing to be ashamed of, nothing!"

Heather twisted on her side, curling her knees to her chest. "How can you look at me and not think of him—of James Elliot? How can you look at me and not be reminded that my father is a murderer?"

Victoria's hand stroked her shoulder. "You ask that as if you think I have no answer. But I would tell you this, Heather. I look at you and I see *you.* No one else, Heather, no one but you. I see what you are, the sweet, loving child you always were. So giving . . . never asking for anything. I see . . . what I've always seen. A beautiful young girl whose soul is filled with goodness . . . a woman who has overcome so very much . . . a woman whose strength rivals that of the most powerful man . . . I see my daughter, who makes me so proud I feel I could burst. That has not changed, love. It never will."

She bestowed on her a smile that was almost whimsical. "I say that because I love you, Heather, the same way your father loves you. No, you are not a child of my womb, not a child of his loins, but you are a child of my heart—of our hearts. No child of mine, of ours, could be more our own than you. What Miles did, he did out of love. Never forget that, sweet. Never lose faith in us . . . or in yourself."

Heather's eyes had slowly lifted. Warm, wet tears trickled down her cheeks and dripped from her chin. She didn't bother to wipe them away. What she glimpsed in Victoria's eyes in that moment would live on in her forever. A hot ache filled her throat as she sought to grapple with all that filled her heart.

Reaching out, she hugged her mother fiercely. "I—I love you, Mama," she choked out.

Neither knew that Miles had slipped into the room as well. He could not help but feel left out and alone. But a rustle of his clothing alerted them to his presence.

Heather sat up and bravely wiped the wetness from her face. Her smile was misty. Wordlessly she held out her hand.

Miles was too choked up to utter a sound. But he couldn't withhold the tears that sprang to his eyes . . . nor did he try to.

Eighteen

A morning mist hung close to the ground, for the sun had yet to pierce the low-hanging clouds. All around the London street vendors hawked their wares in the damp morning air.

A sleek, ruby-red carriage clattered on the cobblestone street, then cleanly rounded the next corner.

Gleaming avarice shone in the eyes that followed the vehicle until it disappeared from view. The boy to whom they belonged was a street urchin known as Jack Scavenger. His shirt was threadbare, his too-short breeches held up by a knotted rope, his scrawny feet bare. He made his living day-to-day—begging, stealing, peddling what goods his wits and quick hands brought him. He slept in alleys, under doorways, wherever he could find a place from which he'd not be chased.

"Now there's a man wot I'd like to be," Jack remarked to the fellow next to him. "Come from America, 'e did, only to find his elder brother dead. Next thing 'e knows 'e's stepped into his brother's shoes—and his brother an earl, no less!" The man gave a cackling laugh. "Can ye imagine? The bloke probably danced a merry jig atop his brother's grave! A bleedin' shame it 'appened to 'im instead o' me!"

James Elliot turned sharply in the direction of the coach. "You know that man?" he demanded.

Jack shrugged. "Well, I don't know 'im personal-like, but I know who 'e is."

"That's what I asked!" Elliot had no patience with imbeciles. He seized the boy by the collar and dragged him forward.

"'Ey! No need to take on so! 'e's the bloody Earl of Deverell, that's who 'e is!"

Stunned, James Elliot released him. Jack scurried backward. Elliot's mind was racing. Charles Tremayne's voice echoed through his head.

Never again will I see my boys, Giles and Damien.

So this was the younger son. He'd only recently heard tales of how the one called Damien had made his way to America years earlier. It had crossed his mind more than once that perhaps the jewel case might be with the younger son instead. He'd been trying to learn more, but with an ocean between them—and a shortage of money—it was difficult. But now it seemed he need search no more. . . .

"The earl is living 'ere in London, is 'e?"

"I believe so," Jack answered sullenly.

Elliot reached into his pocket and slipped the lad a coin. "Remember me, lad. If you learn more about the earl—where 'e goes, who 'e sees—there's more where that came from."

Elliot sauntered away. A smile as black and sly as his heart rimmed his lips.

This was news. Good news indeed.

The days that followed were among the most difficult of Heather's life. Her pride was both her ally and her bane. It was a struggle to reconcile the truth about her parenthood—knowing that she was the spawn of an evil, unscrupulous man was difficult, but with one day into the next, it was easier. But where Damien was concerned . . .

Her heart was in turmoil.

In the days since she'd left Lockhaven, she had convinced herself he meant nothing to her. She'd convinced herself she despised him, for he'd made her achingly aware of all that was lacking in her life . . . all that would never be hers—a husband and children. She didn't want to need him. She didn't want to *love* him.

But now he'd appeared once more. He was back in her life . . . and in her heart.

And she knew not what to do about it.

He was the first man to kiss her, the first man to make love to her . . . the first to hurt her. Perhaps it would be better for them both if he left her alone. . . .

He couldn't. The very idea was unbearable.

He called on her the very next afternoon. The message came down through the butler that she was otherwise engaged. It was repeated the next day and the next. The fourth day, it was Victoria who came down the stairs, who crossed the gold-flecked marble floor to greet him.

His hands laced behind his back, he rocked up on his heels and back. "Let me guess, my lady," he drawled. "She is indisposed."

The merest smile grazed Victoria's lips. "Actually, my lord—"

"Damien," he corrected curtly.

"Well, Damien, in all honesty, her speech was quite explicit. She refuses to see you under any circumstances."

"Indeed." Damien clenched his gloves in his fist. His eyes narrowed. Unless he was mistaken, there was a glimmer of amusement in the countess's eyes. He was abruptly irritated. "I do not mean to be rude, my lady, but I do not find this situation humorous."

Her smile faded. "No," she sighed. "It's hardly that, is it? And please, there's no need to stand on formality here. Call me Victoria."

His irritation fled as suddenly as it had made itself known. "If it pleases you, Victoria it is, then." There was a small pause. "How is she?"

Victoria's hesitation was marked. "Coping as well as can be expected, I suppose. Some days are better than others. At times she feels she doesn't know herself very well. You must understand, this is a trying time for her. She doesn't know what she wants—"

"Only that she does not want to see me." He couldn't disguise his bitter frustration.

Victoria's expression had turned cloudy. "May I speak plainly, Damien? Just between you and me?"

"Of course, madam. I would have it no other way."

She laid a beseeching hand on his sleeve. "If Heather is important to you—I pray you correct me if I am wrong, for I truly believe she is—then you must give her time. Be patient. In a sense she is finding her way again."

Damien's jaw was bunched and knotted. Time, he thought darkly. That he had—an abundance of it, as it were. But patience was a virtue he'd never learned to master.

He gave her a low bow. "Thank you, Countess. I trust we shall see each other again"—his smile did not quite reach his eyes—"in time." With that he departed.

He tried to keep her counsel firmly entrenched in his mind, but he was not a man to stand idle. Victoria seemed sympathetic, but . . .

Three days later, Heather received a summons early in the afternoon. A maid rapped on her door, then opened it. "Excuse me, Miss Heather, but Lady Beatrice requests your presence in the garden."

Heather glanced up from the book she'd been reading. "Now?"

The maid nodded. "She stressed that it was a matter most urgent."

Heather frowned but got up and reached for her cane. Had Bea gotten herself into some sort of trouble? Such a request was most unusual; she hurried outside.

But the garden was deserted. There was no one present save a fat, noisy robin. Puzzled, Heather glanced down a twisting row of pristine white and blood-red roses. Stupefied, she gazed all around. "Bea?" she called.

From just behind her, she caught a flash of movement. A hand clapped over her mouth, stifling her cry of alarm. A steely arm wrapped around her waist. The world tilted crazily as she was borne from her feet and dumped with little ceremony onto the velvet seat of a coach.

As she scrambled upright, the coach lurched forward so suddenly she had to grasp the seat for balance.

Damien sprawled across from her on the opposite side of the coach, a study in indolent grace. He gazed across at her, his smile lazy. He was obviously quite pleased with himself.

Her gaze went straight to the door. She licked her lips. It was locked, but that was no barrier. She had only to ease a little to her left . . .

"Don't even think about it." His warning was icily polite.

Heather gritted her teeth. "What is the meaning of this?" she demanded.

"You would not see me," he said, as if that explained everything.

"And so you abducted me?"

He laughed at her closed, angry features. "An unfortunate choice of words," he said mildly. "I prefer to think of it as an outing."

"An outing," she said through her teeth. "And where is this outing taking us?"

"Oh, not terribly far. To the country just outside the city."

She glared her outrage. "The last time you took me to the country was a disaster."

Regret flashed in his eyes. "This one will not be, I promise."

"My family thinks I'm upstairs reading. They'll be frantic when they realize I'm gone."

His mouth quirked. "No," he said dryly. "They won't."

Heather's jaw clamped together. "Let me guess. Beatrice?"

He nodded, a faint twinkle dancing in those silver depths. "Wonderfully helpful, that girl."

Heather fumed. The little traitor! By Jove, she vowed, she'd see that Bea did not pull such a stunt again.

He crooked a finger at her. "Come here."

Panic blazed high and bright in her breast. If he touched her—if he touched her she would surely shatter into a million pieces. She would be completely, utterly lost.

She shook her head, huddling even farther into the corner.

"Very well, then. I'll come to you."

He was beside her in an instant, moving with the lithe, effortless grace she had once envied. Tugging her from her niche, he proceeded to pull her back against his chest. Long arms curled around her from behind, spanning her waist, caging her in a tender prison.

Heather froze, her hands extended almost straight out before her.

"None of that, now," he scolded gently. "All I want is to hold you. Nothing more, I promise."

Hah! she thought, for their position was shockingly intimate. She was lying in his lap, her hips snug between the notch of strong, hard thighs.

Yet there was nothing sexual or threatening in his hold; it was loose and passionless. Letting out a long, shaky breath, her hands fluttered atop his. She stared, for the contrast was riveting. His hands were wonderfully masculine, his fingers long and lean and dark against the paleness of her own. A little quiver tore through her.

"Just relax," he whispered. "Don't think about anything, Heather. Don't worry or fret. Just lie back and enjoy the moment."

She wanted to, she realized wistfully. The past weeks had been fraught with tension. And it felt so good to be held, tight and safe and warm, as she hadn't been in such a long, long time.

The coach bounced along the roadway. Her body rocked gently against his. Gradually her limbs relinquished all resistance. His jaw scraped lightly against the tender skin of her temple, but she didn't mind.

Warm breath stirred her hair. "You looked beautiful the other night, Heather. Enchanting. Like a fairy princess."

A wisp of a smile lifted her lips. "That's what Bea said."

"She was right." His tone was husky. "I remember thinking I'd never seen anyone quite so lovely in all my life. But then, I shouldn't be surprised. You're beautiful, no matter where you are, no matter what you wear. As the princess you were the other evening. As the gypsy I first met at Lockhaven."

Her head ducked down. "Don't," she said very low. "Don't—don't say such things."

"Why not?"

She twisted around so she could see him. She spoke with hesitant words . . . and hesitant heart. "Damien, I—I have been trying to understand why you did . . . what you did . . . at Lockhaven. But there is a part of me that feels betrayed."

His regard was steady. "I can understand that, Heather."

"From the start, I felt you were . . . a man of conviction. A man of honor. I—I would have no more duplicity between us. So if it's guilt that prompts such flattery—"

"Disabuse yourself of that notion here and now, Heather." His tone had gone hard.

All at once Heather shivered. The hairs on the back of her neck prickled eerily.

Damien frowned. A surge of fierce protectiveness shot through him. "What is it? What are you thinking?"

"I was thinking . . . of him."

"You mean James Elliot." His arms had gone as brittle as his voice.

She nodded.

"What of him?"

His expression was so forbidding that she was momentarily afraid to speak. "I think he is a horrible, odious man—the man who killed your brother." Dark, sinister features flashed before her. She spoke haltingly. "Remember . . . I told you about . . . the terrible man in my dream?"

"You said if you made a sound, he would punish you. He'd hurt you." Dear God, how could he forget?

"He did," she said in a voice that made his blood run cold. Tensely he waited.

"You asked me once . . . if the man in the dream was my father. I—I do not know if that man is James Elliot. God help me, I—I don't want to believe it." Her hand came out to touch the mangled surface of her knee. "But the man in the dream. I . . . I think he did this. He—he raised something high above his head. And then he—he hit me. . . ."

Damien's blood had gone to boiling. Rage stole over him, a rage so potent he shook with the force of it. Heather might doubt the identity of her father, but he did not. If James Elliot were before him now, he would tear him limb from limb without a second thought. Not only for what he'd done to Giles . . . but for what he'd done to Heather, to the poor, innocent child who could not defend herself against him.

Staring up into his face, Heather went cold to the tips of her toes. His features were harsh and taut, his eyes empty of emotion. Yet in that mind-splitting instant she sensed a ruthlessness about him that was almost frightening.

She blanched. "Dear God," she said faintly. "You're going to kill him, aren't you? When you find James Elliot, you're going to—to kill him."

His lips were ominously thin. "When I find him, he'll be punished. I'll say no more."

She didn't recoil from him, yet she wore her horror like a wounded animal.

"Don't tell me you would have him spared! Heather, he murdered my brother!"

Her breath tumbled out in a rush. "Yes . . . no. Oh, don't you see? I don't know! I don't know what to think! Is there no forgiveness for the damned? No mercy for the weak? Will you kill him without knowing for certain he is the one?" She tried to tear herself free of his embrace. He wouldn't let her.

He closed his arms around her and buried his face in the shining black cloud of her hair, fighting a violent tug-of-war inside.

He lifted his head. "Heather." Her name erupted on a long, tense breath of air. "Heather, please. Do not torture yourself, for this I promise. An innocent man will not pay for my brother's death. Though James Elliot has already killed two men, if he is the one who murdered Giles, I will have it from his lips."

Her troubled gaze sought his. "I have questions, too, Damien. I would know if he is indeed my father. And if he is, then I—I would know why my mother traveled without him that long-ago night. I would know why he did not seek out his daughter after twenty years in Newgate. Indeed, I've been thinking an investigation of my own—"

"No. If he should find out someone else is making inquiries, that might well send him even farther into hiding. Besides, he is a violent man."

Heather went very still inside. "Would it put you in danger, if he knew someone other than you were looking for him?"

"In all honesty, I don't know, Heather. But I suppose it could."

And that was something she would not do, no

matter what. Heather chafed inside, even as her heart cried out. How much longer could she stand not knowing if this horrible man were truly her father?

Damien sensed her distress. "In time, your questions will be answered, all of them," he said quietly. "Now, may we not speak of this again? May we not even think of him this day?" He pressed his thumb against the softness of his lips. "I wanted to take you away from everything, Heather. I wanted you to have a day with no cares, no worries, no distress." His eyes darkened. "But most of all, I wanted to have you all to myself. Will you let me?"

His low, husky murmur turned her inside out. Disarmed her. Stole her will from her as if it had never been her own to possess.

Tenderness lurked in his gaze—a world of it— a tenderness she was still so afraid to believe in. . . . Yet she nodded, unable to tear her gaze from the sight of it.

It was the most wondrous day of her life.

He took her to a place near a small lake, surrounded by woodland. They shared a leisurely luncheon beside a fallen tree trunk near the shore—and with the family of chipmunks that resided within. Heather laughed at their antics as she hadn't since she was a child. They watched clouds drift across a powder-blue sky. Together they strolled hand in hand near the shore, watching dappled sunlight dance upon the waters. It was a day filled with quiet contentment, occasional laughter and undemanding camaraderie . . .

The stuff of which dreams were made.

So it was that she wished the day would never end. Yet all too soon, streaks of pale pink painted the horizon, and a purple haze gathered above the treetops.

She was pierced by a bittersweet ache when the coach drew to a halt before her parents' London house. Damien led her into the garden, near the spot to which he'd lured her this morning.

He drew her into his arms.

On guard, her hands came up between them. They stood so close that her slippers were wedged between his booted feet. The tips of her breasts brushed the fabric of his jacket.

Lean fingers stole beneath the fall of her hair. A hazy sensuality glimmered deep in the crystalline depths of his eyes.

Alarm raced through her, yet she was plagued by a paralyzing uncertainty and couldn't move. Her fingers curled and uncurled on the plane of his chest. She confined her attention to the wiry tangle of hairs at the base of his throat.

"Damien, please," she said shakily. "Please do not do this."

"Why not?"

Her heart faltered. Her resolve crumpled. "Because I can't fight this," she cried softly. "I can't fight you."

His fingers slid down her throat. "Nor can I," he whispered just before his mouth closed over hers.

His kiss was all a kiss should be. Sweetly persuasive. Hotly passionate. Heady and devouring. A kiss of remembrance . . . a kiss of promise. With naught but the pressure of his mouth he coaxed from her a response she was helpless to withhold. With a low moan she wrapped her arms around him and clung. He made a sound low in his throat; his arms were tight and hard around her back.

Reluctantly he released her mouth. His thumb beneath her chin, he brought her face to his. "Do you know," he murmured, "I have been waiting for that since the moment I saw you again at Lady Seton's ball."

His quiet declaration made her want to cry. She averted her face before she embarrassed herself totally and completely. She tried to step back.

He wouldn't let her. His hands snared her waist. There was a heated silence before he spoke.

"Do you think," he asked softly, "that what I feel is less than what you do?" His fingers caught at hers, bringing her hand up between them. Slowly he wove his fingers through hers, palm to palm. "I assure you, sweet, it is not."

Heather trembled. She had no weapon to fight such tenderness—such gentleness. She had no strength to vie against his will—or her own traitorous longing.

"Damien, please, if there can be nothing else, at least let there be honesty."

"I would have it no other way, Heather."

"Then let me speak plainly. Damien, I—I've lain with no other man. You know that. But you . . . oh, I'm not such a fool as to believe there have been no other women in your life."

She swallowed, unable to look any higher than the hollow of his throat. Then all at once the words were tumbling out, one after the other. "You are a man of the world—a man of experience. And I know I cannot compare to all the other women you've known—"

"Stop," he said. "You assume there have been scores of women in my life. There have not."

Her gaze came back to his. "Truly?" she whispered.

"I will not lie to you, Heather. I am a man, and I have not lived a celibate existence for nearly thirty years. Of course there have been other women in my life. And yes, I've had a deeper affection for some than for others—but nothing lasting." He paused, and his gaze delved deep into hers. "There's never been anyone like you, Heather, *never*. You're"—he hesitated—"you're different from every woman I've ever known."

She made a faint, choked sound. "Yes, and we both know why—"

Anger kindled in his voice. "Don't!" he said almost roughly. "Your limp doesn't matter to me; it never has. Don't you know that?"

Her eyes clung to his. She wanted to believe him. But there was so much at risk here. Her very heart . . .

His hands came up to cup her shoulders. "You're kind and sweet and good. You're bright and beautiful. Heather, you—you're different," he said again. "In every way that's good. In every way that's *right*."

She trembled. "But what about now? Damien,

you are the toast of London." It hurt to hear the words aloud, yet Heather could withhold them no longer. "You could be with any number of beautiful women. You could *have* any woman—"

"I want only you, Heather. Only you."

Even as the words sent joy winging through her, she plummeted to the depths of despair. She shook her head. "No. This . . . it's not possible. We must put these feelings aside, for this can never be—"

"And what about the night we spent together? Or have you forgotten?"

A pang swept through her. Dear God, how could she? She relived those wondrous moments in the stark loneliness of her bed, in the hours where memory filled the empty corners of her soul. She would cherish them, hold them close in her heart forevermore.

"I have not." Her voice was but a breath. "But we are not the same people we were then, neither of us. You were Damien Lewis—not the Earl of Deverell. And I was simply Heather Duval. But now"—she swallowed, steeling herself against a wrench of pain—"now it may well be that I am the daughter of a murderer."

Something flashed in his eyes; she glimpsed an arrogance in him that was foreign to her. "You forget; I knew who you were then. And it doesn't matter that you knew me as Damien Lewis. You cannot dismiss this so easily, Heather. You cannot dismiss *me* so easily."

She was swept into his arms. His mouth trailed fire along the curve of her cheek, the corner of lips that parted in sweet surprise. And then he claimed her mouth in a hot, blazing stamp of possession that plumbed the very depths of her being and left her dizzy and breathless.

He let her go so suddenly she nearly stumbled. Strong arms caught at her anew and brought her close—so close they shared the very same breath. Stunned at his intensity, she stared up into fiercely glowing eyes.

His regard was unsmiling. "I am going to court you, Heather. I am going to woo you." His eyes darkened. "And I am going to win you."

There was scarcely time to catch hold of the thought. Another wild, mind-stealing kiss was bestowed on her lips . . . and then he was gone.

Nineteen

He meant it, for Damien Tremayne, Earl of Deverell, was a man who would stop at nothing to get what he wanted.

And what he wanted was her.

It was impossible. Unthinkable. Unbelievable. And wholly wonderful.

Heather had never been so terrified in her life.

She couldn't give in to him—she couldn't. Deep inside, she was afraid she didn't have what it took to keep a man like Damien—indeed, any man. Oh, she did not doubt her worth as a person. She was quick-witted and intelligent, staunch and independent in an age where women were seldom afforded such opportunity; Lockhaven was the proof, for she ran her estate with an eye to detail that many a man would have envied, and she was proud of it. But when it came to being a woman . . .

That was another matter entirely.

She was not a perfect little beauty, like those

who paraded through Hyde Park. Like those who graced the elegant drawing rooms of Society's most elite citizens, in the company of the most handsome of men. She was not . . . whole.

She admitted her desperate fear only to herself.

In time, she would lose him. In time, he would not want her. He was surrounded by the most beautiful women in all England. What need had he of her? Wasn't it better to keep her distance, to know the pang of loss now, than to experience heartache later?

It was a battle she waged daily.

But Damien was persistent. Relentless. He called on her often. Nor did her family make it any easier on her. Many were the evenings that Damien shared supper with them as well, at Mama or Papa's invitation. When he occasionally went riding or hunting with Papa, he inevitably stayed afterward.

Whenever Damien chanced to be near, a secret glimmer of approval shone in Mama's eyes before she demurely lowered her lashes. Almost daily, Bea declared how wonderfully romantic it was to be pursued by someone as dashing as Damien. Papa enjoyed having port and cigars with him after supper—the privacy of their conversations alerted Heather's suspicions that one of the subjects discussed was James Elliot, a subject she sensed everyone went to great pains to avoid in her presence.

Yet indeed, Heather speculated in mingled frustration and resignation, it would have done little good to refuse Damien entrance into their home, for Mama or Papa or Bea would surely have invited him in—or even one of the servants, whom he now called by name!

He did not shower her with flowers, or bonbons, or simpering poetry. But his eyes were ever upon her. . . . She lost count of the times she had only to glance over at him to meet his gaze full upon her, burning and direct. It was disconcerting. Distracting.

Thrilling, beyond all measure.

Little wonder that she was so torn. . . .

But these were the least of her worries, for Heather harbored a secret, a secret she could share with no one . . .

For their one night together had yielded a consequence she'd never dreamed would happen—not to her. And she wasn't certain if she was terrified or elated. . . .

One evening she was to attend the opera with Mama and Papa. Unfortunately, by midafternoon, Mama was not feeling well. Papa asked if she would mind crying off, for he hated to leave Mama at home in such a state. Heather hid her disappointment, for the evening was one she had looked forward to. Damien called soon afterward; it was Papa who spied him in the drawing room with Heather.

"Have you plans for the evening?" he asked, striding boldly as was his way.

"None," Damien assured him.

"Then perhaps you'd be willing to escort Heather to the opera tonight at Covent Garden. Victoria and I had planned to attend as well, but Victoria is unwell—"

"Papa!" Heather couldn't hide her distress. "I cannot believe you would be so forward—"

"Forward?" To her horror, Miles appeared vaguely amused. "My dear, Damien is hardly a stranger. Besides, you're a friend of the family." He glanced at Damien. "What do you say? Are you free?"

Damien's gaze was on Heather, who could not bear to look at him. Her cheeks were flaming. "I would be honored to escort her, sir."

Heather's pulse was fluttering madly. She wanted to refuse . . . but she longed to spend the evening with Damien far more. . . .

Such was the nature of her wayward heart.

She dressed carefully that night. The gown of burgundy velvet she wore lent her the courage to go through with the evening . . . a courage she was about to discover she would sorely need.

Damien was waiting in the entrance hall when she came downstairs, dark and striking in evening dress, his hands behind his back. At the swish of her skirts, he turned and looked up. Hunger blazed in the silver of his eyes, a hunger that made her weak in the knees.

"Ready?" he murmured.

Heather nodded, unable to do more. He dropped a matching cape around her shoulders, his fingers skimming the bare skin of her upper arms in a warm and fleeting caress.

She tensed as they approached the Royal Opera House. This was the first time she'd been alone in public with him, and the strain on her nerves was almost more than she could stand.

But it appeared that no one took notice of them; the crowd streamed all around, and they were swept inside the vestibule along with the others.

Their box was in the upper tier. When they reached it, Heather sank gratefully into the plush seats. In the pit, the orchestra had begun to tune their instruments. The crowd scurried to find their seats before the performance began. Beside her, Damien chatted politely. Stiff with apprehension, Heather nodded now and again, her smile frozen in place, only half aware of what he said. Then, finally, the crimson draperies parted, and all else was forgotten. She leaned forward, enraptured as the strains of a lilting soprano aria filled the air.

She sighed in envy when the first act ended. Damien turned to her. "Shall we go down for refreshments?"

Dark brows lifted slightly, as if in challenge. Though Heather longed to decline, she didn't dare. If she did, he would accuse her of hiding away. . . .

Her chin tipped. "Certainly," she replied. As she placed gloved fingertips lightly on his arm, she thought she detected a gleam of admiration.

Delicate lace fans fluttered like butterflies in the spring. Brocade and satin rustled as women flitted like peacocks, showing off their finery. Diamonds and gold flashed brightly beneath crystal chandeliers. But as they slowly descended the wide staircase, color rose high and bright to her cheeks. Heads were turning; opera glasses were raised to many an eye. Inside she cringed, for she could almost hear the horrified whispers that had already begun. *Whatever is that lame girl doing with the Earl of Deverell? No doubt he feels sorry for her. Indeed, why else would he be with her?*

The worst moment came when Damien briefly left her to fetch a glass of wine. One woman walked past, staring at her boldly, her expression fairly hostile. Heather felt herself pale. Her hands were shaking, her fingers as cold as if she'd plunged them in ice.

Damien handed her the glass of wine. "Pay no attention to them," he murmured. He took her cane and tucked her free hand into his elbow.

"I cannot help it. I—I dislike being on display."

His hand came to rest atop her own. She knew he could feel her trembling. "Besides," he said lightly, "I confess, I find I rather like this."

Heather blinked. "You *like* being stared at?"

"I like showing you off." His voice took on a note of huskiness. "I'm the envy of every man here, you know. They'll go home and tonight, and they'll lie beside their dowdy wives—"

"Dowdy! Why, I doubt any woman here tonight is dowdy."

"Hush, sweet." His head lowered. He spoke for her ears alone. "They'll lie beside their dowdy wives, but they'll be thinking of you. They'll wonder what it would be like to be with you—this very night. They'll imagine what it would be like to strip your gown from you, little by little. They'll wonder how small your feet are, how long and white are your legs. They'll wonder whether your nipples are pink or brown, tilt up or outward."

Heather couldn't help it. Though she was secretly scandalized, she listened, mutely fascinated by this glimpse into the male psyche. "Men are utterly captivated by the size of women's breasts, you know. Why, they've even been known to place wagers on the size and shape of a woman's breasts—whether they'll fit into a champagne glass, like Helen of Troy, or if they're the size of ripe melons . . . don't look so shocked, my dear. Women are no different. In secret they whisper to each other, speculating about the size and endowments of whomever they plan to take on as lover that night. Is he the size of a shriveled carrot, or—"

Heather gasped. Her gaze shot to his face, only to find his eyes alight with amusement. As her expression changed from shock to a righteous indignation, Damien laughed softly.

Unbelievably, she found her lips twitching in return. She knew then what he was about—he'd merely been trying to take her mind away from her anxiety. "You are incorrigible," she accused without heat.

He clicked his heels and brought her hand to his lips. "I stand guilty as charged, m'lady."

The crowd had begun to disperse, heading back to their seats. Damien cocked his head toward the staircase. "Shall we?"

She nodded, turning a smug smile his way. "I knew you were lying," she informed him loftily. "Of course a gentleman would never think such outrageous things about a lady."

Damien nearly groaned. If she only knew what had been going through his mind these past weeks . . .

The rest of the evening passed without incident. When they were home, he escorted her to the door. His gaze roved her features, one by one, coming to rest on her lips. Her heart knocked wildly. Heather held her breath, awaiting the moment he would draw her into his arms. But he merely lifted her hand to his lips, the proper young gentleman. . . . She made her way to her room, vastly disappointed that he hadn't kissed her mouth.

Her dreams were most improper that night, so much so that she debated the possibility that Damien had not been exaggerating after all. . . .

The next day at breakfast, Bea filched Papa's copy of the *Gazette*. Of particular interest to her was the social column. Heather always laughed at her, for she gobbled up the juicy tidbits as a child would a sweet treat. Mama merely smiled indulgently. But Bea's eyes nearly fell from her head as she caught sight of a familiar name. In earnest, she read on:

It was not the opera on stage at Covent Garden last evening that had all comers agog—it was the sight of Damien Tremayne, Earl of Deverell. The earl chose to shower his attentions on one Miss Heather Duval, raven-haired ward of Miles Grayson, Earl of Stonehurst, to the envy of many a younger miss, who may have well had her hopes dashed. Many a matchmaking mama—indeed, all London—shall await the outcome of this dalliance.

Beatrice lowered the paper to her plate. "Oh, my," she breathed.

Victoria glanced up from her croissant. "What is it, Bea?"

Bea couldn't say a word. All she could do was thrust the paper at her mother. Miles leaned over as well.

The dishes leaped from the table as he slammed a hand down. "Damn!" he swore, his face like a thundercloud. "This is why I hate London!"

Bea look unhappy. "Why must they be so unkind? Heather is not old!"

Victoria sighed. "It does little good to complain, dear. 'Tis simply the nature of the gossips."

Miles had begun to pace. "This is my fault. I was the one who asked him to escort her."

"Papa," Bea spoke quickly, "don't let Heather see this."

"Don't let Heather see what?"

It was too late. Heather stood at the door. Her gaze slipped from one to the other.

It was Victoria who rose and handed her the paper. "I'm afraid you and Damien have made the news, dear," she said softly. "Take heart, love. It happens to all of us at one time or another."

Heather's cheeks grew pale as she read the column. When she was done, she laid it aside. "We did attract any number of glances" was all she said, reaching for the teapot.

Miles and Victoria exchanged glances. Beatrice blinked at her aplomb. "Heather! You act as if it doesn't bother you in the slightest!"

Heather smiled slightly. "Oh, it does, Bea. But at least they didn't mention my limp." She poured a generous dollop of cream into her tea.

Bea was in a state. "Well, if he had, I should march down to the *Gazette*, find who wrote this column, cut off his leg and see how *he* likes it!"

Victoria's brows shot up. "And if you don't learn to curb your tongue, Bea," she said dryly, "you'll soon find yourself the subject of that very same column."

Bea tossed her head. "Well, as you said, Mama, it's bound to happen to all of us! Perhaps it's best if I become accustomed to it now."

Victoria sent Miles a look that said "Heaven help us." Heather hid a smile in her teacup. But it appeared that was not the end of the morning's excitement. They were just rising from the table a short time later when the butler came in with a letter for Miles.

"It's from Lyndermere," Miles said with a frown. He broke open the seal and scanned it quickly. His expression sober, his eyes sought Victoria's.

"There's been an accident, love. A fire in the kitchens. Several of the servants were injured" —he laid a restraining hand on her arm when he spied the leap of fear in her eyes—"but Arthur and Christina are unhurt."

She nodded. "I think we'd best return at once, Miles."

"I agree, love. We can leave this afternoon and have the rest of our things sent on later."

"I'll have the maids start packing," Bea said quickly.

"Yes. Yes, please do, Bea."

"I'll have the carriage readied." Miles was already striding through the doorway.

Victoria began to follow him, only to whirl around. She pressed her hands to her cheeks. "Oh, no!" she cried. "It completely slipped my mind. Sophie's ball is tonight. Of course we can't stay . . . I know she'll be disappointed, but it can't be helped." She glanced toward the study. "I must send a note—"

"Don't worry, Mama. I'll tell her myself. Tonight." Heather could see that Victoria was in a tizzy.

It was a moment before the full import of her words reached Victoria. "You won't be returning with us, Heather?"

"No, Mama. I'd like to remain on here in case . . . in case James Elliot is found."

Victoria looked at her sharply. "Are you certain that's wise, dear?"

"It's something I have to do, Mama." Heather was quietly determined.

Victoria nodded. "What about tonight? You're certain you don't mind attending Sophie's ball alone?"

Heather's mind sped straight to Damien. "I've no wish to hide away, Mama."

"And I don't think you should. That would simply fuel more gossip."

"Besides, Paige will be there." And Damien, too, no doubt, though Heather didn't mention

his name aloud. But Mama had let it drop that
Sophie had invited him.

Several hours later Heather stood near the
street, waving the trio off. Her smile faded as she
watched the carriage rattle away. She'd said she
would attend Sophie's ball, and so she would.
But inside she was a quivering bundle of nerves.
After this morning's column in the *Gazette*, there
would probably be even more gossip. . . .

Damien had seen the column as well. He
didn't give a damn what was said about him, but
he was furious at the affront to Heather. He
paced before the windows in his study, while
Cameron Lindsey looked on.

"I should have known this would happen," he
fumed. "Can no one do anything in this town
without someone catching wind of it? By God, I
can see why Heather prefers to stay in the
country."

Cameron stroked his jaw. "It occurs to me, my
lord," he said suddenly, "that this could be a
boon."

Damien rounded on him. "A boon? Are you
mad, Cameron?"

"Think," Cameron said quietly. "You wanted
to make your presence known. But what if Elliot
doesn't know you're here yet? What if he didn't
realize she was in Lancashire? Perhaps that's
why he didn't seek her out there. On the other
hand, if it's known that the two of you are being
seen together . . . she is his daughter! If he rea-
lizes who she is—"

"I see your point, Cameron. But you forget,
it's been over twenty years since he's seen her."

Cameron regarded him quietly. "I mean no dishonor toward the lady when I say this, my lord. But Heather Duval's limp is rather uncommon. It might easily jar his memory."

"So you think he might come to reunite with her."

"Exactly."

"So you think I should squire her about for all to see. For all to bandy her name about."

"And yours," Cameron pointed out. "It might well increase your chances of finding Elliot."

Damien fell broodingly silent. A certain grimness had settled on his features. Cameron was right. If Elliot recognized Heather, it could well bring him near. Yet what Cameron proposed seemed so cold—so callous.

No. *No.* He couldn't use her like this. He *wouldn't.*

Cameron watched him closely. "You want to find him, don't you?"

"I will find him." Both Damien's tone and his expression brooked no argument. "But I won't use Heather like this, Cameron, and that's all I have to say on the matter."

Jack Scavenger didn't have a difficult time locating James Elliot. Elliot had a reputation for meanness; his vile temper and penchant for drink were becoming well known in London's back alleys.

He rapped sharply on Elliot's door. It rattled on its hinges, then opened a crack. Elliot peered without, his eyes bloodshot, his face unshaven.

"What do ya want?" came the whiskey-laden voice.

"It's me, Jack Scavenger. I've news o' the earl."

The door was flung wide. Jack stepped into a tiny, filthy room. Envy shot through him, for he'd have given anything to call a place such as this his own.

"What news?" Elliot demanded.

"Ye wanted to know where 'e goes, right? Who 'e sees?"

"That I did, boy." Elliot raised a bottle to his lips. Liquid seeped from the corner of his mouth. He wiped it away with the back of his hand.

"Well, I've seen 'im 'ere and about. Seems to spend a 'ole lot o' time at the 'ome o' the Earl o' Stonehurst."

Elliot scoffed. "That's all ye got to tell me?"

Jack grinned. "Gossip says 'e's got a ladybird, too."

"I could care less who the bastard ruts with!"

Jack's smile vanished. "Well, ye said ye wanted to know who 'e saw and where 'e went," he said indignantly. "Now do ye want to know or not?"

Elliot gestured for him to proceed.

Jack's smile reappeared, this time sly. "Just so 'appens I saw 'im the other night at Covent Garden—some easy pickin's that night, I must say—and I saw 'im with his ladybird." Jack scratched his head. "A beauty, all right. But 'twas odd to see one such as her with a gent like 'im, if ya know what I mean."

Elliot grew impatient. "Why?"

"'Cause the girl's a cripple, that's why! Limped like this." Jack gave an exaggerated mimic of her slow gait.

The bottle stopped halfway to Elliot's lips. Slowly he lowered it. Sweet Christ. It couldn't possibly be . . . or could it?

"This girl," he demanded. "Did ye get a look at her? What did she look like? How old was she?"

"Now 'ow would I know? But I did see 'er. Dressed to the nines, she was—small, with hair as black as midnight—just like I said, a beauty. And I 'eard someone say somethin' 'bout her eyes—the shade of violets, I think."

Elliot surged to his feet. Heather, he thought. *Heather.*

"Do ye know anything more about this girl?"

"Aye," Jack said smugly. "But it'll cost ye."

Elliot dug into his pockets and tossed him a coin. Jack held it up to the dingy light of the window, then shoved it deep in his breeches.

"Seems she's the ward o' the Earl o' Stonehurst. Doesn't come to London often, so they say, either of 'em. Live in Lancashire, they do."

Lancashire. Bloody hell, it was her. It had to be. For an instant a vile rage flamed in Elliot's veins, a rage so potent he shook with it. Had the brat spent all these years living in luxury?

Belatedly it struck him . . . she had been with Damien Tremayne. . . . A cunning smile spread slowly across his face. So the whining little brat was all grown-up, was she? Well, perhaps it was time the little bitch was of some use to him. . . .

First, he would see for himself if it was her.
And then . . . well, he wasn't certain. But he
would come up with something . . .

Only this time—this time he would be more
careful than he'd been with Giles Tremayne.

Were it not for the fact that Heather had told
Mama she would relay her message to Sophie,
she might well have lost her nerve and decided
not to attend Sophie's ball. But Sophie was
Mama's dearest friend in all the world, and she
would not disappoint her.

The ball was in full swing when Heather
arrived that evening. Panic raced up her spine as
she entered the home of the Viscount and Viscountess Wyburn. Could she do this alone? Society could be cruel. When she was with Mama
and Papa, those she encountered were charming
and polite, for no one would dare risk the wrath
of the Earl of Stonehurst. But this was different.
There was every chance she would be cut cold,
and she did not relish the prospect.

It was Sophie who spotted her first. "Heather!"
she cried, giving a wave and rushing across the
salon. Sophie took her hand and stepped back.

"There, now. Let me look at you." Soft brown
eyes swept her up and down. "Oh, Heather, you
look smashing!" Her husband, Donald, had
joined them as well. "Doesn't she, Donald?"

The viscount gave Heather a low bow. "She
does indeed, my love."

Heather smiled her thanks. She wore a gown of
shimmering white satin, shot through with silver

threads. The hem of the full skirt was caught up here and there in embroidered bunches of pale lavender wildflowers. Once again, she felt half naked, for the gown exposed a considerable amount of decolletage. Her sable tresses were caught up in a loose topknot on her crown.

"Excuse me, ladies," said the viscount, "but I see Jeremy Wyndham craves a word with me."

Sophie turned to Heather. "Are Miles and Victoria on their way?"

Heather shook her head and quickly explained about the accident at Lyndermere. "A pity," Sophie said, guiding her to the side of the ballroom. "But I'm so glad you came, Heather." She cast a quick glance in either direction to make certain no one was listening. "I was afraid that silly column in this morning's *Gazette* might keep you away." Sophie's eyes flashed angrily. "I confess, I saw red. Why, I was nearly your age when I wed. Everyone said I was on the shelf, but as you can see, they were wrong. And you should have seen the scandal when Victoria wed Miles. The gossips were hopping for weeks!"

She squeezed Heather's shoulder. "I do run on at times, don't I? All I mean to say is this, Heather—don't let it trouble you, for no doubt tomorrow tongues will be wagging about someone else."

Paige joined them, and the conversation turned elsewhere. Eventually she and Paige moved into the ballroom to sit. It was then that Heather spotted Damien. Her heart vaulted. He looked stunning, dressed all in black except for the dazzling white of his shirt. He spoke briefly with Donald. When Donald departed, the scope of his gaze encompassed the guests.

Their eyes locked. The contact lasted but an instant; then he turned away to talk to a group of gentlemen.

For one awful moment Heather experienced the sheer, stark pain of rejection. Yet she knew in her heart it was better this way; after the article in the *Gazette*, the less talk about the two of them, the better.

Paige hadn't noticed Damien's presence. But others had, and already Heather could see heads bending. Turning. The flutter of fans. The hiss of whispers . . . a feeling of deja vu poured over her. It was just like it had been last evening at the opera. Only Damien wasn't there to bolster her courage.

Beside her, Paige said brightly, "Oh, look. Sophie's signaled the orchestra to start the dancing."

Dimly she heard the strains of a waltz. As yet no one had moved to the dance floor. It was then she noticed that Damien had disengaged himself from the group of gentlemen. But a lovely blonde had snared his arm. His head was bowed low; it almost appeared as if hers lay nestled on his shoulder. The blonde darted a coy glance at Heather. A smile curved those crimson red lips—oh, a smile of sweet malice!

Heather tore her gaze away. There was a devastating wedge of tightness trapped in her chest. She had no claim over him, she reminded herself. Yet neither did she have the stomach to watch him with another woman. Should she leave? The bend of her mind so inclined, she got to her feet.

Beside her, Paige tugged at her sleeve. "Heather," she whispered.

Heather was busy reaching for her cane.

"Heather!" Paige spoke more loudly. She twined her fingers in one wide satin sleeve and tugged hard. Finally Heather took notice. She glanced down at Paige, who was nodding almost frantically toward the dance floor.

Puzzled, Heather turned slightly to see what she was about.

Damien stood there, in the center of the ballroom floor.

In some distant corner of her mind she knew the guests had gone utterly quiet. It was as if the entire world held its breath. Every eye in the ballroom was turned upon him . . . upon her.

But Damien . . . his gaze spoke to her alone.

Never in all her days would she forget his expression. It was a look that made her melt inside—a look that made the ground move beneath her feet.

And then he did something she never would have expected. Indeed, the last thing on earth she expected . . .

He held out his hand.

Twenty

The world spun crazily. Heather felt she would surely faint. He couldn't possibly want her to . . . to dance with him.

But the hold of his eyes was utterly commanding. Utterly irresistible.

She never even noticed that Paige had slipped her cane from her grasp.

Not ten steps separated them. . . . Swallowing, certain that her heart was lodged permanently in her throat, she felt herself begin to move.

He met her halfway.

Still, Heather was overwhelmingly conscious that they had captured the scrutiny of everyone present. At the very last moment, her strength seemed to desert her. She swayed.

Strong fingers closed around hers, warm and reassuring. A hard arm swept her close.

Her fingers fluttered on the broad sweep of his shoulder. "This is . . . absurd," she said weakly.

No, he nearly said. *This is love.*

Even the orchestra had been held spellbound. At a signal from Sophie, they began to play.

Damien arched a brow. "Shall we?" he murmured.

It all came back in a flash. Her feet began to move. Damien's voice echoed in her mind. *One, two, three. Tiny, tiny steps.*

By then Sophie had snagged her husband and tugged him onto the floor. The smile she sent Heather was blindingly triumphant. One by one, other couples drifted onto the floor.

The tension that had nearly sapped her courage was suddenly gone.

"You're doing splendidly," he murmured in her ear.

"Ah, but I had an excellent teacher." Her smile was dazzling.

His was quite wicked. "Oh, but it's not quite the same as before, is it? As I recall, we were slightly less . . . encumbered."

The remembrance of how they'd danced naked in her room flooded her. Two bright spots of color stained her cheeks, but her laugh was breathless. "We were, weren't we?"

His arm tightened. He bent his head so that his mouth brushed her ear. Tiny shivers played over her skin. "Do you have any idea what I'd like to do to you, Miss Heather Duval?"

The huskiness in his voice made her feel beautiful and feminine, and it was a whole new feeling for her.

"Perhaps you'd like to tell me." Her own daring was shocking—but delightfully so.

He kissed the side of her neck. "Oh, I'll do

much better than that," he said solemnly. "I'll show you." It was a promise, one he intended to fulfill to his most fervent, wanton desire . . . as well as hers.

As if on cue, the music ended. He pulled her hand into the crook of his arm. "Now, I would very much like to leave this place. I predict the gossips will have a feeding frenzy tomorrow, but I don't care a whit."

Heather turned shining eyes to his. "Nor do I."

Good-byes to Sophie and Paige were quickly made. Within minutes they were heading outside toward Damien's carriage. Heather's heart was singing, and her feet felt light as air.

In the carriage, she sat next to him, her head tipped against his shoulder. Where they were going, she had no idea. Nor did she care. A sense of calm inevitability had come over her. They were together, and that was all that mattered.

It wasn't long before the carriage drew to a halt. Heather stirred, raising a hand to push aside the velvet curtains. They'd stopped before a brick-fronted mansion with tall windows.

She glanced over at Damien. He watched her closely. "Where are we?" she asked.

"My home." He opened the door and leaped lightly to the ground, then turned and held out his hand. "Don't worry," he said when she hesitated. "No one will know. My staff is very discreet."

Heather placed her hand in his. "I am hardly a model of propriety for Bea, am I?" she murmured with a faint smile.

A short, balding butler admitted them.

"Thank you, William," said Damien. "That will be all for the night." The butler bowed and retreated.

Heather's fingers were still laced tightly within his. She relied more on his touch than on sight as he pulled her through the shadows. She caught a glimpse of a magnificent staircase that split in either direction at the landing; then they passed through a set of double doors into a ballroom with a high, arched ceiling. Delicate scrollwork and dainty rosettes decorated the walls. The sweet scent of roses perfumed the air. An array of candles placed around the perimeter of the room spilled its golden aura all around. In the center of the floor were a round, lace-covered table and two gilt-trimmed chairs. There was fruit, a bottle of wine, and two crystal glasses.

Heather caught her breath. He'd planned this. He'd planned all along to bring her here. She felt suddenly giddy. Reckless. Dangerous. What else would the night bring? she wondered.

She couldn't wait to find out.

Her gaze returned to Damien, only to find his regard hadn't wavered.

A hint of a smile curled his lips. "I thought we'd have a celebration of our own. Do you mind?"

She shook her head. She felt strangely shy, yet awash with anticipation, too.

He poured the wine and extended a glass to her. "Are you hungry?"

Their fingers brushed as she took it. Current seemed to leap from the place where their skin met. *Yes*, she thought yearningly. *For you.*

She sipped the wine and nibbled on the grapes, then reached for a plump, ripe strawberry. On the last bite, juice dribbled down her chin as she bit into it. With the tip of her finger, she swiped at it, intending to bring the sweet liquid to her lips to lick it away. But at the last instant, Damien reached out and snared her wrist.

Questioning violet eyes met his.

"Let me," he said. His eyes never leaving hers, he brought her fingertip to his mouth. He sucked gently, the tip of his tongue rough and wet. Everything inside her went weak. If she'd been standing, she'd surely have fallen into an igno-minious heap.

"Thank you," she whispered.

The waver of the candlelight cast intriguing shadows over the planes and hollows of his face. His tone was very grave. "You're quite wel-come."

Standing, he pulled her to her feet and drew her into his arms. He smiled down into her startled features. "It wouldn't be a ball without dancing."

"But . . . we've already done so."

"Ah, but we had an audience then. I much prefer it this way."

He whirled her around in a tiny circle, just as before. Then all at once his arms came hard around her back. He lifted her full off the ground and spun her around and around in circles until she was dizzy and breathless and laughing, the sound chiming in the air like bells on a warm spring morn. She braced her fingertips against his forearms, her head cast back, the long arch of her neck graceful and white and fragile. When at last he came to a whirling halt, she was still laughing.

He was not.

Her heart seemed to stop. Her laughter snagged in her throat. His expression was fierce and intent, almost hungry.

He let her slide down his body; for one heart-stopping instant, their hips were bound together. There was a stab of heat low in her middle. Even through the silk of her skirts, she could feel the aroused thickness of his manhood hard against her belly.

Time swung away.

The world narrowed into that one moment. His gaze seemed to possess her, reaching clear inside her very soul.

Then, with a muffled exclamation, he swung her up and into his arms.

Heather's heart was beating so hard it threatened to choke her. Her breath tumbled out in a shaky rush. "Where are you taking me?"

There was a heated rush of silence. "To bed," he said softly. "Any objections?"

A smile flirted at the corner of her mouth. "Just one," she ventured.

He hiked a brow.

She linked her fingers behind his nape. "*Hurry.*"

Her fervent whisper nearly snapped his control. His arms almost crushed her. His head descended. He sealed their lips in a fiery kiss.

Their tongues danced together in an unbridled duel where each was the victor. They were both gasping when at last he dragged his mouth away.

With an odd little laugh he lowered her. The tips of her slippers grazed the floor. "To the devil with bed." Warm breath raced past her ear. "I don't think I can wait that long."

His fingers were in her hair. In seconds it tumbled down her back. Lean hands cupped her shoulders. Heather felt her dress slide down her torso, slipping past her hips. Her chemise met the same fate. Soon she was naked.

Eyes like silver flames pored over her nakedness. Though he'd said he couldn't wait, his regard was slow and thorough, a languid exploration that left no part of her untouched. Beneath the heat in his gaze, her nipples grew tight and tingly. His gaze lingered long and hard at the dark thicket at the base of her thighs; a restless questing began to pulse in that secret place hidden deep inside.

An arm hard about her back, he drew her to him. She shivered with delight when, with his thumbs, he traced slow, maddening circles around her breasts. At last he flicked her nipples; they sprang taut and hard, yet still it wasn't enough. She wanted the hot, wet suction of his mouth there on those quivering peaks.

She gave a cry of frustrated yearning. "Damien!"

He kissed the baby-soft skin behind her ear. "What is it, sweet?"

She felt like pounding her fists against his chest. "I—I thought you had no patience!"

He smiled against her lips. "I suddenly find I'm blessed with an abundance of it."

This time she did pound her fists against his chest. "Damien, please!"

In answer he lowered himself to his knees.

He filled his hands with the jutting bounty of her breasts. With his tongue he grazed the pouting tip of one breast. She cried out, a sharp sound of ecstasy. He made a low sound deep in his throat and tugged first one deep, straining circle into his mouth, then the other, leaving her nipples glistening and damp with the warmth of his tongue, his play a divine rapture.

But there was more.

His knuckles grazed the hollow of her belly. He trailed a line of scorching fire clear to the place that guarded her womanhood. Lean fingers slowly unfurled, tangling in thick, dark fleece.

His mouth traced the same shattering pathway.

With his hands he parted slender white thighs. With his thumbs he opened soft, pink folds.

Heather's eyes were wide and dazed. His intent ripped through her brain. No, she thought fuzzily. Oh, no . . .

His breath wafted across the tender bud bared within . . . and then she felt the seductive sweep of his tongue.

A jolt of wanton sensation tore through her. Even as her mind rebelled, her body welcomed him. A quickening heat stormed all through her. She clutched at him, lest she tumble to the floor.

His tongue was a brazen, relentless invader, a dart of sheer flame, dauntless in its quest, ceaseless in its pursuit. With torrid, lashing strokes, he plied pink, weeping flesh, the tiny kernel of flesh hidden in her cleft. Her fingers coiled in his hair. She arched against him, desperate for that elusive torment. Then at last she found it. Her limbs trembled, her body twisted as ecstasy exploded inside her. Piercing cries of bliss burst from her throat.

Damien caught her as she sank to the floor. He eased her down against the silken pile of her clothing. He disrobed quickly, pulling his clothing from his body. A crimson haze of passion surrounded him. His body was ablaze, his shaft pounding.

Heather's eyes, smoky and dazed, drifted open as he eased down beside her. Triumph surged in his breast, for he knew he'd just given her the ultimate pleasure. He kissed her, his mouth wide, tasting anew her essence on his lips.

He exalted in the way her arms crept round his neck, the way she pressed her lithe young body against the heat and hardness of his. Only now it appeared that the tables had turned . . .

And indeed, a reckless abandon washed through Heather. With the pressure of her palm against the heavy satin of his shoulder, she eased him back so that she lay poised above him. The temptation to explore his body as he had explored hers was irresistible. She longed to return the splendor he evoked in her—longed to return it in full measure.

Her fingers slid over the smoothness of his shoulders, thrilling to the sleekness of his skin, loving the tight play of muscle beneath. One small hand coasted down his chest, combing through the wiry mat of hair. Her knuckles skimmed the taut drum of his belly, an exploration that came ever closer to the part of him that held such fascination. His manhood surged, as if to seek her touch.

Heather stared in mingled amazement and admiration. Their outrageous conversation of the night before flooded back.

Her heart was in her throat. "Damien," she whispered, "is there truly a difference? Are some men . . . larger than others?"

Damien half laughed, half groaned. His rod swelled still further, lengthening yet another inch.

Heather was in awe. "Oh, my," she said faintly. "I cannot imagine that anyone would be larger than—than you."

Her innocent words aroused him almost past bearing. "Touch me," he said raggedly. He caught at her hand and dragged it down to that part of him she so inflamed, filling her palm, guiding cool fingers around his burning member. She needed no further urging.

And it seemed he'd taught her well.

The rhythm of her strokes brought him to the brink of rapture. He gasped with pleasure, struggling against the need to turn her over and plunge hot and hard in the damp silken prison of her flesh.

Nor was she finished.

A hand on his chest, she pushed herself upward. He'd thought her beautiful before, but she was exquisite. Slight, but with delectably full breasts tipped with rose-hued nipples that were as sweet as they looked. Her hips flared out from a waist that was incredibly narrow. For one soul-stopping moment, she was poised above him, slender hands resting on her thighs.

The merest glimmer of a smile curved her lips. Slowly she bent forward. Her hair feathered over his thighs, the grid of his belly. Damien's breath dammed in his chest. Dear God, surely she would not . . .

With the tip of her tongue, she touched him.

His heart slammed to a halt.

His hands twisted into the silk of her gown. He gritted his teeth against a pleasure so intense it bordered on pain. She played him like a master, swirling and dipping, the soft suction of her mouth an exquisite torture he wanted never to end. He bore it with his head cast back, features taut and strained, his breath whistling through his teeth.

"Heather," he said thickly, and then again: "*Heather.*"

He could stand no more. In one swift move he dragged her to his chest. Then she felt the sweep of powerful arms around her. In a surge of power he stood upright. Two steps took him to one of the velvet chairs. He sat, strong hands clamped around her buttocks. Heather blinked, for she was sitting atop him; her thighs imprisoned his.

For one mind-splitting instant, his eyes flicked open. His stare sheared directly into hers, silver and hot. Deep within the fiercely glowing depths of his eyes was a burning demand she didn't fully comprehend.

She gaped down at him. Her hands fluttered on his shoulders. The muscles of his arms were knotted and bulging. She could feel him huge and stiff against her cove of damp, feminine flesh. She drew a deep, shuddering breath. "Damien—"

"Hush, sweet. Hush."

His fingers delved through damp, dark curls. With his fingers he spread her wide. He lifted her, bringing her down at the same instant he plunged upward.

She clutched at his arms, filled with the rigid thickness of his rod.

"Take me, Heather. Take me." It was a hoarse, ragged whisper.

Her eyes half closed. A heady sense of power caught her in its tide. She discovered that with the tensing of her thighs, the sway of her hips, the rise and fall of her loins, she controlled the tempo of their loving.

Her lips parted breathlessly. She began to pant and churn. The sensations bombarding her were incredible. His fingers dug into the soft skin of her hips. Damien groaned. He lunged almost wildly. Stretching. Driving. Seeking.

Her nails dug into the knotted hardness of his shoulders. Each thrust pushed them closer to the edge. A scaling pleasure carried them higher, ever higher. Then at last it came. Her body convulsed around his. Spasms of release carried her to the heavens and beyond. His seed spilled hot and thick and molten at the gate of her womb.

They drifted slowly down to earth. When his

breathing had slowed, Damien carried her to his bed, slipping in beside her and drawing the covers over them both.

Heather pillowed her head against the hollow of his shoulder. But all at once she shivered.

"What is it, Heather? What's wrong?" Concern etched his brow. One hand between the span of her shoulder blades, he waited.

Her voice came haltingly. "I was just thinking—about the jewel case."

The tension that invaded him was palpable; she could feel it in every muscle of his body. When he finally spoke, his tone was guarded. "What of it?"

"We've never spoken of this, Damien . . . but I would know. Why were you so convinced it was your mother's jewel case?"

He hesitated. Sitting up, he ran his fingers through his hair. He was clearly torn. Heather sat up as well, drawing the sheet up over her bare breasts.

His hands settled on either side of her arms. "Heather," he said quietly, "I want nothing to ruin this night. But I must be honest. The jewel case is the same. I know it belonged to my mother."

Heather opened her mouth. His fingers against her lips, he stifled her protest. "I know you doubt me, but in my heart, I know I am right. I admit, it's been many, many years since I last saw it—I was just a boy then. But the memory of that jewel case is one that will stand out in my mind forever. My parents loved each other very much,

Heather—it's much the same with yours. One can not only see it, one can *feel* it."

Heather's gaze was steady on his face. "Go on," she murmured.

"The jewel case was a present to my mother from my father; it was her most treasured possession. I don't know why, but I was already fascinated with it. I used to sneak into her room to look at it, for I knew I would never be allowed to play with it. But one day, I decided I didn't care. I climbed up onto her dressing table and opened it. But I was fearful I would be caught, and I was not careful. I broke one of the hinges, and just as it happened, my mother walked in. I knew what I'd done, and though she did not chastise me for breaking it, tears sprang to her eyes, tears she thought I didn't see. I had made my mother cry, and I felt guilty for days afterward."

"What happened then?"

"My father took the jewel case to London to be repaired. It was then that he died. I'd forgotten until I saw it again, but I don't remember seeing it after the day he left for London."

"So it wasn't among his possessions when he died?"

"I cannot say for certain. I only know that I never saw it again."

An odd tingle sped down Heather's spine. "How did your father die?"

"A sudden illness took him during his trip to London. He never returned to our home in Yorkshire."

"Is it possible the jewel case was returned to

your mother and you simply never saw it? Perhaps she hid it away because the memories it evoked were simply too painful."

"That's possible," he admitted.

"But it doesn't explain how my mother came to have it." Heather's voice was very low.

Damien said nothing. He sensed her anguish—she didn't want to believe her mother was a thief. Indeed, he had no proof.

"It's possible my mother sold it, and I simply wasn't aware of it," he said. "Perhaps that's how Justine came by it."

"Perhaps," she said slowly. "It's just so—so bizarre that you came to Lockhaven to find my father. And instead you found your mother's jewel case." She shook her head. "It's so strange," she said again. "And I can't help but wonder if it's somehow connected with—with my father."

Damien maintained his silence. The very same notion had occurred to him as well.

"I brought it with me from Lockhaven, you know. You should have it," she said suddenly.

He was startled. "The jewel case?"

"Yes. I can return it tonight, if you'd like—"

He cut her off. "Heather, that's not necessary."

"But it was your mother's. And now it's yours—"

"And what would I do with it?" He took both hands within his own. "Heather, it's belonged to you for years. I want you to have it."

"But I don't feel right keeping it! Besides, it—it's not the same."

She couldn't quite keep the hurt from her voice. He understood in a flash. A finger beneath her chin, he guided her eyes to his.

"It's always been precious to you, hasn't it?"

She nodded.

"Then let me do this. It's my gift to you, Heather. Do you hear? I give it to you here and now, and I pray it will remain just as precious—but for a different reason."

He was right, she realized. He, too, had lost his mother. And she had always treasured the jewel case because it had belonged to her mother. But now—now she would treasure it because it had belonged to *his* mother. . . .

But in the very next instant, her despair ripened anew.

Her tongue came out to moisten her lips. Her words were not what he expected. "What will you do when this is all over?"

"You mean when I find James Elliot?"

She nodded. Her eyes clung to his. "Will you return to America? To Bayberry?" He'd told her of his home the day they'd spent together at the lake. "Or will you stay in England?"

He expelled a long sigh. "I don't know," he said finally. "To be honest, I really haven't given it much thought."

Without warning a tear slipped from the corner of her eye. He stared. "Heather, I told you I will do nothing without—"

"It's not that." She gave a choked little cry.

Exasperated, he was at a loss to explain her tears. "What, then?"

Her gaze nearly slipped. She swallowed bravely. "Damien," she said softly, "I'm going to have your baby."

Twenty-one

He went deadly still. She almost thought he hadn't heard, but then she felt the tension that invaded him.

"Dear God," he said in an odd, strangled voice. His gaze slid down to her belly, as if to test for himself the truth of her words. In that mind-splitting instant when his eyes returned to hers, she glimpsed in his a horrified shock he couldn't hide.

The world was a watery blur. Heather forced back the hollow ache gathering in her breast. "I knew it!" she cried. "I knew I shouldn't tell you. But I thought . . . I wanted no more lies between us!"

She tried to wrench back, but he snared her wrists in an iron hold. "Heather, no! It's not what you think."

"Of course it is." Her voice betrayed a scathing denunciation. "It's one thing to bed the daughter of your brother's murderer. It's quite another for her to be carrying your child."

His jaw snapped shut. "That's not it and you know it."

"Do I?" A strange cold note crept into her voice. "And how would I know it, Damien?"

Damien bit back an oath. This was his fault. He knew it. He'd just never expected it . . . another mistake, he realized grimly. But before he could say a word, there was a knock on the door.

"My lord!" called a voice. "Cameron Lindsey requests your presence below stairs."

He gave an impatient exclamation. "Not now, William."

"My lord, he says he has news you are anxiously awaiting."

Damien surged upright and threw on a dressing gown. "Stay here," he ordered curtly. "We'll continue this discussion when I return."

But Heather had no intention of standing idly by and waiting. He'd made his feelings about her condition quite clear. What need was there to wait? The door had no sooner closed than she slipped from the bed.

Her clothing was still in the ballroom. Wrapping a sheet around herself, she found her way downstairs.

Below, in the study, Cameron was on his feet as soon as Damien strode in. His dispatch was brief and direct.

"He knows you're here."

Damien stopped short. "Elliot knows? Elliot knows I'm in London?"

"Yes. He's been asking questions about the younger brother of Giles Tremayne."

Damien couldn't hide his mounting excitement. "Yes. *Yes!*"

"Indeed, my lord. Apparently he learned the two of you were at Covent Garden the other evening. It seems he was"—Cameron laughed softly—"quite interested in this news. The streets have been abuzz with questions about you—and her. I must say, your being seen with her at Covent Garden does seem to have done the trick. I knew it would."

Damien seized Cameron by the shoulders. "It's finally coming to pass. Cameron, he'll soon be mine, and this will all be over!"

Neither knew that a figure had paused just outside the door, which was slightly ajar.

Before long Damien saw Cameron to the front door. A smile of satisfaction rimming his lips, he turned, only to find his way barred.

"You bastard," she said feelingly.

His gaze ran over her. Her hair tumbled over her shoulders and down her back. Her ball gown was hastily donned; it hung crookedly from one bare shoulder.

The pure violet of her eyes was the only color in her face. Her skin was chalk white.

"Heather. Heather, for God's sake—" He started to reach for her.

She eluded his touch as if he carried the plague.

"Do not pretend such concern! I know better now, Lord Deverell." His name was a blistering curse. "Your concern is naught but a ruse."

Damien was stunned. "Heather! Why are you so angry? That was Cameron Lindsey, my investigator, with word of James Elliot."

She faced him unflinchingly. "So I gathered," she said tightly. "You must be very happy he's aware of your presence."

"Yes," he said. His regard was unwavering. "And I thought you would be as well."

"Oh, I am, my lord. I am."

"Then what is wrong? Why are you so incensed? I apologize for leaving you the way I did—"

"It's not that!"

He was genuinely puzzled. "What, then?"

She was suddenly so angry she was shaking with it. Her lips curled. " 'I must say,' " she quoted, " 'your being seen with her at Covent Garden does seem to have done the trick.' "

Now it was Damien's turn to pale. "You heard."

"Oh, aye." Her tone was falsely hearty. "I heard!"

He inhaled, searching for the right words, praying he could find them. "You put a meaning to those words that is not there, Heather—that only you see. I swear, it's not what you think."

A suffocating heaviness knotted in her breast. Tears scalded the back of her throat. She blinked them back. If only she could believe him—if only she dared! The anguish inside her nearly sapped her strength, but she maintained her composure through a sheer effort of will.

"You use words to advantage, Damien. I—I

know it well. You used *me* to advantage. But the fact remains; you deceived me—twice now. You used me to find my father. You used me when you came to Lockhaven."

A dull flush crept beneath his cheekbones. "That was different, Heather. Everything has changed—"

"Nothing has changed, nothing! That—that stupid dance at Sophie's, for all to watch! I—I was moved to the marrow of my bones. I thought it so tender, so very romantic!"

She dashed away the tears that rose unbidden. "But I know now it was just a—a calculated move. You only wanted the gossips to take note, that all London would be filled with talk about the two of us, that *he* might hear. God, but I was a fool to think it was me you cared about!"

"I do care. Heather, I do. I will not lie— Cameron *did* want me to use you to lure your father out from hiding. I refused. Indeed, I meant to keep my distance until later . . . but then I saw you—Heather, you were so beautiful! And suddenly I didn't care who saw. I didn't care about anything but holding you in my arms and giving you something I knew you'd always wanted. Heather, you have to believe me!" With his eyes, he implored her. With his hand, he reached for her.

She slapped it away. Did he truly believe she was such a fool? This time she'd not be misled so easily. "You're a liar," she accused flatly. "You've lied to me all along."

"Not this time, Heather, I swear—"

"Please summon the carriage." She had gathered her skirts in hand—along with an icy dignity. "I would like to go home."

Damien battled a bitter frustration. As he stared at her, it was almost as if he could see her retreating, drifting further and further away. And all at once the distance between them was immense.

She wouldn't listen. She wouldn't even look at him. She'd closed her ears to him . . . and her heart as well.

The cast of his jaw rigid, he did as she requested and summoned the carriage. His posture was wooden as he watched the carriage clatter into the darkness.

Damien slept little that night. The taste of self-disgust was like dust in his mouth. Heather's stricken little cry tore at his insides. *God, but I was a fool to think it was me you cared about*! She had been shattered. Her lips were tremulous; he could see that it took all her strength not to break down. He knew it, and he hated himself for putting that look on her face. He considered going to her, trying to convince her once more of the truth. His mouth twisted. Yet why should she believe him, for indeed the evidence was damning.

Then there was the babe. He'd never considered she might be with child, and in that he'd blundered rather badly. He'd known that in time he would marry and have children. In truth, he'd never married not because of a disdain for the institution, but because he'd never found a wom-

an with whom he longed to spend the rest of his
life . . .

Never until now.

He loved her. He loved the way her hair lay
over her shoulder like the wings of a raven, dark
and sleek. He loved the way her lovely mouth
pursed while she pondered deep and hard, lost in
thought. Her beauty, her inner strength. The way
those deep violet eyes lit up with the warmth of a
thousand suns when she laughed. She possessed
a warmth and a gentleness of spirit that made her
sparkle like the finest jewel. She was so
beautiful . . . and she didn't even know it. For
still she had so little faith in herself as a
woman . . .

Even less in him.

But he liked the idea of his babe curled deep in
Heather's womb. He liked the idea of sharing his
home—his life—with the raven-haired beauty
who captured his every waking thought. And
now she carried his child . . . *his child.* He was
filled with a wondrous elation, even as he was
filled with the bleakest of despair. For he had the
awful feeling that if Heather had anything to say
about it, he would be a father long before he was
a husband.

Indeed, where he was concerned, it seemed
fate would take a turn even more cruel. William
brought the *Gazette* along with his morning
meal. He scowled as he read the fine print:

Miss Heather Duval was seen yet again in the
company of the Earl of Deverell. Before an
astonished crowd, he whisked the young miss

onto the ballroom floor. Indeed, it appeared as
if the earl had eyes for no other. A dalliance?
we wonder, yet again. Perhaps not.

With a blatantly obscene expletive, he hurled
the paper to the floor.

He allowed a day for her temper to cool, and
then he went to her the next evening.

Nelson shuffled toward the back of the house.
He reappeared a few minutes later. "My lord,"
he said sheepishly, clearing his throat, "I fear
Miss Heather will not see you."

Damien was not surprised. "Thank you for
passing on her message, Nelson," he said to the
stoop-shouldered butler. Bold as you please, he
stepped inside and closed the door himself.

Nelson's mouth opened and closed. He was
clearly in a quandary.

Damien glanced down the long hallway. He
clapped the old man on the shoulder and lowered
his voice. "You've not betrayed her, Nelson," he
murmured. "But I wonder . . . could she be in
the garden?"

Relief flashed in the old man's faded blue eyes.
He nodded.

He found her sitting on an old stone bench
near a small gurgling fountain. She was staring
out across the maze of flowers, her profile solemn
and unsmiling, stark and lonely. Her hands were
linked together in her lap. The thought vaulted
through his mind that her heart was as empty as
his arms. . . . So intent was she in her musings
that she didn't hear his approach.

He stopped. "Heather," he said quietly.

She looked up. Her gaze scraped over him. "Who let you in?" she demanded.

He smiled thinly. "I happen to be on excellent terms with the servants."

She glared her displeasure. "Well, you may charm them but you won't charm me. You may as well leave. I have nothing to say to you."

He shrugged. "No matter," he said lightly. "But I have quite a lot to say to you."

Digging her cane into the dirt, she pushed herself upright . . . straight into his arms.

Deliberately she turned her face aside. "Please remove your hands from my person."

His smile was frugal. "So prim. So proper. But I think not, love."

Love. Heather wanted to slap him for daring to say that to her. But his hands on her waist were disturbingly warm. As always, the power of his presence was a potent force. She fought against it and rallied.

"We didn't finish our discussion last night," he went on. "There's a very important matter between us that needs to be settled."

Her chin climbed high. "There's nothing between us!"

"No?" His laughter held no mirth. "Now that's where you're wrong. There's *this* between us." His hand moved before she could stop him. He splayed his fingers wide across the hollow of her belly.

Heather gasped. She tried to push him away, but it was no use. He clamped her hips between his hands and brought her close, so close her slippered feet lay squarely between his booted feet.

"The way I see it, there's only one thing to be done. You'll have to marry me."

You'll have to marry me. The world teetered. All conscious thought fled her mind. For the space of a heartbeat, all she could do was gape numbly.

If only she could have remained numb . . . all at once pain descended, swift and merciless. She trembled in reaction, feeling as if she were bleeding inside.

Marriage to Damien . . . Her breath came raggedly. God in heaven, that was all she ever wanted. She hadn't known it until that moment. But there was a rending pain in her heart. He didn't speak of love . . . and little wonder, she thought bitterly.

He didn't love her. He would never love her—and the knowledge was like a knife slicing through to her soul. He felt obliged to marry her. He was a gentleman, and he would do the honorable thing.

Perhaps she should have respected him for it. But now she almost hated him for it.

Straightening her shoulders, she looked him full in the eye.

"I wouldn't marry you if you were the last man on earth."

But he was the *only* man for her. In the instant between one breath and the next, he'd seen it. She loved him. But she wouldn't admit it.

"And what about the babe?" If he was ruthless, he didn't care. "I would remind you this is my child you're carrying. Do you think I want no part in his upbringing?"

Her eyes blazed defiance. "This is *my* child. You made your feelings about this babe quite clear last night."

"I did no such thing. You left before we could discuss it."

"How generous of you, my lord. But there's no need to make such a"—she mocked him almost sweetly—"such a sacrifice."

"You're a fool if you think I'll let you go."

She scoffed openly. "What, my lord! Do you think I don't know where this offer comes from? No doubt you think I'm unfit to be the mother of your child. I am, after all, the daughter of a murderer. You think that because I—I'm lame that I cannot take care of a child."

He released her, only to cross his arms over his chest. He raised an arrogant brow. "Well, which is it, I ask? Are you unfit to be the mother of my child because you are lame? Or because you are the daughter of a murderer?"

He knew he mocked her most cruelly. Heather's spine was rigid. "You tell me," she stated levelly.

"Oh, I'll tell you, sweet. But I've no doubt you won't like what you hear. I think both are an excuse . . . an excuse to hide from yourself—and your feelings about me."

"My feelings? You delude yourself," she said flatly. "My feelings in no way resemble that of a wife toward her future husband."

"Indeed." His tone grew soft. "Your lips say

no, Heather. But your eyes . . . I see something else entirely in your eyes."

Heather quivered. Was she truly so transparent, then?

"You are a lovely, desirable woman, Heather. Yet you refuse to see it. . . ."

She wanted to believe him. She wanted to, so much it hurt inside. But there was so much to lose—*too* much.

"It's not wrong to want someone, Heather. To need someone. . . ."

But it was wrong to love him. Wrong to love someone who would never love her in return. . . .

He ran a finger down the fragile curve of her jaw. He smiled. She could see that he thought he'd won. His voice turned cajoling. "I'm not asking for an answer now—"

"Well, I'm giving you one. I will not marry you, Damien. I don't even want to see you again."

Those words hung between them endlessly.

He clenched his jaw tight. "But you want to find your father—you want to see James Elliot, don't you?"

She narrowed her eyes. The rogue! Would he blackmail her? "You know I do," she snapped.

His smile was a travesty. "Then I'm afraid you're simply going to have to tolerate me a while longer, Heather."

Heather glared at him as he proceeded to saunter away. By Jove, she thought furiously, he wouldn't get away with it. If necessary, she would hire her own investigator . . .

The thought progressed no further.

From out of nowhere came a loud popping sound. An acrid odor reached her nostrils, like something burning. She glanced down and saw the shoulder of her gown fluttering in the breeze. Her skin gleamed pale in the sunlight. There was a faint buzzing in her ears; it was growing louder. Her vision swam mistily. She blinked, reaching out a fingertip to touch a dark blotch on her outer arm.

It came away streaked with blood.

Twenty-two

Her stomach lurched. She didn't black out, though she thought she might. Her arm had begun to sting mightily. Blackness rimmed her vision. As if in slow motion, she felt herself turn. The next thing she knew she was hurtling through the air. She landed on her back with a dull thud. Her head cracked against the ground. A kaleidoscope of lights and colors danced behind her eyelids.

"Heather," a familiar masculine voice yelled into her ear. "Heather, are you all right?"

There was a massive weight atop her chest. Stunned, she found herself staring into Damien's grim-faced visage. The frantic fear on his face sent terror winging through her anew. "I've been shot," she said shakily. "Damien, I've been shot!"

His fingers were already tearing at her sleeve. "It looks like it's gone completely through, thank God," he muttered. "But it's bleeding like the devil." His face intent, he whipped out a hand-kerchief and tied it above the wound, so tightly she bit her lip to keep from crying out.

His eyes flashed up to hers. "I'm sorry, sweet," he muttered. "But the bleeding must be stopped."

Heather was trembling from head to toe. "Who would do this? Who?"

Damien scarcely heard. He wanted to leap up and search out the fiend, but he was afraid to leave her alone. His expression angrily intent, Damien scanned the endless maze of greenery. A vile curse hovered on his lips, for he could see no sign of the perpetrator. Before long, a bird began trilling a warbly tune. It was almost as if it had never happened.

But there was someone out there. Someone who waited . . . and watched. . . .

He gave no answer but lowered his mouth to her ear. "Be still," he warned, the words no more than a breath, "for I'll not risk making you a target again. We must wait here and stay low. When it's safe, we'll crawl back inside."

Heather nodded and ducked her head into his shoulder. Her fingers crept up to tangle in the front of his jacket. He was right. All they could do was wait.

A slow curl of smoke drifted lazily upward. From beneath the limbs of a drooping willow, ebony eyes watched . . . and waited.

He'd caught a glimpse of her as she'd left Tremayne's house last eve. Jack Scavenger had been right—it was her. There was no mistaking that rich wealth of hair or those wide, thick-lashed eyes. But James Elliot was not a man to see beauty . . . he saw only opportunity.

All these years he'd thought the brat was probably dead, yet she was alive and living a life of comfort and affluence with the Earl of Stonehurst. At first he'd been furious, for *he* had been rotting away in a filthy cell in Newgate. The very idea made his every muscle vibrate with rage.

But his inquiries about her had yielded a bounty he'd not expected. It seemed she'd never married. Little wonder, he snorted, for who would want a cripple such as she? He'd thought she still made her home with the earl, but indeed it was not so . . .

On the occasion of her twenty-first birthday, Stonehurst had gifted her with lands of her own—lands that, from all accounts, were worth a pretty penny indeed. . . .

The idea had come to him suddenly, in the dead of night. If he found the jewel case, so much the better. But if he didn't, he had something far better. A daughter . . . a daughter whose wealth far exceeded his wildest dreams.

Stonehurst had been generous with her. Per-haps it was time the little bitch was generous with her father. . . .

It had seemed so easy, so much easier than searching for that blasted jewel case. But now he'd failed, and he cursed roundly—he'd only wounded her. The stub of his thumb curled around the butt of the pistol. He slapped it against his palm. Why was it the bitch would not die? he raved. If only that bastard Tremayne hadn't shown up. . . .

His dark head came up in a flash. That was it! Perhaps this was a blessing after all. A crafty smile curled his lips. Perhaps this was not the right time for Heather to leave this earth. . . .

Aye, he thought. There was a better way . . . a way he could have both the jewel case *and* his daughter's wealth.

He threw back his head and chortled at his genius.

It wasn't long before darkness fell, and Heather and Damien were able to creep inside. In her room, he gently wiped away the blackened gunpowder and blood. A sigh of profound relief escaped as he examined her. Though the wound had bled profusely, it was not nearly as deep as he had feared. He cleansed it and sprinkled a healing powder over the reddened flesh, then bound it with strips of clean, white cloth.

A heavy cloak of silence hung in the room while he worked. But though his lips were quiet, his mind was not.

Who had done this? Who would try to kill her? The shot had not been meant for him—of that he was certain. He had left her alone when the shot rang out. . . .

All at once his blood ran cold.

A sickly coil of dread tightened deep within him. Dear God . . . Cameron had been right. James Elliot might very well come to Heather.

But not for the reason Cameron thought—not because he longed to reunite with the daughter he'd not seen in twenty years.

But because she was rich.

Self-loathing poured through him like boiling oil. This was his fault. He had involved her in his plan to locate James Elliot, and now her very life might well be at risk.

He prayed she would forgive him. That God would forgive him. Because if anything happened to her, he would never forgive himself.

So deep in thought was he that it gave him a start to see Heather's gaze fixed widely on his face. "What are you thinking?" she murmured.

He gave a terse shake of his head. "Nothing."

Her eyes were cloudy. "Damien, tell me. There have been too many lies already."

"Heather . . ." His soul was in turmoil. His hand hovered near her shoulder. He was unsure whether to touch her—whether she wanted him to.

He dropped his arm to his side. "I should never have come to Lockhaven," he said heavily. "I should never have involved you in this whole scheme to find my brother's murderer."

She made no response. Instead she searched his face as if to plumb the very depths of his being. "There's something you're not telling me."

His silence terrified her as nothing else. All at once a numbing cold seeped into her breast.

"Dear God," she said faintly. "You think it's he, don't you? You think my father . . ."

His silence declared his answer.

Heather's jaw didn't want to work properly. "But why? Why would he want to shoot me . . . his own daughter?"

"It's just a guess, Heather. Of course I can't be certain it was he—"

A shudder tore through her. "It is. I—I can feel it." She clutched at his sleeve. "But I—I don't understand why. What possible reason could he have for . . ." She stopped, unable to voice the thought aloud.

"A very good one," Damien said very quietly. "Money." When she frowned, he went on. "Miles told me once that Lockhaven was deeded solely to you."

Her eyes were huge on his face. "It is," she whispered.

"And what if James Elliot found out you have an estate in Lancashire—a very profitable estate?" He fell quiet for a moment. "He is your only living relative, Heather. With you gone, he could try to claim Lockhaven for himself."

Heather blanched. Unknowingly she flung out a hand. Damien captured it between his own; it was ice-cold.

"Listen to me, Heather." He turned her toward him. A finger beneath her chin, he demanded she look at him. "It's not safe here. I want you to come home with me tonight."

Heather nodded, too shaken to argue.

Several hours later she was installed in a guest room on the third floor of Damien's home. She waited for sleep to come, but the silence raked at her nerves. She lay there in the night-drenched stillness, her emotions a seething tangle inside her. So much had happened. The shock of Damien's proposal. Then the shot . . .

The sound of footsteps outside in the corridor made her jump.

The door opened. A sliver of light spread onto the carpet. Heather sat up. "Damien?" she whispered.

He came to stand near the bed. "Why aren't you asleep?"

She shrugged her shoulders, offering no other reply.

"Are you all right?" The mattress dipped as he sat.

Heather lowered her gaze. "I'm fine," she murmured.

"Does your arm pain you?"

"A little," she admitted.

An awkward silence drifted between them. Neither seemed to know what to say.

It was Heather who broke it. "I had a letter from Bridget today," she murmured.

"How is she?"

"Quite good, actually. She's begun working at the manor house again." For the first time that evening, the makings of a smile graced Heather's lips. "She's just discovered she's with child again."

Damien's brows shot up. "She and Robert didn't waste any time, did they?"

"That's what I thought," Heather admitted. "But I—I'm very glad for them. I only pray this babe is born fine and healthy."

The silence was renewed. Only then did Heather wish she'd kept Bridget's news to herself, for it was inevitable that they be reminded that she, too, expected a child. . . .

His hand lay very near hers on the counterpane, close to it, but not touching. Then, all at once, he reached for her; he began toying idly with her fingers.

"Why won't you marry me, Heather?"

The hurt in his tone was almost her undoing. Her heart cried out. Why? he asked. Because she couldn't allow herself to believe that his offer stemmed from anything more than guilt and responsibility over the fact that she carried his child. And now there was yet another reason.

"If I did, the threat from my father would be gone, wouldn't it? Lockhaven would not pass to him?"

He seemed reluctant to answer. "Lockhaven would become your husband's," he said finally. "But if that's why you think I want to marry you, you're mistaken. I've no need for land or wealth, Heather." His gaze burned into hers.

"I—I wasn't going to say that."

He sighed heavily. Heather lapsed into silence again. Lowering her head, she shielded her expression from him through the shining curtain of her hair.

He stopped playing with her fingers. "Would marriage to me be such a hardship?"

Her breasts rose and fell quickly with every breath. She wanted to cry that marriage to him would be no hardship at all . . . if only he loved her as she loved him. Madly. Passionately. Forever. She knew she could settle for no less.

Tearing her eyes from his, she shook her head.

Her control was perilous. She had the awful
sensation that if she said a word—if she looked
at him again—the tears would start and never
stop.

He weaved his fingers through hers and let
them rest against the hollow of her belly, there
where their child dwelled. The gesture moved
her as nothing else could have. But she was still
so afraid. . . .

The pitch of his voice was very low. "I'd be a
good husband, Heather. You'd want for nothing,
I swear. You—you should not be alone at such a
time." There was a note in his voice she'd never
before heard. "I'd be a good father. I'd love this
child, and any others we might have."

And what about me, she wanted to cry. Was it
selfish to want to be loved by him? Raw pain
stabbed in her breast. She didn't want the quiet
affection so many husbands had for their wives,
solely because they were the mothers of their
children. It wouldn't be enough . . . it would
never be enough.

She wanted to be loved for herself . . . all the
love he had to give . . . and more.

Yet his quiet intensity made her tremble inside. Slowly she raised her head. The silvery
trickle of moonlight through the draperies
etched his strong profile in an ethereal hue. She
ached with the need to reach out, to feel his
presence, trace the jutting blade of his nose, the
squareness of his jaw, the beautiful, masculine
shape of his mouth.

She spoke haltingly. "I don't know, Damien. I
need . . . time. Time to think on this . . ."

He withdrew his hand. In an instant he was on his feet. He gave her a low bow, his tone coldly formal. "I'll say good night, then."

He didn't offer to stay. She didn't ask. It was almost as if they were strangers.

She watched as he closed the door, stung by the oddest sensation that she'd wounded him. But such was not possible. He offered his honor and his name . . .

But never his heart.

A dry sob escaped her as she lay back on the pillow. Only then did she let loose the flood of tears dammed in her breast.

She saw little of Damien the next day. The maid who helped her with her morning bath relayed the message that the master had asked that she remain indoors today.

Heather was not inclined to argue. Her shoulder ached, and she was nervous and jittery. A cold shiver rushed through her whenever she thought of her close call the previous day. And there was a peculiar hum in the air, a sense of sizzling expectancy that she couldn't shake no matter how she tried.

It was midafternoon when she heard the front door open. Heather stood near the grand staircase. Her gaze swung around and fell upon Damien. He spared no greeting but beckoned her forward. Wordlessly she followed him into his study.

"I've just made arrangements for you to return to Lockhaven." He spoke the instant the doors were shut.

Heather's spine went stiff. "Indeed," she said coolly. "On whose authority, I wonder."

His mood was not easy. A storm already brewed in those clear gray eyes. "You're not the sort to throw tantrums," he said curtly. "I pray you won't start now." He began to pace back and forth.

But her temper was crackling. "And have I no choice in the matter?"

"Dammit, Heather, do not argue!" He spun around, looking as if he might explode. "It's too dangerous for you to remain in London. I want you out of harm's way."

"And what about what I want? I think this is a decision that belongs in my hands, not yours!" She tipped her chin up defiantly. "And I say I will stay in London."

His hands clamped down on her shoulders. "Do you forget so soon, Heather? You've another life inside you to think of."

Though she was secretly stung by the bite in his tone, there was a note of truth in what he said. She could take no chances with the life of her unborn child. Shoulders sagging, she nodded miserably.

He released her. "Normally I dislike traveling at night. But under the circumstances, I'll take no chances that Elliot might see you leaving here. The carriage will leave shortly before midnight."

The evening meal was strained and silent. Heather excused herself, then retired to her room to prepare for the trip. She had no means to fight the debilitating sense of loss that slipped over her, like a shroud of blackest night. Damien had given her so much, she realized helplessly. He had done what no other had done; he'd made her feel cherished and desired and beautiful.

And now she must leave him. She must leave him alone to face the unknown.

Alone to face her father.

Alone to face a murderer.

An ominous foreboding crept over her. She shivered, unable to shake it.

Damien was waiting in the entrance hall when she descended the stairs. She bowed her head low and evaded his gaze, and it took him but one look to discover why. Her cheeks were pale and streaked with tears.

He gave a muffled exclamation. "Heather! Heather, please do not do this!" With a groan he dragged her into his arms.

She clung to him shamelessly. "Don't make me go," she choked out. "Please do not make me!"

"Heather!" He stroked the shining cap of her hair, his hand not entirely steady. "Oh, love, don't you see, if anything happened to you, I'd never forgive myself. This will all be over soon. Please don't be afraid. You'll be all right, I promise."

She gave a dry, jagged sob. "It's not me I'm worried about. He killed your brother, Damien. What if he tries to kill you, too? I—I'm so afraid for you." She buried her face against his throat. "I—I love you," she cried. "Damien, I—I love you."

Damien went utterly still. His fingers caught at her chin. He raised her face to his, staring down

into misty depths of violet. Heather didn't flinch
from the intense probe of his eyes, and in that
mind-splitting instant, she bared her very soul to
him.

He whispered her name, a ragged sound, as if
he were in agony, and then he crushed her
against him. The emotion that rushed through
him almost brought him to his knees. *And I love
you.* The words burned on his tongue. In his
heart. But he was afraid that if he said the words
aloud, she wouldn't leave. And she was far too
precious for him to risk losing her. And so he
kissed her again and again, with fierce and shattering desperation, pouring into the fusion of
their mouths all he held deep in his heart.

They were both trembling when at last he
released her. Taking her hand, he led her outside,
where the coach waited. There he cradled her
face between his palms. He kissed her tenderly
one last time, then raised his head.

"I'll come for you." His whisper was low and
fervent. "Will you wait for me?"

She nodded, unable to speak for the tightness
in her throat. Somehow she managed a tremulous smile. He lifted her into the coach, then
closed the door.

The coach lurched forward. Heather leaned
back against the cushions, the hurt in her chest
almost unbearable.

He hadn't said he loved her. But there had
been something . . . was it enough? It had to be.
It had to be. Her hand came to rest on her belly.
She wanted their child to have both mother *and*

father. She must trust in him—trust that he was right, that this would soon be over.

Despite the frail tendril of hope that curled deep in her heart, scalding tears slipped down her cheeks. She dropped her forehead against the velvet-draped wall, feeling utterly drained.

But they hadn't gone far when the carriage swerved abruptly, then jolted to a halt. Heather heard shouts and then a thud. Panic leaped in her breast, bringing her to the edge of her seat.

The door snapped open. She glimpsed the dull glint of a pistol, and then claw-like fingers dug painfully into her arm, yanking her from her berth in the coach and whirling her around.

A shabbily dressed man confronted her, a man with hair as black as the night and eyes that gleamed like the very pits of hell. His grin was twisted and leering.

Her garbled scream died in her throat. Horror stripped her mind of all thought. She knew that face—knew it well indeed . . .

It was the man from her dream.

Twenty-three

Heather's throat was frozen. She made no outcry, but she went cold to the tips of her fingers.

A beefy hand shot out. Heather braced herself for a blow but held her ground. The blow never came. Instead, he gave a guttural laugh, for he'd seen her flinch. A grimy fingertip swiped at the dampness on her cheek.

He sneered. "You haven't changed a bit, have ye, missy? Still a sniveling little brat."

So this was her father. This was James Elliot. He was as evil as she remembered.

Her heart skipped a beat. It resumed with thick, uneven strokes. Inside she was terrified, but she was determined not to show it.

Bravely she raised her chin. "What do you want with me?"

Those black eyes rounded. "Such cultured speech! Think ye're better 'n me, eh, girl? Well, not for long." He dragged her toward a horse hobbled just behind him. It was then that Heather spied the driver. He lay sprawled facedown in the road. Heather gave a sharp cry and would have gone to him, but Elliot wrenched her back.

"He's not dead, missy, though when 'e wakes up, 'e'll probably wish 'e was." He cackled. "Better to worry 'bout yerself, lass."

Heather matched his bold stare. "It was you who tried to shoot me yesterday, wasn't it? Why? Why would you try to kill your own daughter?"

"Ye're worth more to me dead than alive, girlie. Ye see, I still 'ave some friends. And with the right piece in the right pocket, I found out me little girl has amassed quite a fortune." Black eyes gleamed. "I understand it's quite an estate ye have in Lancashire."

So Damien had been right. "And you thought it would be yours if I were dead?"

He smiled his assent. "And who else would it go to? I may not know as much as you, girlie, but I'm not a dimwit, either. I'm yer only blood relative."

Heather's lips tightened. "And who would believe you?" she scoffed. "Who would believe you were really my father after all these years?"

" 'Twouldn't be hard to lay my hands on yer birth record, missy, or that of my marriage to yer mother. Nor would it be hard to prove ye're the little cripple who was with 'er when she died, now would it?" He grinned his satisfaction.

Heather found herself seized by a reckless anger. "If you intend to kill me, just—just do it and be done with the deed!"

His eyes glinted. "You've your mother's feisty

spirit, don't ye, girl? But I've decided to be generous and let ye live a while longer," he drawled. "It occurred to me p'rhaps I was a bit hasty when I tried to snuff ye, girl. I always thought you were a useless little brat. But it appears I was wrong."

With that cryptic statement, he heaved her onto the back of the horse, then climbed on behind her. A cold knot of dread lay heavy in the pit of her belly. What did he mean? What did he want of her? With his arm anchored around her waist in a bone-crushing grip, she saw no chance for escape. When he turned the animal and headed back toward London, she was stunned. It wasn't long before he reined to a halt—in front of Damien's mansion.

She knew then . . . knew he was after Damien. Despair seized her like a clamp. "No," she cried. "No!"

"Yes, missy, yes!" His breath, fetid and hot, nearly made her gag. He wrested her from the horse's back and dragged her up the stairs. Bold as you please, he pounded on the brass knocker.

But it wasn't William who opened the door. It was Damien. At his side he held a pistol. His eyes ran over the tall, black-haired stranger on the doorstep.

"James Elliot, I presume?"

"At your service, sir." With a gusty laugh, Elliot jerked Heather out from behind him. He held her before him like a shield. His lips flattened in something that bore little resemblance to a smile. He nodded at Damien's pistol. "I'll just take that if ye don't mind, laddie. And then let's just take this cozy little reunion inside."

Damien's face was grim. He handed the pistol to Elliot, who shoved it in his breeches, then nudged Heather before him as Damien stepped aside.

The sound of the door closing was a hollow, empty sound. Once they were inside the entrance hall, Damien looked at Heather. "Are you all right, love?"

Heather's eyes clung to his. His expression was grim—so very grim. She started to speak, to assure him that she was fine, but Elliot twisted her arm behind her back so cruelly she gasped. Then he flung her to the floor.

When Damien would have gone to her, Elliot swung the pistol up level with his chest. "Stay where you are, laddie!" He leered at Heather as she pushed herself awkwardly to her feet.

"What's wrong, lame little cripple? But I suppose I should have a look at ye, proper-like." He walked round her, then stopped. With the barrel of the pistol, he prodded her right leg through her skirts.

Damien clenched his fists. "You did that to her, didn't you?"

"That I did. Took a poker and smashed her kneecap." Elliot seemed almost proud. "Always cryin', she was. Always stickin' her nose in where she didn't belong." His smile was nasty. "Pity it never healed right, ain't it? But it kept ye from pokin' round where ye shouldn't, at least for a time."

Rage seared Damien's veins. To think that a man could be so cruel to his own daughter . . .

He clenched his fists. "It's me you want," he said to Elliot. "Let her go."

"What! Already? Oh, I think not, laddie. I think not." His laugh was malicious. "Ye know, ye weren't so smart as ye thought, boy. I knew ye'd taken a fancy to my girl, here, and I thought ye might send 'er on 'er way. All I had to do was watch. . . . But I suspect ye'll see things my way as long as she's 'ere. Besides, all these years I thought she died along with 'er mother. Seems only right we should 'ave some time together, eh?"

Heather wet her lips. "Why did she leave you?" she asked. "Why did my mother leave you? And who was the man with her?"

Elliot's grin vanished. "How the blazes should I know? Most likely 'e was 'er latest lover. I knew she was spreadin' her thighs fer somebody." He scowled. "She's lucky she died in that accident, 'cause if she hadn't I swear I'd 'ave killed her with my bare hands for daring to steal from me, 'er own husband!" A brooding darkness slipped over his features for an instant. Then he transferred his gaze to Damien. "And that's why I'm 'ere, laddie. To retrieve what's mine."

"I have nothing of yours."

"Oh, now that's where ye're wrong. I know ye have it. Yer brother didn't, so ye're the one who must."

Damien's entire body had gone tense. "I've no idea what you're talking about," he stated flatly. "I've no idea what you *want* from me."

Elliot erupted into laughter. "Why, what else? The jewel case!"

Stunned, Damien managed to hide his dismay. Heather's eyes were huge. Elliot's laugh sent a prickle of warning across his skin. When Elliot tossed his head back, Damien gave a tiny shake of his head, signaling Heather to keep silent.

He felt his way carefully. "So it's my mother's jewel case you're after."

"Aye, laddie." Elliot jeered. "Ye didn't know I was at yer father's bedside when 'e died, did ye?"

"No." Damien's voice was taut.

Elliot shot him a black look. "Oh, I didn't kill 'em, if that's what yer thinkin'." His lip curled. "I worked at the inn where 'e stayed in London. I fed 'im when 'e was too blasted weak to hold a spoon! I cleaned his slop and changed his pissy sheets, and what thanks did I get for it?" He shook with rage.

"My father had the jewel case in London to have it repaired. Is that when you saw it?" Damien held his breath and waited.

Elliot nodded. "It was just before 'e breathed his last that 'e told me of the jewel case. It was hidden in a cloth sack in the corner. Why, all that time and I never knew it was there. But 'e wanted his wife to 'ave it, 'e said. 'E asked me to take it to 'er when 'e was gone." Elliot's eyes gleamed. "'Ere's what 'e said. ''Idden within the case is my legacy to my wife, a treasure beyond price,'" he quoted.

Treasure? Damien reeled. What on earth had his father been referring to? Was it simply the rambling of a sick man? But he dared not speculate aloud, for Elliot's temper was too volatile, too unpredictable.

"So my father died. And you took the jewel case."

"Aye. I took it 'ome with me, intending to search for the treasure later. But fool that I was, I told Justine." His face contorted. "When I woke up the next morn, she was gone—the brat and the jewel case along with 'er! Stole it, she did, the bitch! I found out she'd 'ired a coach, and I followed 'er to Lancashire, but she was already dead when I got there."

Damien's mind was racing. "Only the jewel case wasn't with her."

"No." Elliot's response was sullen, but then he smiled. "'Course I knew yer family must have managed to get it back some'ow. The jailer at Newgate said I was mad," he boasted, "but I knew I was right. I knew your family must 'ave discovered I'd stolen it. But I knew I'd find it someday."

"So when you were released, you sought out Giles."

"Aye," he said sullenly. "But the bastard swore he knew nothing of it! And it was nowhere to be found . . ." He smirked. "Then suddenly you showed up in London. 'Course I knew then it must be you that 'ad it."

The jailer in Newgate was right, Damien thought vaguely. Elliot *was* mad. The jewel case could have been anywhere—with anyone—and the fool had pursued it with a singlemindedness that had cost Giles his life. . . .

Damien felt sick inside. There was a part of

him that longed to lash out—to flaunt the fact
that the jewel case had been with his own daughter all these years . . . only the bastard had never
bothered to find out if his own child had lived or
died. . . .

He didn't dare disclose this. Not yet . . .

"So now you've finally come for it."

"Aye." Elliot gloated. "I'll 'ave the treasure in
the jewel case . . . and my poor daughter's fortune when she meets with an accident—just like
'er poor mother!" His laughter was chilling.

All at once he stopped, with a suddenness that
was eerie. The pistol veered sharply to Damien's
chest again. "Where is it?" he demanded.

Damien's mind worked frantically. Time. He
need time. Time to somehow gain the upper
hand . . .

His eyes collided with Heather's. Her face was
pasty white. There was something pleading in
those deep violet depths, yet it was not a plea for
help . . . no, it was more as if she sought to tell
him something. . . .

"I won't ask again," Elliot barked. "Where is
it?"

Damien nodded toward the staircase. "It's in
my bedchamber."

Elliot grabbed Heather's arm and jerked her
before him. He thrust the pistol against her
cheek. "Lead the way. But no tricks, laddie," he
warned. "Else we both know what lies in store
for our little 'eather."

Damien moved slowly up the stairs. If he
could just get to his room, there was another
pistol hidden in a drawer. . . . Behind him he

heard Heather stumble. His heart stopped. He glanced over his shoulder just as Elliot wrenched her arm behind her back. She let loose a sharp cry of pain. Damien seethed, wanting nothing more than to leap for Elliot's throat. But the time was not yet right.

He advanced farther up the steps. Behind him he could hear Heather's sobbing breaths. Just as the pair reached the landing where the staircase divided, Heather cried out sharply, "Wait!"

Damien half turned. From the corner of his eye he saw her lunge down, as if to grasp for her injured knee. Then all at once that same arm came up and back in a wide arc. Caught off guard, Elliot wasn't expecting the blow to his forearm—it knocked the pistol from his grasp. It went skidding across the marble floor.

Damien dove for it. He snatched it up and whirled.

Heather's blow had toppled Elliot's balance— the heel of one foot was hanging off the top step. His arms flailed wildly. His lips drew back across his teeth. "Bitch!" he cursed, even as he teetered, slanting backward. Damien saw that Elliot was aware he was going to fall . . .

But it seemed he'd decided he wasn't going alone.

Something burst in Damien's brain as the events played out before him. It all happened in a split second. Even as Damien lunged into motion, driven by raw fury, Elliot's hand shot out. He grabbed a fistful of Heather's skirts. With a strangled cry, she pitched violently to the side, dragged by the force of Elliot's downward motion.

Together they tumbled wildly down the stairs.

Elliot landed first. He lay sprawled on his back. Heather lay facedown atop his body.

Neither moved nor made a sound.

Fear wrapped a stranglehold around Damien's chest. "Jesus," he breathed, plunging down the stairs.

He gave but a cursory glance toward Elliot. His head was bent at an odd angle; his neck, broken. His hand was still clamped onto her skirts.

Damien fell to his knees beside her. He thrust Elliot's lifeless hand aside. Carefully he turned her over. Her head lolled back on his arm. What he saw sent sheer terror arrowing into his chest.

"Heather," he cried hoarsely. "Heather!"

Her skin was bled of all color. A massive, ugly bruise had already begun to swell on her temple. She was limp in his arms, like a puppet whose strings had been severed. His heart pumping in fear, he bent and pressed his ear to her lips.

She was breathing, but just barely.

Twenty-four

The physician returned to the Grayson town house for the seventh day in a row. An expression of defeated resignation on his lined face, he stepped into the hallway outside Heather's bedroom. As the door clicked quietly shut, four somber faces turned anxiously toward him.

He cleared his throat. "My lords, my lady, I'm afraid there's little hope. The injury to her head is simply too traumatic."

"There's no hope at all." This came from Damien.

The physician hesitated. "I've heard of cases where a patient might awaken days—even weeks—after. But in Heather's case"—he shook his head—"'tis my belief that day will never come."

Victoria turned her face into Miles's shoulder and wept. Beatrice pressed a handkerchief to her lips and stepped close to her father. Miles slipped an arm around each of them.

"Thank you, doctor," he said heavily.

Damien spoke not a word. He whirled and disappeared into the bedroom. Resuming his seat at Heather's bedside, he tenderly brushed his fingers across her brow. The pallor in her skin was deathly. Her lashes lay like thick, black crescents on her cheeks. One side of her face was swollen and black.

When Miles and Victoria entered the bedroom hours later, he hadn't moved. His face was gaunt and drawn. Her heart bleeding, Victoria laid comforting fingertips on his shoulder.

Only then did he acknowledge their presence. "Move her back to Lockhaven." His voice was low and grating.

Miles hesitated. "Damien," he began gently.

"If she is to recover, it will be there." He turned burning eyes upon the pair.

Miles and Victoria cast a helpless look in each other's direction.

"Please." The word was rough, vibrant with his plea. "She"—his voice broke—"she loves it there."

Victoria's eyes filled with tears. Seeking her husband's gaze, her wordless plea joined Damien's.

Miles raised a hand, then let it fall to his side. "You're right," he said quietly. "I'll make the arrangements."

Within a matter of days, the mistress of Lockhaven returned to her beloved home. The days passed, bright and sunny and warm. The fields flourished, and birds trilled cheerfully outside the room where Heather lay unmoving. But there was no laughter in the manor house; there was only a silence that seemed to penetrate the very walls.

Nearly two weeks had passed since her fall down the stairs. All the while, Damien kept vigil in a chair at her bedside, never releasing her hand. The ugly bruise that swelled one side of her face had faded so that it was scarcely visible.

And still she did not awake.

And on this day, the despair he sought to avoid descended, swift and merciless. Bitterly he cursed the fates that would take her from him. He'd found love, only to see it slip from his grasp forever. . . .

His gaze roved over her face, as if to brand it into his memory forever. She was heartbreakingly beautiful, he thought wistfully. But she was so still and white . . . fear pierced the depth of his soul. Shaking inside, he pushed back the cuff of the white linen nightgown she wore. His fingers sought the pulse in her wrist. It was barely there, thready and weak. He didn't know whether to give thanks . . . or give up.

He reached for her, gripping her hand within his as if to instill his own lifeblood within her. He could scarcely breathe for the fiery ache in his chest.

"Oh, Heather," he cried hoarsely. "Don't leave me. Please don't. I know I've hurt you . . . I'll make it up to you, if only you'll stay. Please fight, sweetheart. Please," he begged. "I need you so much. I want the chance to make you happy. You never told me if you'd marry me, Heather. But I want you to be my wife—forever. I want to grow old with you, love. I want to watch our child grow straight and tall. I want to give you dozens and dozens more children. Do you hear me, love? Dozens and dozens . . ." Tears choked his voice. He buried his head against her breast, unable to go on.

And then he felt it . . . a barely perceptible caress upon his nape. He raised his head to find her lashes fluttering. Her eyes opened, the color of heather in full bloom.

Her lips parted. Her whisper was so faint he had to bend low to hear it. "Will you . . . dance with me again?"

He whispered her name, a searing little sound that held a world of intensity. Catching her hand, he brought it to his cheek. "Yes . . . oh, yes! I love you, Heather." He kissed her, a sensation that was painfully sweet for them both. When he drew back, his eyes delved deep into hers. "I never got the chance to tell you, but . . . I love you. God, how I love you. . . ."

A faint smile grazed her lips. "And I never got the chance to tell you . . . I will marry you, Damien."

Tears misted his vision. He dropped his head against her hand and wept.

Heather drifted in and out of wakefulness throughout the rest of the day. Every time she awoke, Damien was there by the bedside, hold-ing her hand, his concern keenly evident in those clear, gray eyes.

By the next morning, she was well enough to move about the room for a few minutes. By evening, she was ravenous. Having just consumed her first solid meal in days, she leaned back against the pillows, feeling quite content.

The physician pronounced her recovery miraculous. She'd been stunned to learn she'd been unconscious for nearly two weeks. At first she'd been terrified that she'd lost the babe, but the physician had assured her that since there had been no signs to indicate otherwise, their child appeared to be in no danger.

At times, she couldn't help but think of James Elliot. She regretted his passing, for despite his evil nature, he had been her father. She mourned for the father who had never wanted her, who had never cared. But she could not grieve for this man who had abandoned her, when Miles had loved her as his own. And so she sought to keep reminders of James Elliot at bay, for she had no wish to linger on the past—not when the future loomed so brightly before her.

Damien loved her. *He loved her.* At times she felt like pinching herself to see if it was real, or but a dream.

The very subject of her thoughts had just pulled up his chair. He availed himself of the sweetness of her lips, then sat. "When will you marry me?" he asked without preamble.

Heather blinked, then took his strong, brown hand in hers and pressed it against her belly. "Well," she said lightly, "there is a need for haste."

His eyes began to gleam. Settling his gaze on her lips, he murmured, "I quite agree."

Heather wrinkled her nose playfully.

His expression sobered. "Actually, I was thinking we ought to wed as soon as it can be arranged." Watching her closely, he continued, "Would you mind terribly if it's not a grand London affair?"

The tenderness in his gaze left her breathless. "Not at all. In fact, I'd much prefer the village church."

He squeezed her fingers. "Consider it done."

Heather smiled across at him. "You never did tell me. Were Mama and Papa shocked when they found out I'm with child?"

"Well," he said dryly, "Miles looked as if he would quite cheerfully like to throttle me, but I think Victoria was able to redirect his excitement."

Heather smiled knowingly. "She has a way of taking him well in hand."

For the space of a heartbeat, she noticed that a faint wistfulness dwelled on his face. "My parents were much the same," he murmured. Suddenly he straightened. "Good God, I completely forgot about the jewel case. What was it Elliot said my father told him?"

"Something about a treasure being hidden inside, I believe it was—his legacy to his wife, and something about a treasure beyond price."

"That's it, love."

She watched curiously as Damien strode across to her bureau and retrieved the jewel case. He brought it back to the bed and placed it between them.

"Do you really think there's a treasure?" Heather emptied it of its contents so he could examine it more fully.

"Frankly, no," he admitted. "I suspect it was simply the ramblings of a grievously ill man." His dark head was bent as he slid lean fingers along the inside corner of the compartments. When that inspection yielded nothing, he turned his attention to the outside.

Finally he sighed. "I hate to disappoint you, but—" All at once he stopped. His brow furrowed. His expression was intent. His fingers were on a side panel of silver.

All at once it slid free in his hands.

"By God," he muttered in awe, "Elliot was right. There's a tiny compartment. . . ."

"Do you see anything inside?" Heather breathed. "It's not very big, but there could be a small pouch of jewels. Diamonds, do you think?" She was as anxious as he.

But it was neither jewel nor gem that Damien withdrew. Instead it was a folded sheaf of paper, dry and yellow with age.

His pulse suddenly pounding, Damien opened it. "It's a letter," he said in an odd, strained voice. "A letter from my father to my mother." He swallowed and began to read aloud.

My dearest Sylvia,

It is with the greatest sorrow that I write this, my last letter to you. I am ill, my love, and I fear I shall not survive the coming days. I should have sent word long ago, but I thought this malady would pass, and now it is too late.

By the time this reaches you, I shall be gone. No longer will the letters we've exchanged here in this secret place light my life like the most precious of treasures. But I pray that I will live on within your memories, as you dwell within mine. And so I leave you with my greatest legacy. . . . My heart, forever yours. My love, eternally in your hands. My soul, yours alone.

Damien was silent a moment. "So this is the treasure Elliot was so determined to find."

Heather was touched beyond words. "Your father was right," she whispered. "It's a bequeathal. . . . Can you imagine, they must have hidden letters to each other here."

Damien folded the letter and replaced it in its hiding place, for that was where it belonged. When that was done, he carried the jewel case back to Heather's bureau, then returned to the bedside.

He was stunned to find that her eyes glistened with tears. "Heather! What's wrong, love?"

Heather's heart twisted. A jagged sob escaped from her. "It's just so—so sad. Don't you see, your mother never saw this letter. Damien, I've never heard anything so—so moving in all my life! But she never had the chance to read it."

Damien smoothed a tangle of hair from her cheek. "It doesn't matter," he said gently.

Misty violet eyes lifted to his. "Damien! How can you say such a thing?"

"Don't you see, sweet? She already knew." With the pad of his thumb, he tenderly wiped away her tears. "She knew long before then how much he loved her."

Understanding slowly replaced the sadness in Heather's expressive eyes.

"Yes. Yes, you're right." She smiled mistily.

"It's much the same with us, I think," he said softly. He pulled her into his embrace. "Knowing you love me is a feeling unlike any other." He smiled against her lips. "And I can imagine no greater treasure."

Epilogue

They were married a scant ten days later in the village church, surrounded by masses and masses of sweet-scented wildflowers. Escorted by Miles, Heather walked proudly down the aisle where Damien awaited her. The dress she wore was of antique white, cascading from her tiny waist in shimmering folds of satin and lace. The bodice was adorned with hundreds of tiny white pearls. On her head was a veil of sheer white lace.

At Damien's request, she carried a simple bouquet of violets, the exact shade of her eyes.

No bride had ever looked more beautiful, he decided.

No bride had ever *felt* more beautiful, she was certain.

Indeed, Heather counted that day the happiest in her life. But as she discovered, it was just the beginning of many to follow.

Their son was born on a blustery March night. Though the midwife pronounced such behavior unheard of, Damien insisted on being at her side

throughout her labor—and at the moment one
Wesley Charles Tremayne made his entrance into
the world.

Less than two short months later, Bridget and
Robert MacTavish became the proud parents of
a healthy baby boy. As she had before, it was
Heather who delivered the babe. Once again, she
cried along with Bridget—only this time they
were tears of joy.

Heather and Damien divided their time between Damien's estate in Yorkshire, and Lockhaven. Not long after their marriage, Damien
had quietly sold Bayberry, his plantation in
Virginia. As he'd told Heather, his place was in
England—with her.

But it was Lockhaven that would always be
home to both of them. And on this sunny summer day in early June, she, Damien, and Wesley
had spread a blanket on the very spot where
Heather and Damien had first met over two
years before.

Damien sat with his back propped against a
stout oak tree, muscled legs stretched out before
him, booted feet crossed at the ankles. Wesley lay
on his father's torso, his chubby legs drawn up
beneath his tummy so that his little rump stuck
high in the air. His cheek pressed against Damien's chest, Wesley curled one small fist next to
his mouth, which even now was as beautifully
shaped as his father's.

Heather's eyes grew soft. Poor little lamb. He'd
worn himself out scooting around the field with
his father at his heels. He'd walked at the age of
ten months and was soon on his feet nearly every

waking moment, much to his mother's occasional dismay and his father's delight.

Her sketchbook in hand, Heather sought to capture the strength of the bond between father and son. She couldn't help but remember the day she had first sketched Damien—how very different he looked now! The pain shuttered deep in his soul was no more. His eyes held no shadows . . .

His heart no secrets.

She watched as that strong, brown hand slid up and down the curve of Wesley's spine, occasionally drifting up to tenderly cup dark curls the color of midnight. Unaware of her scrutiny, he pressed his lips to the baby's scalp. He turned his head, and their eyes meshed.

Heather's heart melted.

So did his.

His gaze never left hers as he set aside his precious burden, then proceeded to set aside her sketchbook and pencil.

"I'm working!" Her protest was halfhearted.

"So am I." He was busy unlacing the front of her bodice. She'd dressed in a faded muslin gown that had seen far better days. Her hair tumbled free and loose around her shoulders and down her back. Even her feet were bare.

Damien drew back slowly. His eyes wandered down, then back up to her face. He smiled. "You look like a gypsy," he said.

"And you look like a sheep farmer."

"I *am* a sheep farmer." His grin was boyishly crooked. "But I suppose 'tis better to look like one than to smell like one."

As he spoke, he tugged the shoulders of her bodice halfway down her arms.

Heather swallowed. All at once her mouth was dry. "Damien."

"Hmmm." His mouth brushed the pale swell of one full breast.

Her hand hovered just above his nape. "Wait," she whispered.

The urgency in her tone brought his head up. He searched her features. "What is it, love?"

Heather brushed a lock of dark hair from his forehead. Her heart was suddenly pounding. "Remember you once said you wanted dozens and dozens of children?"

"I do indeed," he said softly. "It was the day I thought I'd lost you. The day you came back to me."

Heather smiled shakily. Her eyes clung to his. "Did you mean it?"

His body had gone utterly still. Comprehension flashed across his face. His hand slid down to the flatness of her belly; his eyes followed. Now it was he who swallowed.

"Why?" His voice was but a breath. "Is there . . . are you . . . ?"

She nodded.

He dragged her into his arms. His grin was totally unrepentant. "Well," he murmured just before his mouth came down on hers, "I did warn you . . ."

America Loves Lindsey!

The Timeless Romances
of #1 Bestselling Author

KEEPER OF THE HEART	77493-3/$6.99 US/$8.99 Can
THE MAGIC OF YOU	75629-3/$5.99 US/$6.99 Can
ANGEL	75628-5/$6.99 US/$8.99 Can
PRISONER OF MY DESIRE	75627-7/$6.99 US/$8.99 Can
ONCE A PRINCESS	75625-0/$6.50 US/$8.50 Can
WARRIOR'S WOMAN	75301-4/$6.99 US/$8.99 Can
MAN OF MY DREAMS	75626-9/$6.99 US/$8.99 Can
SURRENDER MY LOVE	76256-0/$6.50 US/$7.50 Can
YOU BELONG TO ME	76258-7/$6.99 US/$8.99 Can
UNTIL FOREVER	76259-5/$6.50 US/$8.50 Can
LOVE ME FOREVER	72570-3/$6.99 US/$8.99 Can

Coming Soon in Hardcover
SAY YOU LOVE ME